THE COMING OF AGE OF
ELIZABETH BENNET

A PRIDE AND PREJUDICE VARIATION

CAITLIN WILLIAMS

For Rob

and

Seaweed

With special thanks to Claudine.
www.Justjane1813.com

for all your help and encouragement

A novel in four volumes

Volume One: Fifteen

One

Some love stories are simple - a dance, a walk in the shrubbery, a clasp of hands and it is done. If affection, fortune and situation are equal enough not to cause any great offence, the business may be concluded very quickly and without much trouble to anyone. A courtship, a nervous application to the father and then the lovers might marry and spend the rest of their lives in regret or joy, feeling their luck, or cursing their choices. For happiness in marriage, as Elizabeth Bennet was later to learn, is entirely a matter of chance.

Born in the year of Our Lord, Seventeen-Ninety-Four, the second daughter of a country gentleman, hers should have been the easiest of tales to tell. Her circumstances suggested she was bound for a future as the wife of a parson, or a well-to-do solicitor, perhaps even a naval or army officer should have been her destiny. Death, however, can have an even greater influence over us than love, and Mr Bennet's demise, in her fifteenth year, saw Elizabeth's life diverge down an unusual path.

As she'd watched her father's last journey, from Longbourn to the churchyard, through an upstairs window, her whole being had burned with fury and she'd felt a keen sense of injustice. With her father's body had gone her protection, her comfort and her home. She had not cried at the loss of the man yet, however, any tears she'd shed were angry ones. Having always thought of herself as his favourite child, her father's most final decisions made no sense to her at all. Hadn't he always praised her quick mind, her ability to recall Coleridge or Shakespeare, her knowledge of Latin? Wasn't she the daughter who made him smile with pride when she mastered a new skill, while the younger ones made him shake his head in despair? He had taught her French and chess, geography and philosophy. While her mother scolded and harried her, he had been her well of unconditional love. So why had he chosen to punish her so?

Why decide to send her away?

She spent the weeks following Mr Bennet's burial in continuous, lethargic contemplation of this question. She walked about, or else sat around, in misery and shock while the house was packed around her. Though her father had told her he would die, and had spoken of the arrangements he had made for them all, Elizabeth had simply not believed him. She had truly thought he would recover and thought it typical of his humour to play such a great joke on them all. Yet now she was forced to look on, as her mother and sisters filled a multitude of trunks with belongings and clothes, while she wanted to scream at their futile efforts. As if trinkets and baubles and lace mattered; you could not put memories and happiness in a box and take them somewhere else, there was no point in *things*.

Letters went from London to Derbyshire and back again, bringing the news that a date for her own departure had been set. She received it with a most determined silence while her elder sister, Jane, smiled and tried to reassure her. Elizabeth was not fooled and noticed the way Jane's hands had shaken as they gripped the paper. "Mr Darcy writes that the park around Pemberley is ten miles round, you'll enjoy walking in it, I am sure, and he says he has a very good library, one of the finest in England."

At Elizabeth's continued silence her mother had thrown her napkin onto the breakfast table. "And now she has nothing to say for herself. Miss Lizzy, who came into the world kicking and screaming - and who I daresay has barely stopped talking to take a breath since - now says nothing, when she ought to be thankful. You do not deserve your luck, child. Your father thought of your interests before he did ours. Where will I be, when Mr and Mrs Collins come to evict me? Reduced beyond what is bearable. Oh 'tis all so horrible, I cannot speak of it. Do not ask me to, I will not say another word." Yet speak of it she did, in great minute, between wails and to anyone who had the patience to listen.

Elizabeth could not listen. Not to Jane's sweet attempts to convince her of a rosy future or to any of her mother's noisy complaints. Even her own thoughts became too loud and she would sit in the attic, amongst her father's childhood possessions and cover her ears against them. She would pinch her skin at the wrists, squeezing it tightly between her thumb and forefinger, but no matter how hard she tried, she could not wake herself up. Her father was dead, Jane was to go and live with their Uncle and Aunt Gardiner in London, while her mother was to take her three younger sisters to a cottage in Meryton, and she was to be sent two hundred miles away to live with strangers. She wished for time to stop, but it caught her up, of course. It ticked and tocked and taunted and terrorised her, and on the day when she was to leave, it chased her up once again into the attic. She made herself a bed of old clothes and curled herself up into a ball, which is where she might have remained, if Jane had not come to find her.

"There you are, Lizzy," her sister said, coming to stand at the top of the attic stairs and sighing when she saw Elizabeth was still in her nightgown. "Why are you not dressed? Mr Darcy and his son will be here in an hour or so. You must be ready."

"I know," Elizabeth replied, but did not move.

Jane came further into the room and crouched beside her. "I understand you do not want to go, but it is what Papa chose. You must not see it as a punishment."

Elizabeth nodded dully, but could not speak. She could not put any of the horrible, selfish things she felt into words; for she wished it were Jane being sent away to Derbyshire and that she might take Jane's place at their Uncle Gardiner's house. She ought to have been pleased for her sister, who had always been so kind to her, that she was going to a home where she would be loved and cared for but instead resentment and unwarranted jealousy nestled in her breast.

Jane looked around at their father's possessions. "You might take some of Papa's things with you. I am sure there are a few books here, and in his library, that you would like to have. Steal them away and put them in your trunks, but come on now, you must get ready."

"I will get dressed, Jane, I promise you faithfully, I will, just leave me alone for a few more moments."

Combing back Elizabeth's long dark curls from her face, Jane kissed her forehead and went back downstairs. After she had gone, Elizabeth pulled her hair back over her face and looked through it, playing with the strands, while her heart thudded frantically against her chest. An hour or two! It was not long. Mad, dangerous thoughts and ideas began to intrude and she wondered where she might find a pair of scissors.

Stopped at an inn on the road between London and Hertfordshire, Fitzwilliam Darcy inspected the shine on his boots. A few feet away from him stood Miss Temple, a governess newly employed by his father. They had been left alone outside while the carriage was being brought round but he knew not what to say to the lady. To avoid having to think of something, he attempted to look as if his attention was taken by other things. He examined his pocket watch for some time and then took out his handkerchief and slowly re-folded it into a neat square, before putting it back into the pocket of his waistcoat. They had been in a carriage together for above two hours but she was still mostly unknown to him and from a different social standing. He felt he would have nothing in common with her and dreaded the efforts he would have to make to uphold his end of any conversation they might begin. He simply did not like new people. Or rather, he was not good at making himself agreeable to them. He could never seem to catch the right tone or fall into any kind of meaningful exchange with them. He frequently said exactly the wrong thing or not very much at all. He preferred to allow others to talk, only coming to the fore when he had something he truly wished to say.

Miss Temple was a pretty lady of around thirty, slim of figure and with a calm, melodic voice. She was obviously intelligent and had come highly recommended by the Earl of Wiltshire. Darcy wondered briefly why she had never married and guessed some dire circumstances must have caused her to seek employment.

She eventually leaned forward and caught his eye, forcing him to speak. He mumbled something about the weather, a comment she agreed with, before smiling softly.

"You must tell me a little of my new charges, Mr Darcy. What kind of girls are they?"

"My sister, Georgiana, is eleven. She is currently at school as my father thought it might be good for her to be amongst other girls her own age. She has been desperately unhappy there, however, and so begged to be allowed to return home," Darcy said. "She is a quiet girl but I believe you'll find her well-behaved and attentive to her studies. Of Miss Bennet I can tell you nothing as I have never met her. Though I understand she has recently lost her father which has left her family in financial difficulties, and that is why she is to come to Pemberley."

"Your father must be a charitable man," Miss Temple said, as the carriage finally appeared and rolled to a stop before them.

"Perhaps *too* charitable," Darcy replied.

"Is it possible to be too charitable, Mr Darcy? Can a person be too kind?"

"Not all the beneficiaries of his benevolence have shown themselves worthy of it," he replied evenly. He was spared from saying anything further by his father coming from the inn towards them.

George Darcy apologised to Miss Temple for keeping her waiting before handing her up into the carriage. He then looked steadily at his son. "You'll be kind to Elizabeth Bennet, Fitzwilliam. I don't know what has happened lately, to give you that sour look, trouble with a woman no doubt, but I'll have you remember your manners and treat this young girl as a sister."

"She is *not* a sister and though you do not care for my opinion, I will say again that to take her to Pemberley, without any knowledge of her character or disposition, is madness. What if she is to become a bad influence on Georgiana?"

His father dismissed his concerns. "I knew my old friend Bennet and that is good enough for me. He was very decent to me once and I owe him a debt of gratitude."

"Then offer Mrs Bennet some kind of financial recompense instead. I am sure she would be better pleased with that, rather than us taking her daughter away."

George Darcy laughed. "As she told me in her last letter, she has five of them, so she can easily spare one. Can you imagine, Fitzwilliam, a house of six women! Poor Bennet, I suppose he never concerned himself with the entail of his estate and the welfare of his family until he knew he was not long for this world. We men have such a vain belief in our own potent virility. No doubt he fully expected to father a son and now it is all to go to some distant cousin. Anyway shall we get on and go meet young Elizabeth? I think she will be a fine addition to our family party. She is apparently lively and has a little more wit than most girls her age."

Darcy shook his head. "She sounds like trouble."

As his well-sprung, fine-liveried carriage rolled through Hertfordshire, George Darcy sat back and contemplated his only son. There was much to approve of. Now three and twenty, Fitzwilliam was tall, slim and handsome. There had been some silliness when he had first left Cambridge, over-imbibing and carousing, which might have been expected of any young man let loose in London after four years of study, and in Fitzwilliam's case he had been encouraged and badly influenced by George Wickham. Yet after some stern lectures and a few hard lessons learned, the wildness had been curbed, and a serious, steady young man was emerging. George Darcy was satisfied that when the time eventually came for him to present himself at the gates of St Peter, he would be leaving Pemberley and Georgiana in a safe pair of hands. He did wonder lately, though, if perhaps his son was now a little *too* serious. He seemed to take no enjoyment in life and was bereft of smiles or jests.

Seeing Miss Temple engaged in admiring the scenery, he leaned across and spoke to Fitzwilliam quietly.

"Your Aunt de Bourgh would appreciate a visit soon. You were missed at Easter and Anne specifically asked after you. Will you go soon?"

"I will try."

"She would be a good choice." At his son's exasperated look, George Darcy held up his hands. "I will not try to persuade you, I just remind you of the advantages, but there is plenty of time, you are a young man yet." Then in a whisper, he asked, "is there another, someone else you prefer?"

Darcy gave a brief and vehement shake of his head.

His father sat back in the carriage unconvinced, but not of a mind to pry further.

Oh how Elizabeth ran, till her chest burned, her legs ached and her mouth and throat were scratchy with dust. It was just as well she knew enough of the surrounding countryside to be able to make her way through it without thought; her mind was too panicked for her to concentrate on anything but putting one foot in front of the other. What had she done? What was she daring to do? She'd climbed quickly over stiles and sprinted over fields but had not yet put enough miles between her and Longbourn to feel completely safe.

She ran to the Jones's farm and burst into their yard, scattering chickens and making the dog bark. Henry looked up from his work, smiled at first, but then took her to the nearby barn and shut the heavy door, throwing them into near darkness.

"What sort of game is this now? Why are you dressed like that?" he asked tugging at the boys clothes she wore.

"'Tis no game, I will not be sent to Derbyshire. Will you find a cap for me and tell me where I can catch the stage?"

"Lizzy, when they find you, they'll send you to bedlam, not Derbyshire," he said.

"They won't catch me."

"Where will you go?"

Elizabeth had to admit she did not know. "Please Henry, haven't we always been friends? Find me a cap." She drew a pair of scissors from her pocket, "and cut my hair shorter. I could not get to it all myself."

"I'll not touch your hair, I couldn't bear to do such a thing," he said, looking at the short curls that now brushed her cheeks. The skinny boy Elizabeth had played with as a child was now a broad-chested young man, fair of face. He crossed his arms and considered Elizabeth for a few moments, before taking the cap from his own head and putting it on hers.

She tucked what remained of her dark locks under it and stood with her feet apart. "How do I look?"

"Like Lizzy Bennet in breeches," he laughed. "Go home."

"I have no home, Mr and Mrs Collins come in three days to take it."

Henry sighed and walked away from her to sit on a bale of hay. "Say you manage to get to the stage, what then?"

"I'll go to the coast, I might join the Navy."

"You'd be found out in two minutes."

"Well then, I shall go to London and be some rich man's mistress."

Henry guffawed loudly, setting the dog outside to barking again. "What do you know of men?"

"I know that I am sick of them telling me where I must go and what I must do. If I were a mistress I'd have my own house and income and be able to do whatever I wished." Even as she spoke Elizabeth knew she sounded ridiculous, but held her chin high anyway.

"You're sweet, Lizzy, but I don't think you are what those gentlemen of the ton are looking for." His eyes swept over her and she became indignant. She knew she was lacking in hips and bust; if the mirror did not constantly remind her of it, her mother was always certain to. Her figure showed few signs womanhood yet. Her sister Mary, at thirteen, was more developed than she. Elizabeth had never minded much, she took pride in being the clever sister rather than the beautiful one. Yet to have Henry, her dearest and oldest friend, tease her for it, was unbearable. "You've never even been kissed," he said.

Without thought she marched over and knelt in front of him, pressing her mouth fully against his for a few moments. "There, now I have." For a moment she thought he was going to take hold of her and kiss her again. Instead he licked his lips and looked at her sternly.

"You shouldn't have done that, Lizzy."

Her cheeks aflame with embarrassment and fury, Elizabeth turned and fled, throwing open the barn door and running out through the yard. Henry muttered an oath before going after her.

Two

There was a terrifying high-pitched scream from the road outside, followed by whinnying from the horses and the scraping and sliding of their hooves as they were pulled back. The carriage came to a violent and sudden stop. Miss Temple had reacted quickly and grabbed for the handrail. She was thrown about a bit but managed to keep her seat. The carriage lurched again and there was some yelling from the coachman as he jumped down from the driver's seat. Darcy saw his father had suffered no ill effects and appeared as calm as ever.

"Go and see what the problem is, my boy," he instructed, before turning to the governess to check on her welfare.

Darcy flung open the door and jumped down into the road to see the coachman, John, with his whip over his head, shouting at a young boy who had fallen on the road in front of the carriage. The boy was scurrying fearfully backwards across the ground.

"Are you soft-headed, lad?" John yelled. "Don't you know to look out for carriages? What d'you mean by running straight out? You might have overturned the coach and we'd all be dead. By God, I ought to whip you." The whip was raised to shoulder height and brought down on the dirt road with a thunderous crack, narrowly missing the boy's legs.

"That's enough, John," Darcy commanded, before striding over and pulling the boy up by his collar. He was oddly dressed, in an old-fashioned suit of velvet breeches and a short jacket. Beneath this, he wore a shirt that had come untucked on one side and hung down almost to the child's bony knees. The fancy breeches and jacket looked incongruous next to the farmer's cap the boy wore on his head. Darcy took hold of him by his shoulders to look at him properly. "Are you hurt?"

The boy shook his head and opened his mouth, but was unable to speak. He was a slight, skinny lad with a thin face and delicate features. Darcy wondered if he was mute, or indeed, did suffer from some kind of malady of the mind, as

John had suggested. "You deserve the driver's rebuke, child. You should take more care," he said, speaking slowly and directly, so as to make himself more easily understood.

Another older youth came crashing through the trees onto the road, breathing heavily, as if he had been involved in a chase. He was a much stouter lad of sixteen or seventeen.

"Is this child with you?" Darcy demanded of the older boy.

"Aye, sir, run off from me," he replied, taking hold of the child's sleeve.

"Well then, you both ought to get off home. There was almost an accident. Your younger brother here ran out and came within a hare's breath of being trampled by the horses. It is fortunate no tragedy occurred."

Removing his cap, the older boy offered a small, apologetic bow. "I beg your pardon, sir, we'll go home directly."

"See that you do," Darcy instructed. He turned to the coachman and signalled with a brusque wave of his hand that they should be on their way. John climbed up to his seat and took hold of the reins as Darcy walked back to the carriage. While he was taking his seat, Darcy looked out though the window at the smaller lad, who was staring back at him. There was something about the boy's eyes that shocked him. They were full of fire and boldness and Darcy found he could not look away.

"He's not my brother," the boy called out, speaking for the first time. The older lad shushed him and grabbed the child's arm more firmly, pulling him towards a natural path between the tall trees.

The carriage had moved off before Darcy realised his error. He had been momentarily fooled, but now he was certain the younger boy had not been a boy at all. He kept thinking of the boots the child had worn. They had been decidedly feminine, dainty walking boots, not the sort of heavy, thick-soled boots a farmer's son or servant might wear. And the facial features had been too delicate, a small upturned nose, a pouty rosebud mouth, and those dark angry eyes had been framed by exceptionally long lashes. Her appearance ought to have given rise to suspicion but only the high, feminine pitch of her voice had finally alerted him to the truth. Darcy ran a hand over his mouth and considered briefly stopping the carriage and turning it around so he might ask further questions of the pair. But then, he reasoned, it was none of his business. He had no appetite for country drama, and if his father were to become involved, they would no doubt be there all day. He resolved to put the matter out of his mind and within ten minutes they were rolling into the park of a small estate.

"'Tis Longbourn, sir," John called out as the carriage came to a stop.

Darcy peered out at the house and saw a long sandstone building. It was pretty, but unimpressive and the park was embarrassingly small. If he were to guess, he would have said the income from it would have been two or three thousand a year. By the front door was a welcoming committee; a lady and one, two, three, four of her daughters, all clad in the dark colours of mourning. Darcy and his father exited the carriage and bowed before them. The lady of the house came forward, curtseying three or four times between each step.

"Mr Darcy, you are very welcome to Longbourn, such a fine carriage, sir, though I am sure it is only one of your many fine equipages. How gracious of you to come fetch Lizzy, for I would have been quite happy to set her off on the stage with a servant. Your coming here in person shows such great condescension and I know you will take the very best of care with her."

His father introduced Miss Temple, amidst more overflowing thanks. No speech was required of him, so Darcy remained silent. Mrs Bennet did not leave much room for response in any case. Her girls she named by order of their ages and they gawped and smiled and dropped quick, excited curtsies.

When Mrs Bennet at last paused for breath, George Darcy took the opportunity to ask after his new charge, "and young Miss Elizabeth, she is not here?" They were being shown through the hall down to a poky parlour, which was full of trinkets and baubles and so much furniture as to make Darcy feel uncomfortable and slightly unwell. Longbourn's ceilings were low and its windows small, so there was a lack of natural light. He was used to grander settings, more airy habitats.

"Oh of course Lizzy is here. She is all packed and prepared for her journey. I have sent the housekeeper to fetch her down," Mrs Bennet said, while she fidgeted and fussed and asked them thrice if they would take some refreshment. Darcy breathed a sigh of relief when his father refused on all three occasions. He didn't want anything prolonging their stay and the tea would no doubt be of middling quality.

On and on Mrs Bennet prattled, her manners were countrified, her voice unrefined and her questions of the rather vulgar variety. Darcy was not in the room with her for above ten minutes before concluding she was a woman of mean understanding, little information and uncertain temper. He watched impatiently while his father treated Mrs Bennet with far more graciousness than she deserved and began a lengthy speech of condolence, lyrically expounding on Mr Bennet's finer qualities, as if he had been a prince or a great leader, rather than a country squire of no particular note. Darcy fought hard not to roll his eyes. Then, however, with no small amount of skill and in a way that caused no offence, George Darcy began to speak of the rooms he had booked at the White Hart outside Reading. He neatly mentioned they had five and thirty miles to cover yet and said again how anxious he was to meet Elizabeth.

Mrs Bennet looked flustered and spoke about what fine weather it was for travelling, before the housekeeper entered the room rather breathlessly, her hand pressed to her chest. "I've searched the whole house, madam, and there's no sign."

The eldest Bennet girl, by far the most handsome and genteel, put her hand on her mother's arm to still and quiet her, perhaps fearing an outburst of hysterics. "Did you check the attic, Hill?" she enquired of the housekeeper. "Lizzy has been up there often of late, going through Papa's things."

"Yes, everything has been gone through up there, but there is no Miss Lizzy and cook says she saw her running out the side door a while back. She says she was..." she looked askance at the Darcys and Miss Temple but then carried on, "not properly dressed."

Miss Temple bit her lip and looked towards Darcy. "The young people we saw on the road, perhaps..."

Darcy cut the governess off. "I think we are of the same opinion, Miss Temple." He went to stand before Jane Bennet. "What was in the attic, your father's clothes?"

"There were some clothes, yes, from when he was a boy, with his books and papers. He had been at Longbourn all his life. He grew up here."

"And now it is all lost," Mrs Bennet wailed. "Those despicable Collins' people gave us only six weeks to quit the place. They would have us thrown into the hedgerows. They are hard people, Mr Darcy, totally without compassion."

"Mamma, you have never met them," said one of the other Bennets, a mousy-looking girl in glasses. "To condemn a man, with such little knowledge of his character or circumstances, does not show great Christian spirit."

"Oh shush, Mary, nobody wants your sermons now, not when Lizzy is out there in the wilds, facing who knows what dangers, without coat or bonnet."

"Mrs Bennet, when your housekeeper said your daughter was not properly dressed, I believe she meant she has donned breeches, jacket and cap, not simply that she might be without a coat."

"That's right, sir," confirmed the housekeeper. "Cook said she looked like a boy and at first she wasn't certain it was Miss Lizzy, but now she has had time to think on it and Miss Lizzy is missing, she is sure enough."

"That wilful, obstinate child has no compassion on my poor nerves. I am certain she will be the death of me. No doubt that farmer's boy has something to do with this. I warned your father about letting her run around with the tenants' children all these years, for it was certain no good could have come from it." Then, as if suddenly remembering Mr Darcy was in the room, Mrs Bennet gave him an ingratiating smile. "Though, there is nothing truly bad, nothing that cannot be corrected. A year or so at Pemberley, and a good governess, will set her just right."

Before his father could speak, Darcy intervened. "Pray, do not be overly concerned, Miss Bennet, Mrs Bennet. I believe she is little more than a half-mile along the road. I'll fetch her back readily if you can supply a horse?"

Jane Bennet nodded at the housekeeper, who rushed out to find a stable lad, while George Darcy gave him a look of caution and drew him over to the window so they might speak privately. "Be careful and circumspect."

"There is nothing to be concerned about. It was Elizabeth Bennet who nearly fell under the wheels of the coach, she is not far away."

"Yes I know, but if you do not find her quickly, come back and seek help," his father advised.

"I'll have no trouble at all. If I am not back in an hour or so, go on with Miss Temple. Your priority must be to collect Georgiana from school tomorrow, she is expecting you. The girl and I will catch you up on the road."

His father eventually nodded. "Very well, but I must remind you not to travel alone with Miss Bennet. While she might be running around the countryside in boys clothes and in less than desirable company, she is still a young lady."

Darcy quickly dampened down his father's concerns. "Credit me with some sense. I will make whatever arrangements are necessary. I doubt anyone cares about the comings and goings of a disobedient little country madam in any case."

"Go on then, but do not go courting trouble," George Darcy said, waving him away.

Darcy walked quickly from the room, Jane Bennet was hard on his heels and he turned briefly to face her. "Your mother mentioned someone, and there was an older boy with your sister, Miss Bennet? Do you know who he might be?"

"It will have been Henry Jones. They are, in fact, both just fifteen. Lizzy is small for her age. Henry is one of our tenant's sons; they were born days apart and have played together since they were children. It is perhaps not an ideal association for her, but my father allowed it since they were very great friends. If she were to confide in someone, or ask for assistance, she would go to him."

They went through the front door and Darcy tapped his stick impatiently against his boot whilst he waited for the horse.

"Mr Darcy, Lizzy was very upset at the thought of being sent away from her family, but will you please believe me when I tell you that her only faults are youth and impulsiveness. She has never done anything like this before. Her grief has made her angry and angry people are not always wise. She has a most kind and generous nature and is a most beloved sister to me. I hope you will not blame her too much for the trouble she has put you and your father to."

He looked into Miss Bennet's lovely, sincere face for a while before nodding. He had the odd thought that she would make someone a very good wife in a few years. "Miss Bennet, where would your sister go? Where is the nearest village?"

"Meryton, but if she truly means to run off, she would not go there. We are too well known for her to go unnoticed."

"Then to London?"

"Perhaps, but she is not overly fond of London. If I had to guess, but, no…it is ridiculous," she said, shaking her head.

"Go on."

"She has never been to the coast. One of her dearest wishes has been to see the ocean. My father once promised to take her, but his health has been too poor these recent years. He spoke of them going to Kent."

"The fastest route to the Kent coast from here would be to take the stage or a cart to London, and then another to Dover or Folkestone," Darcy said, thinking out loud.

Miss Bennet swallowed hard and looked as if she might cry.

"She will not get that far though, Miss Bennet, I assure you."

The horse was brought round and Darcy thanked the stable lad brusquely as he took the reins and hoisted himself into the saddle. He pressed his heels into the mount's side to signal that a gallop was required. The horse was not young, but it was biddable and strong, and took off at a reasonably good speed. It would suffice for the purpose of recovering a silly young girl and returning her home. As he rode out of Longbourn, he realised his mouth was curved into a small smile. There he had been, less than an hour ago, telling himself not get involved in a country drama and yet, here he was, right in the middle of one anyway, and there was a strange thrill in it. After the long, painful months he had spent in London, clearing up the horrible messes left by Wickham, it was invigorating to be racing down a winding lane with a breeze at his face. The horse kicked up clouds of dust as he ducked under branches, steered around roots and hedges, and Darcy felt more alive than he had done for a good long while.

Three

Henry Jones would not be shaken off. Though he could not forcibly drag Elizabeth back to Longbourn, he would not give up trying to persuade her to go back of her own accord.

She threw him a look of annoyance over her shoulder. "Go home, Henry, your father will want your help on the farm at this time of day."

"I am sorry, Lizzy. I am sorry to have laughed at you. I don't know how many times I must say it before you'll believe me. But you cannot take off with just a few shillings in your pocket and not a bite to eat, and not an idea of where you are going, or what you'll do when you get there." He caught her elbow and stopped her, turning her around to face him. "You're the daughter of a gentleman. You shouldn't be running here and there, dressed like this." He gave the brim of her cap a gentle tug, making her smile in spite of herself.

Then, remembering what had happened in the barn, she was cross at him again. "It is none of your business what I do."

"No, that's right, because we are not the same, and I don't mean to pretend we might be. What did you go and kiss me for?" When she looked away and wouldn't answer, he sighed, "Lord, Lizzy, if the world was a different place maybe I'd be offering to take you to Gretna, but you are something I will never be. I can't see you raising pigs and chickens, with a dozen babies hanging off your skirts, can you?"

She looked back at him at last. Though he was uneducated, his thoughts were wise, perhaps badly expressed, but true. She should no more be kissing a farmer, than she could run for Parliament. "I don't want to go to Gretna Green with you. I don't want to marry anyone, not for ten years at least, but you are right, I should go back, come on."

As soon as they had taken a few steps, however, she saw a monotonous life of needlework, the pianoforte and pouring tea for morning callers stretching out before her and it made her feel so very desperate and reckless. She wanted and prayed for something different for herself, but did not know quite what it was.

"I have to excuse myself," she said, stopping suddenly.

Henry looked bemused. "Why's that?"

"I require a few moments of privacy."

"Oh I see," he said, finally understanding. "I'll wait here while you…I'll wait here for you, shall I?"

"Very well." She smiled affectionately at him before walking off into the woods, knowing it would probably be the last time she ever saw him. Because she went not to answer a call of nature, but to silence the howling of her empty heart and she had no intention of ever coming back.

Darcy heard a shout in the distance. He could not determine the words, but changed course, steering his horse towards it. Instinct and luck caused him to happen upon Henry Jones before too long and Darcy's good memory served him well. He recognised the lad straight away. "You, boy, stop there."

Henry's eyes flickered upwards briefly as he passed Darcy's horse, but he did not stop.

"I asked you to wait, you ought to pay attention when a gentleman addresses you," Darcy snapped, turning his mount.

"Begging your pardon, sir, but you are not my master and I am keen to get back home."

"Where's the girl who was with you, Elizabeth Bennet? I heard a shout just now, what have you done with her?"

Henry squared his shoulders, stopping at last on the lane. "I haven't done anything with her. I was calling her, but she's run off, given me the slip."

"The slip! I hope for your sake, boy, you have not harmed her in any way?"

"Course not. I would never harm her and what's more, I would kill any man who tried to do so."

Taken aback by the vehemence of this statement, Darcy considered the boy for a few moments. He had an open, honest sort of countenance. His spirited defence of himself, and of Elizabeth Bennet, made Darcy suspect Henry Jones was a little in love with her and the thought made him smile. The farm boy aspiring to the gentleman's daughter, what a sweet, impossible attachment it was. Henry Jones deserved a little pity and patience but Darcy had none to spare. "I am to take Miss Bennet back home and then to Derbyshire. I am Mr Darcy's son. Which way was she headed?"

Henry remained silent.

"If I do not recover her in time and something terrible should happen, I'll return to lay the blame squarely at your door, Master Jones."

"To Redbourn, to catch the stage," Henry finally blurted out, begrudgingly.

"In which direction, south for London?"

"Yes."

"And then to Kent?"

"I honestly don't know, sir, I don't think Lizzy does either."

Darcy fished in his pocket and pulled out a coin. "Here, take this for your trouble." He threw the money, a generous half crown, expecting the boy to catch it, but Henry's hands remained firmly in his pockets and he let the coin fall at his feet. He looked at the money and then Darcy, with disdain, before walking away.

When she had reached the point of near exhaustion, Elizabeth flung herself down at the base of a great oak to catch her breath and rest for a few moments. She hoped Henry did not think too badly of her for deceiving him.

They'd once had an oak tree very like this one, a tree they had thought of as theirs - a place where they had met to climb and swing and hide. The tree had been as much of a friend to each of them, as they had been to each other; growing slowly over the years, while they had grown quickly. It had sheltered them from the heat of summer, the rains of autumn and the harsh winds of winter, protecting them while

29

they played and quarrelled, talked and laughed. But now was not the time to dwell on such thoughts, she needed to think of what to do next.

What did she have?

Henry had talked of a few shillings, but in fact she had nearly five pounds in her possession; the result of diligent saving from her pocket allowance over many months. She also had food. In one pocket of her father's old jacket she had a slice of bread and a generous chunk of cheese, wrapped up together in her handkerchief. In the other pocket she had an apple. It was enough for the rest of the day, yet she was very thirsty. A long drink of cordial would have been very welcome, but Longbourn's well-stocked kitchens were far behind her now. Wary of drinking from streams, knowing it was a sure way to make her ill, she decided to head towards the village of Kings Walden, whose main road boasted a well as its principle feature.

Some of her curls had come loose and she pushed them hurriedly back under the brim of the rough cap as she got up. She still needed to crop it, make it as short as Henry's, and she would have to train her voice a few octaves lower. She had a light, feminine, girlish tone that would never help her pass for a boy, even one whose voice had not yet broken.

Only a few hours of daylight remained, and so fully recovered from running so far and so fast, she got to her feet and carried on in the direction of King's Walden, walking at a brisk pace, munching on the apple and grateful for the juice it provided.

Darcy had searched for three hours, criss-crossing lanes, traversing fields and giving every traveller he came across a description but he was no closer to finding Elizabeth Bennet. He had not taken his father's advice. He should have returned to Longbourn as soon as it was obvious she would not be immediately recovered, yet he was loath to give up. However, both he and his mount were tired and hungry and needed to rest for a while. Seeing a village that looked just about large enough to justify a public house, he turned onto its main road. He found a decent enough looking inn and dismounted, handing the reins to a boy employed to tend to the horses, giving him instructions and a few coins.

He did not like to concede defeat at anything but was beginning to suspect he would have no choice but to alert the authorities. His mind was so occupied in this thought, that when he turned and saw her, no more than thirty yards away, he started in surprise.

Just when he had the least expectation of any measure of success for his endeavours, there she was! He blinked and doubted himself but surely there could be no one else wandering around Hertfordshire in such a peculiar outfit. No, it was her. She must have felt his gaze because she looked up at him from under her cap and their eyes met. Darcy was reminded of a deer-hunting expedition he had once undertaken in the Highlands. Her eyes were doe-like, wide in their uncertainty and fear. Neither of them moved and everything was still. She had been leaning over the village well, her hands in its bucket, cupping water in her palms and about to bring it up to her lips. Instead, the water seeped through her fingers. He was certain that as soon as he moved she would take flight, but there was nothing else to be done, he would have to go towards her.

It took only a twitch of his boot to set her running. By the time he had reached the well she'd disappeared down a narrow passage at the side of a sad-looking milliner's shop and Darcy was forced to break into a run. The passage narrowed and twisted to the left and though she was out of sight, he knew she would not get far. There wasn't anywhere for her to run to, the village being nothing but a short string of tiny shops.

He was breathing heavily and struggling to remember the last occasion when he had moved at anything faster than a brisk walk. He fenced, he rode and even boxed occasionally, but running was a pastime he had left behind with childhood and it felt odd to have to move his legs so quickly. He rounded another corner and saw her again in the distance. She had made good ground on him and he was

31

astonished at how nimble and quick she was. It was only when the thin soles of her too-dainty boots skidded on a smooth flagstone and she fell abruptly, that he thought he might catch her. She was nearly within his grasp and he came within inches of grabbing her by the collar of her jacket, when she sprung up and was on her feet again, moving with even greater alacrity than she had gone down. He began to think he might lose her after all but then she turned into the yard of the public house and found herself trapped on all three sides by high walls. The only way out was to go back past him. He saw her glance quickly at a barrel and some wooden crates stacked up in the furthest corner of the yard, as if she were seriously considering climbing up on them to vault the wall. Then her shoulders sagged in defeat, as if she had accepted it was too wild an idea and she turned to face him. Her stance indicated surrender, but her eyes were full of defiance.

"Do not touch me," she shouted.

He stopped a few yards short of where she stood and took a deep, much needed, breath of air before replying. "I have no wish to touch you, but I shall take you back to Longbourn, with or without your cooperation. If you do not do exactly as I say, you will be thrown over my shoulder and taken back by force, do we understand one another?"

"You would not dare."

"Try me, child. You'll find my patience does not extend very far towards young misses who are bent on ruining themselves and embarrassing their families."

"You are Mr Darcy's son," she guessed.

"I am. He has taken responsibility for you and tasked me with bringing you to Pemberley."

She stared at him for a good while, as if taking his measure, before there was a slight tilt of her head that seemed to indicate her agreement.

"Good. Come along with you now, the game is over."

He took her to the inn, where she sat in some astonishment, her head bent to the floor and her cap pulled down as far as it would go, as instructed by Mr Darcy, who left her at a table while he went to speak to the inn-keeper. He had sat her behind a large timber post, where they would be hidden from view and attract as little attention as possible. Elizabeth could not, however, resist an occasional peek around the post to look at the farmers, shopkeepers, bakers and labourers who sat with their metal tankards, telling stories and laughing. They were grimy and dirty from whatever toil had filled their days, their bellies were full of ale and the general absence of women made them raucous and loud. There was the inn-keepers wife behind the bar, and a toothless old crone who sat in a corner, rocking and sipping, well in her cups, talking only to herself, but otherwise it was truly a male domain and fascinating to witness.

Mr Darcy came back bearing two tankards. He sat on the stool opposite her and pushed one of the cups across the table in her direction. "There is only one private room here and it is taken, this will have to do, perhaps it is for the best. We really ought not to be seen alone. Is anyone likely to recognise you?" he asked.

"No, I have been to Kings Walden before, to collect medicine from the apothecary for my father, but I have no acquaintance here. Is this ale?"

"Cider."

Still thirsty, Elizabeth took a long, grateful gulp, but the pungent brew took her by surprise, burning her throat and bringing tears to her eyes. She coughed and spluttered. He handed her a pristine white handkerchief which she pressed to her mouth. When she had recovered enough to speak, she cleared her throat. "'Tis a little stronger than anything I have had before."

Mr Darcy said nothing, but brushed some dust from his elegant trousers, crossed his legs at the ankles and sat back in his chair, giving Elizabeth the chance to study him. He was a fine-looking young man and tall. He carried himself well - with a great air of self-assurance and dignity - but there was also something a little ridiculous about him. He had dark curly hair, which was (since her appointment with the scissors), longer even than her own and he had a thin moustache that did not suit him at all. His waistcoat was gaudy and garish, something only the dandiest of young fops might wear. Yet he had not the cheerfulness to match the bright colours, or the lively air to complement its patterns. He was very serious indeed and looked at those about him with a frown of disapproval. The worst of these frowns were reserved for her.

"We will journey to Longbourn on horseback and make further arrangements from there. The inn-keeper tells me he has a spare mount I might hire for your use. One of your mother's servants can return it. We won't arrive back until gone nightfall, but that cannot be helped, at least there will be less chance of us being noticed."

"I do not ride, sir."

His disapprobation grew deeper. "What do you mean?"

"I mean exactly what I say. My father put me on a horse when I was a child, but I did not care for it. I don't ride, I do not know how."

Mr Darcy muttered a word under his breath which she did not catch. "Very well, I will have to sit you on my horse with me. If it must be so, it must. The circumstances dictate it."

Elizabeth said nothing and took another careful sip of the cider.

"Are you hungry?"

She shook her head.

"May I ask what you were thinking of to run away so? Do you not feel your luck? You should be grateful for the condescension and charity shown to you by my father. He has invited you to live at Pemberley, to be raised alongside his own daughter. I am sure you would be treated almost as if you were a daughter too."

"I do not feel very fortunate at the moment, Mr Darcy."

"Your new situation will be much superior to the one you have left. You will be much elevated by association."

As there was no situation, in Elizabeth's mind at least, that could be better than Longbourn before her father's death; a place where she'd been in receipt of such loving guidance and benevolent, gentle parenting, she was a little stupefied by his words, and disgusted at his suggestion that her father's death, and her family's being made to leave their home, was something to thank the heavens for. She did not know how to express her fury appropriately though and feared her words would come out in a jumbled, incoherent blaze of anger, so instead she shuffled in her seat and looked sullenly down at the table.

"My father has hired a governess for you and my sister, Georgiana, so you might continue your education."

"I do not require a governess."

He laughed a little, but his expression barely changed. "I see, so at fifteen you know everything there is to know. There is nothing a well-educated woman of good breeding, a woman who has instructed the children of nobility can teach you? You know, to be thought of as being accomplished, a lady must have a thorough knowledge of music, singing, drawing, dancing and the modern languages. How is your French?"

"Mon Français est assez bon, Monsieur Darcy, mais il faudrait que je travaille un peu mon accent. J'espère bien un jour aller en France ce qui me permettrait sans doute d'améliorer ma prononciation. Mais je pense que je sais lire et écrire le français plutôt bien. Quel dommage que cette guerre empêche de se rendre en Europe en ce moment et que le traité d'Amiens ait été rompu. Et maintenant on dit que Napoléon a l'intention d'envahir la Russie; mais comment peut - il espérer gagner la guerre contre un pays aussi puissant?"

Elizabeth suspected she had impressed him, and was pleased, though the only evidence of it was a barely discernible raise of his brow.

"And how is your Italian?"

"I do not speak Italian," she admitted, quickly deflated after her little triumph.

"So there are still some things you might master. My sister is learning three languages. She will be a very accomplished young lady and much admired and sought after when she comes out. She'll make a very good marriage."

"I am sure she will. So when selecting a partner, a gentleman's chief consideration is whether she will be able to translate for him at the opera. I had no idea, how surprising! I always assumed that such decisions were based on admiration, love and affection."

"Has anyone ever told you that you are impertinent?"

"Oui, Monsieur Darcy, ils ont."

He opened his mouth to say something further, then closed it again and abruptly got to his feet. "I will see whether the horse is ready. Do not move from this spot while I am gone, speak to no-one and do not even look at anyone."

He required no reply, so Elizabeth took another sip of the cider.

Mr Darcy was not gone for more than a minute before a farmer from a nearby table leaned over and nodded at her. "Your master looks a very fine sort, lad. Rich is he?"

"I suppose," she replied, trying to lower her voice. Then she nibbled on her lower lip and told a terrible lie, while at the same time promising herself she would attend church on Sunday and apologise to the Good Lord in person. "He beats me though, he can be terribly cruel. I ran off, but he has caught me here and is taking me back up north."

"No! You don't say? Well, that's a bad business and no mistake. And, are you needing to get away again, lad? If you are, I am leaving myself soon. Cart is loaded up outside. I won't be checking it before I drive off." The farmer dropped a heavy wink, before pushing aside his ale and standing up to leave.

A few minutes later, she too had left the inn and was sat atop a rough blanket, on the back of a very bumpy cart, as it pulled out of King's Walden. She was astounded at her own daring and boldness. Hearing a shout of 'stop', she looked back to see Mr Darcy in the distance, his hat in his hand, stood in the middle of the road. He did not attempt to race after the cart, perhaps knowing his efforts would be in vain. She was too far away to see his expression, but his stance and the set of his shoulders gave her a notion of just how angry he was. The cart rounded a corner and as it was about to disappear from view, the devil made her raise her hand and wave at him.

Four

Darcy had slept ill. Dirty sheets, sticky surfaces, a lack of hot water and the constant clatter of the coaching inn at Redbourn had all combined to make him restless and angry. Bells and horns sounded regularly throughout the night, announcing the comings and goings of coaches, while passengers tramped up and down the stairs.

Coachmen and maids hollered instructions at each other and dragged trunks hither and thither without any regard for those whose only prayer was for a few hours rest. He had drifted off eventually but had woken again just before dawn to some shouting coming from the yard below. He rose from the bed and walked to the window to watch the commotion, where there was a dispute over a fare. He watched the fight with mild interest, but his mind was elsewhere.

Damn Elizabeth Bennet. When she had waved at him from the back of the cart the previous evening, he had immediately resolved to abandon his search, return to Longbourn, and leave the Bennets to deal with her. What a disrespectful, petulant young hellion she was. If she was silly enough not to see the dangers she was subjecting herself to and the opportunities she was spurning, why should he bother himself any further? Something, however, had made him carry on to Redbourn. Perhaps it was because she was now supposed to be under his father's care that he felt responsible for her, but he suspected it was more his own determination not to be outfoxed that kept him searching. Nobody at the inn at King's Walden had known the cart's destination. Its owner had been passing through the village and was not a local man. Darcy's horse had not yet been readied, so immediate chase had not been possible. He had lost her. After hurrying to Redbourn and making some fruitless enquiries, he had taken a horrible room, ate a bad dinner and slept in a dreadful bed.

Redbourn was ideally positioned on the main road between London and all the northern cities and so had two or three coaching inns. Darcy had chosen to stay at the White

Hart, knowing there was a stage from Leeds that would stop there at half past nine in the morning. He hated to think where Elizabeth Bennet might have spent the night, but she would have to journey from wherever she had hidden herself to Redbourn, and the half past nine stage would suit her purposes well. He felt hungry but would forego breakfast and keep watch for her. He didn't think he could stomach another meal at the White Hart in any case. He was used to far better. When Darcy travelled it was in a Darcy carriage, and the very best of inns were used for overnight stays. It was the very first occasion he'd had cause to use a general coaching inn and he vowed it would be the very last.

Moving from the window to the door, he called out for a porter and ordered some water and a razor in order to clean himself up a bit. What had started out the previous afternoon as an amusing little hunt for a missing charge was becoming a serious tax on his time, not to mention his standards of dress and hygiene. Such was his irritation that when the razor arrived, he botched the job and not only nicked his chin but fumbled with the blade and then stupidly grabbed for it as it fell. It cut into his palm, slicing a long, shallow groove through his skin. The sting of it made him shout loudly and grab for a cloth which he wrapped around his hand tightly for a few moments to stem the flow. The blood was quickly gotten under control, but he had no such hopes of controlling his temper. Damn and blast her – when he did find the girl and manage to get her into a carriage and to Pemberley, his first task would be to convince his father of the mistake he had made in believing her a suitable companion for Georgiana. What Elizabeth Bennet required was a long stay at the strictest of schools, where her manners and wildness would be checked into order. He unwrapped the cloth from around his hands and threw it carelessly onto the bed.

Elizabeth woke slowly on a blanket of hay and blinked into the semi-darkness.

The farmer whose cart she had caught a lift on the previous afternoon had offered her some food and ushered her into his kitchen. His seven children had been sat around a table that seemed too small to accommodate them, but at their father's instruction they had shuffled up along a thin bench to make room for her. The farmer's wife had not been so welcoming and had looked hard at Elizabeth for a long time, examining her from head to toe. "What's your name, boy?"

"E…Edward," she had stammered, almost forgetting herself and just about falling short of blurting out her real name.

"Well Edward, you can sup with us tonight, and sleep in the barn, but you're to be gone tomorrow. I've got enough mouths to feed and I don't relish the kind of trouble that will be brought to my door if your master comes looking for you."

Elizabeth had nodded and ducked her head, sensing the farmer's wife was aware she was no boy, or at least had an inkling that everything was not as it seemed. Luckily, and for whatever reason, the woman took pity on her and said no more, but pushed a steaming bowl of broth Elizabeth's way. It was mostly vegetables, with some tiny pieces of meat floating amongst them. To Elizabeth, who had been out in the fresh air all day and who had walked and ran many miles, it tasted heavenly. She ate quickly and quietly before she was given a thin blanket and shown to the barn.

Though it had been strange and frightening, laying in the dark and listening to the animals move around her, she had been surprisingly warm and had slept deeply for a few hours.

Knowing she had beaten the rising of the sun by only a few minutes, she got to her feet and descended the ladder of the hayloft. It would not be long before the occupants of the farmhouse started to rise and dress.

As she crossed from the barn back to the farmhouse, her boots grew wet from the dew on the grass and she considered going home. It was the most sensible course of action, and if she set off now she might make Longbourn by late afternoon. She did not know the exact route but if she kept walking north she could not go far wrong. But then, her home was no more, everyone would be gone within the week.

Never again would she and her sisters all live together, and if she allowed herself to be taken to Derbyshire, she doubted she would see any of them from one year to the next. The loss was more than her sensibilities could withstand. Though her two youngest sisters' noise and silliness could be irksome, and Mary's oddly serious, pious nature could test her patience, they were still her family and she loved them dearly, and while Elizabeth was often the chief recipient of her mother's shrill scolds and criticisms, all she could think of now was how wonderful it would be to be ensconced in her embrace. Oh, what a soothing pillow her Mamma's voluminous, ridiculous bosom would make at this very moment. But whether she went home, or kept running, that comfort was to be taken from her too.

She peered through the kitchen window of the farmhouse. Nobody was up yet and the room was in darkness. She tried the rough metal catch and finding the door unlocked, pulled it open and crept inside. There was a makeshift washing line strung across the hearth and a pair of woollen trousers and jerkin hung from it. Sat next to the now spent fire was a pair of sturdy boots that had been put out to dry overnight. Elizabeth examined the clothes quickly. They no doubt belonged to one of the boys she had ate broth with the night before. While not as fine as the breeches and jacket she now wore, they were serviceable and much more modern. She would draw far less attention in workable clothes, such as these. Listening carefully and hearing no sounds from above the stairs, she pulled the trousers from the line and quickly changed and then swapped her boots for the sturdier pair. They were a decent fit and well-worn enough to be comfortable.

She sent whoever she had made shoeless for the day a silent apology and fished a generous amount of coins out of her pocket. She left them on the table. The money was enough to replace the items she had taken ten times over and helped to appease her conscience as she slipped out of the kitchen. She was a quarter mile down the road before the sun began to rise and the farm's cockerel crowed.

41

Emma! Of all the people to see, Emma! How that name had once caused Darcy's heart to leap with hope, and how the sight of her had once caused his palms to sweat. Was she a strange apparition brought on by too little sleep? Was it merely someone who looked a little like her? When she passed by not twenty feet in front of him, he saw it was indeed her, but he retreated back into the doorway of the post office, so as not to be seen. What was she doing here? Not travelling on the stage, surely? A lady of her situation would always travel post! She would not wish to share a carriage with tradesman and gentleman farmers, or to have to listen to the row of the lower classes on the outside seats, nor the clatter and bad language and smell of the labourers, maids and general hoi polloi who clung to the roof. Darcy looked around for a smarter, smaller carriage, but none seemed to be in existence.

He had met each incoming coach in good time and watched the boarding, changing of horses and re-boarding of passengers. So far, there was no sign of Elizabeth Bennet, but this was the half-past-nine coach, the one he had a strong inkling she would want to catch. Lady Emma Balcombe's presence was a complication he could have done without. He watched her tall, elegant frame as she moved from the coach to the inn, dressed in the latest fashions - a very fine coat and an elegant hat with a great feather protruding from the top of it. Her hair was so fair, as to be almost white, and her face so pale that her blue eyes were ever the more striking. She drew the stares and admiration of everyone she passed. He stared too, his mouth hung open with wonder and he had to shake himself. *Concentrate Darcy, be mindful of the reason you are here, attend to your business.*

Once Lady Balcombe was inside the inn, he stepped from the doorway and looked across the road. There were two possible directions from which Elizabeth Bennet might emerge, and he saw he might do better to take up a position a little further down the way, from where he would see her no matter which way she came. She would have to pay the coachman, giving him ample time to intercept her. He took up the more favourable vantage point and studied his watch. He was startled by a call of his name and turned to see Lady Constance Balcombe, standing a few yards away, regarding him with curiosity. He bowed and she gave a perfunctory curtsey in return.

"Darcy, how odd to see you here, are you on your way to Pemberley?"

"In a roundabout way, yes."

Her smile was warm, though recent events made their meeting a little embarrassing. "And, are you well?" He saw her eyes travel the length of him, from the cut on his chin, to the makeshift bandage around his palm. She noted his crumpled clothes.

"I am quite well, thank you. Though I know I look a little wild. Dressing myself appears to be a hazardous business."

"You're here without your valet, Darcy? I am all amazement."

"As am I, believe me."

"Emma and I are on our way to Bristol. We sail to Ireland in the morning."

Darcy looked away. "I did happen to see your sister. I am sorry."

"Oh *you* owe me no apology, nothing was your fault. My sister is entirely responsible for her own foolish decisions."

"Yet he was my friend."

"And he betrayed you both."

"I suppose she goes to get away from the talk?" Darcy asked.

"Oh, there is not much talk. These days, it takes a lot more than a daughter of the nobility making a fool of herself over a penniless nothing to get society going."

Darcy let out a bitter laugh. "'Tis true, there are so many fine ladies going to the dogs these days..." He stopped and cursed himself.

Constance merely laughed at his mortification and put her hand on his arm. "Walk me to the door of the inn, Darcy. I shall not see you for two years or more I expect."

They began the short stroll. Darcy glanced over his shoulder once or twice as they went. "Two years, so long?"

"My father is exceedingly angry. Not only are we to be sent to our dreadful Aunt Violet, in deepest, darkest Cork, but we are travelling by the stage, with naught but a couple of servants."

"Is your father not worried something may befall you on the journey?"

"Perhaps he is hoping something might," she laughed, though it was not amusing in the least, "to Emma in any case."

"And you are to be punished alongside her?"

Constance gave a dismissive wave of her hand. "It'll save my family the bother of wondering what to do with me. What better use to make of me, than as companion to Emma?"

Darcy felt aggrieved on her behalf. Constance was the eldest Balcombe sister, yet despite her sizeable dowry, wonderful accomplishments and excellent nature, she had been surpassed and overlooked for Emma. The younger sister's beauty was universally praised and she had been allowed to come out four years previously, at only sixteen, despite Constance being unmarried and only nineteen at the time. There were two older brothers, one who would inherit his father's estate and title, and another who was in Parliament. And in amongst these shining stars, largely ignored by her parents and everybody else, was Constance - a steady girl and by no means horribly unattractive, but of stout build and large features. She stood taller than most gentlemen; Darcy being one of few who could look down at her. This, coupled with her plain way of speaking and direct manners, made her unpopular in society, where false sentiment reigned supreme. Darcy liked Constance though, she was one of a very small number of women in whose company he felt easy. How many mornings had he sat in their mother's parlour, talking with Constance, but looking at Emma? And she, bless her heart, had never minded that his gaze would always wander. Instead, she had gently and kindly teased him about his admiration, encouraged his hopes and told him how much she would like him for a brother - but it had all come to naught. It had all ended in disaster.

He stopped and turned to face her when they reached the door of the inn. "I shall have to take leave of you here. I have some business to attend to, please accept my best wishes for your future health and happiness."

"You won't come in and take refreshment with us?"

His smile was wry. "I don't think I would be welcomed by your sister, but you are kind to suggest it."

"Well, goodbye then. Let me say, Darcy, as we part, that Emma is a foolish girl to have sought what she did, when she could have had so much more."

Darcy thanked her and gave his compliments, walking back to his position further along the street, from where he could keep better watch. Despite his best efforts to remain focussed on the task at hand, seeing Emma Balcombe, and then Constance, had distracted him. So much so, that when Elizabeth Bennet walked directly past him just a few minutes later, he did not notice her.

Elizabeth went not to the inn, but the stables, where she thought she might find somewhere to conceal herself until the coach was ready to leave. She would present herself only at the last moment and pay to sit on the outside seats. The stables were thankfully quiet. Two carriage drivers stood by the door talking, each with a tankard of ale in hand, but she slipped nonchalantly past them and they spared her not a second look. She put herself in the furthest, darkest corner she could find, but she was still able to see the coaches in the yard through the gaps in the slats of wood. Her hands shook and her heart thumped violently in her chest at the thought of what she was about to do. To board a coach to London, unaccompanied, was not only shocking, but possibly foolhardy too. Reaching into the pocket of the jerkin, she pulled out the small pouch which contained her money and began to count out into her palm the amount of coins she might need for the fare. Sensing another presence, she looked up and realised her mistake. A lad of nineteen or twenty, dark haired and dark skinned, tall and rangy, pursed his lips and offered her a smile that should have been friendly, yet it made the hairs on the back of Elizabeth's neck stand on end. His eyes flicked to the pouch containing her money and then he smiled again.

"Looking to take the coach to London are you?"

Elizabeth tried to walk away, to move past him, but he stepped to the side to block her path.

"Now don't be scared, I mean you no harm, I just wanted to offer a bit of advice. You see the ladder yonder?" He pointed to the back of the stables. "It takes you up to the hay store. There is a window from where you can jump. You'll hit the roof of the London stage, 'tis only two feet or so. If you time it right, you can sit snug there in the middle of the trunks and nobody complains much. Give the porter in Town a couple of bob when you get off and he'll look the other way."

Unaccustomed to being addressed by men she had not being introduced to, Elizabeth did not know whether to answer him. Such rules and niceties obviously did not apply in these quarters.

"It'll save you half a crown, if you're looking to spare your money." He nodded at the velvet pouch she still held in her hand.

She put the pouch firmly in her pocket. "May I get past?"

The lad's smile was taunting. "May you?" he mimicked her accent. "Oh, I daresay you may."

"Please get out of my way."

His teeth were brown and he smelt of the horses. He moved closer to her and she instinctively moved backwards, stupidly trapping herself in the corner. "That's a pretty heavy purse you've got there, my little lord. Hand it over and I won't tell anyone you were here. Where you run off from then?"

"It's none of your business."

His attack was fast and furious. She was grabbed by both arms and put against the wood of the stables. All the breath left her body or she might have screamed. He used his forearm to hold her in place while his other hand delved into her pocket and pulled out the velvet pouch.

"It is mine, give it back."

"What's going on here?" A deeper, older voice, common and coarse came from behind Elizabeth's attacker and for a moment she thought she would be saved. He was one of the drivers she had seen at the door. "What's up, Fred?"

"Boy's got over four pounds on him."

"Has he now! Where did you steal that from?"

"Nowhere, it is mine, I saved it," Elizabeth said.

They both laughed at her. The driver's eyes narrowed and he pulled the cap from her head. Her curls fell down about her face and he laughed again. "You ain't no boy. I'll be damned if there's anything in the front of them trousers." He pulled her towards him and began tugging at her clothes. Elizabeth, terrified and trapped, kicked out, her foot hitting his shin. He let out a yelp of pain and whilst he was momentarily stunned, she tried to slip past him, but he recovered quickly and hauled her back and then grabbed the folds of her shirt, trying to pull it apart at the front. She struggled, lost her footing and fell to the ground.

There was then a great shout of 'desist' and the driver was felled too, dropping onto his knees and clutching his forearm. Mr Darcy loomed imposingly over all of them, a bandaged hand clenched around his stick. "Get out, before I whip you and speak to your employers," he told the driver.

"Now, sir, let me explain."

"The child is with me, get out…"

His voice was deep and threatening. It reverberated around the stables. The driver held up his hands, palms upwards in a conciliatory gesture and then made for the door. Mr Darcy took a few steps after him, making sure he was definitely gone.

The young lad, still stood over Elizabeth, reached out while Mr Darcy was distracted and took hold of the thin gold chain around her neck. He snatched at it, yanking hard. The chain broke and she cried out, grabbing for his hand, which now held her cross, trying to prise it back from him, but he shrugged her off easily and fled, brushing by Mr Darcy, who had not entirely seen what had happened and had no reason to stop him. Elizabeth got to her feet to give chase and shouted, but was prevented from running after them by Mr Darcy throwing his arms about her before she got to the door.

"Let them go, it is a mere trifle, I'll replace it," he hissed in her ear.

"It cannot be replaced. Not everything can be bought, no matter how rich you are."

As soon as she stopped struggling, he set her free and she walked a few steps away where she sagged against a post, the fight having truly left her.

"Straighten yourself up. Tuck the shirt in."

Looking down at herself, she turned away from him and quickly did as she was bid. The shirt had not been completely pulled open in the struggle, just loosened, yet Elizabeth found herself blushing in any case and noticed her hands shook as she redid the ties at her throat. "He took my cross," she said, numbly.

"Rather than worrying about trinkets, you ought to be thankful I happened upon you in time." His countenance was grim and stern, and he then astounded her by taking her elbow and marching her out of the stables and across the yard of the inn. He moved quickly, ushering her on. They attracted some attention, but he looked angry, past the point of caring what others might think. She was directed up the stairs and into a room. "You will stay here."

Astounded by his forcefulness and too shocked by recent events to do anything but nod, Elizabeth went and sat in a chair by the window. Mr Darcy paced and then ran a hand over his mouth. "We require some assistance. I need to leave you to make some arrangements. Can I trust you to remain here?"

"Upon my honour, I promise, I will not move," she said and meant it. Having fallen into a world far beyond her knowledge or experience, where danger, thievery and violence were abundant and where men were not gentlemen, she saw she did not have the skills to negotiate it properly. She bore no inclination to be out in it on her own again any time soon.

Mr Darcy gave her a curt nod and left.

Five

Floundering for a while, not quite knowing where to start, Darcy saw Constance Balcombe on the stairs and relief flooded through him. Here was someone he might trust, implicitly.

She laughed at the sight of him. "Darcy, they say our driver has run off and we shall have to wait for another to be found. Can you believe such a thing? What could make a man abandon his living and fifteen passengers?"

He shook his head as if he had no idea. "Constance, I value your friendship, but I fear I may have to involve you in a situation that is improper. Can I count on your discretion?"

"Always, Darcy, whatever is the matter?"

On the way back to his room, he briefly explained Miss Bennet's circumstances, the dire straits he found himself in and the assistance he required.

"Goodness," Constance replied.

"I require clothes for her."

"Of course and I will assist if I can, but you say she has been accosted by these men. Darcy, she must be very upset, take me to her."

She walked up the stairs in front of him and he pointed to his chamber door.

Elizabeth Bennet jumped in fear at their entrance. Darcy immediately felt like the most boorish, crassest man on earth, as Constance crossed the room and knelt at Elizabeth's feet. She introduced herself simply by her first name and asked the only questions that were really important, the enquiries he had failed to make of her. "Are you well? Are you hurt?"

"I am well." Elizabeth swiped at her eyes with the sleeve of her jacket. "I am merely upset at having lost my necklace and cross. They were a present from my father, it is only that which bothers me."

Constance hid a smile at this attempt at bravado and pressed a handkerchief from her reticule into Elizabeth's hands. "But of course. Now, Mr Darcy is going to procure you a glass of wine for the shock and see to the hiring of a carriage, for we must get you out of here as soon as possible. He has flattered me by asking for my help with clothes, but he shows the usual male ignorance in these matters, for I am at least twice your size and a good deal taller, my gowns will never do." Constance thought for a moment, tapping a finger against her lips. "I have a maid who is very petite. She may have a Sunday gown. I shall ask."

Constance got to her feet again and left them. Darcy looked to remove himself too and put a hand on the doorknob but Elizabeth's voice stopped him.

"How did you know where to find me?"

"Your little admirer, Henry Jones, told me you would be taking the stage."

Elizabeth wrinkled her nose. "I did not think he was to be so little trusted."

"Perhaps he knows what's better for you than you do yourself. I specifically asked you to remain at the inn at King's Walden and wait for me. My father is a good and lenient man but I am quite certain he will not tolerate such outright disobedience in his house."

She received this scolding with her mouth set in a firm line, her eyes towards the window and did not reply. He left the room, closing the door a little too firmly behind him, causing the wood to rattle.

Elizabeth hugged herself when they had gone. Exhausted, filthy and itchy in the rough hessian trousers and shirt, she longed for a bath and familiar food. She wanted to sit in front of a roaring fire with one of her father's books open on her lap and not to have Mr Darcy berating her. She could see now how foolish and ridiculous she had been in running off. She did not need him to keep reminding her about her lack of judgement. She had defied her elders, lied to almost everyone and stolen clothes. Her father would have been mightily ashamed of her.

There were physical, as well as emotional reminders, of her folly too; her knees hurt from where she had been pulled over in the barn and there was a stinging about her throat where her necklace had been ripped from her.

Mr Darcy's friend returned after a little more than ten minutes, with a gown thrown over one arm and a bonnet and cloak over the other. "Now, I am sure they are not as fine as you are used to, but needs must."

Constance had a friendly smile and Elizabeth found herself returning it.

"You are very kind. You do not know me."

"But I know Mr Darcy and he has asked for my help," Constance said. "You are to go to Pemberley, I understand?"

Elizabeth gave a small nod.

"You will like it, you know, it is very lovely."

"No doubt, you are going to tell me how grateful I should be; how lucky I am, as everyone else does?"

"I will not presume to tell you how you must feel, but there are worse situations a young lady could find herself in than to be a ward of the Darcys, such as the one you have just come from." Constance paused. "How old are you, thirteen, fourteen?"

"Fifteen," Elizabeth replied proudly, rankling a little that Constance thought she might be as young as thirteen.

"Oh that is terrible. Fifteen is quite terrible." Constance made a face and Elizabeth laughed, instantly liking her again. "Who knows what to think or feel, or who we are supposed to be at fifteen? Shouldn't it just be abolished and we go from fourteen to sixteen in one jump? Though you will get there, I promise. Spring, you see, always becomes summer eventually and all that seems confusing and unbearable now will not be so hard at sixteen, or seventeen or eighteen." She squeezed Elizabeth's hand. "You are far too pretty to pass for a boy, you know?"

"Oh, I am very ordinary looking next to Jane; my elder sister is the pretty one in our family. She is very handsome."

"I see. I have a 'very handsome' sister too."

There was a rap on the door and a maid brought in fresh water. Once she had washed the grime from her face and hands, Elizabeth allowed Constance to help her dress.

Though she had only been without them for two days, it felt odd to be in skirts again. There was no corset to be had, but truthfully, she did not much regret the absence of that particular garment. Her mother insisted, but Elizabeth had always struggled and itched and pulled at hers, seeing it as an evil without necessity - after all, she had nothing that required holding in and very little to be pushing up. The gown hung loosely about her body, despite the string ties being pulled in as far as they would go, but Constance's maid must have been as short of stature as she, for it was the right length and once the cloak was put around her and the bonnet pulled down low, she felt almost like a young lady of Longbourn again.

Try as he might, Darcy could not find a private coach or driver for hire. Some of the passengers from the northbound stage, which had been delayed due to the driver having fled after the confrontation in the barn, had secured the services of what seemed to be the only rentable barouche in town. He paced and fumed. Money, in this case, could not help. He could not buy something that was simply not available and time was of the essence. The facts were that he was a single man with a strangely attired, very young girl, sequestered in a room he had stupidly taken under his real name. They needed to leave and very soon. Darcy felt the threat of scandal breathing down his neck and was not inclined to let it catch up with him.

He cursed and did something that made him shudder. He did not know how he would bear the smells, the hot breath and the course manners he would encounter, but feeling he had no other choice, he went to pay the coachman for two seats on the London bound stage. Once this was done, he secured a glass of wine and climbed the stairs again. He knocked on the door and admittance was granted. He blinked a little at the sight of Elizabeth Bennet in cloak and bonnet, such was the alteration in her appearance, and stood stupidly, with the door open behind him for several moments, before coming to his senses and shutting it.

"Do you have relatives in London, Miss Bennet?"

"Yes, Mr Darcy. My Uncle Gardiner, my mother's brother."

"He's a married man?" Darcy asked.

"Yes, he is married and has two children."

"And does he keep a respectable house?"

"Certainly."

She looked offended but Darcy had no time to spare on her sensibilities. "Good, then I believe the best course of action will be to take you there. We must go by stage, 'tis unavoidable. It leaves at half-past the hour, I will expect you downstairs at five and twenty past." He put the wine on a table, nodded curtly, bowed deeply towards Constance and went to quit the room again.

As he threw the door wide open in great haste, sheer bad luck brought Emma Balcombe passing by. They both started in surprise at the sight of one another.

"Darcy!"

He could not move or speak as her eyes flittered over his shoulder, then widened when she saw Constance behind him.

"Well…" she floundered.

"Lady Balcombe."

They had spoken at the same time. All the polite enquiries normally associated with the coming across of an acquaintance by accident, seemed not only unnecessary, but absurd.

Constance came forward, leading Elizabeth by the hand and trying to make light of the situation. "Emma, I was just assisting Mr Darcy for a few moments with his young charge here, he required a chaperone. What are you doing upstairs? You ought to have remained in the parlour."

"I was looking for you." Emma Balcombe stared at them all, her eyes moving around, back into the room they were now coming from.

"Well, you have found me. I shall be with you shortly, after I have seen this young lady downstairs, and then we might have some tea."

As Constance tried to pass, Emma stepped in their way and looked carefully at Elizabeth.

"Forgive me, my dear, have we met before? I am sure we must have, are you not Millicent Reynolds, we met at the Bertram's dinner? You must remember me, Lady Balcombe?"

"No, I think you have me confused with someone else, I am Elizabeth Bennet of Longbourn, Hertfordshire. I have never met you."

Lady Emma's glacial blue eyes narrowed and a smirk formed at the corners of her mouth. Darcy saw Elizabeth realise her mistake as soon as the words had fallen from her mouth and she looked mortified at her gaucheness.

He smiled at Emma Balcombe and tried to look unbothered. "Miss Bennet is my father's ward. Now, we really must be away, Lady Balcombe. We are catching the London stage."

"Of course, Mr Darcy, travelling by stage, how daring of you!"

"It seems to be the fashion nowadays."

"I must beg a few moments of your time, though. Constance and Miss Bennet may go ahead and secure your seats."

"I..."

"You would not deny me, sir? I have something important to say."

"Of course." He nodded at Constance and she took the stairs with Elizabeth. Emma, to his surprise, strode into his room and looked about.

He stood in the doorway, keeping it firmly open with one boot. "You should not be in there."

"Oh, I am banished to Ireland in any case. Who is she, the little chit?"

"She is nobody, my father's ward, as I have said. What is it you wish to say to me, I am in a very great hurry?"

Emma smiled at him and he could not help but admire her, she was decidedly handsome. "If I promised to be sorry for the rest of my days, would you reconsider? Didn't you love me once, Darcy?"

"You knew what my feelings were."

"Did I? You are a guarded man. What did I know with any certainty? I had no promise, no declaration, all you did was stare at me. Is it any wonder I became impatient?"

"This is a rather wasted conversation, I am afraid. I cannot forget so easily, nor ignore things."

She grew angry. "Oh, look at you, so pompous. So sure of your rightness in all things, and yet, you are no better than I. How old is that girl you have had in your room with you?"

"It is not how it appears. I have done nothing I ought to be ashamed of."

"There is no need to pretend with me. I would only question your taste. Darcy, you have erred and so have I. We might still make a good match."

Unable to help it, he laughed at her absurdity and she, perhaps seeing the hopelessness of her suit, quit the room, pushing past him.

Darcy waited a few moments before going downstairs himself. He arrived in the yard to see Constance standing beside the stage. Elizabeth was already seated within.

"I will talk to Emma and persuade her, if I can, not to speak of our meeting you here. I will beg her silence," she assured him.

He thanked her and they shared a fond look.

"Very best of luck, Darcy."

"And to you, Constance," he said, boarding the coach and taking a seat opposite Elizabeth. He sighed as a woman of large proportions and two of her squawking offspring sat beside him. Three gentlemen farmers, all slightly in their cups and talking overly loud, filled the rest of the carriage, and then they were off with a lurch that made the children cry louder and the drunkards cheer. Darcy resolved never, ever, to travel anywhere ever again in anything other than his own very private carriages.

It was ten minutes before Elizabeth leaned forward and whispered. "Why do we go to London?"

He looked around at his fellow passengers and seeing them occupied, answered honestly, in a rushed, discreet whisper. "You have been missing overnight, London is better."

"Oh, I have no objections, I was just curious. I am very fond of my uncle and aunt and Jane is to go them permanently, perhaps I might stay there for a few weeks?"

Darcy was astonished at her lack of conscience. "If they will have you. Do you have no notion of the trouble you have put people to? I should imagine your uncle will not be best pleased with you. Where were you bound for in any case, the Indies, or the Americas perhaps? Am I permitted to know the details of the plan I have foiled?"

"I did not actually have a destination in mind. I was not running towards anything, Mr Darcy, I think instead, I was running *from* things…thoughts in my head that I could not banish," she said quietly and looked down, pulling the borrowed cloak more tightly around her.

There was clarity then and understanding. He too had once watched a beloved parent slip away, and though time had dulled the pain, the memory was still vivid enough to catch him unawares now and then; to make his chest tighten and his breath catch. His mother's passing had begun slowly, with some loss of appetite, a struggle to rise and dress each morning and an all-consuming tiredness which worsened over time. She had arrived in the drawing room later and later in the day, and then her correspondence had started to go unanswered and the household affairs had become too much for her. His father had not stood idly by and watched. George Darcy had spared no expense and sent for an endless stream of doctors. Men from all over the country and all walks of life, who arrived full of promises and boasts but inevitably left a few weeks later, having exhausted all their ideas; their smiles sympathetic but their pockets full. Crippling pain had eventually made Lady Anne take to her bed permanently, and day by day, hour by hour, minute by minute, she had drifted from this world to another. He had loathed the feeling of helplessness. He had been unable to do anything but read to her, soothe her brow and pray for some miraculous recovery. His prayers had gone unanswered and his hopes had been sunk altogether by the knock on his chamber door in the very early hours of a crisp, bright morning; a morning she would have adored. As he'd walked to his mother's room, a magnificent sunrise had been visible through the long window at the far end of the corridor, bathing everything in warmth, yet her cheek had been horribly cold when he had bestowed his last kiss.

He supposed he had been lost in thought for some time, as when he looked back again, Elizabeth Bennet had fallen fast asleep with her head back against the cushion, her mouth ever so slightly parted. He could not fathom how she could rest in such a poorly sprung coach, but perhaps she'd had an even more restless night than he. Lord knows where she had laid herself down. Despite the bumping and jostling, and the rowdy men and crying children, she slept on peacefully, looking even younger in repose. As he watched her Darcy felt a startling, overpowering feeling of protectiveness but could not fathom from where it came.

They arrived in London without incident, Elizabeth waking when the stage came to a stop. She followed Mr Darcy wordlessly through a small passageway to a carriage hire company, where he secured them a more private mode of transport for the rest of their journey. He said not a word, other than to ask her for her uncle's address, which she gave, noting afterwards the look of distaste that crossed his features when she mentioned Gracechurch Street.

"Perhaps your father will not want me in his house after all, because I have behaved so badly, and I shall not go to Pemberley," she said.

"Was that your intention?"

"No, I honestly had no intention, of anything."

Mr Darcy's mouth twisted into a ghost of a smile. "My father is not so easily put off his responsibilities. One way or another, Miss Bennet, before ere long, I'm quite certain you will go to Pemberley."

Though her arrival at the Gardiners was received with shock, there was also relief, for she soon learnt an express had been sent from Longbourn with news of her disappearance. Her aunt clasped Elizabeth to her and stroked her arms and kissed her cheek. Her uncle began a great lecture but was quietened with a look from his wife, who merely said 'later'.

A bath was ordered and Elizabeth was led upstairs. She took a few steps before turning, remembering Mr Darcy and supposing she ought to offer him some sort of apology; she had led him a merry dance after all, and he had saved her from Lord knows what back at the inn. When she looked back, he was still in the hallway, looking uncomfortable and as if he wished himself a million miles away. All the expressions of genuine regret she might have made would somehow not form on her lips.

"Goodbye, Mr Darcy," was all she could manage. Despite what he had said in the carriage, Elizabeth fully intended that it would be the last she ever saw of him.

He offered her nothing but a small bow in return and she hurried away up the stairs.

Her Aunt Gardiner, good kind woman that she was, shooed her own young children away and gave them over to the care of a nursemaid, before fussing over Elizabeth. She helped her out of her gown, striped her down to her underclothes and wrapped her in a blanket whilst the tin bath was brought up and jug after jug of hot water was poured into it. "Your uncle goes to Longbourn on Tuesday to fetch Jane, he will have to bring your clothes also."

Elizabeth nodded dully. Gowns and pelisses seemed very unimportant. "So will I stay here for a while?"

"That is a decision for your uncle and Mr Darcy," her aunt sighed. "We are very fond of you, Lizzy, but for us to take care of you and Jane, well, it is a lot to ask of your uncle. We have two young children of our own, and I think maybe another on the way. He has so much to concern him already."

"But I might share a room with Jane, and her old clothes might be altered to fit me and…"

Her aunt interrupted her with a laugh. "Yes and you might eat scraps from the kitchen and only bathe once a month."

Elizabeth ignored the teasing and pressed her case. "I would not be disobedient, or impertinent. I would certainly never run away again."

"I am glad to hear it, whatever made you do such a foolish thing? You are lucky you did not come to any harm."

That she'd been robbed, and might have been beaten too, if Mr Darcy had not rescued her, she did not say. Her aunt would be horrified. "I cannot explain it. I suppose I lost my mind, momentarily."

"And your hair…" her Aunt Gardiner said as she stroked the short dark curls that fell about Elizabeth's face, "but it will grow again. In the meantime we shall have to pin it back as best we can. It is too short to go up. Your Mamma will take to her bed for a week when she sees it.

Elizabeth let out a long yawn. "How am I so tired when I slept the whole way here?"

"Let's get you washed and changed. You can have some supper on a tray and then to bed. You will need a good night's sleep to endure the lengthy and strident lecture your uncle will give you tomorrow," Mrs Gardiner warned with a smile.

Six

Darcy spent the evening of his return from Hertfordshire mostly in the confines of his study. He wrote a very long letter to his father, giving a largely faithful account of what had transpired thus far and intended to wait for a response, before deciding how and when Elizabeth Bennet should make the journey to Pemberley.

The housekeeper and butler had looked at him with some astonishment when he had returned home unexpectedly. Having shut the Darcy's London house up only the day before, they were then faced with the task of reopening it again and although they performed their duties without any overt complaint, he saw resentment in their eyes. The family always repaired to Pemberley for the summer months and they no doubt had expected several easy weeks of simple caretaking before them. Now the young Mr Darcy was back and could give them no immediate idea of when he might go away again. Though he understood their disappointment, their obvious umbrage gave him cause to feel more than a little irked.

He went to bed in a state of exhaustion and anxiousness, his conversation with Emma Balcombe running through his mind, over and over, while he wondered whether he might have handled her better.

Several hours of sleep felt like only a few moments and when he woke in the morning his first thoughts, oddly, were of Elizabeth Bennet. He could not help but wonder how the girl fared. She *was* such a little hellion and so far removed from his idea of what a young lady ought to be, but still, he couldn't help but admire her fortitude. She had been attacked, manhandled and stolen from, yet she had not panicked or been overcome with hysterics. Her composure had been admirable. He ought to be more irritated with her than he was; instead he hoped she did not suffer any ill effects from her tomfoolery.

Not being prone to idleness, however, he did not ponder her for long. He decided he would spend the day hunting down a book he had been meaning to read. There was a bookseller near Hyde Park who might be able to procure it for him. Happily, he had no business to attend to, nor any social obligations. Nobody knew he had been forced to return to London. There would be no callers, or invitations to beckon him hither and thither. If he avoided his club and the smarter parts of Town, he might indulge in a short holiday of sorts. For a whole day, perhaps even two, or three, depending how long it took for letters to go back and forth to Derbyshire, he was entirely at leisure and able to do exactly as he pleased.

The next day saw Elizabeth being fitted into an old gown of her aunt's by a maid with excellent sewing skills, after which she had sat before her Uncle Gardiner and received a telling off she would not have believed him capable of, had she not been the unfortunate recipient of it. Sternness did not come naturally to him. Mr Gardiner was a jovial, warm-spirited man and though he took to the task of her dressing down with professional gusto, he looked as relieved as she was when it was finally over. Escaping his study, she then embarked upon a plan of making herself so indispensable within the household that the Gardiners would absolutely insist to the Darcys that she remain with them – she was to be so helpful they could not possibly spare her and so pleasant and amiable, they would not want to either.

She wrote dinner invitations for her aunt, poured tea when a visitor came and then took herself off to the nursery to entertain the children, only to be shooed away an hour later when Mr Gardiner complained of a headache brought on by the noise. On reflection, maybe she had entertained them a little *too* much and they *were* a little over excited and boisterous, but surely her efforts would not go unrewarded. Over dinner, Mr Gardiner informed them he would be travelling into Hertfordshire at first light the next day and would be bringing Jane back with him. It had always been the day she was to come and 'Lizzy's little adventure' as he referred to it, would not alter the arrangement. The joy Elizabeth felt at hearing this was great - to be reunited with

Jane; her confidant, her guide, her friend and dearest sister! No news had ever been more welcome. Though in reality, it had been only a couple of days, the separation felt of much longer duration.

She did not move from the window seat in the drawing room the following afternoon, not until her uncle's modest coach came into sight and stopped at the door. She then raced down the stairs and met her sister in the hallway, throwing her arms about her. Jane laughed at her exuberance, but then as she held her away to look at her, her expression was one of dismay. "Oh Lizzy, your lovely hair, it is so short!"

Embarrassed, Elizabeth shrugged. "It does not matter."

"Of course it matters, oh, and it is so thick and has such a curl in it that I fear it will take months to grow back."

"And I will be in mourning for many months yet, so you see, I can hide away until it does."

Elizabeth went with her sister to the room they would share and helped her change out of her travelling clothes but soon grew cross at Jane's sidelong glances. "Please stop looking at me that way. It *will* grow back. Tell me, how is everyone at Longbourn. Is Mamma well?"

"She is better now, though she was in her room for two days, sick with worry."

"About me?" Elizabeth was taken aback. She and her mother were so different; there was no physical resemblance between them at all and they certainly did not share the same disposition or humour. Oh, she knew her mother loved her, but she always supposed it was in the same way that she cared for the family dog, or for Longbourn's cook, who prepared her mutton just so. Her mother's greatest displays of affection were reserved for Jane, who she believed would marry very well and save them from their current financial predicament, and for ten-year-old Lydia, her youngest daughter and greatest pet.

"Of course about you!" Jane said. "Do you not know that the house has been in uproar? Uncle Phillips was out in his cart about the countryside looking for you, the groom and stable boy likewise. I know you did not want to go and live with the Darcys, Lizzy, but do you not think it was very selfish of you to run off so?"

"Oh, don't you give me a scolding too, Jane. I have already had one off Mr Darcy and our uncle."

"Mr Darcy scolded you?"

"It was very brief, he is a man of few words," Elizabeth smiled but Jane seemed in an unusually dour mood. "Please be of good cheer, Jane. All is well now."

Jane turned suddenly from where she had been arranging her things on the nightstand. "All is not well," she snapped, "everything is different and you are very fortunate not to have made it worse for us all."

Elizabeth did not know what to say and looked at the floor. Jane was normally so sanguine, so calm tempered and kind in her dealings with everyone. Such sharpness was not like her.

"I am sorry," Jane said, after a pause. "I know you miss Papa, but you are not the only one grieving, Lizzy. You do not hold the monopoly on despair and your actions, well, they might have had disastrous consequences. Did you not think? We already have so little to recommend us, a thousand pounds each, and our charms. If the talk prevails in Meryton it will have an effect on Mary, Kitty and Lydia."

Elizabeth noticed how her sister was only concerned for their younger siblings and not at all for herself. She was all noble indifference to her own reputation. "Is there talk?"

"Yes, that you ran off with Henry Jones, but then he came back after a while and that you made your way to London alone."

"Oh, well that is hardly a great scandal. Remember what Papa always used to say? *'For what do we live, but to make sport for our neighbours, and laugh at them in our turn?'*"

"And you are just like him. Thinking the world is a joke, that everyone and everything is to be laughed at; that we are all here for your amusement."

"I do not. I do not laugh at you, Jane and I could not bear it if you were to remain cross at me." Elizabeth threw

63

herself down upon the bed in a childish show of distress and gave a huge heavy sigh to garner her sister's attention and sympathy. Jane could not help but smile and shake her head. She too sat on the bed and gathered Elizabeth up in her arms.

"We have no father now, and the world's least sensible mother. We must be careful and cautious, not silly and unguarded. Do you promise me, Lizzy?"

Jane seemed suddenly older and sadder; responsibility for her younger siblings now weighed heavy on her shoulders. They sat and said nothing for a while, Elizabeth happy just to be held in a steady pair of arms. It was a welcome relief to her when the world seemed to be constantly changing and shifting. Oh, what a worthless creature she was in comparison to Jane. All she knew how to do was kick and scream and run. "I promise, Jane. I promise I'll cause no trouble from now on."

Seven

Those at the centre of a scandal are usually the last to know of it. While Fitzwilliam Darcy had spent an indulgent day amongst leather bound volumes in a tiny shop in West London, breathing in the heavenly scent that was peculiar only to old books, and Elizabeth Bennet had used all her charm and diligence in order to try and prove herself an indispensable, welcome addition to the Gardiner's comfortable home, letters of a most vicious nature had found their way from Hertfordshire to London. They were letters deliberately meant to wound, and of a sort that could only be written by a woman who felt herself ill-used, rejected and cast off. Lady Emma Balcombe had felt no compunction in exacting her retribution and could hardly believe the opportunity for revenge had come along so quickly. There was to be no years of seething and plotting for her, she had dealt her blow and now had nothing to do but sit back and laugh at the sheer deliciousness of it. She chose the recipients of her letters well, selecting those members of society least known for their discretion or prudence, those more prone to idleness than industry and those to whom such news was traded like currency – the more terrible the rumour, the greater its worth and the further its reach.

By turns appalled, amused and shocked, society exclaimed, tittered and repeated the tale. Even those who found it hard to believe of Darcy, and who called themselves his friend, passed it on to everyone they met, prefixed with '*I suppose it is not true, but I have heard...*' thus what had been related to just a few in the morning post, came to be common knowledge by supper time.

Colonel Fitzwilliam came to know of it via a chance encounter with George Wickham, a man he verily detested. It was unusual for the Colonel, second son of the Earl of Matlock and Darcy's cousin, to dislike anyone, but Wickham had behaved so abominably, despite all the favour shown to him, that the Colonel would not have spat Wickham's way if he had been passing by and seen the man on fire. He understood, to a certain degree, Wickham's jealousy of

Darcy. He, as a younger son, knew something of self-denial and dependence on others. His own life was one of limitation - he had a lack of money, a lack of good looks and a lack of stature. But unlike Wickham, he knew a man ought to count his blessings and not covet what he could not have, lest he be eaten alive with envy. And the Colonel did have much in his favour after all; he was nobly born into an excellent family and had the easy manners which meant he had formed a large circle of friends. He was never short of somewhere or someone to eat dinner with. Invitations to shooting weekends and house parties flowed thick and fast and were too numerous for him to accept them all. And the fact that nobody seemed particularly interested in marrying him did not upset him in the least. He rather enjoyed being excluded from the marriage mart. He was able to flirt with impunity, dance with whomever he pleased, while wearing a dashing red uniform and nobody expected anything from him. Life was good and generally there were very few things in it to cause him pain, but the sight of George Wickham at the gaming tables, wasting away the Darcy's money, was one of them.

He bent low, surprising Wickham, who jumped slightly in his chair at the sound of the Colonel's voice. "Be careful, you villain. Once it is gone, it is gone, there'll be no more."

Wickham turned, recovering his composure quickly, and offered the Colonel a smug smile. "Who says I am going to lose? I am feeling particularly lucky tonight. I became a father this morning, so you see, it is a fortuitous day for me."

"Well, congratulations. I trust mother and child are in good health?"

"Doing very well, I hear."

"You have not been to see them as yet?"

"And interrupt a winning streak? Besides a man is no use to anybody in such situations, but I hear he is a beautiful boy."

"Well, you are lucky indeed. I hope your son will feel fortunate himself, when he is older, to have had you for a father. Your son is blessed because Mr Darcy had enough money to coerce you into doing the right thing."

Wickham shot up from his chair and for a moment the Colonel thought he was about to be asked to step outside. If the truth be told, he would have relished a physical confrontation. Wickham was a head taller than him, but the Colonel was an excellent fighter, quick and surprisingly strong, a very fine pugilist. He would knock the pretty scoundrel on his arse, and maybe break his nose into the bargain. But it seemed Wickham was neither brave enough, nor stupid enough, to call him out. Instead he took a swipe of a verbal nature. "You doubt my honour, sir, but we are all human. You should look to your own family and save your censure for your cousin, for it seems he is quite the scoundrel himself."

"What are you talking of?"

"Have you not heard? You must be the last to know."

"Spit it out, Wickham."

And so he did, smirking and laughing all the while.

Darcy had taken a leisurely walk back from Hyde Park, not looking forward to being at home, and sure enough, when he arrived, the Grosvenor Street house felt empty, silent and not very welcoming. This spurred a decision to dine out and he had dressed quickly, without the assistance of his valet, who was probably now arrived at Pemberley and would stay there until he received any further instructions.

He was in the hall, with his stick and hat in his hands, when Colonel Fitzwilliam arrived, looking pale and troubled. "Where do you go, Darcy?"

"My club."

"Do not. I beg you, do not. Go nowhere. Let us speak in private," Colonel Fitzwilliam said, with a look at the butler, whose eyes were averted, but whose interest was obviously piqued.

Seeing that there was something terribly wrong, Darcy did not ask any further questions and they went to a downstairs study, a masculine room full of books and papers, dark furnishings and a great heavy desk. "Pour yourself something, Darcy."

"You know I am not a great drinker these days."

"Make an exception. A large exception, you will need it."

He poured his cousin a glass but still did not measure out anything for himself. "Tell me, what's amiss?"

The Colonel spoke quickly and directly and once he had finished they sat in silence. Darcy's expression did not change, causing the Colonel to wonder if he had been half-expecting such news, and if he had, did that mean the story was partly true? He could not believe it was all accurate, though. His cousin and friend, Fitzwilliam Darcy, was most certainly not a defiler of young girls.

"So Wickham is a father?" Darcy said at last, running a hand along the edge of the desk. "Yes, it would have been about this time the girl would have been due."

"He looked more pleased with his progress at the card table than he was in fathering a son."

"I did not accept the faults in him till it was too late. I touted George Wickham around Town, ignoring my own doubts. I introduced him to the Balcombes, as if he were a gentleman." Darcy let out a short laugh. "He does not know the meaning of the word." It pained Darcy to think he had been so wrong and he wondered if he had overlooked Wickham's unscrupulous character because it had suited his own ends. Wickham's charm, the way he could engage people and make them feel at ease, make them smile so readily, had amazed Darcy and he had liked to have the man by his side for social engagements. There were so many ways in which he could best Wickham. He was more skilled with a sword, his horsemanship was second to none - he was so far above Wickham academically it was laughable - and of course, as a Darcy, he was the rightful heir to a vast estate, grandson of an earl and nephew of a judge, while Wickham was the son of a steward. Yet Wickham could meet another man and be fast friends with him within hours and he could flirt with a woman in such a way as to not make them feel ill-used when his attentions wandered elsewhere. Darcy had found it very convenient to hide behind his friend's affability. When Wickham had spoken, Darcy might remain silent. This had been the real success and the true basis of their friendship. They had used each other, in many ways.

"Enough of Wickham, though. We have exhausted too much time and energy on that cretin already. This is nothing to do with him," Colonel Fitzwilliam asserted.

"It is everything to do with him, for I am certain these reports have come via Emma Balcombe. And if you arrived here expecting me to tell you that it is all lies, I am sorry to say you will be disappointed, I cannot. Elizabeth Bennet was in my room at an inn, albeit very briefly, and there were perhaps a few moments when we were alone."

"Darcy, how have you let this happen? Ever since that incident with Miss Watson, when you were but a lad, you have been so careful."

"I foolishly thought I could manage it all, but things happened so quickly, and the situation became more desperate every moment. Miss Bennet had run off from her family before my father and I arrived to collect her. It took me some time, but I found her. Though when I did, she was being accosted by two men. She was robbed and they were pulling at her clothing..." Darcy stopped. "She's an odd little thing, I don't know if she really saw what they were about, but I am quite sure that she would have been...," he stopped again, unable to say the words out loud.

"Molested?" the colonel supplied in his direct way.

"Her clothing was in disarray. I took her to my room in order that she might make herself presentable and to recover from the shock. I enlisted the help of Constance Balcombe. Perhaps Emma Balcombe noticed her sister's comings and goings, I do not know, but she saw Elizabeth Bennet in my room."

"The blood on your bedclothes was from Miss Bennet's injuries then?"

"No, that was mine. I cut my hand while grabbing the blade of a razor and threw the cloth I used to clean it up with onto the bed."

"What a mess, Darcy. What a terrible mess."

Darcy got to his feet. "Will it make the papers?"

"Wickham is telling everyone he knows. I should think so."

"I'll go to Mr Raymond, see if he might prevent it."

"He is just one proprietor, Darcy. What of the others, the less reputable rags? They'll print and be damned. You know how they love a good society scandal."

"The alternative though is to sit and do nothing. I must try. Will you come?"

"I am entirely at your disposal. I'll assist where I can."

Darcy shook his cousin's hand, grateful for his support and friendship.

Jane and Elizabeth had been summoned to the drawing room at Gracechurch Street and within it were two people whose names were extremely familiar to them, but whose faces were not. They had heard much about Mr and Mrs Hogarth Collins but had never met them. Hogarth Collins was their late father's cousin and heir to Longbourn. He wore a clerical collar, was of stern countenance and possessed hard, sharp features. Elizabeth recalled her papa once referring to him as a narrow-minded, pious nitwit. She took a seat between her Aunt Gardiner and Jane, feeling both wary and curious.

Introductions were made but there were no exclamations of pleasure.

"We are passing through Town to take possession of Longbourn and had no notion of calling on you but for these terrible reports that have reached our ears," Mr Collins said.

Elizabeth, fearing something had happened to one of her sisters, felt a shiver of terror creep down her spine and reached for Jane's hand, but it seemed Mr Collins had come to Gracechurch Street to talk only of her running off.

His voice was low and disapproving. "In the absence of your father, Miss Elizabeth, I fear I am now the head of your family and I find myself in the unenviable position of having to shroud your sisters and mother from the shame you have brought upon them."

"The shame you have brought upon them," his wife repeated, with a nod.

Hogarth Collins leaned over Elizabeth and fixed her with an appraising look. "Yes, indeed, now I look upon you, I see there is a sinner within, a terrible badness."

"A badness," agreed Mrs Collins, who appeared to have nothing of her own to say and could only reinforce her husband's opinions, in an even slower, deeper tone than he used.

As she had said nothing but 'hello' when she had entered the room, Elizabeth was quite astounded by the accusations and assumptions regarding her character. She looked to her other aunt for help and Mrs Gardiner did look as if she might speak, but before she could, Mr Collins began again on his tirade.

"Yes, those eyes know too much, innocence is lost and your soul is destined for damnation."

"Destined for damnation," Mrs Collins repeated.

Elizabeth fought back a terrible urge to laugh.

"Salvation will only be yours if you beg to the Lord. You must pray daily, on your knees, repent, repent, repent."

"Repent, repent, repent," said Mrs Collins.

She did giggle then - it burst forth from her uncontrollably and earned her a look of disapprobation from her Aunt Gardiner and a gasp from her Uncle Collins, who pointed a long, bony finger in her direction.

"See how she laughs at her malefactions; the devil is on her shoulder. I'm not sure the Good Lord will ever be able accept her into his house again, not without a great many years of penitence. Come Mrs Collins, I cannot have you in the presence of such unashamed immorality."

Having delivered their hearty disapproval and condemnation, they departed henceforth, in great haste and with no bows or curtseys, scuttling from the room. Elizabeth looked up at her Aunt Gardiner whose face had sunk into her hands. "When do you think they will return to burn me at the stake?"

"I am sorry, Lizzy. I thought they had come merely to pay a social call, a call of condolence. I had no idea he had heard the talk."

"What talk?" Jane enquired.

Mrs Gardiner looked at her eldest niece. "There is something I need to speak to Lizzy about, Jane. Will you leave us for a few moments?"

Elizabeth watched her sister rise and leave the room and waited, sitting on her hands, hoping her aunt would enlighten her.

"I must ask you a question, which I expect you to answer honestly. I promise not to judge you on your answer. Where were you, the night you were away, before Mr Darcy brought you to us?"

Elizabeth was surprised by the question but answered it truthfully, as requested. "I spent the night in a hayloft, on a farm."

"Alone?"

"Of course."

"You were seen in a room Mr Darcy had taken at an inn. Were you ever alone with him in that room?"

"Perhaps, very briefly." Elizabeth felt herself starting to colour a little, a blush rising into her cheeks. "All he did was shout at me."

Her aunt fussed at the back of her hair, clearly uncomfortable at having to perform such an intimate interrogation. "There are scratches and bruises on you, Lizzy. I saw them the other night, when I helped you undress."

"Oh. You must not think they are anything to do with Mr Darcy, he has not harmed me. He has, I think, a tendency to proudness and pomposity, but I don't believe he would be capable of hurting me, or anyone. Is this the talk, that I was in his room; alone with him overnight?"

Her aunt sat down beside her and took one of Elizabeth's hands between both of her own. "It is the polite version, and if that was all there was to it, it might be a case of outwaiting the storm and hoping people would forget. However, there is a nasty edge to the story, a salacious detail that has given it horrific credence and I know not how to explain it to you. I don't know how much you would understand, or what your mother might have told you."

Elizabeth took her hands from her aunt's clasp and stood. She walked the length of the room and stopped before the window, not seeing the scene outside it though, her mind too perturbed to focus on the carriages and walkers that went by.

"Tell me."

"To repeat such vulgarity pains me."

"But I must know, Aunt. Surely if I am old enough to be implicated in a rumour, I am old enough to hear a complete account of it. I would hate to not know what is being said about me."

Mrs Gardiner took a deep breath and then her words came out in a rushed whisper. "Someone saw blood on his sheets the next morning."

"Oh."

"Do you see? Do you understand?"

Elizabeth nodded. "Yes, I think I do. They are saying he has had me. That I have lain with him as a man might lie with his wife. That is the salacious detail?"

Her aunt closed her eyes. "Mr Darcy will proclaim it malicious falsehood, I am sure."

"I did not, you know. I have not..."

"I know."

"I do not even particularly like him," Elizabeth said, with a touch of desperation in her voice.

Her aunt laughed a little.

"But, now I think of it, there was blood on his sheets," Elizabeth admitted, "I know not how it got there, but I do remember it. The blood was not mine, you do believe me?"

"Of course, I have every faith in you, but others will not. It is hard to stop a rumour when there is some element of truth attached to it, and unfortunately, Mr Darcy is such a public figure that word has spread with great alacrity, far and wide."

"What will happen?"

Her aunt shook her head. "It is too soon to say, but you must understand that if something is to be done, it will most likely be done quickly. I know of the Darcys, Elizabeth, they are a most excellent family and will not tolerate such a besmirching of their name, a solution will be found, and with the utmost expediency."

73

Elizabeth rested her forehead against the window pane. "'Tis all my fault," she said, not to her aunt, but to herself, her breath misting up the glass.

She saw him arrive. All day there had been comings and goings, hushed whispers behind doors, followed by notes, expresses and letters. Jane had gone to assist in keeping the children amused but Elizabeth sat at the top of the stairs, in a state of bewilderment and misery, wondering what would happen to her. Pemberley seemed very unlikely now, but she also suspected she might not be able to return to Meryton, or be allowed to remain in London, where talk was apparently rife. She would be sent away, somewhere very remote, she was sure of it.

The sounds of a grand carriage rolling to a stop outside the door roused her from her reverie and she looked over the bannisters to be met with the sight of his very shiny boots and dark head in the hallway below her. The deep timbre of his voice made her shiver as he asked for her uncle. He sounded very much like the harbinger of doom. Elizabeth's eye was drawn to a flash of bright red and she realised Mr Darcy had not come alone. She could see his companion better than him, a pleasant looking man in regimentals, but not handsome or very tall. He seemed to sense her gaze on him and he looked up sharply, caught her eye and gave her a little nod. Realising she had been caught spying, she coloured and was a little ashamed. She rushed off but not before she had seen the amused smile playing around the corners of the soldier's mouth.

Mr Darcy was with her uncle for a very long time, while she had lain on her bed with a book. Then she heard doors opening and closing and soon after, she was summoned by a maid. Her uncle's study was empty apart from her uncle and aunt. The guests, if they could be described as such, had obviously departed.

Her uncle spoke plainly, directly and laid all that had transpired between him and Mr Darcy before her, and then left her to digest the news.

74

"I will not," was her response, when she had gathered her wits, aghast that such a thing should even be suggested. "I will not," she said again, more emphatically. "I shall bear the shame of it instead."

"And what of your sisters and your mother, have they not suffered enough? They are already reduced to a state of genteel poverty. Do you wish to make them lower?" Mr Gardiner asked. "Your sisters' chances of making good marriages will be materially damaged by your disgrace. No-one of good standing will wish to solicit their society. No respectable man will want anything to do with them, or you. What will become of you?"

Her uncle's words pierced Elizabeth's heart. She looked to Mrs Gardiner for her opinion. "Would it truly be that bad? Have I really injured the others so?"

Her aunt did not answer. Instead she swallowed and looked sympathetic, but turned her head away, leaving the matter to her husband. Elizabeth felt betrayed.

"You are not truly wise to the ways of the world, Lizzy. You do not understand what a harsh place it can be for a young lady whose virtue has been called into question, or how cruel society can be when one is cast out from it. What your aunt and I ask of you is to see that this is the only truly sensible way forward, the only adequate solution to an ominous situation; and you are indeed a lucky girl to have been offered this rescue. I could not have demanded such a thing, of such a man. I have no power over him. He had no reason to be afraid of my threats. Yet, he has come forward, done you great honour and I insist you do not embarrass this family by a refusal."

She was a little speechless in the face of such persuasive argument, and could only burst out, uncontrollably. "You cannot make me. I will not. I would be the one who would have to stand before God and say the words; you cannot force the necessary promises from my mouth."

Mr Gardiner grew angry and looked as if he were about to launch into another tirade, but then calmed suddenly and sighed, smiling sadly. "Heavens, Lizzy, I am sorry to be raging at you. It is the last thing in the world I would wish for you, but you are too young to be able to make a sensible decision for yourself. Though I think your father will be turning in his grave and be as horrified as you are at the thought of it, even he would see the necessity of a marriage in these circumstances. What is the alternative, my dear child, shame and disgrace?"

Her world was shifting and changing again, her head spun, her emotions swirled. She looked at the door and the window, but knew flight was not an option. Indeed, her impulse to run was what had gotten her into such a situation in the first place. When her uncle asked it of her again, she found herself nodding. Indeed, she almost *saw* herself nodding, as if she were outside of herself, looking in. She saw a young girl in a dark gown rise from her chair and leave the room in a sort of stupor. As she always did in times of trouble, she sought out Jane, and found her coming out of the nursery, laughing at the antics of her niece and nephew. One look at Elizabeth's face, however, was enough to stall her in the hallway.

"You look as if you have seen a ghost, Lizzy."

"Oh, it is worse than that. I am to be married, Jane, married to Mr Darcy!"

"Just how old is this girl, Darcy?" the Colonel asked as they left Gracechurch Street by carriage, "only the way her uncle spoke of her and his reluctance…"

"Fifteen."

Darcy saw the shock on the Colonel's face, but his cousin immediately tried to hide it with a smile of commiseration.

"Well, I suppose many girls are out at sixteen, some marry soon after. My mother was barely seventeen when she married, and girls seem so mature these days, most of them look far older than they actually are."

"There is no need to sugar coat it for me, cousin, and this one certainly does not look older than her years. She is as skinny as a rake and does not even reach my shoulder.

She'd sooner pass for twelve than twenty. I will find myself a laughing stock. She is very young in her ways too. She is an unruly, disobedient little hellion. Impertinent to the point of rudeness, very spoilt. I fear she has been much indulged."

The Colonel looked half-horrified and half-amused. "Well, how fortunate that you'll have the management of her, so the next time she is naughty you might put her over your knee."

Darcy glowered at him. "If you had not just been of great service to me, cousin, I would hurl you from the carriage for that remark."

"I am sorry, my dear Darcy, but perhaps you will find life less trying if you try to see the humour in situations. Sometimes, when it all goes wrong, the only thing we are left with is the ability to laugh."

"I cannot laugh at this. It is so far removed from what I wanted."

"Come now, men marry for all kinds of reasons, for connections, advancement or property. I myself will have to be practical when it comes to choosing a bride. I hope I find someone I can love for reasons other than the size of her dowry, but I fear prudence may have to come before passion. So you will have a country wife, many men do."

"A country wife?" Darcy frowned.

"Keep her at Pemberley and busy with babies, and have your own life in Town. You may have other…pursuits."

"I have always been disgusted by such behaviour."

"Are you sure there is no other option?"

"No, no other option. Not without loss of honour, or reputation." Looking out of the window as they left Cheapside, Darcy shuddered. "She has some inferior connections, as you have seen, this will have to be managed. The uncle we have just met is in trade."

"Though the house seems respectable and they had excellent manners, I don't feel there is much to be feared in that direction, though I can well imagine my mother's reaction, and Lady Catherine's! Still, Darcy, I suppose it gets you out of marrying Anne de Bourgh."

Darcy shook his head. "I would never have married Anne, no matter how much my mother wished for it; no matter how much Lady Catherine might have sought to persuade me. What I wished for was a handsome woman, with intelligence, extremely accomplished, with good connections, perfect manners, someone who would be an active and useful mistress of Pemberley."

"That's quite a list, does such a paragon exist? Did you believe Emma Balcombe to be that woman?"

"For a time I suppose I did. I was foolishly blinded by her beauty and being already amongst our acquaintance - their home being in Derbyshire - she seemed the ideal choice."

"Well I am of a mind to think that while Wickham meant to wound you, he ended up doing you a great favour. You saw her true character before you had committed yourself. Though, now you have to marry young Miss Bennet. Is there no other way?"

"I have tried to think of a thousand different solutions; of sending her away to school, or of going away myself for a good while. I have considered wild ideas, but in the end, it all comes down to a question of honour and what is the right thing to do."

"Well, it seems harsh to me, when the rumours are false and you did nothing wrong."

"Perhaps, but cousin, I feel the fault might be partially mine too. I acted rashly. I suppose I wanted to play the hero. I enjoyed it all too much, the thrill of the chase, but in the midst of it all, I sat alone with her at an inn and I did take her to my room. I was foolish to think I would get away with it."

"You probably would have done, but for Emma Balcombe."

Darcy let out a short laugh. "Yes, it is a good job that lady is now in Ireland and far out of my reach, I daresay any affection I might have once felt for her is well and truly dead."

Eight

Elizabeth had been instructed to wait in the Gardiner's parlour, where she paced, unable to concentrate on anything, though there was frequently a book in her hand. She had read the first page twenty times but could not recall a single word of it. Mr Darcy was to call, specifically upon her. She supposed it would be the first of several visits, when they would get to know each other before they were married. Married! Oh, how ridiculous it all was.

She had started the day with a slight hope of escape in regards to her mother's approval, which she was told had been sent for the previous day. It was a thin hope, for Elizabeth knew Mrs Bennet spent a good many hours of her days deciding which young men in the neighbourhood might make eligible matches for her daughters. She had spoken with enthusiasm of 'getting them all well married' long before Jane had even come out. And her mother was unlikely to raise any objections on account of her age. When there had been tutting in Meryton at the rushing to the altar of sixteen-year-old Susan Bridges, her mother, in contrast to the generally accepted view that it was all a bit disgraceful, had exclaimed that she thought the girl had done 'extremely well'. As she had feared, when the answer did come from Meryton, Mrs Bennet's consent was roundly and vociferously given and Elizabeth's heart had sunk into her shoes. She was given sight of her mother's note, in which Mrs Bennet bid her brother Gardiner, to *'give her clever girl a kiss from me'* and to *'tell Elizabeth to write as soon as she reaches Pemberley to let me know how many bedrooms there are so that I might tell Lady Lucas'*.

Elizabeth's next course of action had been an attack on the sympathies of her aunt, which she made by shamelessly crying and pleading. Mrs Gardiner was affected by her entreaties, visibly so, but batted them away with platitudes, *'all will be well in time'*, *'ours is not to reason why'*, *'what's done is done'*, *'life is not fair'* - and who could argue against such calm, over-used assurances? She went to Jane, who listened and sympathised, but being only a little over seventeen herself, could offer no practical assistance. Her Uncle Gardiner went out, apparently for the purpose of meeting with Mr Darcy. They were to go and procure a licence together. Elizabeth had felt a little sick and faint as she'd watched him leave and now they were back. She heard the front door open and voices in the hall. Mr Darcy's was very distinctive.

"Mr Darcy would like to see you, Lizzy," her aunt said with a look that told her she was to be polite and deport herself in a ladylike manner. Mrs Gardiner needn't have bothered with such warnings. Elizabeth had no intention of being anything other than conciliatory and the very essence of decorum. If she really was going to have to spend the next thirty years or so with the man, it would not do to start off on a bad footing.

He bowed deeply and with grave formality. She ruined her chances of creating an excellent, more favourable impression than he had hitherto formed of her, by forgetting to curtsey in return. She stood frozen for a while until her aunt's cough reminded her of the established etiquette. In the end her greeting was a botched, rushed, dip that she was afraid looked more like a stumble.

"The door will remain ajar," Mrs Gardiner said, before leaving them alone, rather ridiculously, Elizabeth thought, as if they were a pair of star-crossed lovers from a novel who would leap on each other with unrestrainable passion the moment nobody else was near.

Mr Darcy came further into the room with a determined tread and stopped suddenly before her but then seemed not to know what to do. Elizabeth could not meet his eyes and inspected her shoes closely, while running a finger along the edge of her book.

"Your uncle has spoken to you I suppose?" he asked.

She wanted to laugh at his directness, there were no enquiries into her health or remarks on the pleasantness of the day; he was all about his business, his tone clipped and abrupt. She wanted to say something witty, to seem worldly-wise. Instead, she merely nodded.

"I have made the necessary arrangements and we will travel to Hempstead tomorrow, and from there onto Pemberley."

"Tomorrow!" she cried. Had she misheard him? She had expected to be consulted, to be granted leave to set her own date. She had known it must be soon, but tomorrow!

"I fear so. We must act with great expediency, so the marriage announcement might be made. Any delay would do further damage to my reputation."

"And mine, I suppose."

He waved a hand in the air, as if her dire situation was of no consequence at all. She frowned at him and he returned it with one of his own, before walking away to stand behind a chair, putting two or three yards between them. "You need not look so horrified, Miss Bennet. You will not be mistreated. I will see to your comfort in every respect."

"Sir, I am sorry if my countenance suggested otherwise, but I have no concerns as regards my treatment, it is just that I did not expect to be married now, at my age. I feel...ill-prepared. You can understand my reluctance, I am sure."

His expression was stern and his eyes were cold. "Many women might think themselves most fortunate to be in receipt of my offer."

She was quite disgusted by his arrogance, but tried to soften her temper, though she was aware her cheeks were starting to burn with crossness. "I am told I ought to be thankful."

He strode forward, grasped her hand and took it to his lips, where he bestowed the quickest of kisses, taking her by surprise, she had never before been in receipt of such an intimate gesture from anyone other than a close relation and did not know how to respond, but it seemed no response was necessary in any case. He had turned and was gone, stating he would see her on the 'morrow, leaving her ample time to reflect upon their brief meeting. She did so mostly in a state of displeasure.

As Elizabeth sat reeling in the parlour, her aunt begged a few moments of Mr Darcy's time while she saw him out onto the street. He was focussed on his pocket watch and paid her little attention, but Mrs Gardiner did not give in so easily and her repeated entreaties for a few words could not be ignored completely.

"Sir, I feel I really must speak to you regarding Elizabeth?"

He stood aside from his carriage and his silence seemed tacit agreement enough for her to continue.

"Some girls of fifteen are quite worldly-wise, grown up. Lizzy, though, at a time when she might have been learning some of the more polished ways acceptable to society has been tending to a sick father. She can be somewhat gauche, lacking a little in refinement, perhaps. She is clever though and will be quick to learn what is required of her." Mrs Gardiner took a deep breath and went on. "But she will need your patience and guidance, and I ask you to be generous with both. I spent a good deal of my childhood in Lambton and am aware of the station Mrs Darcy will occupy."

They had grown up within five miles of each other, this man and her, and yet he gave her no acknowledgement, there was no discussion of coincidence or remembrance of places they both knew. No light-hearted references to the smallness of the world. He looked at her blankly, this man who would soon be a relation, and then said shortly, in a tone that suggested he was offended by her interference, "you need not fear for her wellbeing."

"No, I do not, not her wellbeing as such…"

Before she could go on, he had bowed and excused himself, and was boarding his carriage.

Mrs Gardiner watched the carriage roll away with a heavy heart. How on earth would her niece cope with this brusque, inhibited man? Before her father's death, Lizzy had been of a playful, merry disposition. Though grief had subdued her, she would return to what she had once been - and what opposites she and Mr Darcy were. How could they possibly even be companions for one another, let alone friends and lovers?

This last thought made Mrs Gardiner realise there was another difficult conversation to be had with Elizabeth; another onerous task to perform. Though she suspected Mr Darcy was very conscious of her age, and not of a mind to be instantly demanding his conjugal rights, her aunt decided it might be best to ensure the girl was not completely unprepared for the marriage bed.

Nine

Darcy had spent an exhausting day. There had been visits to the bank, and to the tailors to collect a coat he had ordered weeks ago, without knowing it would be the one he would wear to his wedding. Then he had dashed to meet Mr Gardiner at a small attorney's office where the articles of marriage were inspected, approved and signed. He had shaken the businessman's hand and known then that his fate was sealed. There was nothing else to be done but to order the packing of some further attire for travelling in, write some quick notes, and then he had paced the house, going from room to room in a state of restlessness, walking the corridors without settling anywhere, much to the annoyance of the butler and housekeeper - who tried either to follow him, or anticipate his movements, moving candles and refreshments around with him. He had fallen asleep in a chair in the study and woken before dawn with a crick in his neck. After breakfast, where he ate little, he dressed with particular care and was stood in the hallway when an express rider came knocking on the door and breathlessly handed over a letter and a parcel.

He thanked the man, gave him a few coins and tore the parcel open with relief. He had feared it would not get here in time. He might have married her without it, of course. He might have picked up a ring from any jewellers in Town, or might have indeed been wed without bestowing a band upon her. But having this particular ring seemed important, and he enjoyed the weight of it when it fell out of the paper and into his hand. It represented his eagerness to do something right, when everything else was wrong. The return address on the package was Pemberley. A brief, cold note from his father accompanied it. It merely told him he had better 'marry the girl, all things considered' and that he would meet them at Haddon Hall, the Fitzwilliams' country seat. He tore the note into small pieces and put the remnants into the hand of the footman who was still stood at the door. The ring he put into his coat pocket, where it sat alongside the special licence Colonel Fitzwilliam and Mr Gardiner had discreetly helped him procure from the Archbishop the previous day. Then he asked for the carriage to be brought round and stepped outside.

Darcy banged his stick impatiently against his boot. Now he only awaited the arrival of his cousin, but it was a full ten minutes before Colonel Fitzwilliam came strolling along the street, looking carefree and indolent.

"At last! We should have departed five minutes ago if we are to make Hempstead on time."

The Colonel's smile was wide. "How nice to see you so keen to greet your blushing bride."

"She's more petulant than blushing. Were you at the club last night?"

"Yes, and Almacks, and Mrs Arlington's drawing rooms. I have socialised tirelessly for your sake. You owe me a great favour - perhaps a nice little living when I am too old for soldiering?"

"And...what is the talk now?"

"That you have shocked all your friends and family by falling hopelessly in love with a young country miss, and that you married her in secret two weeks ago. The elder members of your family are exceedingly angry with you."

Darcy nodded. "I suppose 'tis better than the rumour that preceded it."

"Aye, now you are merely stupid and romantic, rather than a complete blackguard." Seeing Darcy wince, the Colonel patted his arm.

"You did not mention her age, I hope? Or a date?"

"Of course not."

"Good, and was it believed?"

"You doubt my acting skills! I made a wonderful Othello at Cambridge. I think it was generally believed, yes. I gave it a few dramatic touches. Your father has threatened you with disinheritance. You were so heartbroken over Lady Balcombe that you had lost your mind, etcetera, etcetera... and have sought consolation in the arms of a country girl, whose charms are simple and sweet."

"Simple and sweet? You have clearly never met Miss Bennet."

"No, but I am very keen to do so. Shall we?"

Darcy pulled his coat around him, patted the pocket that held the licence and ring, and boarded the carriage that was to take him to his wedding.

It all went off as expected. A very quick, straightforward ceremony conducted by a man of the cloth who had bowed before the groom reverently before he began to direct them in their vows. Mrs Gardiner suspected he enjoyed the patronage of the Darcys and his living was bestowed by them. For the vicar did not question why a special licence was required. Nor did he raise an eyebrow at the tender age of the bride, or the palpable lack of attention her groom gave her.

Mr Darcy stood with a very straight back, one booted foot slightly in front of the other and a hand on his lapel throughout the ceremony. Elizabeth glanced nervously over her shoulder now and then. Her aunt gave her the most encouraging smile she could muster in the subdued, tense atmosphere of the church.

The morning had passed oddly. Elizabeth had risen early, refused breakfast and then requested permission to walk out in a nearby park. Mr Gardiner had protested on the grounds that London was not as safe as the country lanes of Hertfordshire, but Mrs Gardiner had persuaded him that their niece ought to be given a little half hour of freedom, in which she might compose herself. Though she had admittedly been very relieved when Elizabeth had reappeared again at the expected time, half-fearing she would take the opportunity to run away again. But Elizabeth had re-entered the house less angry after her walk. Indeed, when it came to her *'I will'* she said it rather firmly, with a glance up at Mr Darcy, as if she had decided her fighting spirit might be better directed in favour of making a go of her odd marriage, rather than in resisting it.

The ring was placed on her finger, they were declared man and wife and the necessary entry was made in the parish register, but once outside, nobody threw rice and there were no hearty congratulations or slightly bawdy jokes.

They were all introduced to the gentleman who had stood up with Mr Darcy, his cousin, Colonel Fitzwilliam. He appeared to be an affable man; and was in his person and address, most truly the gentleman. If she had to be sending her niece off with either of the two relations, Mrs Gardiner was struck by the thought that she'd much rather it be the Colonel, who gallantly bent over Elizabeth's hand, welcomed her into the family and called her Mrs Darcy. Both the bride and groom wrinkled their noses in distaste at the appellation and Mrs Gardiner sighed and worried, but it was done, for better or worse.

After Elizabeth's meagre belongings had been removed from the Gardiner's carriage to the Darcy one, and it was time for them to depart, she crushed Elizabeth to her and made her promise to write as soon as she reached Derbyshire. Jane cried at the moment of goodbye but Elizabeth remained largely silent. Mrs Gardiner suspected her bravura was a veneer that was wearing thinner by the moment and in some respects it was fortunate that Mr Darcy hastened her quickly into the carriage, for she was not a girl who liked to lose her composure. She was more the kind to pretend everything was well and did not like to admit to being afraid.

While they watched the Darcy carriage roll away, Mrs Gardiner's husband caught her hand and threaded her arm through the crook of his elbow. "It is a good match, however it has come about. She might never have aspired to such a man and such a family in ordinary circumstances."

Mrs Gardiner shook her head. "My niece is the future mistress of Pemberley! I should not have imagined it in a thousand years. Yet I do not think she would have aspired to it, not under any circumstances. Despite her faults, she is a caring and affectionate girl, and I am sure that is what she would have wished for in a marriage - for what is there to life if we cannot love and be loved in return?"

"Do not distress yourself, my dear. I have spent some time in the young man's company these last few days, and though a little proud, I think underneath his reserve lies a good man. A kind man, even, and he has done the right thing by her. Love can grow."

The only thing growing, however, in the carriage occupied by the new Mr and Mrs Darcy was a great, stretching silence. His dark head was turned towards the window, his gaze fixed on the passing scenery, while hers was fixed on her lap. What she was waiting, or wishing for him to say, she was not sure. Perhaps some acknowledgement of what had just come to pass, some sort of reassurance, or even a jest, but there was nothing.

"It was a pleasure to make the acquaintance of your cousin, sir. He seems a pleasant man, are you quite close to him?" she ventured when she found she could bear it no longer and the silence had reached deafening proportions. She offered him a small smile but it was not returned.

"Yes. We spent much of our childhood together."

Elizabeth waited for this sentence to be expanded on but it was not. "He mentioned about riding on ahead?"

"He is also travelling north, to his family's estate near Matlock. He will see us at the inn."

She might have carried her enquiries further and asked more about their journey, where they would stop and how long it would take, but he looked so annoyed by her questions that she fell quiet again. Her tight bonnet itched against her head and the ribbons under her chin were suddenly suffocating. She pulled it loose and threw it onto the seat beside her. Mr Darcy frowned a little but she ignored his disapproval, it was much cooler and more comfortable without it. Besides, he had removed his hat and they were in an enclosed carriage and would be for several hours yet. "'Tis very warm for April, don't you think?"

"I suppose," he agreed, and returned to watching the scenery.

"Shall I open the window?"

"If you would find it more comfortable, please do so."

She did and then sat back, breathing in the very welcome fresh air, although there was not much of a breeze, the air was thick with humidity, almost as if a storm were brewing. "I think spring is my favourite time of the year. What is yours?"

"I had never really thought on it."

"I enjoy seeing the flowers come into bloom. Is Derbyshire pretty in April?"

"As much as anywhere I should imagine."

"Perhaps I should have brought a book," Elizabeth said with a sigh. "Do you like to read?"

"Yes."

Exasperated, she knew not what subject to try next. Music? Or dare she even try politics? Literature, family and the weather had gotten her nowhere. She saw Mr Darcy's eyes drift down to her boots and realised she had unconsciously been swinging a foot back and forth, lightly scraping the floor of the carriage with each downward motion. She stilled her feet but then began feeling warm again. She freed her right hand from its glove and then began to pull at the left one. She tugged at the tight fitting apparel to no avail at first but then the glove came off suddenly and the motion dislodged the gold band he had placed upon her third finger, less than an hour ago. They both watched in horror as the wedding ring sailed through the air, struck the frame of the carriage's window with a clink, and then bounced through the open portal onto the road.

His expression was thunderous. All she could say was, "oh".

Mr Darcy banged on the roof of the carriage with his stick and shouted for it to stop.

"Was it terribly expensive?"

"It was my mother's."

"Oh," she repeated, her hand rising up to cover her mouth.

He flung open the door of the carriage and jumped down onto the lane. Elizabeth followed him but was promptly told to get back in.

"I ought to help you look, sir. Two pairs of eyes are surely better than one."

He again told her to return to the carriage, but she ignored his request and began to scour the ground around them for any sight of the ring. They spent a good half an hour in such a fashion, the carriage driver and footman joined them, and they walked up and down the lane several times without success. Elizabeth left the lane and began to look in the neighbouring field, unmindful that her petticoat was now gathering grass stains to add to the dust from the road. Mr Darcy stood at the edge of the field with his arms crossed. "Come out of there, it is lost. We shall have to go now if we are to make the inn by dinner."

"Oh, I could not go yet. I am sure it must be here somewhere."

"Elizabeth."

She looked up in surprise at his use of her given name. He had the right to address her so now, of course, but it was still somehow astonishing.

"Elizabeth," he said again, more firmly. "Come on now, it is starting to rain. Let us go."

"But it was your mother's ring. We cannot give up."

He trudged down into the field and stood next to her. "You will get wet. You are already filthy. You have no bonnet or gloves, what might anyone who sees you think? Come, get into the carriage."

"I would never forgive myself if we did not find it."

"Did you not just stand up in a church and promise to obey me?" he asked with no small amount of exasperation.

The heavens opened with a great crash of thunder that made them both jump. The rain was heavy and they began to get soaked, but just when Elizabeth was about to yield and do what he asked of her, she found the precious piece of jewellery, hidden between long grasses. She recovered it and held it up to him, between her thumb and forefinger, with a triumphant look, then felt rather foolish, because she did not know what to do with it. Mr Darcy plucked it from her fingers with a dark look.

"I shall have it altered, 'tis obviously too big."

With that, they ran to get out of the rain. The footman held open the door and Mr Darcy rather threw her up into the carriage and clambered in after her. She took her seat again and now it was over, the whole business diverted her and she laughed and smiled at Mr Darcy, whose hair was wet through and jacket soaked.

He did not seemingly share in her amusement and silently passed her a travelling rug, with which she might dry herself off a little. "This is funny to you? That we will now be damp and chilled for three or four more hours till we reach our destination; that we will arrive in such a dishevelled state?"

Elizabeth tried to school her features into a more sombre mien. "No, I suppose there is no humour in it at all."

Ten

Colonel Fitzwilliam had spent an agreeable couple of hours in the company of some travelling naval officers and had won a few shillings at cards. The coins clinked pleasantly around in his pockets and the ale he had drunk had made him pleasantly merry. He checked his pocket watch and wondered at Darcy not yet having arrived. His cousin was such a punctual man. They had left Hempstead at the same time, and even though he had ridden ahead and enjoyed the freedom of horseback, he would still have expected the carriage by now. He had strolled into the yard of the inn two or three times for a spot of fresh air, but was still without a single sight of the Darcy's elegant coach. He had just settled down for another round of cards when Darcy's gruff coachman appeared at his elbow and informed the Colonel that the Darcys had arrived; they had a private upstairs parlour for dinner and would be happy for him to join them. When the Colonel entered the room, however, he found only Darcy, sitting before a decanter of wine and a glass. This was a surprise in itself, because his cousin was well known for his sobriety.

"Where's the missus?"

Darcy ignored his jesting tone and fetched another glass, into which he poured some wine for the Colonel, "changing."

"For dinner on the road at an inn, isn't that a little formal?"

"We got wet."

"Ah yes, the rain. I took shelter for a half hour and avoided it. I'm happy to drink with you, Darcy, any time you wish, but I wonder at your sudden need for wine?"

"I was cold. It is making me warmer."

"Hmmm, well do not over imbibe, you are not used to it lately and a man would not wish to be too overcome on his wedding night."

Darcy looked at him in horror. "She is fifteen!"

"Yes, of course. I am sorry. It was a bad joke." The Colonel recalled his first glance of the new Mrs Darcy on the stairs at the Gardiner's house. When he had looked up, after sensing he was being spied upon, he had thought her one of the Gardiner's children, not Darcy's future bride, and now he knew his mistake, he was more than able to see Darcy's objections and understand his embarrassment. "I have been flippant. Of course, you consider her too young, I was not thinking."

"Let us be clear, I would not...I have no desire where she is concerned."

"None, not even in a couple of years? Oh, I know you prefer the tall, fair, alabaster look, the voluptuous types, but I think she has a sweet face, your little lady, and her eyes have a delightful sparkle in them - and as for the figure, well, maybe she will be a late bloomer."

Darcy gave him a disbelieving look.

"Oh come now, man, do you not think her even slightly pretty?"

"She is tolerable, I suppose, but not handsome enough to tempt me," Darcy snapped.

Sensing movement in the doorway, both men turned to see that Elizabeth had entered. Her countenance left neither of them in any doubt that she had heard the slight, but she did not cry, flush, or become enraged by it. She gave a small curtsey and advanced towards the table. "I am sorry, gentlemen, if I have kept you waiting." Though she addressed them both, she did not look at Darcy.

"Some ladies are worth the wait," said Colonel Fitzwilliam, with too much chivalry and too low a bow.

Elizabeth smiled her thanks for his attentions and sympathy, but took her seat with her head bent.

The meal was ordered while the two gentlemen chatted. She remained silent and when the food was brought, squirmed in her seat without taking a bite. It was rough, country fare; a slab of fatty meat and some raw potatoes, whilst the vegetables, in contrast, were overcooked. Elizabeth spent ten minutes pushing it around her plate before begging to be excused, claiming tiredness.

Darcy jumped from his chair. "I shall escort you to your room, should you wish to retire."

"There is no need. It is only a few yards walk."

She was gone before he could raise any further objections, leaving them in a swish of skirts and with a bad taste in their mouths, caused not just by the tough, fatty mutton.

"Go, speak to her," the Colonel said. "You know she heard you."

Darcy shrugged. "Then there will be no misunderstanding. She can now perfectly comprehend my expectations and wishes. Do you expect me to pretend to an affection I do not feel?"

"No, but I find a little kindness never goes amiss."

"I am kind. I have done her the greatest kindness by marrying her."

"You pretend altruism now, do you? Your reputation was as ruined as hers."

Darcy said nothing but reached for the decanter of wine and refilled his now empty glass, determined to forget it all. The horrible day, the rain, her sad little face when she had overheard his remark, there was nothing good about any of it.

Elizabeth had fumed and raged for two or more hours after excusing herself from the table. Oh, how she missed her Papa. He would not have persuaded her that this was the right thing to do; he would have found a solution to their troubles that did not involve her having to be married. But then, she would not have found herself in this situation if her Papa had still been alive. She would never have felt the need or impulse to run from Longbourn, and she would have now been ensconced safely in her bed there, listening to Jane breathing heavily in her sleep and warming her cold feet upon her legs in the night. What a rude man she was now tied to. Rude and haughty, and to think, she had been feeling some sympathy for him earlier. When they had been standing at the side of the road with the rain coming down on them - what a sight she must have made! The poor man was saddled with a girl who covered herself in dirt, had terrible hair and flung family heirlooms from carriage windows. Thinking him as despondent and as discombobulated by the situation as she was, she had gone to dinner determined to be friendly and to act with the utmost decorum; to show him he might not always have cause to be embarrassed by her and that she did have some notion of how a lady ought to behave, only to have walked in and overheard *that* remark. Oh, it wasn't that she had any great notion of being anything *more* than merely tolerable, but to hear it said out loud was mortifying.

Despite all her tumultuous thoughts, the long, emotional day had taken its toll and she eventually fell asleep, though was rudely woken from her slumbers, after an hour or so, by a loud banging on her chamber door.

Her heart thumped loudly in her chest and she sat bolt upright in the dark room. The candle had long ago burned out and fear choked her, making her unable to speak. She didn't know what scared her more, the thought it might be a stranger, robbers - or Mr Darcy, come to claim what was rightfully his, despite her 'tolerability'. It was only when there was another loud banging that she found the courage to call out in response and ask who was there. A gruff voice informed her it was the inn's chief porter. She pulled a robe about her, opened the door to him and at his bidding went along the hall to the private parlour where they had supped. There she found Mr Darcy slumped over the table with his head on his hands, asleep in his chair.

"You'll excuse us for disturbing you. We've tried rousing him, but he's about as blind drunk as any man I've ever seen. He's your husband, ain't he? We'll carry him up."

Mr Darcy had his own room, she was sure of it, but as soon as they had arrived at the inn, he had gravely and silently shown her to the door of hers and left her, she had no idea where his chamber was. The porter looked at her expectantly and she gave a little nod of assent, not knowing what else to do and feeling perhaps Mr Darcy was too drunk to be safely left alone in any case.

She might sleep on the chair in her room with some blankets if need be. Mr Darcy grumbled as the porters hauled him to his feet and supported him by taking an arm each around their shoulders. He was half dragged and half walked along the corridor in such a fashion.

Once inside her room, he shouted incoherently, threw the men off him, and staggered around blindly for a few moments. The men left, wishing her good luck and good night. Elizabeth closed the door behind them and turned, leaning against the wood for support. Now what to do!

Darcy woke slowly, with a groan of pain. His head thumped and protested loudly about something. He found himself flat on the floor of an unfamiliar bedchamber. His right leg was hooked around a chair leg, his left arm was stretched out under the bed, while his fingers dangled in a chamber pot. The pot was thankfully empty, but nevertheless, he quickly removed his hand, and his leg too, which made the chair fall sideways and clatter to the ground.

Somebody had propped his head up by laying his folded coat beneath it. Had she done that? Memories of the last few days and the knowledge of exactly where he was and why, slowly dawned upon him. He lifted himself onto his elbows, wondering if she was still in the room. She had been there last night, he thought. He remembered vaguely seeing her face and feeling it was all wrong. He looked up at the bed and saw her gazing down at him with unabashed curiosity, her head tilted to the side, her chin balanced on an upturned palm.

He ignored her scrutiny and sat up straighter. To his profound relief, he found that, excepting his coat, he was fully clothed, but he had lost a button from his waistcoat and his trousers were stained with wine. He smelt of drink, horribly - reeked of it - the stench made his stomach turn.

"Are you going to be ill?" Elizabeth asked.

"Certainly not!" Though his answer sounded decisive, he was not altogether certain. His stomach might betray him yet.

He slowly got to his feet. The room spun and tilted and he leaned on the dresser to steady himself, his eyes blinking and adjusting to the daylight that was filtering through a gap in the curtains.

She wore a maidenly white nightgown; a plain, billowy garment. Her hair was a mass of messy short curls. It was odd, but she seemed entirely unconcerned at him seeing her in such a state of undress and about being alone in a room with him. Her expression was a mixture of petulance and acrimony, there was no fear. She clambered off the bed and the movement caused her loose nightgown to fall off one shoulder. He quickly averted his eyes while she tugged it unconsciously back into place.

"You ought not to drink so much," she suggested, when he at last looked at her again.

He straightened his clothing and tugged at the cuffs of his shirt, knowing how dishevelled he must look and trying desperately to regain some dignity. "Usually I do not," he said. "Sometimes, though, a man is driven to it. Do you have any further advice for me?"

"Well, since you have asked, I think your waistcoats are gaudy and your knots are too fussy, they do not suit you."

"Thank you," he uttered, his teeth gritted. *How dare she?* "Is there anything else that offends?" She smirked and raised an eyebrow. Smirked at him! He could see the direction in which her thoughts tended and spoke before she could. "Perhaps if I supply you with pen and paper, you might make a list."

"I need no paper. There is no list. But if you absolutely insist on knowing all my complaints then I shall have to tell you I find your moustache a touch ridiculous. Oh, and your hair is too long."

Darcy felt positively murderous, a bad mood to add to his bad head. Fifteen-year-old daughters of country squires had no right to be mocking him. How dearly he wished to rid her of her self-sufficient, confident air, even if for just a few moments. He idly wondered what she might do if he bid her to lay back down on the bed and open for him. Would she obey? Had she any idea what to do? He didn't want to bed her any more than he had the night before. The idea was repulsive to him, but the request might be enough to discompose her briefly. In the end, though, he felt too ill to even trifle with her and although cross, he did not wish to be truly cruel. He walked towards the door, where he paused to check his pocket watch.

"We leave at eight sharp, Elizabeth. I shall expect you to be ready."

Eleven

The rocking and noise of the carriage on the road only exacerbated Darcy's headache and mild nausea. The only thing that eased his suffering at all was to sit by the window, lean his head back on the seat and close his eyes. Every so often he would doze off and then awake to the sound of their inane chatter. His cousin had decided to join them in the carriage due to recurring April showers and he and Elizabeth were talking agreeably to each other, of Kent and Hertfordshire, of travelling and staying at home, of new books and music, with so much spirit, energy and flow as to astound him. What on earth could the colonel have in common with this slip of a girl, a badly bred young lady at that? Yet on and on they prattled, laughing every now and again at something one or the other of them had said. He was amazed and a little annoyed at the easy intimacy they had struck up, and eventually sat upright to listen properly for a while.

The colonel was telling her of his family and their country seat when Darcy interrupted them. "We should reach Matlock by dinner. I ought to warn you, Elizabeth, that they will probably consider ours a reprehensible connection and will be displeased and heartily disapprove, though I trust they will understand this could not be avoided and will not treat you with any overt unkindness. I hope you will not be too much intimidated by their company."

Her eyebrows rose and she looked at him directly. Her tongue darted out to wet her lips and though it seemed as if she had something to say the colonel spoke on her behalf, frowning at Darcy. "Elizabeth does not seem intimidated by my company, Darcy. Am I not of that family?"

"You cannot pretend, cousin, that they will be pleased in any way. They would have wished for me to marry someone from the same social sphere."

The colonel shook his head and looked incredulous, and Darcy did wonder why he had spoken so bluntly. While there was nothing but truth in his words, he might have expressed himself better, or at least in softer tones. Elizabeth blinked rapidly and her hands were clenched in her lap. He saw that she was struggling to gain control of her temper.

His words had the effect of destroying any hopes of civilised, cheery conversation and all three of them fell silent. After a few minutes or so, Darcy saw Elizabeth's foot begin to swing back and forth, underneath her gown, the sole of her boot scraping the carriage floor; a habit of hers he well remembered from the hellish journey of the previous day. He sighed at the thought of having to bear her endless fidgeting for another thirty or so miles.

They did indeed make Matlock in time for dinner. Darcy was thankful that some drizzling rain meant there was no welcoming party outside Haddon Hall. Only the housekeeper greeted them at the doors, an umbrella held over her miserable head. Darcy noted the swiftest look of uncertainty cross Elizabeth's features as he handed her out of the carriage. She stood looking up at the imposing grey walls, turrets and large wooden doors and he heard her draw a long, steadying breath. Haddon was an imposing fortified manor house that had survived from the medieval age, and in truth, Darcy himself had never felt entirely comfortable there; it was certainly not homely or welcoming. He was gripped by a sudden urge to take her hand, to squeeze her fingers in reassurance. Despite all their differences, she still somehow managed to stir him into protectiveness. Yet he did not move closer, doubting, due to the acrimony of the day, that she would welcome his touch.

Though there had been no welcoming party outside, their arrival had obviously been anticipated and they were told the family were assembled together waiting for them. They were relieved of their coats and hats in the entrance hall and Elizabeth smoothed down her dress and licked her lips in preparation for meeting her new relations. Inside her head, she heard her mother's voice telling her to pinch her cheeks to get a little bloom in them and it made her smile, but she did not follow the advice. Though nervous, she was not truly afraid, for hers was a strong character and her estimation of herself did not easily rise or fall on the opinion of others.

Mr Darcy hung back with the dour looking housekeeper, quietly giving instructions, while she and the colonel followed the servants through an ante-chamber to a parlour of fine proportions and grand ornaments. There were five occupants of the room. The colonel introduced her to his brother, Walter, a rather stupid looking man, who grinned inanely. He was much older than the colonel, perhaps almost forty, and held the title of Lord Ripley but invited her to address him however she liked, *'people call me all sorts of names, most of 'em not complimentary and you shall have to tell me yours six dozen times before I remember it'*, he laughed, but nobody joined him in it. His wife was not so jovial or approachable. Lady Ripley's first name was Beatrice. She wore her hair piled high and round on top of her head like it was a hat. Without compunction, she examined Elizabeth from head to toe, her face displaying her distaste, before she turned away with no more than a cursory hello.

Then there was the Earl, small and round, who was quite aged and quite deaf and did not seem to understand who she was or why she was there, and was quite put out to have a stranger addressing him. The elder Mr Darcy, she could not immediately fathom, he was tall and lean, with a full head of white hair. His voice was deep and stern, though he was polite enough and expressed his deepest sympathies to her, in the most elegant manner, as regards her father's passing. He was distant though and appraised her just as Beatrice had done a few moments before. There was no outright show of disapproval, but his gaze was critical. Elizabeth felt he found her wanting and was left with the impression that though he would have been quite happy to have her live at Pemberley as a charitable concern, he was not at all pleased to have her married to his son.

The last person to greet her was the Countess of Matlock, Lady Fitzwilliam. She was a short, rotund lady who walked with a limp and leaned heavily on a stick as she approached. She smiled but Elizabeth was not fooled for a moment, for when their eyes met - the countess's were shockingly blue - Elizabeth saw the depth and breadth of the lady's experience and strength. This elderly matron, who pretended meekness, promised to be a formidable opponent if crossed. Elizabeth silently vowed not to make an enemy of her and dipped into her lowest, most respectful curtsey. This earned her a measured nod of Lady Fitzwilliam's head in return.

"Where is Georgiana?" Mr Darcy enquired from somewhere behind her, having now joined them.

"She'll be down shortly, Fitzwilliam," his father answered, "with Miss Temple."

"We should allow Mr and Mrs Darcy some time to settle in before dinner," the countess said, dismissing both him and Elizabeth from her presence. Mr Darcy motioned at Elizabeth and she followed him, feeling much like a dog brought to heel at his command. They ascended the stairs, she having to hurry to match his long strides. The upstairs corridors were long, thin and dark, requiring candles in order for them to find their way, even though there was still some daylight outside. He stopped abruptly at a door and turned the knob, opening it for her. When he did not immediately leave, she momentarily thought he was going to enter the bedroom with her and her heart and stomach lurched at the thought.

"Miss Bennet," he stopped and smiled at his faux pas. It was the first upturn in his expression she had witnessed in two days. "Forgive me."

She met his smile with a wary one of her own. "I admit I am having some trouble with the change in title myself; every time someone refers to Mrs Darcy, I fight the urge to look around to see who they are addressing."

"And your nose wrinkles in disgust when you realise they mean you."

"As does yours," she said.

His face became stern again. "Elizabeth, it has been a strange day and I have not been myself due to the amount of wine I consumed last night. I can assure you I am not usually a drunkard. In fact, I normally only take a very little wine, an occasional brandy. I hope that my behaviour last

102

night..." He stopped and cleared his throat. "I know not how I came to be in your room, but.."

"The porters brought you there," she blurted out. "They found you asleep and insensible."

"Oh."

He did not remember! The possibilities this presented for teasing him. And she was briefly tempted by the idea, but then what was the point in having fun at the expense of such a humourless man. She told him the truth. "You took off your coat, staggered about and then fell to the floor. I put your coat under your head and left you there."

"That is all?"

"That is all."

"Well, in any case, I must apologise."

She shrugged. Of all the things she felt he might apologise for, falling over on her bedroom floor seemed of very small consequence. If only he might say sorry for some of the awful words that had fallen from his mouth, then she might feel a little more disposed towards him.

"I shall leave you to ready yourself for dinner. Will a half hour be sufficient?"

She agreed it would be and then jumped at the shout of a young girl, who ran down the gloomy corridor towards them and went to throw herself into Mr Darcy's arms. "Oh Brother. How good it is to see you again."

Mr Darcy acknowledged her by calling her name, but shrugged out of the embrace she was obviously keen to give him. It seemed he was as undemonstrative and cold with his family, as he was with strangers.

The child looked at Elizabeth and hid behind her brother's shoulder.

"This is my sister, Georgiana. Georgiana, I am sure our father has spoken to you...this is..."

Elizabeth spoke before he could finish, fearing the strange appellation of Mrs Darcy was about to fall from his mouth again. "'Tis a great pleasure to meet you. May I call you Georgiana? I hope I will be Elizabeth to you, or my other sisters call me Lizzy, whichever you prefer. We are to become familiar and I hope good friends, so we should start as we mean to go on." She immediately feared she had been too forward, too enthusiastic, but had almost felt the need to make up for Mr Darcy's reticence.

Georgiana sank further behind her brother and he frowned.

"You'll forgive Georgiana, she is but eleven."

"Of course." Elizabeth thought of her youngest sisters. Kitty, at twelve and Lydia at ten, neither of them hid behind anyone, both were boisterous and forward.

Miss Temple had been following her charge on their way to their drawing room. The introduction to this lady was somewhat awkward, given that the governess had originally been employed to tutor Elizabeth, as well as Miss Darcy, but Miss Temple was all serenity and easiness, and clever too; for she offered no congratulations, sensing they were not in order, but merely her best wishes and hopes for their future felicity. Elizabeth and Mr Darcy looked at each other quickly and then sharply away again. Future felicity! There was more chance of snow in June.

Elizabeth was ready to leave her eerie little room well before the half-hour appointed for her toilette. She had washed her face and tried to tidy her hair, but it had gotten even wilder in the damp weather and there was unfortunately little to be done with it, other than comb it through and refasten the pins that held it back. She examined her reflection. She looked pale from tiredness and the deep grey of her gown did nothing to offset her pallor, but rather exacerbated it. She had no wish to face *him* again today, or any of the new family that awaited her downstairs and briefly considered feigning illness and asking to remain in her room, brightening at the thought that they might even send a tray with some bread or fruit on it, in lieu of dinner, as would have happened at Longbourn. But a look around the horrible little room made her decide it might be better to go down - or else she might be driven out of her wits. The floors creaked, the closet doors groaned, the candles flickered and draughts were everywhere. It would make a perfect setting for a gothic horror novel and Elizabeth shuddered and dreaded having to fall asleep alone in it.

The sight of Mr Darcy, standing in the hallway, waiting to walk her down to dinner, surprised her. He inspected her gown and seemed as if he wanted to say something, but instead wordlessly offered his arm, which she took.

"I'm sorry I have nothing finer, sir. I'm in mourning. All my gowns are much the same, changing would have made little difference."

"Do not trouble yourself," he replied, but to Elizabeth it sounded very much like a reprimand for not having taken much trouble at all.

Dinner was taken at a large oak table and promised to be exceedingly handsome, with many servants and many courses. Elizabeth, though, did not recognise any of the dishes put before her and with every remove lost more and more hope of finding something she found palatable - oily fish and bowls of spicy, gloopy stew (which she heard referred to as a regout) were so different from what she was used to. She consoled herself with the thought of dessert. That could not be too odd, surely? How could a pudding or pie be strange? Alas, when her favourite course came, it was fruit set in a peculiar jelly, and such was the odd texture of it that she did well not to spit it out into her napkin. She forced one mouthful down with a sip of her wine and water and did not care to try another. The discourse at the table was not so much a conversation, as a series of pronouncements, which were then remarked on by one or two of the assembled party, before heavy silence fell again - while someone else would think of something to say. She pined for Longbourn and those dinners where everyone spoke over each other and laughed and teased, until her father would gently bring them to order. He had struggled to join them for dinner during those last few months and his absence had made them rowdier and noisier, but Elizabeth would have much preferred the chaos of the Bennet table to the sedate Fitzwilliam one. Not shy, Elizabeth was ready to speak if it proved necessary, but she was seated between young Georgiana, whose eyes were as wide as the side plates with fear, and the half-asleep Earl; the former said nothing for fear of being noticed and the latter never looked her way. Mr Darcy was directly across from her. Now and again he would look around the candles to ask her if she might try something or other.

Would she have some rabbits liver?
No, thank you.
Some pigeon?
No, thank you, sir.
The codsounds?
She shook her head.

When the meal was nearing its end and some candied orange and other dried fruit were brought in and he saw her take some, he stretched a long arm out and pushed the bowl from the centre of the table towards her so she might reach it with ease, but he did not look her way, nor did he acknowledge her mumbled thanks. Lord, but he was odd.

The countess stood to lead the ladies out and bid Elizabeth to lend her arm for support, and once in the drawing room, the elder lady kept her near. Her reason for her wanting to do so soon became clear. There came an interrogation. How many siblings did Elizabeth have, boys or girls, older or younger, were they handsome? What carriages did the family keep? What had been her mother's maiden name? Elizabeth answered her with as much composure as she could muster and the countess looked neither pleased nor displeased, but merely nodded and absorbed all that she was told.

The men came in and shortly afterwards Miss Temple rose to take Georgiana away. No sooner was the governess out of the room than Beatrice Fitzwilliam said, "Well, thank goodness, and now we may be just family. I do not see why she ought to dine with us. Why does she afford that right? It is not 'de rigour' in Town, amongst families of quality, to have someone who is, after all, an employee at the table."

Elizabeth's new father came to Miss Temple's defence. "I do not care what the current views or practices are of any family but my own. It has always been the Darcy way that a governess enjoys the privilege of a good dinner, with good company. She is here to guide and care for Georgiana, and if my daughter is at dinner, so will Miss Temple be. She's a gentlewoman, after all. I don't see why you take exception, Beatrice."

Beatrice looked around the room for someone to support her in the matter. "Mrs Darcy, Elizabeth, pray tell me, did your governess eat with the family?"

"We never had any governess."

"No governess!" Lady Fitzwilliam exclaimed. "Five daughters brought up at home without a governess! Your mother must have been quite a slave to your education."

Elizabeth wanted to laugh at this idea and assured the countess it was not the case.

"Well then who taught you? You must have had some sort of instruction."

She blushed when she realised the attention of the whole room was on her but sought to explain. "My father had quite modern ideas on education. He believed that learning had to be self-motivated to be truly effective. My sisters and I had no formal learning, it is true, but if we took an interest in certain subjects, we were given the means and time to pursue them."

The elder Mr Darcy gave a little laugh. "Your father was an interesting man, so odd a mixture of quick parts, capricious by nature - how he loved to debate - and he would win a great many of them, his sarcasm cut his opponents to the quick. He had a fine mind, and if had not been so reserved, he would have done well in public life, I think."

Elizabeth was a little mesmerized by this speech. How wonderful it was to hear her father talked about in such a way; described by someone who really seemed to know him. She wanted to hear more, but there were too many people in the room, and Mr Darcy too far away from her to carry it on in anything other than a very public way. In any case, the younger Mr Darcy spoke before she had a chance to.

"Nothing is to be done in education without steady and regular instruction, which a governess brings. It seems to me that if it is not insisted upon in those of undiligent character, then ignorance and idleness will win out." He was not looking at her, but at the fire. Elizabeth seethed at his comments, which felt like an attack on her kind and gentle father. However, she had a niggling feeling he might have the truth of it. Kitty and Lydia, in particular, could be idle and wrote horrible letters, full of errors, and there were woeful gaps in their knowledge. She could not remember the last time she had seen either of them with a book. Still, did he have to make it sound like her dear Papa had shamefully neglected them all?

Thankfully, the subject was dropped and music called for. Beatrice obliged and moved to the instrument. Obviously, they were all now under the impression that she was an uneducated, unaccomplished country miss, with not a single talent to her name, as nobody bothered asking her if she played. Elizabeth was relieved. She could play but only in a very simple way. Masters had been employed for her benefit, and Mary's, but while Mary was constantly at the instrument, trying to force from it by industry what natural talent had denied her, Elizabeth only went near it to amuse herself or her sisters, despite the entreaties of the earnest young music master that she practice more diligently, and not waste the feel and ear for music that God had given her.

She sat and listened to the music in silence, Mr Darcy's views on idleness occupying her thoughts. It was calm and soothing, and to her shame she thought she might have fallen asleep for a few minutes, because the next thing she heard was quiet applause and the chink of the tea things being brought in. A cup was pressed into her hand by Colonel Fitzwilliam before she could rouse herself enough to offer her assistance in pouring it. Though she sipped the tea, her eyes felt dreadfully heavy. Mr Darcy moved behind her, she sensed him at her shoulder, before he bent to speak quietly to her.

"If you are tired, Elizabeth, excuse yourself and go to bed. Nobody shall mind."

No, she supposed nobody would. No-one wanted her there and in her absence they might pretend she didn't exist.

His words felt much like a dismissal and part of her wanted to remain in the room till at least supper, just to spite him, but she *was* bone tired; to the point where she might cry with exhaustion. She nodded at Mr Darcy and he made the announcement that she would retire, for which she was grateful, and all that remained for her to do before quitting the room was to give a simple goodnight.

Mr Darcy said he would walk her up. She demurred, he insisted, and they took the stairs together again. "We go to Pemberley tomorrow. It is no more than two hours travel and there is no requirement to leave particularly early. You may sleep as late as you choose."

He saw her to the door of her room, gave her a very quick bow and left.

Twelve

Elizabeth woke early and lay in bed for a while, trying to remember where she was. The events of the last two days were relived and considered as she sat up and looked around her. The room was not quite as terrible in the daylight as it had been in the darkness, but she would rather have been anywhere else in the world right now. Married! She thought with disbelief. I have a husband! A cold, proud husband, to whom I am *tolerable*! And to think her Aunt Gardiner had gone through all that embarrassment of talking to her of the marital bed and a 'man's needs'. Her aunt had wanted to ensure she knew the signs that she might be with child, and also had given her some advice on how to try and avoid becoming so, if she felt unequal to motherhood just yet, given her age. It had been mortifying for both of them and Elizabeth had tried to wave her aunt away, but Mrs Gardiner would not be deterred, explaining that she did not want things to be as much of a mystery to Elizabeth, as they had been for her. Oddly enough though, what would happen in the bedchamber had been the least of her concerns, *that* had just seemed like something else to be borne, in amongst her dismay at the thought of being shackled to a man not of her choosing for the next thirty or so years. Though the length of her incarceration might of course be longer - it would be just her luck that they would both live till they were eighty.

She got out of bed and tiptoed across the cold floor to the window. It was very early indeed. The air in the house had the chill of a late spring morning before the sun had fully risen to warm its windows and walls. Outside there was dew on the grass. When she looked up beyond the manicured lawn she gave a little gasp of surprise. What she hadn't seen yesterday, or bothered to look at, was the entirety of the park, for just past the formal lawns, were woods and a stream (there was a maze too, and a folly and all those other adornments one might expect from a great house) but there were also areas where the natural beauty of the surrounding countryside had been allowed to rest and thrive. It was too tempting and besides, she had nothing else to amuse her. No more than ten minutes later, she was hurrying down the stairs, surprising the sleepy eyed maids who were preparing the downstairs fires. The butler, who was in the hallway but still pulling on his jacket, rushed to open the door for her, and then she was outside. She tried to walk sedately but the rustle of the trees beckoned her, the scent of spring wildflowers filled the air, and the breeze whispered her name. As soon as the ground began to slope her legs gathered pace. Her walk became a stride, then her stride became a run. She flung her arms out to the side and let the hill carry her down into the woods - she did not reappear from out of them for some considerable time.

Her ramble ended at the tall folly and she climbed up the steps into the round, open structure, which she hoped would afford her a good view of the countryside surrounding Haddon Hall. She was surprised on reaching the stone floor at the top of the folly to find Lady Fitzwilliam there, sitting on one of the benches, hand on her walking stick, and looking very much as if she had been expecting her.

"We are both early risers then?"

"Yes," Elizabeth curtsied.

"I saw your wild flee across the lawn this morning. I thought perhaps the house was on fire. I was about to order the horses be released from the stables."

"Sorry, you must think me improper." Elizabeth fiddled with the bonnet in her hands and wished it were still on her head.

The elder lady laughed. "Improper? No. I daresay there are worse ways of showing oneself without decorum than having a little gad about the park." Lady Fitzwilliam looked at her for a long while. "Let us decide how things stand between us, shall we? You should know that Mr Darcy has fully enlightened me as to how you came to be married to my nephew. I know what occurred in Hertfordshire and am aware this is a patched-up business, brought about to scotch the rumours that followed you to Town. 'Tis all most unfortunate, for the pair of you, I daresay, because it seems there is little

111

affection in the case. I have not told Beatrice and Walter about your circumstances, as I think it none of their business and the Earl is lucky these days if he remembers that Tuesday follows Monday. What I wish to say, Elizabeth, if I may address you so," Elizabeth nodded and the countess continued, "is that I can bear where you have come from, I can forgive your lack of education and your country manners, but believe me young lady, if you ever embarrass this family in such a way as you embarrassed your family in Hertfordshire, I shall be most seriously displeased. The men in this family like to fancy themselves lord and masters of all they survey, but I can assure you I hold great sway and the force of my displeasure, should it ever have cause to land upon you, will be terrible indeed. Are we clear?"

"Yes, Lady Fitzwilliam."

"Excellent. Close your mouth. 'Tis not ladylike to leave it hanging open so. Now give me your arm, I have walked too far."

Together, they made their way slowly back to the house. The countess gave her a history of the place and pointed out the best views as they walked. Every ten minutes or so they would have to stop so she might catch her breath and when they would begin to walk again, she would wince from the pain in her hip.

"What happened to your leg?"

Smiling at the directness of the question, the countess answered. "I fell from a horse when I was a girl and broke my hip. It healed, but as I have aged, the cold and damp have sought their way into the old injury, so as to give me trouble. What happened to your hair?"

"I cut it," Elizabeth admitted. "It was madness I know. I shall endeavour to better myself, Lady Fitzwilliam. I promise, very soon you shall not know me from how I appear to you now."

The countess stopped and took Elizabeth's chin in her hand, turning her face up to look into her eyes. "Do not wish your life away. What I wouldn't give to be seventeen again."

"I am but fifteen."

"Are you really? Heaven help us."

Elizabeth came across Mr Darcy in the hall after she had helped Lady Fitzwilliam settle into a sunny parlour at the back of the house. He was coming out of the library door with a troubled look upon his face and bade her good morning and asked her how she had slept.

His tone was quiet and polite. She had become so used to being addressed by him sharply that his gentlemanlike manner now astounded her.

"I slept well, sir, thank you."

"You have been out walking?"

"Yes, 'tis a fine day and the grounds are pleasant." She suddenly wished she looked a little tidier and more elegant. His appearance was impeccable. He did not seem to care about her disarray though, he was distracted and she had lost his attention already.

He took out his pocket watch. "Will you ready yourself for the trip to Pemberley? I have just seen my father and he wishes to leave sooner than I had anticipated."

"I'll go upstairs now."

His eyes flittered briefly back to her face. "Have you had breakfast?"

"Oh, I never eat much in the way of breakfast and I have stolen an apple from Lady Fitzwilliam's parlour, she keeps a big bowl of fruit there, see?" She showed him the apple she had been holding behind her back, and then felt a little foolish.

"A *whole* apple, Elizabeth? My goodness," he said with a quizzical smile before walking away.

Thirteen

The journey to Pemberley was made easily, and the carriage was a full and lively one, with three ladies on one side, and he and his father on the other. Darcy remained silent while Miss Temple, Elizabeth and George Darcy chatted easily and Georgiana looked on happily, not daring to add any thoughts or opinions of her own, but glad to be in their company and free of school. She had taken to Miss Temple wholeheartedly, which was something of a relief. He noticed his sister looking at Elizabeth with a sort of reverence, which caused him to smile beneath the cover of his hand. His little sister obviously believed he had *chosen* Elizabeth as his bride and because she so looked up to him, she considered Elizabeth must be far and above all other women. Georgiana stared at her and listened to every word she uttered. When Elizabeth would look her way with a kindly smile, though, she would become embarrassed and blush, hiding her face away.

They sat opposite each other, he and his child bride, so Darcy could observe her without hindrance as she talked to the others. She was freshly bathed and the scent of a flowery soap floated around her. Though her gown was dark and the ribbons on her bonnet were black, she had lost the heavy, gloomy air that had beset her since their first meeting. Today, she was smiling more and he noted she had been blessed with straight, white teeth. Her eyes were alight with intelligence and her complexion was extremely good; unlike many other girls of her age, she possessed not a single blemish. He recalled his cousin saying she had a sweet face and when Darcy bothered to look at her properly, he had to admit that maybe the colonel had the right of it. Cross with her and himself, he had previously only looked at her to criticise, and his determination to find fault had caused him to see her as unattractive, but he now saw she was not ill-favoured, far from it in fact, and he supposed there might yet be a chance of some improvement in her looks, her manners and her figure. But would he ever walk into a London party, a dinner, or to St James' and feel proud to have her on his arm? Would other women envy her beauty, or might other men seethe with jealousy that she was his? The simple answer was no, that would never be. She would be his 'country wife' as the colonel had suggested.

Elizabeth looked in his direction suddenly and arched her brow at him, in a way that belied her delicate years. At her questioning look, he realised he had been staring and shifted his gaze to the window instead.

"We are almost home, Elizabeth," his father said. "We have entered Pemberley Woods."

"Excellent," she replied and then with a sly glance at Darcy, added, "I have heard much of the beauty of the place. In fact, I have been besieged by people wanting to extol its delights. Now if your son will only be quiet, I might enjoy the scenery, for do you not find, Mr Darcy, that he is terribly garrulous? I confess I find his endless chatter and noise a most terrible distraction."

Georgiana was shocked to see someone make sport of her brother. Miss Temple's features were schooled into a well-trained mask, though the hint of a smile tugged at her mouth, his father, however, chuckled merrily.

Darcy rankled at being the subject of her tease, but he also admired her bravado, given that she could not be truly happy herself, so far away from all she knew and those she loved.

She was quiet herself then, after teasing him for being silent, and sank back into the carriage seat to look out of the window. When Pemberley came into view a few minutes later, he watched carefully, but to his surprise, he found her impassive and unusually still. He had been waiting for praise, or a gasp of delight, she just looked.

"Welcome to Pemberley. I hope you will be happy here, Elizabeth, Miss Temple," his father said, ever the gentleman. Nobody would have guessed that only that morning his father had called him into the library and given him a dressing down over his lack of judgement, his foolishness at having been 'caught'. His father had expounded on and on about how badly he had let his family down, and the great wrong he had done Anne de Bourgh.

115

Such was the way with his father; Darcy was either his 'darling boy' or a 'terrible disappointment'.

He leaned forward to catch Elizabeth's attention. "Are you displeased?"

She shook her head. "Oh, forgive me, no. It's the handsomest building I ever saw. Far better than I was expecting."

"What were you expecting?"

"Something like Haddon Hall I suppose." She coloured and stammered. "I...what I mean to say is, that Haddon has its own charms, of course...I would not wish to denigrate...I do not dislike..."

As she blustered and fell quiet again, the carriage descended the hill, crossed a bridge over the lake and drove to the door, where a welcoming party of the foremost servants, from housekeeper and butler, to footmen and upstairs maids, were all arranged in a neat line outside the house. Of course they would come out. Everyone was returning home, the master, the young master, the master's daughter and the new Mrs Darcy! He thanked the heavens it was restricted to just the foremost servants and not every hallboy and kitchen hand had been summoned to pay reverence.

He walked beside Elizabeth once they were out of the carriage. His father would stop at every second or third person to bestow his thanks on them, offer a few words, as was his usual way. Darcy spoke to no one, wishing only to be indoors as quickly as possible, but when he reached the housekeeper, he saw the need for an introduction. Mrs Reynolds had been in their employ for nearly twenty years, it would not do to ignore her and Elizabeth needed to be made aware of her importance amongst the staff.

"Welcome to Pemberley, Mrs Darcy," Mrs Reynolds smiled. She kept her shock under good regulation, but Darcy felt some stares and heard a whisper or two further down the line. He caught Elizabeth's hand and threaded it through the crook of his arm, pulling her close.

Tea was served in the saloon. Darcy left them after a sip or two of coffee, going to a small study kept for his own use on the ground floor, and then sent for the housekeeper.

"Mrs Reynolds, no doubt in our absence, you have approved the menu for tonight's dinner?"

"Yes, everything is arranged."

"I am afraid I may have some alterations to make to it?"

She looked to the door and her brow wrinkled.

"You need not worry about my father, I shall speak to him. What I wondered was whether I might ask that Mrs Small prepare tonight's meal. I know she's now the under-cook, but I'd like it to be good, plain country fare."

"Monsieur Malbec will not be pleased, sir, he was planning quite a feast in celebration of the family all returning."

"I was afraid he was. That was why I wished to speak to you before the preparations go any further. Tonight, I wish for Mrs Small to cook and I want it to be soup, and then some meat and potatoes, local vegetables, and a more traditional pudding. If Monsieur Malbec complains and starts throwing things, please inform me and I will go down to the kitchens myself and shout at him in French."

"Pardon me, sir, but am I right in thinking the new Mrs Darcy prefers a plainer dish?" Mrs Reynolds smiled, obviously thinking him an indulgent, love-struck new husband, eager to please his bride.

"I haven't a clue," he said, abruptly. "But I haven't seen her eat anything substantial for two days. She's skinny enough as it is. I fear she may waste away to nothing, so it's worth a try."

The housekeeper started in surprise and he realised he had been overfamiliar and spoken his thoughts out loud, without guard.

"I'll see to it," Mrs Reynolds replied.

"And Mrs Darcy has been found a good room?"

"The nicest one not already taken, it is…"

Darcy cut her off, "good, good. Mrs Reynolds, I must be blunt. I saw the looks and heard the mutterings outside. I

117

will not tolerate them. Mrs Darcy is full young, but she must be afforded the utmost respect. I will not have her gossiped about, or made a subject of amusement for others. I would ask that the staff have a care when they go into the surrounding villages about how they talk of her. If I hear of anything being said that constitutes an invasion of her privacy, or anything that is less than deferential, then I shall make it my business to know from where it came and that person shall find themselves looking for a new post. Make this clear to everyone."

"I shall speak to them, I am heartily embarrassed, Mr Darcy, if you or Mrs Darcy were offended, I do apologise." Mrs Reynolds wrung her hands together. "Should I offer Mrs Darcy my apologies, also?"

"That will not be necessary. You may go."

When the housekeeper had left him, he leant back in his chair and propped his booted feet upon the desk. He supposed he ought to go back to the saloon again, but he really could not face it just yet. Bringing her home, to Pemberley, had given everything a horrible reality. They were here, she was his wife, and he was now a married man. He sat and grieved for a good while. If only she had the beauty of Emma Balcombe, or the good sense and maturity of Constance Balcombe. What had he done to deserve Elizabeth Bennet? What gods had he angered that he should be punished so? He elected to hide until the dinner hour, he was in no fit state for company in any case.

Fourteen

Her room was beautiful, light and sunny, with thick rugs on the floor and a bed larger and softer than any she had ever known. Elizabeth knelt on the window seat and a smile spread across her face when she saw that her view was lovely too. She could see down to the lake in front of the house, and it was a corner room, so if she went to the other window, she could see the beginnings of the hills and trees behind the house. The park enchanted and delighted her and she could sit and look upon the whole scene, and beyond, up to the woods, to the river and the trees scattered on its banks and the winding valley through the hill they had descended on their way in - everything pleased her. There was natural splendour as far as the eye could see.

"Is everything to your satisfaction, madam?"

She turned on the seat to see Mrs Reynolds behind her, framed by the doorway. She was a respectable-looking elderly woman, much less fine than Elizabeth had expected, and very civil, but with an air of distance. "Oh, yes, it is..." Realising she were about to gush like a girl, she tried to moderate her tone. "It is perfectly charming."

"Your trunks have been brought up. I'll send a maid to help you put away your things, let her know if there is anything else you require."

She gave what she hoped was a dignified nod. "Thank you, Mrs Reynolds."

A great crashing sound, deep and reverberating, made her jump and she looked at the housekeeper for an explanation.

"It's the dinner gong, Mrs Darcy. It's to let everyone know it's time to begin dressing. Dinner will be served in an hour."

"Oh, I see," she said, her hand pressed to her chest to still it, and her ears ringing.

She supposed she had a few moments to herself, between Mrs Reynolds leaving and the maid arriving, but she did not use them industriously by beginning to see to her trunks, she spent them idly admiring everything. Words had failed her in the carriage. She had been truly bewildered by her first sight of Pemberley. If she had been coming there as a stranger to the family - as a mere visitor - she would perhaps have been ebullient and abundant in her praise, for it was undoubtedly a magnificent and grand house. But she had been silent, stupefied by the ominous thought that should the elder Mr Darcy die, the younger Mr Darcy would be master, and she would be mistress - of all this! She offered up a silent prayer for George Darcy's continuing good health. Fortunately, he looked quite robust.

When she left her room for dinner, she met the younger Mr Darcy at the top of the elegant staircase. He wordlessly held out his arm and she realised he had been waiting to escort her downstairs. He looked different. Elizabeth studied his face and figure for a moment before taking the offered arm, but could not put her finger on what the change in his appearance was down to. He said nothing except to ask after her comfort, and she answered that all was well.

The Darcy dinner table was even longer than the Fitzwilliam one had been the night before. Elizabeth felt her heart sink at the sight of it and dreaded course after course of aspic covered meats, thick strong sauces and strange fish. But wonder of wonders, when it arrived, it was glorious and her appetite grew with velocity as her taste buds tingled with delight. She ate every last drop of the simple vegetable soup. The main course was devoured quickly and when the pudding came, the sight and taste of it made her so very stupidly happy, for the first time in weeks. It was an apple pudding, so wonderfully delicious that if both Mr Darcys had not been watching her with curious expressions, she might have picked the bowl up and licked it clean.

So busy was she with these delights, that she paid little attention to the progress of the meal in general, or the conversation. The sweets were served, and then there was some coughing, followed by some pointed stares in her direction. She was all confusion until Miss Temple spoke.

"Mrs Darcy, what a splendid meal. It will be a shame when we ladies have to leave the table, but I suppose all good things must come to an end."

Even young Georgiana was looking at her as if she were quite stupid. She had not realised, not even thought of it as her duty, but as she looked around the table, realisation dawned that she was the now the lady of the house. She rose from her chair, cheeks flushing crimson, to lead the other ladies out.

Once in the drawing room, she approached Miss Temple. "Thank you."

"Whatever for?" Miss Temple replied, feigning ignorance and wanting to pretend nothing had been amiss.

Elizabeth smiled. "I think you know. I forgot my place."

"You shall have a lot to become accustomed to, and such a big house to learn the ways of."

"And I must learn my way about it too. You must draw me a map, Georgiana."

"Even better," said Miss Temple, "she shall give us a tour."

"Me?" the young girl squeaked.

"Yes you," her governess insisted.

They were only left to themselves for half an hour or so, but Elizabeth enjoyed herself and wished it had been longer. Miss Temple was a wonderful conversationalist who could expound on any given subject, and Georgiana slowly began to offer up two or three words at a time, rather than just one or two. The entrance of the gentlemen, however, saw the going away of them. Goodnights were exchanged and Georgiana was taken above stairs for the rest of the evening. Elizabeth half felt as if she should be taken away too.

When they were gone, Mr Darcy and his father stood over a chess board.

"I don't suppose you play, Elizabeth?"

She was surprised and a little delighted, until she returned Mr Darcy's look and realised he was nodding towards a very elegant pianoforte in the corner of the room. A game of chess, where she might engage her mind to forget her troubles, seemed infinitely more preferable than inflicting terrible torture on such a fine instrument. She was sure her playing would please nobody, but could not very well lie. "I do, yes, a little."

"Might you indulge us then?"

Without further ado, he sat down to the chess board opposite his father, as Elizabeth reluctantly crossed the room. She shuffled through the sheet music, but as there was no one to turn pages, she thought she would do better playing something simple that she knew well. The simplicity of the piece was not enough to save her, however, and she winced at every fudged note and cursed every slurred passage. When she had finished, there was some polite applause from the gentlemen, but she took the opportunity of getting up quickly and sitting herself firmly back down upon the sofa, praying they would not ask her to continue.

George Darcy gave her a bland, vague compliment. He was obviously in the habit of hearing the best performers and her dreadful display could not have pleased him in the slightest.

The younger Mr Darcy looked up from the chessboard. "A new music master will be engaged for Georgiana. There would be no difficulty if you should like him to also teach you."

"Thank you." For the second time that evening, she felt her cheeks grow hot. She took a book from a nearby table, opened it wide without reading the title and held it up in front of her face to mask her shame.

"Would you like me to show you to the library? There are some novels and volumes of poetry you might prefer?"

"Oh no," she insisted. "I am already engaged in this one. It is very interesting."

"I see," Mr Darcy said. "Then I shall leave you to enjoy your tome on animal husbandry. There is a chapter on the breeding of bulls you might particularly enjoy."

"I'm sure I shall," she replied from behind the book and then realised her answer meant she was now committed to the blasted book until at least supper time.

It was only when the coffee and tea came and she handed him his cup that she realised what the change in Mr Darcy's appearance was. She had been right earlier, there was something different. He had shaved off his thin little moustache! He must have noticed her looking at his upper lip because he ran his free hand across his mouth in a conscious way and then walked off, as if he was dreading what she might say.

She woke in very fine sheets, in her beautiful room, to a soft knock on the door. When she sat up and answered, a maid came in and began to rebuild her fire, while another followed with a basin of hot water and fresh cloths, and then asked whether she would like anything brought up to her on a tray. Elizabeth rubbed her eyes and tried to straighten her hair a little, thinking that being imprisoned in a marriage with an oddly silent and critical man did have some compensations - hers was a most luxurious kind of incarceration.

Once readied for the day, she asked the maid for directions to the schoolroom, where she found Miss Temple and Georgiana expecting her and they set off on their tour. They did not encounter either Mr Darcy on their travels, except in portrait form in the gallery. Hung in this wide, long corridor, which separated one wing of the house from the other, was a large painting of the younger Mr Darcy and they stopped before it. Elizabeth noted the artist's name and the date of its completion in the corner of the picture, and saw Mr Darcy must have been around nineteen at the time. He looked more carefree on canvas, a small smile playing around the corners of his lips. None of the affectations of dress that he now adopted were present and his mien, though proud, had something more amiable about it. She stopped and looked at it for a good while, wondering at him, before she sensed she had detained her companions too long and they moved onto the next portrait, which portrayed the current master of the house and Lady Anne Fitzwilliam, commissioned on the occasion of their engagement. This scene caused her brows to rise in surprise. Lady Anne, it

123

seemed, had been somewhat older than her husband, and he much handsomer than her. They looked an oddly matched pair, standing far apart from one another, with a horse and three dogs between them. Elizabeth suspected it had been an excellent match in most respects, but sadly, not one of very great affection.

Again, she studied it for too long.

"Are you fond of art, Mrs Darcy?" Miss Temple asked.

"I am afraid I am always more interested in the subject of the pictures, rather than the pictures themselves. And, with landscapes, I confess I would prefer to be outside, enjoying the same view every day, rather than inside looking at renditions of a hundred different scenes."

They moved on, Georgiana rushing them past the master's and the mistress's chambers, with a swift wave towards each door. The first she looked a little afraid of; the sight of the second seemed to give her pain. They went down to the ground floor and passed numerous parlours, a music room and a garden room that might have once been very charming but looked as if it were in need of someone to bring it to life once again. Though the whole house was impressive, there was one room in particular that delighted her and made her gasp in shock and surprise.

"Oh this is not real, surely? How utterly wonderful!"

Miss Temple and Georgiana laughed at her enthusiasm.

"Papa says it is the largest private library in the north of England," Georgiana told her.

It was a huge room, with vaulted ceilings and shelves piled so high with books that steps were required to reach its upper limits. The windows were very large too, providing ample light and there were so many comfortable chairs that she thought it might take her quite some time to find a favourite.

She was interrupted in her raptures by the appearance of a footman, who bowed low and told them he had been sent to find Miss Temple and Georgiana, for the girl was to meet her art master, who had just arrived.

124

"You best go," she told Miss Temple. "I shall be happy to remain here for a while, a week or two should be enough to satisfy me."

She did remain in the library, perusing the collections for some time, but despite her initial excitement, her mood became sombre, as her thoughts began drifting to the subject of her Papa and his beloved book room. Memories, sweet and sad, assailed her so violently as to leave her choking back a sob, and she suddenly felt the need to be anywhere but amongst books.

Going out into the hall, she paced for a while, but there were servants all about giving her curious looks. Seeing the need for occupation and wishing for some sort of connection to those she loved, she went in search of paper and pen. There was a gilded writing desk in the very next room, and she sat at it while, wondering if it were ill-mannered to rummage through the drawers. As she pondered, she was surprised by the master of the house coming through the room. He stopped and stared at her as if he had seen a ghost.

"Good heavens, Elizabeth!"

"Sorry, sir, I did not mean to startle you."

"That was where the previous Mrs Darcy used to sit and write her letters."

Elizabeth made to move and began to apologise.

"Oh no, please stay where you are. She has been gone a long time, you cause no offence."

They smiled at each other uneasily.

"What age was Miss Georgiana, when your wife passed away?" Elizabeth asked, just for something to say.

"Just eight, I am afraid. She was quite a carefree outgoing child before…" He waved an arm and then sighed, as if the rest of the sentence had defeated him.

Elizabeth stroked the top of the desk. "It is a very lovely piece of furniture, but I wonder that Mrs Darcy did not have it moved over there, closer to the window, where the light is better, and she might have looked out upon the view."

George Darcy nodded. "Perhaps she simply never thought of it. She was more the sort of woman who accepted

125

things as they were. In fact, I seem to remember that she heartily disliked change."

"Well, you found me looking for a pen, ink and paper. I promised to write to my aunt as soon as I reached Derbyshire, to let her know of my safe arrival. I should like to send my sister Jane a letter too."

"Have a look in the drawers there, you might find an old pen you can mend and use, and I shall make sure you have plenty of paper and ink."

She thanked him and opened the first drawer. As she was looking through it, she saw the younger Mr Darcy for the first time that day. He walked into the room at a brisk pace but stopped very suddenly upon seeing her at his mother's desk.

He bid her good morning and she returned the greeting awkwardly, then felt the need to explain herself again. "I was looking for the necessary things in order for me to write some letters to my family."

"You need only have asked."

She removed her hands from the drawer and he left for a few moments. The elder Mr Darcy made a few polite enquiries into her wellbeing and comfort before his son returned with writing materials and set them down on the desk without ceremony.

She muttered a thank you.

"Well, if you are busy with your correspondence, Elizabeth, I suppose you will not mind if I steal your husband away for a few hours; in order that I might keep him abreast of some changes on the estate."

"Not at all, Mr Darcy," she said out loud. *Yes take him away,* she said to herself, *take him and his disapproving stares as far from me as possible and leave me in peace.*

Fifteen

She was left in peace. Her first few days at Pemberley passed almost too serenely, for while recent events had been bewildering and difficult, novelty had kept melancholy at bay. Travelling, along with the newness of everything and everyone, had occupied her mind and kept her diverted from her recent sorrows. Though now, without much company and separated from everybody she had been used to, her sadness grew and became acute. Pemberley was a quiet, sedate house and nobody seemed to know what her place in it was. Nobody was unkind, but neither did they put themselves out of their way to secure her happiness.

Georgiana would mostly duck her head and smile politely if she approached, though sometimes would venture a few words if Miss Temple encouraged her. The master was often busy, breakfasting early, before retiring to his study to attend to business, or riding out in the mornings to inspect the estate. He did not seek her out at all, and when he did come across her, he would always look a little confused, as if he had forgotten her existence.

The younger Mr Darcy only approached her twice a day. He would seek her out in the mornings, when she would sit and compose long letters to her family, and ask a few stilted impersonal questions, before moving off and going about his own business, or the business his father concerned him with. He too, often rode away shortly after breakfast and stayed out longer than his father, often not returning until it was time to change for dinner. Their second meeting of the day would always be at the top of the staircase, where he would escort her down to the drawing room for dinner. He seemed to think of this as a duty, but it was one Elizabeth would gladly have relieved him of. They were strangers and the silences were awkward and hard to avoid. However, when she had once politely suggested he need not wait for her if he did not wish to, because she now knew the way well enough on her own, he'd looked offended. So she accepted this odd little routine as part of her new life.

When she wrote to Mrs Gardiner, she spoke of the beauty of Derbyshire and the countryside she had travelled through and made enquiries after her little cousins. When she wrote to Jane, she spoke of the book she was reading and described her new younger sister and new father. When she wrote to her mother, she made sure to mention the number of carriages that were at the family's disposal, the grandeur of Pemberley and the size of the surrounding park. Her mother had now quit Longbourn and removed to the cottage in Meryton. Elizabeth thought brightly that perhaps being able to boast of her daughter's new situation might lessen the pain of her own upheaval.

There were things she did not mention in her letters, recollections of incidents that she did dare not put onto paper and allow to travel through the post, such as her first visit to church as Mrs Darcy, when she had been very briefly carried away with the foolish notion that her new husband had some small regard for her. He'd been solicitous in carrying her prayer book, sat by her side, and given her a small smile when she'd started to sing. But once outside she'd seen the truth of it as he'd hastened her into the carriage, without introducing her to any of their neighbours, or allowing her leave to give her own thanks to the parson. It became plain to her that she was an embarrassment and she realised his smiles during services had been borne of self-consciousness and shame. He had felt the incredulous stares of their fellow parishioners, perhaps thought her singing too loud or off key, and was probably afraid of what nonsense would fall from her mouth in front of the clergyman.

Once inside the carriage, she had crossed her arms over her chest, thrown him an angry look and turned her gaze resolutely to the window. He'd had the temerity to look bewildered by her mood and they had sat in silence while waiting for the rest of their party to catch them up.

Neither could she tell anyone of when she had entered her room one afternoon to fetch her spencer, only to overhear two upstairs maids going through her clothes and sneering over them. She had turned around and left as quietly as she had arrived, so as not to let them know she had overheard, and then she despised herself for her cowardice; annoyed that her usual strength of mind had deserted her.

It would do no good, though, to pass on the level of distress and loneliness she felt to others; there was nothing they could do to assist her, and she would not want to worry them unduly. Her letters were light and airy, full of any witticisms she could conjure up, flippant in their tone. She signed them all with a bold 'Elizabeth Darcy', but when she came to blot her signature, she pressed down on the paper very hard, as if she might press it away completely.

Her one consolation, her only real source of joy, was found in the companionship of Miss Temple. For one hour of the day George Darcy would request his daughter's presence in his study, where they took tea together. During this hour, which was adhered to with great punctuality, Miss Temple would take a stroll in the gardens. She and Elizabeth had met by accident on the first occasion, but they had such a pleasant time together that it soon became a habit. Miss Temple's days at Pemberley were not half as leisurely as Elizabeth's, as almost every moment of Georgiana's life was planned meticulously. There did not seem to be a moment, other than those she spent eating, sleeping, dressing or bathing, when she was not expected to be learning something, which kept her governess very busy. Even at dinner, Georgiana would face the prospect of her father firing questions at her, quizzing her on what instruction she had received that day. Elizabeth suspected the father and daughter tea hour ran on a similar basis. Georgiana's education was a very serious business indeed. Miss Temple was deemed good enough for the academic subjects, but music and art masters were employed also and came almost daily. When Elizabeth made an observation to Miss Temple, during an afternoon stroll in the park, about the heavy demands placed on a girl who had endured the sadness of losing her mother when so young, and who was at an age where she still might like to play and run about, she received a look that showed her the Governess was inclined to agree. Miss Temple was too astute and too aware of her position to voice such an opinion, however, and replied evenly, not wishing to denigrate her employer or say too much. "Mr Darcy has great hopes for her, he expects much, but I think his dedication to her improvement is borne out of love."

"Oh, I daresay it is, I did not mean to suggest him cruel. I just think that if he places even more demands upon her, she may very well soon wish herself back at school."

Miss Temple smiled. "I am told he was just as vigilant with his son. Mr Darcy's education was comprehensive. The responsibilities he will shoulder upon inheriting such a large estate were laid before him at quite a young age. I do not believe his father has made his path easy."

"Ah yes, the poor young man! How abhorrent it must be to know he will one day be in possession of such wealth and property, and how awful to have been given such vast opportunities for learning."

At the Governess' look, Elizabeth laughed off her remark, realising it had been unguarded and a little disrespectful. "I am a terrible wife, am I not?"

Before Miss Temple was spared the awkwardness of finding an answer, a footman came hurrying across the lawn to tell her she was required in the drawing room. Elizabeth followed him and straightened her gown just before the door was opened for her. She learned she had been summoned because there were visitors, a Mr and Mrs Robertson, who were settling themselves on a plump sofa, but were forced to rise again when she entered in order to be introduced. They were neighbours, with a small estate close by. She was pleased to know there was some company to be had, but dismayed that they were so much older than her. Still, they appeared friendly enough.

"When we saw the announcement in the papers, we could not do anything, nor concentrate on nothing, until we had called to give our congratulations. I said to Mr Robertson, we must go; we must be off immediately and meet this young lady who has tempted our young Mr Darcy into marriage. I have known him since he was a babe, Mrs Darcy." Mrs Robertson told her. "And such a handsome baby he was too."

Amused, Elizabeth looked up over the Robertson's heads, but her husband was still stern and walked away to the other side of the room.

She easily managed fifteen minutes or so small talk with them, assisted by the elder Mr Darcy, and then the butler appeared to announce further callers. The Robertsons left and were replaced by the Fosters, who were far more sombre and proper and left Elizabeth, more often than not, lost for words. They went away quickly, after giving their felicitations, but could not have left soon enough for Elizabeth's taste.

"Are we to be visited by the whole of Derbyshire society, do you think?" Mr Darcy complained.

"They waste no time, that's true, t'was in the papers only this morning," George Darcy said. "Perhaps we ought to have arranged to be far from home today."

"I did not know the announcement had been made," Elizabeth said, rather pointlessly, as they both ignored her. She truly wished to see the newspaper for herself - perhaps seeing it set down in black and white might give everything more credence - for she still found herself wondering, from time to time, if she were dreaming. Even now, in the grand saloon, where she could feel the rich fabric of the sofa beneath her hands, and even though her slippers sank into the deep rug they rested on, she still wondered if her senses were playing tricks on her. She blinked long and hard, but when she opened her eyes fully, Mr Darcy was still before her, still frowning in her direction.

The door opened again and the Viscountess Balcombe was announced. Bows and curtseys were deep. Elizabeth sat down only after the great lady had taken a chair. Mr Darcy was obviously impressed enough by this visit to take a seat and pay attention. He sat next to Elizabeth, leaving only a few inches between them. His frame, always straight, always upright, appeared even more so and she realised he was very anxious.

George Darcy thanked the viscountess for her visit most profusely, but she turned her attention to the younger Mr Darcy. "My congratulations."

"I thank you."

"How all the young ladies of society will weep inconsolably at the news of your marriage, Mr Darcy." The viscountess's smile was broad, but not friendly. "I hope you know how many hearts you have disappointed. We all thought you attached before, but yet not enough to tempt you into matrimony, it seems. Tell me, Mrs Darcy, what was your secret, however did you secure him?"

Elizabeth noted how the lady's eyes drifted towards her midriff. She felt her cheeks grow hot, but more out of anger than embarrassment.

"He chased me your ladyship, he would not let me escape," Elizabeth said, both cross and bored with the formality and tedium. She was tired of sitting still, tired of behaving herself, tired of being looked at and judged.

"Is that so?" The viscountess wore an eyeglass on a chain around her neck, and now raised it to her face to peer more closely at them, "how very romantic."

"Yes it was, and then he couldn't wait to marry me. No sooner had he gone to my uncle, with whom I was staying at the time; than he had procured a special licence and we were married the very next day."

Mr Darcy's hand came down hard on her knee and he squeezed it. Elizabeth was shocked and her throat tightened. Her first thought was that he had run mad, not just because of the gesture itself, but of such a display in elegant company. She looked at his very large hand upon her knee and was momentarily fascinated by the way his long, tapered fingers wound around her leg. There was a part of her that wished to squirm away from his strange touch, but she also acknowledged how nice it was to have another person so close to her, how long since anyone had taken her hand? Hugged her, or kissed her cheek? Affection had been rife from where she came. At Pemberley, it seemed non-existent.

Mr Darcy was smiling tightly at her, but his eyes were full of warning. "I think that's enough of that particular story. We wouldn't want to bore the viscountess by telling her every small part of it, would we?" he said.

"Oh, I am not bored at all, Mr Darcy. We ladies love to hear all the little details of a courtship," the great lady

132

replied. "Pray tell me, however did you meet? I have never seen you out in London society, Mrs Darcy."

"I suppose what you mean, Lady Balcombe, is that I am not from the sort of circles that Mr Darcy would normally occupy?"

"Well, I, just…"

Mr Darcy's grip on her knee tightened in warning. Elizabeth gave a small yelp, which earned her an odd look from Lady Balcombe, but she would not be silenced, even at the risk of some colourful bruising. "I suppose to those who place such importance on things, I am pretty much well below you. But you shall all have to put up with me now, so there, bad luck."

"Well, I did not mean to imply…" The viscountess floundered in the face of Elizabeth's directness.

George Darcy intervened. "Mrs Darcy came under the mantle of my care a while back, after her father's passing away, and, well…these two were seemingly bound for one another." He then swiftly steered the conversation away onto safer topics; the state of the roads, the dry weather they were enjoying, and other such tedium.

Mr Darcy released her knee as soon as the viscountess had gone, then took her by the elbow and marched her out of the room, ignoring his father's raised brows. Elizabeth shrugged him off in the hallway. "Let go. Do not haul me about."

"Haul? Your language is as bad as your manners, too much time with farm boys, no doubt."

"Oh, I know far worse words, Mr Darcy."

"I would speak to you in my father's study, follow me," he said, angrily.

Once there, Mr Darcy stood behind the desk and raked a hand through his hair. Elizabeth glared at his hateful locks. "If you have brought me here to chastise me, Mr Darcy, please get on with it. I should prefer it over and done with."

"What was that, in the Saloon, in front of a viscountess, of all people? You were unforgivably rude."

"Not as rude as she."

"She said nothing untoward."

"She implied everything, insults dressed up as niceties. What gives her the right to look at me with such scorn and contempt?"

"She is Lady Balcombe."

"She is a horrible old woman."

"Elizabeth! You shall have to conduct yourself better. To learn how to fend things off. There are ways of replying to such comments without resorting to insolence and impertinence," he said.

They were silent. She chewed on her lower lip thoughtfully, and he moved to the window, seemingly preferring the view outside than to having to look upon her.

"The lady who was kind to me at the inn, Constance Balcombe, the viscountess is her mother?" Elizabeth asked.

"Yes." Mr Darcy nodded.

"And the other lady, Emma Balcombe, was her sister, so also the lady's daughter?"

Mr Darcy nodded again.

Elizabeth saw immediately in his expression that she had touched on a subject he found uncomfortable. She did not have to ask the question, his face when she had mentioned Emma Balcombe, told her all she needed to know - he had been in love with her - who would not be? "You meant to marry her, I suppose, and so now Lady Balcombe is cross with me, and you are cross with me. You might have had that beautiful lady, from a fine family, and instead you are stuck with me." She tried to laugh a little, but there was no humour at all to be had in it.

His gaze moved from the scenery outside back to her. "Yes, we are stuck with each other."

If she were not still so angry with him, she might have felt guilty and truly very sorry. He was a man pining, a man denied love. Instead he had Elizabeth Bennet, and lord knows she had no grand connections, no money, nothing to recommend her and was everything to be ashamed of - young enough to be embarrassing simply by her appearance - and rude to visitors to boot. Elizabeth supposed that as well as being extremely elegant and handsome, Emma Balcombe probably played the pianoforte exquisitely and had a good grasp of Italian. "Mr Darcy, I am sorry if you considered my behaviour particularly bad, but I was always taught that we are all equals, and she did not treat me as such. Don't you think good fortune and elevated position are, more often than not, the result of happenstance, luck of birth, or marriage? My father would not have it that anyone, other than his maker, was his true superior, and I was always told to hold my head high."

"But do we not show ourselves lower, beneath others, Elizabeth, by our behaviour? You might be the daughter of a gentleman, but do not think me ignorant of your mother's origins, your uncles and aunts, their conditions in life. It seems some of their habits and manners may have rubbed off on you. If you are to rise above such inauspicious beginnings, you must improve yourself and learn to think before you speak."

Roused to resentment, she coloured deeply. Just when she would think there was something vaguely likeable about him, he would anger her so as to lose all her compassion. She tried to compose herself, but controlling such strong emotions was something she had yet to master. "I hate you," she burst out, "you are a dreadful man, and I hate you. You speak of manners and yet are so rude to me. I will not be ashamed of my family. You are the most ungentlemanlike man I ever met." Her foot came down hard upon the polished floor.

His countenance betrayed his incredulity. "Please tell me you did not just stomp your foot at me?"

She left, pulling the door shut behind her so violently as to rattle the ornaments. As she made for the stairs, she heard it open again and his voice bellowed through the great hallway. "Do not slam doors." When she picked up her pace, he shouted after her again. "And do not run!"

His father came towards him. "Fitzwilliam, you do realise every servant and occupant of this house can hear you?"

Enraged, Darcy waved a pointed finger in the direction of the first floor of the house, to where Elizabeth had

135

fled. "She calls me ungentlemanlike! While she slams and races her way around the house. Ungentlemanlike, when I gave her my protection."

His father urged him back into the study, pushing him with a gentle hand upon his shoulder. "Calm yourself."

Darcy paced back and forth a few times, till his breath came more evenly and his heart did not race so fiercely. "She will never again be present for callers. She is ill-prepared. No more. She is now withdrawn from society until I say differently."

"That will seem strange, our neighbours will want to call on her."

"I do not care. She is my wife and I will have the management of her. I cannot risk another display like the one with the viscountess."

"I actually thought she conducted herself reasonably well. She is not cowed by anyone, I like that. If she hadn't defended herself so well, I would have done it for her. She is a Darcy now and deserves a respect she was not shown."

"She deserves nothing. She's an ungrateful little madam."

His father chuckled. "I cannot agree with that, but I can see she has a temper. The girl bubbles underneath the surface like a volcano. You must be careful you do not cause her to erupt! Though some men, of course, prefer fireworks. Pour me a drink and tell me what happened in London - the viscountess is unhappy with you. Were you courting Emma Balcombe?"

Darcy closed his eyes against the images that assailed him. Emma and her beautiful smiles, the way she had moved around him in the dance, beckoned him from across the room with her fan. It had all felt so wonderful, he had felt so alive, so happy, had seen a future that involved something more than just duty. He'd glimpsed passion, happiness, a love match. "I suppose it may have looked that way. I did *consider* her. I was on the point of approaching you regarding it and whilst I was deliberating, I made the mistake of introducing her to Wickham."

"And?"

"She prefers a rake, it would seem. She met him in secret."

His father sighed heavily.

"I said nothing, of course, but then received your note about the young lady who had approached you for assistance; the lady who is currently Mrs Wickham - who has now given birth to a healthy baby son - while Wickham gambles and wastes away the money he was persuaded with. When Wickham married, Emma Balcombe tried to turn her attentions back to me. I'm afraid I was rather churlish in response and she has hated me ever since. There was a bit of a scene at a ball, where Wickham was. She has gone away to Ireland now, sent by her father."

"Do the Balcombes know of her affair with Wickham?"

"I don't suppose so. She'd hardly admit it to them."

"So now you are the man who paid their daughter much attention and then embarrassed her by withdrawing it very publicly, seemingly for no reason? Not a good day's work, Fitzwilliam. No wonder Lady Balcombe thinks you used her daughter ill."

"If you did not always favour Wickham so, things might be different. Why do you prefer him? There are dozens of young men who would have been far more worthy of your patronage?"

His father blanched at the question, and then seemingly remembered something. "He is my Godson."

"I warned you of his behaviour in Town. When he was out of your sight, he was quite a different character. He gets away with it all, despite his carousing, dissolute nature, the man's like a cat and lands always on his paws. There is never any punishment for George Wickham. Whereas I, who have done hardly anything wrong, am punished by this ridiculous marriage."

"It is done now, so you shall have to make the best of it. It may not be what you envisioned for yourself, or even what I envisioned for you, but we cannot really plan things. Life is a series of mistakes, chance and vagary. Who's not to say, that one day, this young girl might be the very best thing that happened to you?"

Darcy shook his head. "I know how it was with you and my mother. It was planned for you at a young age and you followed through with it. Her dowry and position, your estate, it was a great match, but as I grew older, I saw the truth you tried to hide, you were not really happy."

His father chuckled. "Show me a married man who truly is. Will you take a drink with me, boy?" When Darcy shook his head, his father poured only one glass out from a decanter on the desk. "Your mother and I were different characters. She was timid and shy, did not like going out. She stuck to family dinners, she liked routine and structure - Matlock at Christmas, Easter at Rosings - I did not understand her at times, but she was an excellent woman, and I grew very fond of her. And she gave me two fine children, did she not?"

Pleased that this seemed to be one occasion when his father meant not to lecture, Darcy smiled, but said nothing.

"Our situations are not so different," his father said.

"Did you not resent the fact that you were denied the chance to follow your heart? You never had the opportunity to fall in love," Darcy said.

"I did, once, but it was not to be. Love makes a mockery of social position, fortune and all practical considerations; it does not discriminate or differentiate. And it is done so easily, a word, a certain look and a man is gone, and I don't believe he ever properly recovers." His father was lost in thought for quite some time before he cleared his throat. "I have a suggestion. We were speaking of our losses at the Scottish estate and the need to identify the problems there. What better way to do so than to make an inspection? You might meet with the steward, and if you find him lacking, get rid and employ a new one. Manage it for a few months for me."

"You mean for me to go and call it home for a while?"

"Exactly so." His father took a long swig of his drink.

"Elizabeth and I would probably kill each other long before we reached the borders."

"Then leave her with me, unless you do wish to take her, but I say, leave her here until the dust settles and then return and make a fresh start of it. The separation will do you both good."

Darcy smoothed his coat down and considered his father's proposal. There was an appeal to it. Peace, solitude, time to gather his thoughts, and an estate to run as if it were his own. The decisions would all be his, he might impress his father if he managed to identify the issues and get it back into profit. "Yes," he said, decisively. "I shall go."

Sixteen

They no longer spoke. Avoiding one another seemed to be a game they could both play with great skill and assiduousness. If occasions arose when it was absolutely necessary to be in the same room, or if they passed by one another accidentally in a corridor, they acknowledged each other only with curt nods. The time they were required to spend together within the course of a day was minimal and mostly centred around mealtimes. She grew ever more silent at dinner, sinking into her chair and looking desperate for the meal to end. When the men entered the drawing room afterwards, and Georgiana was taken away for the evening, she would go to a corner with a book.

Elizabeth, Darcy had discovered, was not one to linger in the breakfast parlour. She would rush in, take a single slice of toast, on which she would pile enough marmalade as to make the bread groan under the weight of it. This would be eaten quickly, without ceremony, usually with her bonnet in her lap and a foot swinging back and forth under the table impatiently, and then she would be off, not just out of the room, but out of the house, to Lord knows where. If they happened to be alone at this time of day, Darcy would shield himself behind a newspaper, but although he could not see her, he could still feel her glowering at him from the other side of the pages.

He had no clear idea of how she spent her days, but if the weather was fine, she would be out somewhere in the park or woods. He was not entirely comfortable with the notion of her wandering about unaccompanied by herself so much, and hoped she did not drift too far beyond the boundaries of the park. Challenging her on the matter, however, would surely only invoke another argument, so he remained silent and could only pray that she applied a little common sense to the length and direction of her rambles and did not venture too far - a hard lesson learned in the stables at the inn at Redbourn would, with any luck, be adhered to. Where she hid herself on the days when dark clouds rolled over the hills behind Pemberley and the early summer showers came, he had yet to discover. It was not the library and neither was she in her room, or the garden room. The downstairs parlours did not tempt her and neither did the downstairs music room, or the practice room upstairs. Not that he looked for her, but she managed to make herself conspicuous by her absence, and he was more than a little curious as to where she had made her bolthole.

The day was fine today, however, and she raced through her morning meal, obviously eager to be away.

"Has the post arrived, Hodges?" she asked the butler.

"I believe so, madam. I shall bring it through?"

"Oh please do not worry, I shall take it from the tray in the hall."

Darcy saw his butler shudder. "With your permission, madam, I shall bring it through in just a moment."

The butler bowed and left the room. Darcy lowered his newspaper, unable to ignore her any longer. "It is part of his duties, Elizabeth, to see to the post."

She looked surprised at his voice, rightly, he supposed, for it had been some time since he had addressed her directly.

"I am quite capable of finding my own letters in the hall."

"Of that I have no doubt." Darcy gave a nod towards the door and the remaining footman left them too. "Let the staff do their work. And actually, while I am about it, I will speak to you on another matter." Ignoring her heavy sigh, he set aside his paper completely. "You were down in the kitchens yesterday?"

"I was..."

"You do not go down there without prior notice to Mrs Reynolds."

She said nothing but shoved her plate aside and made to get to her feet.

"Elizabeth, it is the dominion of the staff. The kitchens and the servant's hall is where they might relax, take some time to themselves, take their coats off and talk. They cannot be at ease if members of the household come wandering in and out with no warning."

"It was not so at Longbourn, I will apologise to Mrs Reynolds."

"I imagine there are quite a few customs and practises which make Pemberley quite different to Longbourn. There is no need to apologise, just do not do so again."

"I will not." Rising, she left the room without a goodbye and he returned to his newspaper.

Elizabeth fully intended to keep her promise to not venture down into the kitchens again. Yesterday's experience had been enough to warn her off the place. Mr Darcy's strictures had been completely unnecessary. She had been feeling hungry, not having eaten since breakfast, and had wandered down to the vast kitchens in search of a slice of bread and butter, or even cake. Her casual entrance had prompted gasps and a great scraping of chairs as they had all stood to attention - for her! Long lines of footmen, hallboys, parlour maids, gardeners and grooms. There had then followed a terrific scrambling for coats and a straightening of skirts, amidst much scurrying around for Mrs Reynolds - nobody else having the courage to address her, and she, likewise, too intimidated by their vast numbers to speak. She had stood in stupid contemplation and disbelief until the housekeeper was found. It seemed the Darcys and the copious amount of servants who waited upon them, occupied very different worlds, separate parts of the house, and with the exception of Mrs Reynolds and Hodges, hardly spoke and knew very little about each other. She could never imagine knowing all of them by name, as she had at Longbourn.

Now she stopped in the hall beside Hodges. He was arranging the morning's letters, with as much care as if they were the crown jewels, on a silver salver for presentation in the breakfast parlour. "I'll take any letters that are for me, Hodges."

"I was just bringing them through, madam."

"Yes, but I am here now. And I have no need to go back to breakfast. Do I have any letters?"

"You do, madam."

"May I have them, then?" she asked with a touch of exasperation.

"I normally take them through to the breakfast parlour."

"Yes, I realise that, but could you give me mine, and take the rest through?"

He looked perplexed and dithered.

Fearing she might scream if the conversation went any further, she took the post and checked through it herself, putting any that were not for her back on the tray.

"Who is this for?" She held up a small piece of paper, folded, but not sealed or addressed.

"'Tis a message for Mr Darcy, to say the music master cannot attend this morning for Miss Darcy's lesson. He is unwell."

"Oh, well please take the note to Mr Darcy, but I shall let Miss Georgiana and Miss Temple know."

"I could not ask you to do that, madam. I'll send a footman."

"You did not ask me, Hodges, I offered. It really is no bother; I saw them taking their morning exercise on the lawn and am going that way."

"I would not want Mr Darcy to think I had sent you on an errand, Mrs Darcy."

"Hodges," she whispered, dramatically. "Shall we make a pact? Shall we neither of us tell him about this shocking business of mine; of my retrieving my own post, and using my own voice and legs to relay a message? Mr Darcy is currently at breakfast and such scandalous behaviour as mine might well disturb his digestion."

The butler looked concerned for a moment, before realising she was teasing and then he gave her an uneasy smile, bowed and went on his way, while Elizabeth went through the great front doors. It was not her normal route to the lawn, but it was the quickest, and her need to be free of the house was growing acute. She could not bear to be inside another moment.

She found Georgiana easily and refused to be put off by her reticence and reserve. "Your music master cannot come, Georgiana, and I do believe that leaves you at leisure for at least an hour, would you say so, Miss Temple?"

"Near enough two, Mrs Darcy."

"Oh, perhaps I might return to my French verbs, Miss Temple."

"Verbs! How horrific," Elizabeth exclaimed. "I have a better suggestion. I noticed when I walked down there the other day that Broad Farm has a litter of piglets. Will you walk over and see them with me?"

"Piglets?"

"They are the sweetest little animals, very funny, I promise they will make you laugh at least ten times in as many minutes."

"But it is such a long walk."

"Not at all, two miles at best if we go through the woods."

Georgiana's eyes widened. "I am not sure my father would like me to walk so far, and to spend time on such an unproductive outing."

"Oh it will not be unproductive at all. It will be excellent exercise and if it shall make you feel better, we will discuss the trees and birds as we go. I am an expert and shall teach you all I know."

Torn between refusing such a request from her brother's wife, and fearful she might receive a scolding from her father, Georgiana looked to her governess for advice.

"Go on, Georgiana. I shall have plenty for you to do this afternoon. Take some time to enjoy yourself."

Elizabeth smiled and took the young girl's hand, pulling her gently away from the great house, determined to make a friend of her.

Colonel Fitzwilliam entered the room unannounced, his presence at Pemberley was so regular that no formalities

144

were required and he walked in quickly, slamming a hand on Darcy's desk. So engrossed had his cousin been in the papers before him that he started in his chair in shock, gasped, and held a hand to his chest.

"You scared me half to death."

"Well if that's all it takes to bring on someone's demise I will do well in Portugal."

"Portugal?"

"I have received orders. I sail Thursday next. I have come to take my leave of you all and mean to invite myself to dinner."

"You are always welcome to dinner. As regards your posting, can you not ask for an exception to be made?"

"I don't wish to. I go around in regimentals and call myself a Colonel, but you see, I should feel a fraud if I never actually saw any action. Not worried about me are you, Darcy? It is the French you ought to be concerned about, they'll not be a man jack of them standing by the time I am done."

"If forced to listen to the drivel you serve up as witty repartee, they'll probably surrender."

The colonel smiled broadly. "I hear you are away yourself, to Scotland. Is it a wedding trip?"

"It is certainly not. Elizabeth remains here."

"I see. And how is your little hellion? Does she give you much trouble?"

Darcy frowned. "Actually no, not much. We have resolved our differences by hardly speaking or seeing each other. We now get along famously."

"Hence Scotland?"

"Yes, although the visit would have needed to be made in any case. The estate is being mismanaged and makes no profit."

They were disturbed by noise from the hallway, girlish voices and laughter.

"Well, that's a nice sound to hear at Pemberley." The colonel rose and opened the door to go out and Darcy followed behind him, only to find himself shocked and angry at seeing Georgiana so filthy. Her hair was wild and her dress covered in grass stains. Her petticoat was three inches deep in mud. Elizabeth's gown and petticoat were no better, and her hair, short as it was and unrestrained by pins, was even wilder.

Georgiana greeted the appearance of the Colonel with a shout of surprise and pleasure and went to embrace him, but he backed away from her, his hands raised, palms upwards, laughing. "Oh do not think of coming anywhere near me, my little cousin, until you have bathed at least twice."

Elizabeth greeted the colonel warmly and promised, before she was warned against it, not to venture anywhere near him.

"What in God's name have you been up to? You look as if you have been in a pig sty." Darcy was astounded by Georgiana's hysterical, fearful giggle and Elizabeth's smile. "Pray, tell me you have not actually been in a pig sty?"

"I will tell you we have not, Mr Darcy, if that is what you wish to hear, but unfortunately, I could not say it with any promise of its truthfulness." Elizabeth lifted her chin, and their eyes met for the first time in days, maybe even weeks. Her face wore a devilish look. Her countenance silently screamed defiance. Not at all cowed, her small shoulders were squarely set and she was ready to sally forth into an argument; her defences were obviously prepared and she looked as if she might relish the prospect.

Darcy opened his mouth to deliver a reproof and closed it again, thinking it was sometimes better to choose your battles. "Upstairs. Go and make yourself presentable."

Georgiana rushed to the stairs on his order, which had been issued in a tone that would ordinarily bear no brooking with, but Elizabeth took the time to bob him a quick curtsey and walked slowly away, throwing a taunting glance over her shoulder.

Darcy went back to his study and the Colonel followed, shutting the door behind him. Knowing Darcy as well as he did, he waited until his cousin had paced a while and gotten his temper back under regulation, resolving not to speak until Darcy had done so.

"And there I was," he said, eventually, "saying she gives me little trouble." He sank into the chair behind the desk.

"It is only mud, Darcy, it washes off. And it is nice to see Georgiana so well amused."

"Yes. Aren't I the considerate older brother? I have married a playmate for my sister."

The colonel went around the desk and patted him on the shoulder. "Be patient. She will not be this age forever. Perhaps you are right to go to Scotland for a while. It seems to me to be one of those matters which might sort itself out, given a little time and distance."

"Yes, I will go to Scotland, and you to Portugal. Do try your very best not to get yourself killed."

The colonel laughed, helped himself to brandy and took a seat.

Seventeen

Darcy spent the days following the colonel's short visit preparing for his trip to Scotland. He had been to the estate on a few occasions as a boy and remembered enjoying its remote wildness. He had created adventures aplenty, running amongst the bracken, chasing the wild horses and deer. He had not cared that it was often cold or wet. What twelve-year-old with a wooden sword tucked into his breeches did? He doubted now, though, that he would find the place as appealing. The manor house was nothing to speak of and he suspected it to be barely habitable. He had little hope of finding any society there, no families of any quality, and though he was of a naturally taciturn nature, he was not insusceptible to loneliness. Even if he did find anybody it would be worth making the acquaintance of, there was no guarantee that he would get along with them. He had always found making friends difficult and could think of only one or two men in whose company he was easy and jovial. His wealth, his position as heir to Pemberley, had made him stand out; his natural reserve often led him to be excluded. No, this trip was not likely to be about anything but work. He would inspect the lands, visit tenants, find a new steward and order any necessary improvements. He was glad his father had enough trust in him to give him autonomy over the decisions that were to be made. The thought of the days pleased him, as did the journey. It was the nights that concerned him, when his only company would likely be books. He would be sure to pack many. At least at Pemberley there were chess games with his father, some conversation with Miss Temple. Sometimes Elizabeth could be persuaded to move to the pianoforte and bash out some lively tune, fudging over the difficult passages, playing all the right notes, just not in the right order. The thought of it brought a smile to his lips unbidden, when he ought to feel exasperation. Her playing was truly un-refined, he had never heard her practice. She just seemed to have reached a certain level of proficiency and was happy to remain there. It was a shame, for she certainly knew how the music was supposed to sound, she had a decent ear, just not the will to apply herself. When he had once asked her to sing in the drawing room, she had refused politely, then scowled at him for almost an hour, though he knew she had a perfectly lovely singing voice as he heard it weekly in church. He supposed she did not wish to perform for him, Lord forbid she give him cause for any pleasure.

He stopped short in these musings, and in his current occupation, which was the selection of his reading material, to think that he ought to try and persuade her once again to take lessons alongside Georgiana. She seemed to be wasting her days away in idleness and surely would be better off improving herself in some way. He sent for Mrs Reynolds and when the housekeeper appeared, he asked her if she knew Mrs Darcy's whereabouts. Mrs Reynolds looked to the window, and seeing the rain falling against the windows, her eyes drifted upwards.

"You might find in her in the old schoolroom."

"She does not go to the schoolroom, Mrs Reynolds."

"No, sir, I meant the old school room, in the older part of the house. 'Tis never used and off a quiet corridor. You know where I mean, sir, you must have taken your lessons there when you were a small boy."

"On the third floor? Near the stairs to the attics?"

"Yes, she likes the quietness of it up there, I think."

Feeling somewhat triumphant that he had discovered where she hid herself on bad weather days, Darcy brushed past the housekeeper and made for the distant corner of the house she referred to. He threw the door open and Elizabeth was indeed there, bent over a writing desk, bottom lip caught between her teeth in concentration. The aspect of the room faced east and though he imagined light and warmth streamed in on good days, today the room was chilly enough for her to have wrapped a shawl about her shoulders as she worked. The furniture was old, but she seemed to have arranged everything neatly to her satisfaction, whereby she might sit and be comfortable. The writing desk wobbled, despite a book having been placed underneath one of the legs in an effort to keep it stable. Darcy observed that the desk would have been of better use if she'd chopped it up and made a fire of it. How she managed to write an even letter on such a useless piece of furniture he did not know. She looked up at him when he entered with raised brows, but gave him no greeting and looked for him to explain his presence there.

"So this is where you hide, there are much better rooms which might have been made available to you. You need only have asked for your own sitting room and I would have allocated you one of the upstairs parlours."

"Thank you, I like it here." She blew on the paper to help dry the ink.

"You have no fire. Why don't you ask for one?"

She shrugged and said no more, though she looked cold, and like she wished him away. He suddenly understood that he had intruded on her privacy, and without even a knock on the door. He had burst into her sad little haven uninvited.

"I wish to speak to you."

She turned in her chair to look up at him properly, expecting to be scolded over something. "What have I done now?"

"Nothing I know of, unless there is something you wish to confess to?"

She smiled at his little jest and for a moment all discord was forgotten. "Oh that would be very foolish of me. I think I shall keep my own counsel. I am sorry, about Georgiana, the other day. I truly did not mean for us to get so muddy."

Surprised by this apology, he nodded. "You should remember that part of your role here is to give good guidance to Georgiana."

"I know, yes. But she has so little free time, so little fun. I just thought we might get a little better acquainted over the course of a long walk. Do you not think your father's schedule for her is gruelling? When does she have time to just be a young girl?"

"You would want her to be idle like you?"

"I am not idle."

He caught her small hands in his and turned them over. Her right thumb and forefinger were stained black with ink. "You write a great many letters, that's true, but it is not a true occupation."

"I like to hear from Jane and Mamma, and my friends at home, and one does not receive letters if one does not take the trouble to write them."

"This is your home now, and I hope you might begin to treat it as such." He realised with a start that he was still holding her hands and released them suddenly. She blushed for some reason, and uncomfortable with her nearness, he moved to the fireplace.

"I am starting to, but it is unsettling, all this talk of Scotland. Am I to go?"

"To Scotland? No, of course not."

"I did not know."

Ashamed that he had not spoken to her directly of it, he went back to stand beside the desk again, leaning over her. "You will remain here with my father."

"Might I go to Town while you are away? I could stay with my Uncle and Aunt Gardiner."

"No. I think it is too soon after all the talk, and the announcement, for you to return to London, or Hertfordshire for that matter. You'd best remain here and find yourself something to do. I am going to ask Georgiana's music master to stay on for another hour with you after her lesson ends." He believed it best to be decisive about the matter. He would have to take charge. She would no doubt do nothing if left to her own devices.

Having delivered this directive, he turned with the intention of quitting the room, but brushed against the wobbly desk, causing a pile of her letters to fall to the floor. They bent to pick them up at the same time. He rescued one that she tried and failed to snatch back from him. He turned it over and saw the return address, and the scratchy, childish male hand it had been written in. "This is from Henry Jones. You correspond with that farmer's boy?"

"Do not refer to him so, he is my friend."

"I'll refer to him how I like, Elizabeth. What are these letters between the two of you? What do you write of?"

"It is my business. They are my letters."

"How many times have you written him?"

"Just once, to tell him what had become of me and that I was well, and to apologise for any trouble I caused him, and then he wrote back to me."

"You'll not write again, Elizabeth. It is not proper. You cannot be corresponding with an unmarried farmer's boy."

She looked at the floor and gave no answer.

"Elizabeth. You must give me your word."

"Yes, very well. Now may I have my letter?"

"I would be well within my rights to read this, you know, to see what this boy has written to you." She looked up at him with huge eyes, round with apprehension and he noticed for the first time that they were not brown, as he had once assumed, but a very deep green. He felt sure that if he were to read the pages he held they would either make him angry, or she very embarrassed. Was no knowledge better than a revelation that would bring pain to both of them? He handed the letter back and her shoulders sagged in relief. "No more, Elizabeth. It stops. Am I understood?"

She nodded and he left the room, but at the doorway, he turned. "And you'll attend the pianoforte lessons. The devil does indeed make work for idle hands. Make sure yours are busy."

Eighteen

Mr Darcy's leave taking was made outside the front doors, with Hodges and Mrs Reynolds, but no other staff in attendance. His father shook his hand, Georgiana clung to him while he told her to pay attention to Miss Temple and adhere to her studies, at which Elizabeth rolled her eyes (as if the poor girl could do anything else with the schedule arranged for her). She had considered not going out to say goodbye at all, certain he would not be bothered by her absence - but her days had so little amusement to them that even someone going was a form of entertainment.

When he was about to board the carriage, he bowed over her hand and kissed it, then pulled her close for a moment, to whisper in her ear. What she was expecting him to say, she was not sure, but his one word, his little warning, was spoken low and right beside her ear. To those watching, it might have looked a little like a whispered sweet nothing, a last message for a beloved wife to see her through a separation of hearts and minds. But all he actually said was 'behave'.

She turned, after he had released her hand, and walked back into the house, rather than remaining to see the carriage drive off, not caring if it was bad mannered. The truth was she wished him away. His disapproval, the way he made her feel she would never match up to the title he had bestowed on her through marriage, was lately more than she could bear. In the vast hall she looked up at the wide, spiralling, intricate staircase and felt as if she could breathe easily for the first time in weeks. After taking a great lungful of air, she took the stairs at speed and ran down the corridors as fast as her legs could carry her. On reaching her room she flung herself down upon the bed and fumed into her pillow. *'Behave!'* Behave, he had said, as if she were a girl of eight or ten. He might as well have been talking to Georgiana as her. And for the very first time since she had arrived at Pemberley, she cried. Big heaving sobs, heavy tears of frustration, sadness, loneliness and rejection. After thoroughly soaking the pillow, she pounded it with her fist in anger for a good long while, until her body relaxed, exhausted with emotion and she fell fast asleep on top of the counterpane.

She left her room only for dinner, her stomach growling and longing for the comfort of Mrs Small's wonderful, tasty meals and her rich, sweet puddings. It was odd not to see Mr Darcy waiting at the top of the stairs for her, with a hand on his lapel, or smoothing down his trousers, tugging at his cuffs, or straightening his cravat. As she turned and took the handrail, she looked askance at the space he would normally occupy and couldn't help the twitch of her left hand, which somehow, involuntarily, sought the crook of his arm.

As she passed the parlour next to the library, she noticed some activity and entered to find two footmen, supervised by Hodges, moving the writing desk to a spot underneath the window; a place she remembered suggesting it should be. She walked in to watch and listen to their huffing and puffing.

"What are they doing, Hodges?"

"The master asked for it to be done this afternoon. He said you might like to write your letters somewhere where there is a view of the lake and the lawn."

"Well, I must thank him." She was amazed at George Darcy, with all he had to remember, all the responsibilities he bore, having paid attention to her comments, and of his acting upon them. He had given his late wife's desk over for her use and put it in a place she would be sure to utilise it. She knew with certainty that she could not hide near the attics any longer, in a cold disused schoolroom, not after he had made such a lovely gesture.

The footmen lowered the desk into position and when satisfied with their work, stepped back. "There is also a gift for you, from Mr Darcy." Hodges put a small wooden box on the desk.

Elizabeth stepped forward and stroked the highly-polished rosewood lid. She opened it to find a writing set, comprising of ink and sand bottles made out of pewter, brushes, delicate pens and pencils, a letter opener and, in fact, every useful and wonderfully luxurious thing she might need. The beauty of the gift almost brought on further tears. The box itself was very fine, inlaid with velvet and all its contents were neatly arranged. She picked up the seal, to find it especially heavy and guessed it to be silver. Turning it over, she saw it would make a pretty circle of interwoven flowers when pushed into molten wax, and in the middle of the flowers would be branded her initials, E.D. The cost of such a gift she could not imagine, she had never seen a more beautiful set. It made the one her father had owned looked very shabby and woeful.

She went to find George Darcy immediately and when entering the drawing room launched into fervent thanks. "I have seen that the desk in the parlour next to the library has been moved and I wanted to express my gratitude, both for your thoughtfulness and for...."

"Oh that, think nothing of it." He waved a dismissive hand in the air, not allowing her to finish.

"But you must allow me to thank you for your generosity, such a gift…"

He was not listening and spoke over her. "Well, Fitzwilliam mentioned you were hiding yourself away upstairs and that will not do. No more thanks are necessary."

"But.."

"Elizabeth please, no more about it. I hear Georgiana and Miss Temple on the stairs. I do not know about you, but I am particularly hungry tonight."

She smiled at him. She had often heard talk of his kindness and charity, but he was obviously uncomfortable with receiving the appreciation that followed his good deeds and seeing that she was giving him pain, she quit the previous subject and agreed that she too, was extremely hungry.

Dinner was a peaceful affair. Now and again one of the party would look to the younger Mr Darcy's chair and seem surprised to find him gone. There was, of course, no separation of the sexes; the master of the house was the only man present and so went with them into the drawing room. Perhaps seeing them all at a bit of a loss, Miss Temple proposed she and Georgiana play them a little duet and they sat at the pianoforte together. The young girl was at first reluctant, blushing with shyness, but was given plenty of encouragement by her father, who wanted to know how she was getting on with her music. They played a pretty, lively piece and Elizabeth enjoyed it. Georgiana was a far better musician than she - even at eleven – the girl was more proficient, and Elizabeth keenly felt her own lack of commitment. Thinking on it, while she listened, she realised that her unwillingness to apply herself to practice had come upon her when her father had begun to be ill. Witnessing his steady decline had lessened the enjoyment she had gotten from many of her former pleasures. She'd never had the patience to sit still for the hours and hours of practice true accomplishment would require, as she saw Georgiana do, yet hadn't she once gained pleasure from playing? Maybe she would again and she quietly resolved to take the lessons that had been arranged for her.

Georgiana was applauded enthusiastically and looked exceedingly delighted with the praise. Their moods were all so sufficiently lightened, that the hour of Georgiana's retirement came far too soon. Elizabeth and her new father were left alone and shared an awkward look before he drifted off to the other side of the drawing room.

"Do not think you need to stay and entertain an old man, Elizabeth, if there is something else you would rather do, but I wondered if you wished to play."

Her heart sank but how could she refuse him when he had shown her such kindness. When she turned around however, he was standing over the chess set, putting the pieces in the right order to begin a game.

"Oh, yes, I would." She took the chair opposite him. "I am not sure I will be as worthy an opponent as your son, however. He plays well."

She blushed at his questioning look.

"You have been taking notice?"

"I like the game. It is not usually considered a particularly feminine pastime though, is it?"

"Let's not worry about that when there's only the two of us here to keep each other company. If we are still alone when the long winter evenings draw in, I might have to teach you billiards."

She laughed readily, taken by surprise, for she had come to know him as such a serious man. He chuckled in response. "Come along then, let this game begin. For all your talk of being an unworthy opponent, I have the dreadful feeling I am about to get trounced."

Volume Two: Sixteen

Nineteen

George Darcy was felled by an acute attack of the heart. They had been picnicking near the Dutch garden and discussing its origins and design. It was a warm afternoon and he had been relaxed enough in their intimate company to think of removing his coat. He got up to do so, shrugged it off and folded it, handing it to Elizabeth, but then a strange look had come across his face and he had walked a hundred yards or so away from them without explanation. Then he had clutched at his left side and toppled over. It was as if a woodsman had taken an axe to a great oak. All was silent for a few moments till Georgiana screamed. Elizabeth knew that if she lived to be eighty, she would never forget the shrill and desperate sound of the girl's terror. Miss Temple had gathered her close while Elizabeth had run towards Mr Darcy. Turning him over, she had loosened his cravat, but seen immediately that he was lost to them. He had not slipped away gently into the good night like her own father had done - but expired so rapidly he would have known very little about it. She went as far as to undo some of the buttons on his waistcoat and put her hand upon his chest, to see if she could detect the beat of his heart, but there was nothing. He did not breathe, he was gone.

Help soon came running in the form of his servants and his steward, but it was all too late. There was nothing to be done but carry his lifeless body inside the house and lay it out in a far parlour as respectfully as they could.

Elizabeth followed and stood and watched them through the doorway, still bowing before their master as they positioned his legs and arms correctly, so as to make him look as proper as possible. Behind her, she heard Mrs Reynolds and Miss Temple ushering Georgiana away.

The shock was great for everyone. Hodges, the butler, when he approached her, looked quite broken, a man floundering without a master to guide him.

"What's to be done, madam?" he asked.

"I..." He was looking to her for instructions she realised and she was stood there quite stupidly, with her mouth agape. She tried to straighten herself up. "Please send for the doctor," she managed at last.

"I think, I am quite certain, it is a little too late…"

"For Miss Georgiana, Hodges. She may need his attendance given what she has witnessed today. I am well aware it is too late for Mr Darcy, may God rest his soul."

"Of course, madam, I'll send for the doctor."

"And will you have a groom stand by with the fastest horse available? I will write a note for Haddon Hall, it is to be taken immediately."

Elizabeth went past him to her desk, a place where she had sat daily for so many months now, to write her letters. Nobody spoke of it belonging to the late Mrs Darcy any more, it was hers. She sat gripping the edges of it for support for a while, before taking out a fresh sheet of paper. There was no time to edge the letter in black, and in any case she rather feared that the Fitzwilliams, on receipt of such a letter, would immediately fear for their son, still at the front in Portugal, fighting Napoleon. George Darcy's passing would be a terrible blow, but she did not wish to frighten them into thinking, even for one moment, that they had lost their son.

The letter was written and sealed quickly and she walked from the front of the house to the back, and then out to the courtyard, where she knew the messenger would be waiting. The groom doffed his cap but did not leave his seat atop a great black hunter, sensing the urgency of his errand. He looked to be a clever, quick-witted lad. "I am no horsewoman, so I am never in the stables, I don't think we have met."

"No, Mrs Darcy, happens we haven't."

"What is your name?"

"Robert."

"Robert, please take this to Haddon Hall as quickly as you can. If you have to stop on the way, please do not mention the master's passing to anyone. His family should know of it first. And when you arrive, please impress on whoever receives you there that the note is for Lady Fitzwilliam, and not the Earl. Between you and I, Robert, the

Earl might read it one moment and forget it the next. You must ensure Lady Fitzwilliam hears the news."

"I will, Mrs Darcy. You can rely on me."

"Yes, I think I can. Now, away with you, God speed."

She watched him until he disappeared from view, galloping madly down the road for a while, before cutting through the woods. The quickest route to Matlock was as the crow flies - be there trees, tors and other obstacles - he had pledged to go quickly and seemed intent on doing just that. Hearing commotion within the house, she turned and went back up the stone steps and through the glass doors, only to be accosted by Hodges once again.

"The household is a little in turmoil, madam, as you might expect. The undercook has fainted away at the news. Monsieur Malbec is wondering what sort of meal will be required, as he insists he cannot go on without her assistance."

"Hodges, there will be no need for dinner. Nobody will feel like eating much of anything I am sure."

"Will I send for the undertaker?"

"I suppose, yes."

"And shall I close the curtains? And the doors?"

How could he keep asking her these questions? *Please no more*, she felt like shouting at him. How on earth was she supposed to know the answers? And yet until help arrived from Matlock, she was alone, left in sole charge of a vast estate, a very grand house, over fifty servants and a newly-orphaned twelve-year-old girl. Her stranger of a husband had been in Scotland for almost a year and a man she had come to love in the last few months, almost as another father, had just died in front of her on the lawn. "Would you please refer any further enquiries to Mrs Reynolds, and any issues regarding the estate should be handled by Mr Darcy's steward. I shall be concerning myself with only two matters and that will be writing to Mr Darcy's son in Scotland, to bring him home, and taking care of Miss Georgiana."

"Yes, madam, if you'll excuse me, I should like to say we are all so very saddened. He was a great man."

"Yes, he was."

She fled before she might cry and went to the master's study to find a direction for the Darcy's Scottish estate, which she located quickly. She then took out a fresh sheet of paper, but pen in hand, found herself paralysed, not knowing how to address the letter. During his long absence she had not written to him, and he not to her. She knew very little of his affairs, though she would see correspondence between him and his father appear occasionally on the silver salver on the hall table, and his father would sometimes give news of him over the dinner table. She knew the Scottish estate had been in a worse condition than at first feared and it had taken him some time to find a suitable steward; he had then written of his wish to remain and oversee some of the planned improvements. Though she supposed no small part of his desire to remain there had been due to his wanting to be far from her, she had not minded. Life had seemed simpler since his going away. The master had, on closer acquaintance, proved an amiable companion. Stern and serious in his expectations for his children, hard on those who flouted his rules or orders, but in essentials a good and kind man, a charitable man. He had been wonderfully understanding towards her, so tolerant and forbearing.

Her hand shook as she lowered the pen towards the paper. How to begin? 'My Dear Sir'? He was *not* dear to her though, no such affection existed and why would she now pretend it did? 'Mr Darcy', however, in such a letter, seemed too formal. She eventually settled on just 'Sir', writing quickly, trying to choose her words with some degree of sensitivity, eager not to give him too much pain, but also with the knowledge that expediency outweighed all other considerations. She dried and blotted her letter, folded and sealed it and was blackening the edges when Hodges came to tell her she had been asked for above stairs. She put her letter into the butler's hands with the order that it be sent by express.

When she rose and passed the window, she could not help but look down towards the Dutch gardens, where he had fallen. A flash of blue caught her eye and she saw that

163

nobody had yet been down to clear up the picnic things. George Darcy's coat was still folded on the blanket where she had placed it. She went out and picked it up, clutching it to her a little, before brushing some imaginary lint from its lapels. She carried it up the stairs with her, not yet wishing to relinquish it to his valet.

Georgiana, when she went to her, was sitting up in bed, still in shock, her expression displaying her inability to comprehend what had happened. "Is he really gone, Elizabeth?"

"Yes, he is really gone. I am very sorry."

"And will Fitzwilliam come home?"

"I have sent for him," she said taking her sister's hand.

"And I suppose, now, we will not go to Scarborough in August, like Papa said we would, and you will be denied your first sight of the sea."

Reaching out a hand to smooth down Georgiana's hair, Elizabeth spoke softly. "You are a good girl to be worrying over my silly dreams at such a time. My dear little sister, I would gladly forego any pleasure in the world, if it meant I could bring him back to you."

Georgiana clutched at her so, that it became easier for Elizabeth to lay down on the bed next to her, and so she did, and so they remained for many hours; crying, talking and soothing, and even laughing on occasion, until Georgiana fell asleep. Elizabeth supposed she might have slept briefly too, for when she woke the room was dark. What had roused her was the sound of carriage wheels on the road below. Easing herself out of Georgiana's now light embrace she went downstairs directly, rubbing her hands over her sore eyes and trying to straighten her hair as she walked.

She was in time to see Lady Fitzwilliam come through the great front doors, limping heavily on her stick. Elizabeth had come to know her better when the Darcys had joined the Fitzwilliams at Haddon Hall at Christmas, for celebrations and services, and she had come to recognise the signs when the countess was in great pain, though she always took care to mask her discomfort. As soon as

Elizabeth rose from her curtsey, the countess bade her to come forward and expressed her sorrow and condolences most eloquently. The earl was taken through directly to the saloon by his man and seated by the fire. He looked as confused and uncertain as ever, not really knowing where he was, recognising no one but his wife and valet.

"You will stay for a while, until Mr Darcy returns?" Elizabeth begged the countess.

"Of course. You have sent for him?"

"Yes, by express."

"Well, God willing it will reach him by tomorrow and we might expect him home the following day, he will not delay a moment, I am sure, once he receives the news."

Elizabeth bit back a sob, but tears pooled in her eyes. "Thank heavens you have come, for everybody looks to me to know what to do, and I cannot advise them."

Her eyes flickering towards two footmen who stood awaiting any orders or summons at the doors to the room, the countess ushered Elizabeth into a quiet corner and spoke in hushed tones. "This is not the time to lose your composure. You are mistress now. You will be looked to for direction, and you must not be found wanting."

George Darcy had given to Elizabeth every respect due to her as the lady of the house, but had not expected her to fulfil any of the associated duties, having been so used to managing matters on his own. Having previously been in such rude health, he had probably not seen the need to give her any instruction on the workings of his home. "You cannot ask this of me, to run Pemberley! I have not the experience or knowledge to cope on my own."

Lady Fitzwilliam sighed. "Why he never married again after Anne's passing, I do not know." Elizabeth had puzzled over this idea many times herself. Anne Darcy had now been gone for many years together and it would have made sense for George Darcy to take a new wife, to have a companion and helpmate beside him. And he would have had little trouble securing one. Despite his age, he had still been a handsome man, and certainly an eligible one. Yet he had chosen the life of a widower. "Although, that is neither here or there now, and does not warrant the time it would take to ponder it out, when there are other more pressing matters to attend to," the countess said. "Have you instructed his man of law? His banker? News must be broken to his tenants too, and Lady Catherine must be written to immediately."

"No, no, I have done none of those things. I have only sent word to the undertaker and my...to my..." She had referred to him as her husband in her thoughts on a good many occasions, but it seemed difficult to say the word aloud.

"The new master?"

"Yes, Lady Fitzwilliam. Do you know that I am still two months and twenty-two days short of my seventeenth birthday? This is all so very wrong. I never asked for this role. I do not know how to do it."

"What does that signify? It matters not if you err or falter, or if you stumble ignorantly, what matters is to *look* as if you know what you are doing. If you give the appearance of consummate competence, nobody will notice the difference."

Elizabeth laughed despite herself and covered her mouth, fearing her amusement was not proper, given the events of the day. "I am scared," she whispered, hating to have to admit to it.

"Of course you are. We are all scared, of everything, every day, but we must fight on. Look at the poor Earl over there. He doesn't know where he is, or what he is about half the time, imagine what a terrifying place the world is for him." Lady Fitzwilliam took one of Elizabeth's shaking hands between her own. "Nothing is as complicated as it first appears and you are a very capable girl. You will manage. I was only seventeen when I became Countess of Matlock."

"I think, perhaps, you were brought up to expect such a station in life. You were always to be a Lady someone or other, to have some grand position or title, I am sure. What was imagined for me was probably that I would marry a clergyman, or some insignificant country gentleman. Anybody with a few hundred a year would have gotten my parents approval."

"And yet, fate has brought you here, for its own reasons. So you must be strong. A great many people now depend on you. Go and call all the servants together, speak to them, reassure them that all will go on as before, that is what Mrs Darcy must do."

"No, forgive me, Lady Fitzwilliam. I cannot."

"You can't, or you don't want to? There is a difference."

Elizabeth had a sudden strong remembrance of leaning over George Darcy on the grass. His eyes open, unblinking, the colour draining rapidly from his face, his mouth twisted into a grimace. She blinked but it was all she could see and all she felt was Georgiana's desperation. All she saw for her future was a tall, forbidding, young man who would return to look at her sternly, upbraid her for her lack of breeding and remind her of her inferiority and failings. She ran from the room.

My Dearest Jane,

It seems I am never to escape the black and grey gowns. No sooner had I started to wear my new yellow one (which I described in the dullest, most excruciating detail to you when I wrote my last) than I have been required to banish it to the back of the closet. The upstairs maid, who often helps me dress, remarked on the shortness of my skirts when she put my deepest black on me, and do you know, Jane? She is right. I have grown an inch and a half, I daresay, since last summer! So you see, today I am feeling very sad, but I am now not so very short. I daresay there is always something to be grateful for!

My triumph in this regard will be short-lived, however, Georgiana will outstrip me in a couple of years (she is all arms and legs and protruding elbows and destined to be long like her brother). Mamma writes that Lydia is already head and shoulders above both Kitty and Mary, so although I am proud of my inch and a half, I am fearful I may have reached my upper limits - 'tis some comfort I suppose, to know nobody will ever be able to accuse me of looking down on them.

George Darcy, a man I have come to have the highest regard in the world for, has left us for a better, more forgiving, place. It seems so cruel, particularly for young Georgiana. I fear this blow will have a lasting impact on the development of her character, having come at a time when she should know nothing but laughter.

The earl and countess are here, along with Walter and his wife - this lady, as you well know, is not a favourite of mine - I find I am spending most of today in avoidance of her. Hence my letter to you, and when I am done, I shall go back up to Georgiana again to see how she does.

We wait the arrival of the younger Mr Darcy with our collective breaths held. We are hoping he is the glue which will fix us all back together, as if we were a broken vase - but I fear that when someone dies, things can never be fully restored to their former state - no matter however careful the repair, on a closer inspection, the cracks will always show.

I am afraid our plans will be altered by these horrible events. We will definitely not be going to Scarborough now, and of course, Mr Darcy was going to grant me my dearest wish by inviting you to stay at Pemberley, after we had returned home, and now I think the plan must be put off, if not abandoned altogether.

Oh, this is too gloomy, now all I can think of is our own Papa, and how we are all in so many pieces and different places. When you write back, talk of happy things. Have you had any more verses from Mr F___, Mr Gardiner's neighbour? He sounds as if he is violently in love with you, but do not rush into loving him back. If he rhymes rose with nose, he is not worthy of you. Write also of the Watson's ball, which I remember you were to attend last Saturday. Tell me of all the dances, I am quite sure you will not have sat down once.

You are thinking what a silly girl I am to be writing such a letter, at such a time. I cannot always keep it in my head to be serious, and with you I know I can be as I am, and not what everyone expects me to be, I miss you.

I love you, I love you, I love you.

Lizzy

Twenty

As he neared Pemberley and turned his mount onto the road that led to the stables, Darcy harboured, within his breast, those feelings which always came upon him when reaching home. A feeling of belonging and pride in the house, the park and the lands around it, assailed him, but these feelings of satisfaction could not overrule other, darker thoughts. Somewhere within the sandstone walls laid the body of his father, waiting to be buried. There was also a young sister for whom he was now guardian and a whole other range of roles and responsibilities he was required to assume. Then, there was the issue of Elizabeth, which occupied his mind more than it probably ought, when perhaps his only emotion should be grief.

Her letter, received late at night by express, when he had been half asleep in bed, had shattered and disturbed him to his very core. He had unsealed it carefully, taking note of the blackened edging, half-expecting to read that his cousin had perished at war. The news of his father's death had, on his first reading it, washed over him. To his shame, he had gotten to the end of the letter and fixed only upon the signature. *Elizabeth Darcy*!

He had screwed the paper up into his fist and walked the length of his bedroom a few times, wondering at the first letter he had ever received from her. So consumed had he been by a fit of temper, that he had been oddly unconcerned by the letter's meaning and contents. It wasn't until he had evened the paper out, smoothed it back down flat upon the desk and read it again, several times over, that he had taken on board the importance of its content, *'my father is dead'*, he told himself several times over, trying to make it a fact, before calling for his man and making preparations to leave. Yet, still her missive irked him and he'd kept returning to look at it. Her hand was astonishingly elegant, beautiful cursive strokes of her pen, conveying her message in such simple, but eloquent language. Yet for all this it was brief and cold, he was 'Sir'; and it was icy enough to chill him just as deeply as the news it contained. Elizabeth Darcy! What angered him more? That she had the right to call herself Elizabeth Darcy, or the manner in which she addressed him?

As he drew nearer to the house, the sight of the drawn curtains in some of the main rooms, and the length of dark silk that had been tied around the door furniture, made everything more tangible. Greetings were exchanged with the servants and where Darcy had always been welcomed with delight as the returning son and heir, now he was treated as master. Deep respectful bows were offered by all. He was told his family were in the drawing room and went through to find the men discussing the newspaper and most of the ladies sewing. Elizabeth was missing. He spoke with them all and promised a delicate Georgiana they would speak privately later. He sat by his aunt.

"Where is Elizabeth?"

"Outdoors I should imagine, I cannot claim to know, I have not seen her today." Lady Fitzwilliam looked up from her work. "The burial will take place tomorrow. There are some papers on the desk in your father's study. His local man of law was holding a letter for you, to be delivered in the event of your father's death, and a copy of his will, which holds no great surprises. You are named as his heir, with provisions for..." Lady Fitzwilliam looked askance at a red-eyed Georgiana, "others."

Darcy nodded. "Thank you."

"She is always scampering about, our dear Elizabeth. I wonder, Mr Darcy, that you do not find it unseemly," Beatrice said.

Darcy made a short reply, offering no opinion. He was entirely in agreement that it was unseemly and a habit he'd hoped she might have outgrown during his absence, but he would reserve the right of criticising Elizabeth's behaviour for himself and was affronted by Beatrice's remark.

"Where is my father, I should like to see him?"

Lady Fitzwilliam stood and they walked the long corridor together, to the parlour where his father had been laid out. He and his aunt leaned on each other for support. Darcy's heart beat wildly with fear, but he had an intense need for a final sight of his father, to say goodbye.

His aunt left him at the door and took a chair outside, while he went inside. He remained within for only a few moments, just to observe that his father looked more peaceful and carefree than he had ever seen him. He made wordless promises to do his duty well, by Pemberley, by Georgiana, and to the rest of their ever-dwindling family. When he came out, he helped his aunt to her feet and they began the walk back to the drawing room.

"I have no fears, Fitzwilliam," his aunt began, "that you will do well as master, and that Pemberley is in good hands. Never has a father better prepared a son for his inheritance."

"Thank you. Does Lady Catherine come?"

"She has written that Anne is too ill to travel, and too ill to be left alone, but has sent a long letter of condolence; which contains much advice to us on how we might observe our period of mourning."

"Is Anne really ill?" Darcy asked. "Or is Lady Catherine still cross at the news of my marriage?"

"She didn't come to Haddon at Christmas and the excuse was the same, make of it what you will. But efforts should be made to heal the divide. I will suggest we go to her at Easter, as is the usual custom, though we were not invited last year, and see how she replies. Elizabeth ought to be introduced. If we do go to Kent, perhaps we might all remove to London after, for a short while. It wouldn't do to present ourselves there at the height of the season, not so soon after your father's death, but a few weeks in April, before everyone has left might suit our purpose well."

"I am not in the happy state of understanding you. Suit what purpose well, exactly?"

"To present Elizabeth to society, to our general acquaintance."

"You think it wise?"

"I think it necessary. I know it will be like throwing her to the lions, but Mrs Darcy holds a position of some standing, and she needs to learn how to negotiate the jungle. I will be with her every step of the way, you needn't worry."

"Necessary? My mother hardly ever went to Town."

Lady Fitzwilliam sighed. "No she did not, but that was her choice. She had been part of society as a girl, and after she was married, she chose to remain at home. Is it Elizabeth's age that stops you, or will you never take her?" At Darcy's look of warning, she inclined her head in apology. "I have overstepped the mark. It is for you to decide, of course."

"You must not think your opinions unwelcome, I will think on it, Aunt, but my inclination is for her to remain at Pemberley for the present time. Unless…tell me, will I find her much improved?"

Darcy was distracted by a movement from the corner of his eye. Through Pemberley's large windows he had seen a flash of dark skirts on the lawn. Although he had not a proper glimpse of her, he knew it was Elizabeth.

"Perhaps you ought to go find out for yourself," Lady Fitzwilliam said. "Go on, I can get back to the drawing room unaided, I walk much further at home."

He bowed and left, striding towards the doors with haste. He came upon Elizabeth by the line of young Spanish chestnut trees which promised to make Pemberley's lawns most decorative in future years. She had been wandering towards the house at a slow pace, her head bent to the ground, and his appearing quite suddenly must have taken her by surprise. She looked up at him with wide eyes.

"Mr Darcy, welcome home, sir."

Having rushed out to speak to her, he now felt a little foolish as no words came, and he looked stupidly upon her in silence for a few moments, his neck sweating under his high collar in the heat. She had grown, but not filled out. She was thinner than ever, he thought, and it made her face look quite dramatic, angular and striking. Her hair was swept up, with only a few curls hanging down at the back, as they should, but she looked even more girlish than he had remembered. Perhaps due to a smattering of freckles across the bridge of her nose, caused no doubt by her time out of doors, and her tendency to do anything with her headwear, other than wear it on her head. Now, a wide straw bonnet, adorned with black ribbons, was tucked under her arm and she had a book in her hand.

"You look surprised. Did you not know I was due back today, I sent a note ahead?"

"Oh yes," she said, casually, as if his presence, or lack of it, mattered not a jot to her either way. "I knew but..." and then, as if sensing he was a little cross at her, she stopped and amended her tone. "I'm sorry I was not here to receive you. I have been into Lambton to collect a book I ordered."

"Lambton! It is nearly five miles each way. On your own?"

She looked over her shoulder, as if doing so might summon up some company, but then glanced back at him. "It is a lovely walk," was all she could offer.

"And what is this book that warrants so great an excursion?" he asked holding out his hand for it. She showed him with a degree of reluctance and blushed as he turned it on its side. It was the third volume of a romantic novel. "I see." He let her have it back and cleared his throat. "Perhaps when you have made yourself presentable again you might join the other ladies in the drawing room."

He made to move off but was stopped by her voice. "I am so sorry, about your father," she said.

Such was the simple sincerity with which she spoke that for a moment he was in danger of being overcome by his emotions. "Thank you," he managed, before he left her.

Darcy spent the rest of the day in his father's study, going over his papers. The letter, he left till last. He had received so many from his father over the years, some lecturing in their tone and full of stricture, others had been overflowing with praise and love. He hardly knew what this one would bring and tore it open with trepidation. It was lengthy and written with great care. He digested the words slowly, having to stop every so often to swipe at his eyes, thinking of how his father, if he were seated opposite him, would tease him and call him soft-headed. He put it aside when he heard the familiar, resounding sound of the gong that warned them to dress for dinner. In his father's large, distinctly masculine study, he leaned back against the soft leather chair. Tomorrow would be a dreadful day, to have to bury the man, and then there would be calls of condolence and meetings with stewards and the foremost tenants to be gotten through. Georgiana would need extra care and reassurance, but all this actually only troubled him in a most perfunctory way. What really occupied his mind was what to do about his wife; that curious little imp whom he had earlier left sewing in the drawing room, wedged between Lady Fitzwilliam and Miss Temple on a gilded sofa, with a work basket in her lap. She had looked so out of place, so uncomfortable. Should he try to mould her into Mrs Darcy with the help of Lady Fitzwilliam? Would such a thing be possible? He thought it unlikely. There was little or no improvement in her that he could see. He expected his father had let her do exactly as she pleased for the past year. She would not go to London, not for another year at least, if ever.

'*Keep her busy with babies*' was what Colonel Fitzwilliam had once suggested. This thought made Darcy colour and pull at his cravat. Babies, indeed, when Elizabeth was still a child herself!

Dinner was got through, though no one except Walter Fitzwilliam ate much. Darcy had not seen him in over a year and he swore the man's stomach had grown two inches, while his hair had receded at the same rate. Elizabeth admittedly, did well enough, by remembering to give deference to his aunt on the way into dinner, and by leading the ladies out smoothly at the appropriate moment. He noticed she had a touch more grace about her when she moved, though she had never been inelegant and was always light of foot, she was now slower and did not dash everywhere.

They were all thinking on the 'morrow and it seemed the sooner everybody was abed and the day was over, the better. Darcy remained in the dining room with Walter and his uncle. The Earl soon fell asleep with his head on his chest and Walter began to run on and on about some investment he had made abroad. Darcy listened half-heartedly, until something began to niggle at him. "You say you have invested money in the West Indies, family money?"

"Yes, Darcy, and I urge you to do likewise. There are large fortunes to be made."

"You have not invested too much, Walter, in one place?"

"I had such a good return on my first investment, Darcy, I could not help myself. I confess, I have rather thrown in my lot, or all that I could access."

"And what sort of business is it?"

"Ships, import, export that sort of thing. I met a man in London who sorts it all out for me, you know I have no head for business."

"Walter, you realise it is not uncommon a practice in London, to lure a gentleman into such a scheme by paying him out well on his first investment; to use his first profit as bait to reel him in with? Who is this man and what do the ships carry?" Darcy was afraid of the answers. He was seized with an intuitive idea that the cargo might be human but hoped it was not the case. He pressed Walter for further details, but his cousin could not really give any and Darcy despaired of him. He'd always thought him something of a nitwit, now it appeared he was an incompetent fool of the highest order. He would have to travel to London and make his own investigations. It was a matter for another day, however. He had other things to immediately occupy him. They rose to join the ladies after shaking the Earl awake. Darcy went immediately to speak to Georgiana. She was quiet and shy of him, not having been in his company for over a year, but he gave her all the reassurances he could think to and squeezed her hand before the time came for her to retire. With his sister gone, his attention wandered around the room and rested upon a small table, where Lady Fitzwilliam and Elizabeth were occupied with their work. Beatrice was with them but not sewing. It was a sweet domestic tableau. He found himself engrossed in the study of Elizabeth's face. She had looked terribly bored earlier when forced into the occupation but now she seemed eager to learn the skill and would stop to watch Lady Fitzwilliam's stitches with a furrowed brow of concentration every now and then, before returning to her own thin square of muslin. She would frequently prick herself with the needle, let out a tiny yelp and suck the end of her finger to stem the flow of blood, before continuing. After some time in observation, he moved closer to stand over her.

"What do you work at so diligently, madam?"

"I am embroidering some handkerchiefs for you." She looked up at him with a mischievous smile, and he suspected she had come up with the answer only upon his asking. "Isn't it one of the duties of a good wife?"

"I see, and will you launder the blood off them first?"

She laughed a little, taking his jest in good humour. She obviously had no conceit regarding her skills with her needle. "Oh no, it adds to the pattern."

He peered down at the work in her hands and frowned. "There is a pattern, I hadn't noticed."

She arched a brow at him but said nothing further. Although he would not have minded continuing the conversation, he could not think of anything else to say. He moved to sit by the fire, with his back to her, content to watch the flames and let them soothe him as best they could.

Despite the arduous journey he had undertaken and the very late hour, Darcy could not yet contemplate sleep and was still in breeches and shirtsleeves, staring out into the nothingness, when a scream broke through the quietness. He knew the owner of it and dashed without thought to her room, throwing open the door. Elizabeth had beaten him to it and when he recovered enough to process the scene before him, he realised she had been quicker because she had already been there, asleep, curled up next to Georgiana, her hair braided down her back, a long voluminous nightgown swamping her thin frame, while his sister sobbed into her breast.

"A nightmare?" he asked, more to himself, than to her.

Elizabeth nodded but said nothing, occupied with soothing Georgiana.

"Can I assist in any way?"

"I think not, Mr Darcy, she is tired, she will go back to sleep again."

He sank into a chair by the window, his breath coming fast with the fright his sister's screaming had given him. "I cannot think what she is going through."

Elizabeth's eyes met his across the room, but she said nothing, and he suspected she too had been asleep before the screaming had begun. Georgiana eventually stilled and breathed deeply, while Elizabeth soothed her hair down and rubbed her shoulders.

"Shall I show you back to your own chambers?" he said at last, when they had been silent for some time and Georgiana seemed to be asleep again. A low-burning candle was all the light between them and it bathed the room in a low, flickering glow, casting ever-changing shadows of themselves on the walls.

"I will stay here. It is easier, if she wakes again."

"She has grown fond of you," he said, his voice no more than a whisper.

"I hope so, and I her."

He might have said much, in the relative privacy of the quiet house, when everybody else was abed, and they were stripped bare but for bits of muslin, but he was a man temporarily lost in grief and uncertainty. He thought of giving assurances that all would be well; that he would try to care for her and they would make a life between them, but he was not certain they were promises he could keep. So, instead, he rose from the chair and went from the room without another word.

Twenty one

Elizabeth stood at the door with the countess and watched the party for the burial move off. Mr Darcy walked with great solemnity and dignity behind the carriage bearing his father's coffin, his back straight, head high and proud. There was, she thought, some alteration in him since his return from Scotland. His hair was much shorter than she remembered, and his neck cloths less fussy and perhaps he was broader in the chest. He looked more man than boy now, but maybe that was something she merely imagined, due to all his new responsibilities. When they were gone out of sight, the countess declared she needed a lie down and went away. Elizabeth shook herself and rushed to the music room, where she found Miss Temple and Georgiana and insisted they go out into the park with her. Although both pupil and teacher were sat at the pianoforte, it looked as if not a single note had yet been played and her little sister trembled. "Georgiana, we still have ten chapters to read. How can you be concerned with scales and practice at such a crucial stage in the book? We must go out onto the lawn right this moment and finish it underneath the Spanish Chestnuts."

"Is it right to read, at such a time?"

"Oh, reading is always right. Opening a book can never be a wrong thing to do," Elizabeth told her.

Miss Temple smiled conspiratorially at Elizabeth. "Yes, let's go out. We all need the distraction."

Once outside, Elizabeth read aloud, while Georgiana listened with a wistful expression on her face. When the story was done and the book was closed, Miss Temple laughed.

"Well, it was very entertaining."

"And so romantic," breathed Georgiana. "How deeply he loved her! To be refused by her, but to still dream and yearn, and then to change his ways for her, and to ask again. How wonderful it must feel be to be loved so completely like that. I don't suppose anyone will ever admire me that much; I don't suppose I'll ever be anyone's idea of perfection."

"Of course you will, you are everything that is good and lovely," Elizabeth told her and then smiled at Miss

Temple. "And thanks to your excellent governess, you will have the required accomplishments to tempt all the handsome young men, and you have, of course, the added virtue of thirty thousand pounds. What could be more perfect than that? How they will all fight over you! I hope you enjoy dancing, for you will never sit down at a ball."

"Sometimes I wish I were poor. If I were poor, then I would know the man who loves me does so only for me."

"Oh, I should be careful what you wish for, Georgiana. A woman entering the state of matrimony should always ensure, if she possibly can, that she has the compensation of a good house and comfortable carriages. The first flush of love must inevitably fade and as they say, familiarity breeds contempt."

Georgiana's brow furrowed. "How can you say such a thing?"

"Your sister teases you, Georgiana," Miss Temple soothed.

"Yes, she must. Elizabeth, how can you not believe in love and passion when your story is such a wonderfully romantic one?"

"Mine?" Elizabeth was no less than astonished.

"Yes, my brother met and fell in love with you so quickly. You had known each other for such a short time. He must have adored you from his very first sight of you; to have carried you off and married you in secret like he did, without a care for your lack of fortune or what anybody would say about it. It's the most romantic thing in the world."

If she had not such a careful regard for the girl's feelings, Elizabeth would have laughed out loud at her misconception. Instead she looked down at the book in her hands and hoped the conversation was now at an end.

"Georgiana," Miss Temple said. "Why do you not run into the house and fetch another book? I shall read this time." Georgiana ran away to do her bidding and the governess looked over at Elizabeth. "It was very kind of you, Mrs Darcy, to walk all the way into Lambton to fetch the last volume for her. It was a lovely story."

"Perhaps I ought not to encourage her so, with such silly nonsense. Her father certainly would not have approved of my filling her head with such tall tales. It is all frothy fantasy."

"There I must disagree with you, Mrs Darcy, if you will permit me, for I do not believe love to be nonsense. Love exists, and very strong deep attachments, ones that stand the test of time, are possible. I have been fortunate enough to fall in love, and I do not wonder at there being so many songs, sonnets, books and plays written about it, because it is a powerful emotion indeed. When one loves, everything that is normally grey bursts into colour, dark clouds are blown away, what is dull and mundane becomes beautiful and glorious. I know it is possible to love someone so much that you cannot bear to be parted from them, and each minute they are gone is torture, each hour they are not near feels like a lifetime. It is possible to love another so much that even their faults and foibles matter not and become as dear to you as their other more admirable qualities."

Elizabeth moved close to her. "And where is he now? If you have felt such things, why are you not with him, Miss Temple?" She hadn't been able to stop herself from asking, but now she felt her question too intrusive. "Forgive me, I should not pry."

"No, it is no great secret. He went to sea, to earn his fortune in the war. He was a young naval captain, and well, he never came back. The ship was sunk."

"That is the saddest thing I ever heard."

"Oh, it was a long time ago," Miss Temple said, "but you see such love is real. I have never forgotten or forsaken him. His memory is still so dear to me. A year or so after his death, my family tried to persuade me to marry elsewhere and there was a suitor, another man who wanted to court me, but I would not have been happy or content with him, as I would have been with Edward. My family were never cruel, but they did not understand that I could never love another. I might have stayed at home and been a spinster sister, daughter and aunt, but I found I did not relish the prospect of spending all my days in a position and place that offered so little variation in circumstances, events or people, so I applied for a position as a governess. If adventures will not befall a young lady in her own village, she must seek them abroad."

"And have you had adventures? Pemberley is often quiet."

"Oh, I have been in many great houses, lived in the most beautiful places. And I have travelled with the families who have employed me. I have been to the continent twice."

Though there was sadness in her story, Miss Temple had chosen a life of independence and autonomy and this was a revelation to Elizabeth, who had always previously assumed young women took up positions out of necessity. She was full of admiration. "But you are not so very old, Miss Temple."

Miss Temple laughed. "Why, thank you."

"You might love again, if you have such faith in the emotion. Can it not be experienced twice in one lifetime?"

"Not for me," Miss Temple said with quiet assurance. "I love Edward still, time has not diminished my feelings, though he has died, my love for him has not, and even though we were together for such a short time, I am still glad I knew what it was to love."

Elizabeth looked at the ground, her spirits overcome. Had Miss Temple not been Georgiana's governess - had it been Jane sitting next to her - Elizabeth might have confessed the thought which overwhelmed her and almost brought her to tears. *I will never know it - I will never know what it is to fall in love.* She would never be the object of someone's most ardent passion. She was married already, not yet seventeen and all that she should have been excitedly anticipating, was lost to her already. She pressed the balls of her palms into her eyes. When she lowered them again and glanced at Miss Temple, she found herself being looked upon with great sympathy. Elizabeth realised words were not necessary for Miss Temple to know the state of her mind. The governess was an astute lady who had been present when she had first run from Longbourn.

At length she recovered her equilibrium and was able to speak again. "I do not believe you should close off your heart or deny the possibility of loving someone again, Miss Temple. You would deprive some poor man of a wife with great kindness and understanding."

"Well, let us make a pact then, Mrs Darcy. I promise to not absolutely close my heart to the possibility of future romance, if you do not either."

Elizabeth shook her head at the nonsense of such a statement before a sudden breeze made her shiver. Thinking they might have been out too long, Elizabeth checked her pocket watch and realised it would not be long before the gentlemen came back from the churchyard. She did not think Mr Darcy would care to see her at leisure in the park and had no wish to subject herself to the very worst of his frowns and lectures; she was not of a mind to do battle with him today. "I think perhaps the morning has run away with us. We ought to be inside."

Miss Temple agreed and they went to seek out Georgiana in the schoolroom, where she was still occupied with the choosing of another book. Elizabeth did not leave them as she could hear commotion downstairs. The gentlemen were returning and she thought the schoolroom was as good a place to hide as any. A maid came up after a while, however, to say Miss Darcy and Mrs Darcy's presence was required in the drawing room. Elizabeth was as surprised and unprepared as Georgiana, but they went down directly. On reaching the threshold of the room, they paused long enough for Miss Temple to instruct her pupil. "Sit quietly and speak only if spoken to, and even then say as little as possible, but remember to thank people for their condolences. It is mostly gentlemen, as is the way with burials, so nobody will expect to engage you in conversation for long. I trust you to remember the most basic of manners and curtsey when introduced. And when coffee and tea is brought in, you will be required to assist in serving." Despite the advice not being directed at her, Elizabeth found herself listening and nodding as if it were. She flushed when Miss Temple noticed and smiled at her.

It was not too long an ordeal. The gentlemen were all of around the late Mr Darcy's age or older, local gentry and people he'd had business dealings with. They were not attended by their wives and spoke mostly amongst themselves of horses and land, money and politics, as Miss Temple had suggested they would. Her husband did not come near her but Elizabeth felt his presence constantly and would often look up to find him staring at her with an inscrutable expression on his face. Feeling certain he looked at her only to criticise, Elizabeth resolved not to allow him to find her lacking and tampered down every insolent thought, bit her lip to prevent even a single impertinent witticism from escaping, and though she was dull, nobody could have excused her of being anything other than exceedingly proper.

The mourners began to drift away after refreshments were taken and the correct amount of sorrow had been expressed. After the last of them had been seen off, Mr Darcy went to his father's study, without a word to anyone, and was not seen again until dinner. When they sat down to the table, he took the master's seat for the first time, his large hands occasionally stroking the armrests of the carver chair his father had used for so many years. After dinner, Elizabeth watched him go to the chess set. It had been left mid-game, she and the late Mr Darcy having not finished their last contest. After studying the board for some time, he set all the pieces back to the beginning, before walking away to the window. His hands hung limply at his sides and Elizabeth sat in contemplation of him for some time. It was not difficult to see that tonight, the weight of his new responsibilities and his grief, were hanging heavily upon him. She crossed the room slowly and quietly, and put her hand in his. The moment their fingers touched, he started and jumped away from her, as if she had meant to hurt him. Embarrassed, she took her offending hand and put it behind her back, lacing it with her other.

"I am sorry."

"You startled me," he blustered.

"I just wished to say…to…" she floundered.

"Yes?"

"It does not matter. I shall go back to my work."

"Ah, yes. How are my handkerchiefs coming along?" he said, brightening a little.

"Rather slowly, there is a difficulty."

"Might I enquire as to the nature of the difficulty?"

"To the long list of all the things in which you find me lacking, Mr Darcy, you should add my skills with a needle."

He looked as if to say something else, but she moved quickly back to her place at the table, every fibre of her being burning with the shame of his aversion to her touch.

Twenty two

The days following the late master's burial saw the house slowly return to a semblance of normality, though of course, they all remained in deepest black and would do so for many weeks more. Mr Darcy, she had scant conversation with; he seemed as cold and distant as he ever was and she quickly resolved not to let it bother her in the slightest. *Let him go about his business and I will mine*, she told herself. She did worry over Georgiana, who seemed to have moved from a state of shock over her father's passing, into a deep melancholic grief, which nobody seemed able to penetrate. No matter how much she read to her, held her or talked to her, the girl was understandably inconsolable and numbed to the outside world by the depth of her pain. She took to staying in bed late, with the covers over her head, and no amount of coaxing could bring her out until nearly noon. She would retire early too and spend her evenings in the same fashion. Miss Temple, when consulted, suggested grief and excessive tiredness often went hand in hand and thought it best to let Georgiana be for now. Between the two of them, they decided not to approach Mr Darcy or Lady Fitzwilliam on the matter unless there was no improvement in a week or so.

Elizabeth began to walk out a lot, as she had done when she had first come to Pemberley. She roamed the park and woods for hours at a time, only coming back when her ankles ached or her stomach growled with hunger.

A comment Mr Darcy made to Lady Fitzwilliam over the breakfast table one morning, however, did give Elizabeth cause to wish to remain inside and petition him for his favour. Having heard him mention that he would be going to London soon, she tossed her bonnet onto the side table and from the bottom of the stairs, watched him go to his study. She paced outside for a while, wondering how to approach him. Mrs Reynolds walked past, looked at her oddly and asked if she might attend her in any way, but Elizabeth shook her head. She almost went away, fearing she looked a little foolish, but gathering her resolve, she knocked on his door.

Hearing his regal command of 'come' she went in. He looked up at her from his seat behind the desk and was as shocked to see her there as he might have done some total stranger who had wandered in from Lambton or Kimpton.

"Elizabeth, is something amiss?"

"Oh no, nothing." Approaching his desk, she picked up a paperweight in her hand and examined it with an absence of mind, before setting it down on the desk again. She then wandered around the room for a while, trying to choose the words she thought might give her the best hope of a favourable response.

Mr Darcy looked pointedly at the paperweight she had moved and put it back to where it had originally been. "Are you only here to move things about, or is there a purpose to your visit?"

"I did want to ask you something." She sank into the chair on the opposite side of the desk. "About London."

"London, well, it is our capital city, it is located in the south of the country and the population..."

She cut him off before he could further amuse himself at her expense. "Mr Darcy, thank you for the Geography lesson. I think even you must believe that I am entirely aware of its location, size and importance. I wanted to ask you about your intended trip there."

He pursed his lips and shook his head. "I see, I am thoughtless, I should have informed you directly. I will go on Thursday and be back within a fortnight. The earl and countess will remain with you and Georgiana until I return, so you need not worry."

"May I go with you?"

He sat back in his chair, clearly shocked by her request. "I am not pleasure bent, Elizabeth. I go to London on business," he said at last.

"Yes, I know, I do not expect you to entertain me. You don't have to take me shopping, or to the theatre, or anything like that. I would be quite content to spend all my days at Gracechurch Street. I would just like to see my sister, Jane."

He put up a hand. "No."

"You are thinking I will be a nuisance, but I will not. You will barely notice me in the carriage. I will not speak a word between Nottingham and Bedford."

A ghost of a smile crossed his face, disappearing as quickly as it arrived. "I have given my answer and it is no."

"No! That is all the response I am to expect?"

"I have good reasons for my refusal."

"And your reasons and preferences outweigh any of my wishes? Do my feelings not matter?"

He looked directly at her and seemed to waver for the briefest of moments before shaking his head. "Do not press me on this, there would be no point, my mind is very firmly made up."

"If not London, you could leave me in Hertfordshire and collect me on your return from London, so I might visit my mother and other sisters."

"You will remain here. Now, as I have already told you, further conversation is pointless. Unless you have any other matters to discuss, I have a great deal of correspondence to attend to."

"You cannot just dismiss me with without a proper explanation," she cried.

"Is this the part where you stamp your foot and tell me you hate me, or have we outgrown that stage?"

Half-tempted to do exactly what he mocked her for, she instead controlled her temper and got up to leave, but at the last moment she turned, unable to resist voicing what was in her head. "You are insufferable, and cruel. I have not seen my family in over a year."

"Think of me as you see fit, Elizabeth, but you do not go to London."

"Never! Am I always to be at Pemberley?"

"I'd say that largely depends on how you choose to conduct yourself. Please take care not to slam the door on your way out, I have a sudden headache." His eyes were dark and his mouth set into a firm line. She might have begged or cried, she might have shouted, or perhaps picked up the paperweight again and thrown at his head, but she knew nothing would make a difference. He was as immovable as a

188

mountain. She dropped a small curtsey of mocking obedience before quitting the room.

When it came time for them to go down to dinner, Elizabeth swept past him with an impressive flick of her skirts and took the steps almost at a run, leaving Darcy to trail in her wake. Although he called her name, she did not stop or look back at him. Once in the drawing room, she put herself between Georgiana and Miss Temple and would not meet his eye for even the briefest of moments. Darcy stood at the fireplace, furious at her show of petulance. There could surely not be a person in the room who did not notice her antipathy towards him, her angry little face wore a permanent pout and her arms were crossed over her chest.

"Well, I am hungry," declared the countess to no one in particular. "The food is always so good here at Pemberley." Receiving no reply, she moved closer to Darcy, lowered her tone and nodded towards the fire. "Maybe you ought to throw another log on, nephew. I detect a certain chill in the air."

"She sulks because I will not take her to London. Georgiana gives me less trouble."

"Oh do not speak too soon, Georgiana is fair young yet, her turn to vex and frustrate you will come. Take a turn about the garden with me before dinner."

They went onto the terrace and the early evening summer air calmed him a little, which he supposed was why the countess had brought him out.

"Why can you not take her to London?" his aunt asked. ˙

"I go on business. I have told you; I wish to see what Walter does with your money."

"Yes, and I thank you for your vigilance and care, but why not take Elizabeth? Spend two days more there, take her shopping, or seek some amusement. There will be nobody of consequence in Town at this time of year, so you will not be bothered with calls or have to make any. She will be company for you."

Darcy raised his brow. "Company! She barely speaks to me. I am apparently cruel and insufferable. Besides, it is too soon for her to go to London; a year is not long enough for people to have forgotten our hasty marriage and the talk surrounding it."

"Oh brave it out. It is known you have taken a very young country nobody as a wife, that is all. The truly terrible gossip was silenced by your having married her."

"Elizabeth has no plans to go shopping in Town. What she wishes for is to visit her aunt and uncle and sister in Gracechurch Street every day, whilst I go about my business. Who knows who she might come into contact with there, unattended and unprotected. I prefer her to be at Pemberley where I know she is safe. I do have a care for her, you know."

"Then be mindful of her wishes, or the angry girl will turn into a resentful woman and woe-betide you then."

"I cannot acquiesce to her over this. I will not yield, either to her scowls or your persuasion. Did you see her petulance? And you, my dear aunt, speak of taking her to London for reasons other than seeing her family. Do you really suppose she would ever cope in a London parlour?"

"Maybe she would surprise you. You rankle her, when you were not here, I saw a different, steadier girl emerging. Your father had smoothed out some of her wilder, rougher edges. I think the shock of losing him and you coming home has set her back some, but I am not without hope where Elizabeth is concerned. She does know how to behave," the countess smiled, "most of the time - and most is surely better than some, or not at all."

"Oh, so I am the one at fault? She is only sullen and childish around me?" Darcy was incredulous.

The countess sighed. "I worry about this family and where the future generations might come from. Anne, I fear, will not live to see thirty. Her mother will make up a match for her, now you have married elsewhere, but I cannot see any children resulting from it. She is so weak. Beatrice and Walter have been married ten years and failed to produce, while my second son is off playing at war and shows no interest in settling down." She poked at his shoes with her stick. "And

190

then we have you and Elizabeth, who can barely look each other in the eye, much less anything else. I should imagine she's as innocent as the day you brought her here."

"Madam, that is an entirely private matter. I cannot believe you would make such a comment."

"Oh, I may say what I like. I am old. You may be as outrageous as you like when you reach my age and pass it off as eccentricity and senility. We ought to go in for dinner, but think on, Fitzwilliam, that little wife of yours is the only lady who can give you a legitimate heir. You might do better to appease her some, now and again."

He did think on it, as he sat at the dining table and looked around at his family. He was shocked to have been reminded that ten years had gone by since Walter and Beatrice had married. The earl was most decidedly entering the last few years of his life and when he passed the title would go to Walter, but it did not seem likely that Beatrice would have a child now, having not done so in the last ten years, and with the Colonel on the front line, where men were dying daily in their hundreds, he saw the basis for the countess' fears and understood them. They were dwindling, the Fitzwilliams and the Darcys, so few of them now. Past generations had regularly produced large families of six or seven children. One poor mistress of Pemberley had been taken to bed with a child a year for eleven years without fail, until she had obviously had enough and banished her husband to his own bedchamber and bolted the door. Georgiana would certainly marry, but that was a decade or so away. His eyes drifted towards Elizabeth, who was not eating, but pushing her fork listlessly around her plate, no doubt awaiting the arrival of pudding.

She was far too young to be a mother, but the countess was right, at some future point there *would* have to be children. He was not the sort of man to take a woman to bed who was not willing; he would most definitely not be striding into her bedroom to demand his marital rights and wrestling her onto the bed. The thought of it made him smile, however, as he imagined himself as the leading character in some dark, gothic romance, who would throw open the door, scoop her up and put her flat on her back. Elizabeth, he surmised, would not swoon and surrender, but more likely kick him in the ankles. When he emerged from this odd little reverie he looked up to find her puzzled gaze upon him and felt himself colour deeply.

The day of his leaving for London came upon him quickly, Darcy having been so busy. Due to some inclement weather, he took his leave in the drawing room. Elizabeth was not present and though he was briefly of a mind to leave without an adieu, he then decided to seek her upstairs, fearing she had retreated to the horrid little room near the attics. Upon passing the music room, however, and on hearing a pretty tune played on the pianoforte, he went inside and found her to be the source of it. She stopped as soon as she caught sight of him and folded her hands in her lap.

"Please do not stop on my account, you play it very well."

"I have had the benefit of an excellent master, this past twelve-month."

"It sounds as if you have employed your time well."

"I am probably still not as diligent as I ought to be. Your sister spends many more hours in this room than I do," she said.

"No one admitted to the privilege of hearing you, can think anything wanting." She looked surprised and he was forced to admit to himself that it might have been the very first compliment he had ever paid her. "I should like to hear that piece in the drawing room one evening, when this initial sadness is over, and we begin to think of music again, and perhaps you might sing for us sometime?"

"So that you may judge and criticise and tell me where I go wrong? Indeed, I will not, Mr Darcy." Her head rose and he saw she was still cross with him for denying her request to go to London. Though the first flush of heated hatred did seem to have abated a little, she still struggled to remain civil. "I will not give you the pleasure of deriding my taste, or voice. I am resolved to cheat you of your

192

premeditated contempt, by not performing in your presence at all. Despise me for it, I do not care."

"Elizabeth...," he began, but seeing her head tossed away from him, gave up all hope of appeasement. Who could argue with such a stubborn, mule-headed girl? He had encouraged her to better herself at the pianoforte and now she had improved, she seemed to almost blame him for it. Darcy had brought a parcel of letters with him, which he then threw on top of the instrument. "Upon going through my father's papers, I found these and thought you might wish to have them. I am leaving very shortly, goodbye." He bowed and left the room at a brisk pace.

Elizabeth, flustered and confused, took the letters and untied the ribbon which held them together. When she saw what they were - letters from her father to Mr Darcy - dozens of them, spanning many years, she was overcome and put a hand to her mouth. The sight of her papa's whispery, spidery handwriting warmed her heart and brought tears to her eyes. She opened the earliest of them and began to read an account of his trip home from the continent as a young man. She broke from his witticisms and recollections only when she heard the sound of a carriage rolling away from the front door. She rose and went to the window to watch it leave and cried a little before returning to her father's letters. Gathering them up in her hands, she went to the window seat to read them and that was where she remained for the rest of the day.

Twenty three

When Darcy returned to Pemberley three weeks later, it was in a carriage travelling at a great pace, drawn by four horses whose hooves thundered along the road, jostling its passengers from side to side. Darcy winced at every cry of pain his cousin tried to stifle and suggested he might order the driver to go slower.

"No Darcy," Colonel Fitzwilliam said. "Do not. I just wish to get there as soon as may be. Once I am there, I can get comfortable and down a stiff brandy. I will be well."

"We enter the woods soon."

"I am so sorry about your father, Darcy. And in the midst of all you have had to deal with recently, you are called to fetch your foolhardy cousin from Dover."

"I would have gone much further, any distance, to fetch you home safely, and you would have performed just such a service for me, if it had ever been necessary. Think nothing of it, cousin. I am glad to have been in London and so close when the message came."

The carriage hit a particularly deep rut in the road and the colonel stifled what would have been a great cry of agony. Darcy looked down at the heavy bandage that was wound tightly around his cousin's thigh and knee and saw that blood was once more beginning to seep through. He would need to summon a doctor as soon as they reached Pemberley. The wound had been caused during a charge on the French cavalry, but ridiculously was the fault of an English soldier, who had stumbled and caught his own commanding officer in the back of the leg with his bayonet. Though he had chided his cousin, Darcy nestled within his breast a glowing pride that the colonel had been at the forefront of the fighting and not hiding behind his rank and connections at the back.

"I can't think of the horrors you must have faced."

Colonel Fitzwilliam grinned through his pain. "Oh it was not all hardship. There were some pleasures to be had on our route down to Portugal. Oh, the ladies of the continent, Darcy, so different to the home-grown filly, so fine and elegant; and the sweet fragrance of them. I had adventures not just on the battlefield. I swear I fell in love twenty times over. You would have been enraptured." Darcy smiled slightly, but did not answer, and his cousin looked at him oddly. "Oh, I forget, you are a married man now. Do you behave yourself?"

Darcy again said nothing.

"You are such a closed book, Darcy." The colonel shook his head at him as the carriage turned into the woods, and free of the restrictions of the public road, John drove the horses even faster. They roared through the trees and broke through into the park at a mad speed and drew to a dramatic, sharp stop in the courtyard behind the house.

The colonel was assisted up into a room he regularly used when visiting Pemberley and his family were soon there to fuss and cry over him. His mother held a hand to her heart at the sight of his wound, while Georgiana burst into tears. Darcy left them to it and went wearily downstairs to ask Hodges to fetch the doctor. What he required was a bath and to change out of his travelling clothes. They had travelled through two nights and he was disgusted by his own grime. He met Miss Temple in the hall who greeted him and asked after the colonel. When he answered that his cousin did well, apart from his wound, the governess expressed her relief and told him how concerned they had all been the previous night after receiving his note.

"Mrs Darcy was very keen to welcome you back, but I fear she spent most of last night in Miss Georgiana's room, and was a great comfort to her after she had suffered a nightmare. Today we were reading in the library and waiting for news of the approach of the carriage, but Mrs Darcy fell asleep with her book, and it is no wonder, considering she had so little rest yesterday."

Darcy nodded, unable to give credit to the idea that Elizabeth had been waiting on him coming home. He was in no doubt that Miss Temple was embellishing or overstating the matter. On his leaving her, though, he went to the library and found his wife asleep against the wing of a comfortable chair, her hand still loosely gripping an open volume of verse in her lap. He took the book and put it quietly onto a nearby table. She did not stir and he saw that exhaustion had well and truly claimed her. The fire was some distance away, so he shrugged off his greatcoat and put it over her. Other than the steady rise and fall of her chest, she was still. He stood observing her for several minutes and found something quite calming and peaceful about watching her. He sank into a nearby armchair and pulled a footstall closer to rest his boots upon. His bath could wait. It was not often he had the opportunity of observing Elizabeth with her face in repose; her countenance was normally so animated with rage. His gaze moved to her eyelashes, where they rested on the top of her cheekbones, so long, dark and fine. He had to admit there *was* something vaguely pretty about her, or at the very least, she had the most extraordinary eyes - there were times when they verily pierced his soul. It was in the midst of this contemplation of her eyes, that his own began to close; sleep pulling him down with an insistence that could not be denied.

Elizabeth woke with a gasp and sat bolt upright. Her hand pressed to her chest in fright. No matter that it rang and reverberated around the house at the same time every afternoon to tell them to change for dinner, she would never get used to the sound of the dressing gong. She then noticed Mr Darcy's presence, sitting up straight in a chair opposite, blinking, as if he too had been startled. His hair was rumpled and stuck up on end, and there was at least two days-worth of stubble on his chin. "You look like a pirate," she said, the words escaping her before she'd had a chance to gain full consciousness of her mouth.

He got to his feet immediately and began to straighten himself up, tugging at his cuffs and smoothing over his hair, to little effect, for it just sprung up again. "Forgive me, I fell asleep."

"If that is a crime then I am afraid I am guilty of it too. I did mean to receive you properly."

"I understand Georgiana passed a bad night, thank you for your continuing kind attentions to her," he said, very formally, backing away.

"Is this your coat?" she asked, folding it up and handing it over to him.

"You looked cold."

"Thank you."

He waved away her thanks and they were silent and awkward for a while. "I suppose we ought to go up and change for dinner."

They went, and on the staircase she thought to ask after the colonel. Mr Darcy told her of his pain, but that he was expected to recover well.

"Oh that is good news, we were all so worried," she said. She then took a deep breath and began to relieve herself from the burden of gratitude felt, but not yet expressed. "Mr Darcy, I wanted to thank you for the letters you gave me, from my father to yours. I can't tell you how much pleasure they have brought me; I have read them many times over and will treasure them forever. They always seemed to me such different characters and I wondered at their friendship having endured as it did, purely through the written word, but on having seen their communications, it is now entirely obvious to me how they amused and entertained each other. I suppose, sometimes, a person with entirely opposite sensibilities, and a seemingly juxtaposed view of the world, can hold a strong fascination for another, who is so fundamentally different to them. My father was such a poor correspondent, yet he must have treasured this particular connection to have been so attentive to it."

Mr Darcy smiled slightly.

Undeterred by his lukewarm response, she went on, "and about London. My childish tantrum was born out of disappointment. I miss my sister, but I have been given to understand; or should I say that I have tried to understand, after speaking to Lady Fitzwilliam, your reasons for not taking me. Can I ask, nay plead with you, I am not too proud to beg, that the next time you go to London, you consider taking me. Upon my honour, I will behave so well. I will speak to no one but the Gardiners and Jane, I promise you, with all my heart."

He ran a hand across his face. "Elizabeth, in London, I made some discoveries which I fear will alter all my future plans, but we will speak soon, of this and everything. Enough for now, let us wait until Richard is up and about, and full of his old tricks."

"Who is Richard?"

He openly laughed at her. "Colonel Fitzwilliam. His first name is Richard."

"It is? I never thought of him as having a first name, everybody always refers to him by his title or last name, but of course, everyone has a given name, I just did not know his."

"*My* first name is Fitzwilliam," he said to her with an earnest expression.

Did he think her so stupid as to not know? "Well, of course I know *your* name."

They had reached the top of the stairs and he gave a small bow. "Well, then, *Elizabeth*. I will see you when it is time to go down for dinner."

"Yes, Mr Darcy, till then."

He sighed and offered her a small bow before walking off. Elizabeth, as she went to her room, had the feeling she had not understood him completely, that there was something about their conversation she had missed in her efforts to be amiable. She truly wanted to be more disposed towards him. What good was fighting and kicking? It had gotten her nowhere after all, and his having given her the letters had dissipated some of the resentment she had felt a few weeks previously. Perhaps he was not totally without feeling towards her, and she resolved on treating him with as much cordiality as she could muster.

Twenty four

The weeks following his and the colonel's return to Pemberley, saw Darcy much engaged with the countess and Walter Fitzwilliam, trying to muddle through the mess that was now their financial affairs. Thankfully, a thorough examination of his own accounts and meetings with the bank and his solicitor in London, had given him nothing to worry about as regards Pemberley or any of the Darcy property. George Darcy had been as efficient as he was scrupulous. Walter's investment in the Indies seemed to be the only dark cloud on the horizon.

The colonel was fortunately growing stronger by the day, but his leg gave him a great deal of pain, and he was in bed for above two weeks while the wound healed.

Darcy visited his cousin's bedside regularly, but was astonished to find Elizabeth sitting with him on one occasion, sewing while the colonel slept.

"I was reading to him but he fell asleep," she said when Darcy entered the room, her head was bent low over her work and her brow furrowed in concentration.

"Should you be here, alone, tending to him while he is in a state of undress? I am not sure it is proper."

Elizabeth shrugged. "Maybe you forget, I am a married woman."

"I do not forget," he said and walked around so they were on the same side of the bed. Darcy's conscience tugged at him, seeing her keep watch over Richard and knowing how much she did to try and console Georgiana, made him remorseful. He had spoken to an uncle in London, a judge, regarding a possible annulment. Only in a conversational way, but he had made enquiries into whether such a thing would be possible, given all the circumstances. Now he felt like a blackguard for it ever having crossed his mind, particularly as she lately seemed to be making some efforts towards peace and accord. She still did not speak much to him, but occasionally he would receive an awkward smile, a civil hello. She deserved better from him.

"Does he sleep easy?" he asked.

"Yes. I think he is well recovered."

"Not well recovered, Elizabeth. He will always limp; will always have to use a stick."

"And yet, the wound might have robbed him of the use of his leg altogether, or it might have become infected and robbed him of his life. He is lucky, in some ways, to be here at all, over four hundred men died in the same battle, or so I have read."

Surprised at her knowing so much, Darcy cocked his head to one side. "This is true I suppose. He is such an outgoing, active man though. I don't know how he will bear it, being incapacitated so, forevermore."

Elizabeth laughed a little and he raised a brow.

"It is a good thing, perhaps, that he is not as gloomy as you."

"I am not gloomy. I am a practical man who prefers to see the world exactly as it is. I do not laugh when there is no occasion to do so, that's true."

"It is very true. I don't think I have ever met a young man more solemn than you."

"You speak of it as if it were a fault of mine."

"Maybe not a fault for you, but a great pity for me, for I dearly love a laugh."

"We are very different, then." he said.

"I sincerely hope that is not a recent observation." Her smile was full of impudence. "Or else I must doubt the formerly good opinion I possessed of your presence of mind."

He walked over to the window. "Perhaps I can be overly serious, but I do try to avoid those weaknesses which often expose a strong understanding to ridicule. Of course, even the wisest and best of men, and all the wisest and best of their actions, can be rendered ridiculous by a person whose first object in life is a joke."

"Undoubtedly," she replied. "And I am sure I detract much from the world by smiling and laughing along with it. I must adopt a little of your philosophy, Mr Darcy, and be more dour from now on. I am sure people would prefer it."

She finished with a swift bat of her eyelids, a look that almost dismissed him and he was temporarily stupefied.

How quickly she could turn an idea around, and rebut him with a perfectly coherent, well-formed sentence. She could do it without pause and he could not help but admire the quickness of her mind. He remembered his father talking of Mr Bennet as being a great debater. It seemed he had taught his daughter a thing or two.

"May I ask to what these questions tend, Elizabeth, this examination of my character?"

"I haven't asked you any questions," she said, all innocence.

When he thought on it, she had not, and yet he felt as if he had been pulled apart and put back together again, and now he did not like himself very much. He looked down at the needlework she had continued with while they had talked. "Will my handkerchiefs be ready by winter do you think?"

She kept her gaze focused on the task at hand. "This winter or the next? I might safely promise them as a Christmas present some winter or another, but I do not feel I ought to tie myself down to a particular year."

He came over to where she was and leaned over to inspect her work. "What is this here? Are those my initials?"

"No, it is a hollyhock."

The colonel opened his eyes and coughed. "As fascinating as this little domestic exchange is to listen to, I wonder if you would take it elsewhere and allow a man to sleep."

Elizabeth smiled and rose to leave, wishing the colonel a good rest. Once she had left, Darcy sat down in the chair she had vacated and took up the book Elizabeth had been reading to his cousin.

"Would you like me to continue with this?"

"No. You do not have such a sweet voice, nor do you smell as nice. The book is not interesting enough for me to endure your recital of it."

"Well, it seems Elizabeth was right. You are well recovered and almost restored to your old objectionable self. We will see you downstairs in no time."

In fact, it was not until a further week had gone by that the colonel came down to the drawing room after dinner, assisted by Mr Darcy on one side, and a walking stick on the other. Elizabeth sat by him, glad beyond all measure to see him able to join the party, and pleased that he was as friendly and affable towards her as she had known him before. When the colonel asked her to play, she agreed and went readily to the pianoforte and even went as far as to sing, which seemed appropriate on such a night of celebration and thankfulness. Everyone applauded politely and gave her genuine compliments. She was truly pleased for a short while, beginning at last to feel part of a family and very much at home. Mr Darcy's countenance, however, was stern. She could not fathom just how she had upset him on this occasion, but perhaps it was merely a case of their recent armistice having lasted for too long and that peace could not reign forever between people with such opposite tempers. It was a shame, Elizabeth thought, because although nothing of great import had been exchanged between them, he had recently begun to offer the occasional pleasant comment and some brief nods of no mean respect, which made their time together far more bearable.

She also idly wondered if he was cross because he still did not think her musical talents bore out her displaying them so readily, but resolving not to let his distemper bother her, she ignored it and sat herself back down beside the colonel for the rest of the evening.

Twenty five

His face turned up towards the summer sun and his eyes closed, Colonel Fitzwilliam was out in the gardens and sat alone on a bench when Darcy found him the next day.

"I am glad to see you outside, cousin. Are you well?"

The colonel answered without opening his eyes. "I'll never be completely well, the muscles in my leg have been damaged in such a way that the doctor believes I will probably always need this damned thing." He patted the walking stick beside him. "So I am out here considering a change of career."

"You will not go back to the army?"

"No, I have no wish to lead men from behind a desk. In fact, I have already written to resign my commission. So here I am, a bit of a cripple, no occupation, no wife or family and no immediate prospect of one. I find myself at a bit of a loss, Darcy."

"You will not become melancholy I hope."

Grinning, Colonel Fitzwilliam finally opened his eyes. "No, I will not, but I do wonder what to do with myself. It is too late to retrain for the law. I think sermon making my only option."

"They do not let such reprobates take orders." Darcy had taken a seat, but he now jumped up again, his mind too full of his plans for his body to be still. "Will you stay here, if I go away?"

"For a bit, though I begin to be thirsty, I might come in for a glass of wine soon."

Darcy laughed out loud. "I do not make myself clear. Would you stay at Pemberley, if I were to go to Antigua with Walter to sort out this business he has got himself into?"

It was such a great question that the colonel could not answer it straight away. "What exactly is it, this business of Walter's? I have heard whispers but nobody will give me the truth."

"I have not wanted to trouble you while you were so ill, but he has made an investment and signed a contract that

203

binds him into giving even more money over to it. It is not the sort of business I should like the family to be in."

"Nothing illegal, I trust."

"Not illegal, but in my view, morally unjust. I can barely speak of it as I am so angry with him for implicating you all by investing so heavily in it."

"A fool and his money are easily parted. My mother shouldn't have trusted him with the family coffers."

"She had little choice, I suppose, what with you being away at war, and your father unable to manage his own affairs. Besides, it will all one day be Walter's, he is the heir. I have advised him to go to the West Indies to sort it out directly, but I feel I ought to go with him, that someone should go with him. I suppose it would have been your job, had you been well."

"Darcy, you have only just returned home from Scotland, and you are needed here. Georgiana..."

"I can do little for Georgiana other than pat her on the head and say 'there, there'. I am useless. Others are far better at giving her comfort than I."

"You are not the most effusive of men, I grant you, but she would miss you nonetheless. I really do not think I am best equipped for running Pemberley in your absence, Darcy. You have been brought up to it. I am just a second son."

Darcy waved away these concerns. "The house and estate run themselves. I have excellent stewards who manage both, I only need you to oversee matters and to take care of Georgiana and Elizabeth."

The colonel was quiet and thoughtful for a while. "It would give me occupation, I suppose. You know, in cases where the master is absent, such duties and responsibilities would normally fall to the mistress. When the King goes off to war, the Queen is sovereign in his place, is she not?"

"She is sixteen."

"Nearly seventeen, she has a birthday coming up, did you know?"

"And she is yet to even order a dinner! She has much growing up to do," Darcy said, with a dismissive wave of his hand.

"I should go, really, to Antigua," the colonel said. They both looked down at his leg. "But I see you are determined. You speak of duty, but I sense a touch of wanderlust. You want to go, Darcy."

Darcy gave him a wry look. "Perhaps I do. I would relish the adventure. I would return within a twelve-month."

"You are grieving; I hope you do not act in haste." There were many more things the colonel wanted to say. He wanted to advise his cousin to give more consideration to remaining at home; he wanted to tell him that it seemed he was running away, and that he ought not to treat his wife in the same manner as he did his twelve-year-old sister, but Darcy was not a man who sought or welcomed advice. He liked to have things his own way, and not to be questioned or doubted.

They were interrupted by the sight of Elizabeth running across the lawn to them. She slowed a little on seeing Darcy and tried to look more sedate, which made the Colonel smile, and then he almost laughed when she spoiled her efforts by throwing herself down on the bench next to him with a none-too-delicate, breathless thud. "The Countess has sent me to fetch you in, she says you have been out too long and is afraid of you catching a chill."

"A chill! How would I catch a chill on such a glorious day?"

"Oh but you must come in, if you do not, I shall have been unsuccessful in my errand. You would not want me to fail so miserably, would you?"

"Never," he promised her, wondering that Darcy could not see what he did; that the prickly, awkward phase she had been in when they had first come to Derbyshire was now almost past and that a lively and lovely young woman, with a pretty face and brilliant smile was emerging - blossoming slowly, that was true - but she was definitely coming into her own.

"Then you must come in, lean on me."

Frowning, Darcy stepped forward and put himself between them. "He'd much better lean on me." He shooed Elizabeth away and she ran gaily on ahead of them.

The colonel watched her go, with her petticoats flapping around her legs in the light breeze and her curls bobbing about, before turning to Darcy. "Do you really want to leave her?"

"Elizabeth?"

"Of course Elizabeth, she is coming up to an age where young girls..." the colonel waved a hand in the air. "Their heads can be turned on the slightest of whims. If she were still Elizabeth Bennet of Hertfordshire, she would normally be coming out, attending her first balls, experiencing her first flush of love."

"And?"

"Do you not feel the danger of leaving her alone at such a time?"

Darcy looked truly puzzled. "She will be here, at Pemberley, no harm will come to her."

"And does that not have its own dangers?"

"I do not follow you."

"She is a girl, who it seems to me, is blessed with a lust for life, an enjoyment of all things. And I would suppose an ability to love beyond reason, beyond everything, if she were bored and neglected."

"What on earth are you suggesting, Richard?"

"I do not know, exactly, except, I would take care of her."

"She wants for nothing."

"That is not what I am saying. Do you have no notion of women? They are different to us, Darcy. Their hearts are not the same; they feel things in quite a different way."

His cousin stopped on the lawn and scoffed. "This! From you! A man who has dalliances at every turn! Who has lovers and knows actresses and courtesans."

"Oh, forget it, Darcy. You are obtuse in all matters of love and ladies." He wanted to add that it was no wonder Emma Balcombe had sought Wickham out, but despite his frustration, he could not be so cruel. He suspected that all had gone wrong in that affair because his cousin had pondered and wondered, and kept himself back, failed to commit and reveal the secrets of his heart. Lady Balcombe had grown tired and seen his reticence as a lack of affection. Wickham's attention had caught and flattered her, made her heart pound in a way that Darcy's cautious admiration could not. "Go on, go to Antigua if you must and I will stay here."

"I see you think it is a jaunt, but truly, Cousin, my aim is to protect and promote your family's prosperity and welfare."

"Then I thank you, Darcy, and let us shake hands." They did. "I will look after your interests and you will look after mine," the colonel said as they slowly crossed the lawns and went back into the house.

Elizabeth sat on her hands, bit her lip, and tried to be still and quiet while the men talked, in order that she could hear them better. As much as she strained her ears, however, she still couldn't make out enough of their conversation to satisfy her. Despite the colonel and Mr Darcy being only a few yards away, they were largely drowned out by another conversation between Lady Fitzwilliam and Beatrice, who were sat either side of Elizabeth on the sofa, talking of long sleeves, short sleeves, the price of this piece of muslin, as opposed to that one and everything dreadfully dull, whereas the men's conversation interested her greatly. She heard Mr Darcy mention London again and again. Was it possible he was making another trip there so soon? There was also talk of the West Indies and some troubles, and the booking of a passage on a ship, but this she found less engrossing, it was the thought of London that excited her and caused her heart to swell in hope. Mr Darcy had said they would talk of it again soon, of her possibly visiting Jane, but he always seemed so busy and she had not not wanted to constantly berate him on the subject - to become such an annoyance that he would again determinedly refuse to take her - so she had been waiting and hoping, and looking for an opportunity to introduce the subject.

When seeing him set down his coffee cup on a side table, she leapt to her feet and took it up, going to the refreshment table to refill it. She brought it back to him with what she hoped was an engaging smile and pressed it into his hand. He gave her an odd look. "I hadn't finished the previous cup. You whisked it away before I had the opportunity."

Her smile faltered but she remained firmly in place by his side, waiting for him to mention his trip again. Mr Darcy, however, remained tight lipped in her presence.

The colonel pushed his own cup her way with a smile and a wink. "I should like another cup please, Elizabeth, if you would not mind."

She agreed and noticed that as soon as she moved away, they began to talk again. It was so vexing. When she brought the colonel's cup back, he thanked her properly and asked if she had walked out today, saying he was surprised to see her in the drawing room mid-afternoon. She replied that she had been out but had come in again quickly, as the skies were dark and she was sure it must rain soon.

The colonel nodded. Mr Darcy looked at her as if she were an irritating fly he wished to swat but was too well-mannered to tell her to go.

"You have been here over a year now, haven't you; I suppose you must know the park and woods very well, as often as you walk out?" the colonel asked.

"I can find my way around well enough, but there are so many different paths to be taken, and of course, our ever changing seasons and our variable weather can make even the most familiar grove fresh and new to my eyes and ears. I don't tire of it. Although, that is not to say, I would not occasionally welcome a change of scene." She took a deep breath and plunged ahead. "Mr Darcy has promised to take me to London with him next time he goes?"

Mr Darcy paled and walked away a little. "That is not what I said, Elizabeth. I said we would only talk about the possibility of your going. I made no promise of the kind, and well you know it."

"You are unfair to me," she burst out, too loudly, and regretted it instantly, sensing she had drawn the attention of the whole room. She sounded like a child, and he regarded her as if she were one.

"We will speak later, in private," he said, in a voice just above a whisper.

"You say that, but you do not speak to me. I know none of your business. I do not know why you go to London, or when, or how long you will be gone."

He flushed red, but it stemmed from anger, not embarrassment. "The drawing room is hardly the place…"

"I just want to see my sister." Her voice sounded strange to her and cracked with emotion. "I have never asked you for anything but this, and you always refuse."

Beatrice got to her feet and put a hand on Elizabeth's shoulder. "Come, my dear. You can't expect Darcy to be calling at Gracechurch Street. You must see why he is reluctant. You cannot help your connections, but you must see how they are an embarrassment for your husband."

Fighting back burning tears of indignation, she glanced at Mr Darcy, who instantly looked away. "An embarrassment?" she repeated, to no one in particular, but it was Beatrice who answered her.

"You must rise above your upbringing now, be assured that we will not hold it against you. But you must seek to improve yourself, and this will not be achieved by your continuing to associate with businessmen and their like."

"Improve myself? To become what, pray tell me, someone like you?"

Beatrice looked pleased with this idea. "Why yes, I should be very pleased to give you guidance and to be an example to you."

Elizabeth heard Mr Darcy say her name, his voice deep and full of warning, but she paid it no mind. "Yes, you would make a fine example to me, of a woman who is as vacuous as she is vain, with a head full of trivial matters and who looks down on good honest people whose only crime is not to have been born with either title or fortune. I would be ashamed to spend money I would not have had the wit, ingenuity or intelligence to amass."

"Elizabeth, apologise to Beatrice and leave the room," Mr Darcy said.

"Yes, sir, I will, as soon as I have an apology from Lady Ripley, who has insulted everything I hold dear and everyone I love."

Beatrice was astounded. "My advice was kindly meant."

"I doubt you ever did a truly kind thing in your whole life."

"Elizabeth." Mr Darcy shouted her name like a high command. "I will see you outside."

"Well is it no wonder poor Darcy hides you away. For shame, you'll be lucky if you ever see any further than Loughborough," Beatrice said.

Elizabeth stepped suddenly towards Beatrice. She had not struck anyone since the age of seven and though her mind could not be controlled, she was still in masterful possession of her limbs and would not have raised her hands. She merely meant to remonstrate further, but Mr Darcy must have supposed she was going to do something very dreadful, for as soon as she moved towards Beatrice she felt herself grabbed around the waist and hauled back into his arms, and then she was propelled, half-dragged and half-carried towards the door, along the corridor and into his study. He kicked the door to with his foot and it reverberated around the room as it slammed into its frame. Still he did not take his arms from around her, and they stood in such a fashion for some time, him bent slightly over her and holding her tightly, their breath coming in deep gasps, until she began to feel the strangeness of it. He had held her thus once before, she remembered, at the stables of the inn at Redbourn, when he had been preventing her from running after the boy who had stolen her cross and chain. She had paid it no mind then, what with all that had gone before it, but it felt odd now and she became aware of his broad chest against her back, his earthy smell and his long arms about her. She had ceased struggling so he had no reason to hold her and yet he didn't let go, not until she, gaining control of her wits, calmly asked him to. He then released her quickly, throwing himself away from her as if she were poisonous.

She wrapped her own arms around her, when his had left her, and stood in the centre of the room waiting for him to speak.

He paced away, looked out of the window, glanced at her, shook his head, and then looked back out of the window again. "I know you to be outspoken, to be quick to temper and to have strong opinions, Elizabeth, but by God, I never thought I would actually have to physically remove you from a room. Everything you said about Beatrice is true, but a lady does not..."

Not wanting to hear his chastisement, she cut him off. "I know, I know." How she missed George Darcy and his sage advice. *'Always keep your temper, choose your moment and your battles, or else the only person you will cut to the quick will be yourself,* he had told her, and how right he had been. He had always delivered his lessons in a measured way, showing her what was right by example. Mr Darcy, in contrast, had launched into a tirade.

"A lady has forbearance, patience and self-control at all times, no matter the provocation. With anger comes loss of rationality. What you ought to have realised is that the person you were livid with was me, not Beatrice."

This was true. Beatrice was a mere irritant; he was the real object of her fury. Though now, she was more cross with herself than any other person alive and ashamed to have let his father down. Beatrice was right about one thing - after such a childish loss of temper she wouldn't go further than Loughborough - she'd be lucky if she made Lambton again. She had been trying, these past weeks, to show him she had matured and could be trusted, and he had seemed to treat her with a little more respect, and now she had undone all her good work. "Forgive me," she said. "But do you not understand why I was so offended? For her to speak so about my family, as if I should forget them all and that you would be too embarrassed to have me call at Gracechurch Street." He said nothing but continued to stare out of the window. "Oh, I see, you are in agreement with her. You *would* be embarrassed. You came to Gracechurch Street before out of necessity, but would not go now, or have me go. I remember you saying once before that your family would consider my connections as reprehensible, but I did not realise you felt the same way. I did not think *you* so bad."

"You cannot deny the situation you came from is most decidedly beneath my own. How can I consider it as anything other than a degradation upon my family name? I suppose you think I ought to flatter or deceive you as regards to this point, but disguise of every sort is my abhorrence."

Elizabeth was disgusted by his arrogance and pride, his horrible words. "If I had known then, what I know now. If I had been blessed with the power of foresight and not been so young, I would have protested more. I would not have gone to the altar with you, sir. You would have been the last man in the world whom I could ever have been prevailed on to marry. I would have kicked and screamed and refused. I would have borne the shame of the scandal, and far worse, rather than be bound to such a conceited man, a man with such selfish disdain for the feelings of others."

"You have said quite enough, madam," he said, his voice as cold as she had ever heard it. "I think we perfectly comprehend each other. Now, wherever it is you go to when you leave this house for hours on end every day, I suggest you quit this room and go there now, for I wish to have no sight of you until dinner, or I really do not think I shall be responsible for whatever I might say or do."

Taking him at his word, she fled.

The rain, as predicted, began to fall at around four o'clock. Darcy watched it from his study window and looked around only briefly at Colonel Fitzwilliam when he appeared at the door.

"Is she back?" his cousin asked.

"No."

"Did she even take a coat or bonnet?"

"I don't believe so."

"You'll have to go after her, Darcy. Saddle a horse. I'd go myself if I could."

"I don't believe I have ever been so angry, Richard."

The colonel came to stand beside him. "Even before you were master of this house, you liked to have your own way, you are used to nothing less than complete deference, and she will challenge you at every turn. I remember once joking with you that you might put her over your knee when she misbehaved, tell me, were you tempted?"

There appeared to Darcy, to be some sort of double meaning in this question; he had the feeling he was being teased and so he stalked away to the door. "I'll go after her. The rain shows no signs of abating."

As he went into the hall though, he heard the sounds of another door opening and the exclamation of a downstairs maid. Elizabeth came through, soaked to the bone, water dripping off her hair, petticoats and skirts clinging to her skin. She gave him one brief look of contempt before moving to the stairs, ascending them rapidly and disappearing from sight.

Darcy stepped forward and beckoned the maid to him. "Have an upstairs maid see to Mrs Darcy's comfort. A hot bath, perhaps, if she wishes, and will you please inform her that she need not come down to dinner. You might have cook prepare her a tray."

The maid looked astounded at being addressed by him because he had never previously given her any notice, and at being asked to convey such a message between master and mistress, but she nodded and scurried away, no doubt to find Mrs Reynolds and repeat the instructions. Darcy looked at the rainwater Elizabeth had trailed across the highly-polished floor and sighed. His thoughts were of a hot sun, long tall ships, plantations, new sights and smells. It could not come soon enough for him.

Twenty six

In the end, Mr Darcy did not go to London. Walter was despatched and discharged with whatever duties were deemed necessary. He took Beatrice with him, and they went the very next day, after lunch, though not before Elizabeth had sought her out and offered an apology for her fit of pique (though she was careful not to make any admission of guilt as to the sentiments and accusations she had put forth, for she still believed she'd had the right of it). Beatrice accepted this half-hearted olive branch, though none too graciously and made a comment about how she had never been so insulted in her whole life. Elizabeth bit her lip to stop the retort that came to mind, so wanting to advise Beatrice that she ought to get out more.

She had been concerned that she had upset Lady Fitzwilliam, but the countess seemed strangely unbothered by all that had passed and even gave her a kiss and a smile when she too departed Pemberley, two days after her eldest son. The earl kissed her too and said he hoped to see her soon, and although he called her Eunice and wished her a Merry Christmas on a bright summer's afternoon, Elizabeth cherished the sentiment anyway.

To Mr Darcy she said nothing for a whole seven days. She could not look at him without abhorrence, remembering the sentiments and opinions he had expressed and thinking him abominably proud. Oh, he might be ashamed of her, but she was equally mortified at being tied to such a man. Her dislike of him was now intense and immovable. He had very little to say to her either. They could not look each other in the eye, nor bear to be in the same company. If he were in a room she entered, she quit it very quickly.

Such a fierce battle of wills could not last forever though. One of them had to break the stifling silence before it strangled them. Elizabeth was surprised at it being Mr Darcy, she had thought she might be the first to give in, but he approached her after dinner one evening as she sorted through music at the pianoforte.

"I was wondering if we might speak."

Not waiting for an answer, he surprised her by taking her hand and leading her to a chair, where he sat her down with a great degree of solicitousness. She was immediately concerned that someone else had died, such was his kind manner. He attended her with a gentleness and courtesy she had hitherto not known from him before. His telling her that he was soon to depart for the West Indies was not so distressing, given the disasters her mind had first imagined, but it was still astonishing. To leave Pemberley when he had just become master, and they were still grieving for his father, seemed inconceivable, but she said nothing.

"I would not like for us to part on such bad terms, might I at least have a few words from you?"

"I suppose, since we are down to a party of five, if we include Georgiana and Miss Temple, which I always like to do, some talking is necessary, if we are not to be miserable."

"Are you?" he asked, looking at her with some solemnity. "Are you wretched? No matter our differences, Elizabeth, I would hate to think you are. If there is something I may do to ensure your happiness here, while I am away, please name it, and if it is within my power to grant it, I will."

She was both touched and annoyed by this speech, and wondered how he could inspire such strong, yet opposing, emotions within her. "The only thing I wish for, sir, the single thing that you could do for me, you have refused to."

He knew very well to what she referred, but rather than acknowledge it, he stared at his shoes for a while, before his head rose and he went back to the subject of his impending absence.

"Colonel Fitzwilliam will remain here with you and Georgiana. I am sure you have no objections to that. You like the colonel, don't you?"

"Yes, of course."

"I thought so. You are always talking freely with him, and are happy to play and sing for him whenever he asks."

His tone was light, but there was an odd quality to his voice that she couldn't quite account for. It sounded as if he almost resented her getting along with his cousin, like he was jealous of it, but then she inwardly scoffed at such a thought.

"I did intend to go to London myself to make arrangements for the journey, but then I decided I might remain here. I have noticed Georgiana's reluctance to rise in the mornings and her decided disinterest in everything of late. I aim to take her riding in the morning." He called over to Colonel Fitzwilliam. "Will you come riding on the 'morrow, Richard?"

Ambling slowly over with the aid of his stick, the colonel looked pleased with the idea, although he had some concern for his injury. "I may need some help mounting and dismounting, but I don't see why not. I would greatly enjoy it. I have not been on horseback for months; I hope I shall not be too much of a hindrance to you, you might have to go easy on my account."

"I have no ambitions beyond a slow amble around the park. Georgiana has not ridden for some time either and Elizabeth will be learning, of course."

"Me?"

"Yes, you," he said, nodding at her.

"I do not ride."

"As I said to the colonel, you will be learning. You need not worry, as I have just the horse for you. We will go out at eleven," he said with determination, implying that the subject was closed.

She, however, could not let the matter go. She was not a puppet to be directed and pulled about by his whims. "Sir, I do not ride," she said, with no small firmness in her manner.

"Elizabeth. You cannot go on scurrying about the countryside on foot like a milk maid, 'tis not dignified. You ought to learn to ride." Undeterred by her frown, he went on. "You would see much more of the countryside on horseback and you might go much further on your excursions if you rode, and it is safer." He then looked directly at her with a raised brow and there was something challenging in his gaze. "Of course, if you are afraid of horses that would be a different matter?"

216

"I am not afraid," she said quickly and then realised she had trapped herself. She ought to have just admitted the reason for her reluctance. She did not like horses, and there *was* an element of fear. He would surely not force a plainly terrified lady onto horseback. But if she would not admit to a certain amount of trepidation, what excuse could she have? "It's just that I do not have the right clothes."

"A cloak and sturdy boots will do for now. Though, I agree, in future you should have full riding habit."

"I prefer walking," she protested. "I see nothing wrong with using one's own two legs to get about."

"Oh, Elizabeth, come on now, the park is ten miles round, walking is no way to see it properly. Riding is excellent exercise and you will enjoy it once you reach a certain level of proficiency."

She looked to Colonel Fitzwilliam for support. He was always so kind, so quietly supportive of her, that she expected to find an ally in him, but instead, he grinned broadly. "I cannot think of anything I would enjoy more. Nothing would give me greater pleasure than for us all to ride out tomorrow. You will not find a better teacher than Darcy, Elizabeth, and I do agree with him, Georgiana is too much in her own room, too occupied with indoor pursuits."

Elizabeth had gone to bed thinking she could always wake in the morning with a terrible headache, one that could only be cured by her staying inside with a good book and a cup of chocolate. She had also been cheered by the thought that it might rain. However, the weather had not been a great friend to her lately, and proved a definite foe now. The morning had broken bright and glorious to spite her. But rather than get up, she pulled a cowardly blanket over her head. When the maid who usually attended her arrived to help her dress, she sent the girl away. Not thirty minutes had passed before Georgiana burst into her room without a knock and flung herself down on the bed next to her.

"Are you very ill?" she asked, peering closely at Elizabeth's face for signs of sickness.

"'Tis just a headache, it will pass, with a little quietness and solitude."

Georgiana failed to take the hint. "Fitzwilliam said we are to go riding, but I told him I would not go if you do not. I shall stay here and take care of you, as you do me, when I am ill."

"Oh, you need not. I shall be better just left to my own devices."

Frowning, Georgiana left the room and Elizabeth pulled the covers back over her head. In truth, the only thing the matter with her was her stomach, which rumbled with hunger. What a shame that one could not pretend to be very ill and still go down to breakfast. She would have to wait until they had all gone before she might sneak downstairs and ask someone to bring her something.

In contemplation of what delights she might partake of later, she was not at all prepared for another intruder in her room and sat upright in shock when the door opened and Mr Darcy's deep voice reverberated off the walls.

"Good morning, Elizabeth."

"What are you doing in my room?"

"I heard you were ill and seeing as I have never known you to have even a mild case of the sniffles, and as you were so lively and in excellent health yesterday evening, I have come to see what the problem is myself. I am exceedingly curious to know what ails you."

"You are not entitled to just come in, without…it is a terrible liberty for you to enter while I am still abed…" She trailed off at seeing the amusement on his face, and pulled the neckline of her nightgown up. She then pulled the counterpane up too for good measure.

"Oh, you see I am. I am very entitled, just because I have never previously done so, does not mean I cannot, or will not do so again, and should the need or desire ever arise, I certainly shall."

His use of the word, 'desire' made her blush, and then he, seemingly realising what he had said, coloured too, although he recovered from the embarrassment of the moment much earlier than she did.

"Georgiana has stated she will not come out riding without you. So unless you are struck down with the plague or leprosy, I want you out of bed, breakfasted and ready to leave by eleven."

She thumped the pillow beside her. "Is a lady not entitled to have a headache?"

"Oh a headache is it? Well, I find the best cure for headache is fresh air and exercise. I'll leave you to change."

"You are overbearing and intolerably dogmatic, sir."

To her very great shock he reached down and grabbed one of her ankles through the covers, holding it firm and looking her in the eye. "About this, yes I aim to be. My sister will not get on a horse without you. The exercise would be entirely beneficial to her. I believe you have more than a passing care for her welfare."

She kicked her leg and he released his hold. "Of course I care for her, you know I do."

"Then I shall leave you to change, Elizabeth, and let us have no more talk of headaches. If you are not downstairs within three quarters of an hour, I will be back and I will use all my husbandly rights to strip you down and dress you myself, are we clear?"

"Mr Darcy, I am not afraid of you," she said, with more conviction than she felt.

"I would not have you so. I will see you downstairs, and today, we ride out."

Whatever she felt about such an affront (and she felt much) Elizabeth did begin to wash and dress when the maid arrived - only minutes after Mr Darcy had left and clearly upon his instructions - reminding herself that the whole purpose of the ride was to encourage Georgiana out of the house. She was also now convinced Mr Darcy was not likely to let the idea of her learning to ride alone, not until he had actually seen for himself how little talent she had for the pursuit and how much she hated everything equine. She resigned herself to the torture that lay ahead. He had, of course, behaved in a brutish and unforgivable manner. She resolved not to pay him the slightest bit of attention.

Oh, and how horribly gay they all were about it as they watched the horses being brought round to the courtyard! They were all smiles and jokes. The colonel was assisted by Mr Darcy and his groom onto a large black hunter, and while this delicate manoeuvre was taking place another groom stepped her way, waiting to assist her onto a much smaller chestnut mare. He said nothing and waited patiently, but when too many moments had passed and she had not moved, he looked directly at her and broke convention by speaking without first being addressed.

He stroked the horse's mane and in a hushed tone, said "you'll have no problems with this little lady, Mrs Darcy, she's as calm as can be. I take her out for exercise daily myself. All you have to do is sit atop and she'll do the rest." He put out his hand, "will you allow me?"

With a nod and an assent made through gritted teeth, she put her hand into his and followed his instructions. Before she knew it, and with far more ease than she had expected, she was in the saddle. She looked down at the young groom and managed a nervous smile. "Thank you, Robert, isn't it?" she asked, remembering that he had been the messenger on the day she'd sent a note to Matlock to inform them of the late Mr Darcy's passing.

"That's right, ma'am, aye," he replied, looking pleased she knew him. "And I remember you saying you were no horsewoman, but I'll be riding right behind yer today, you'll have no trouble."

"You are very reassuring, Robert."

Mr Darcy approached and looked surprised to see her all ready and seated correctly. From her elevated position she could look down at him for once, and took no small pleasure in being able to do so, even though it was a short-lived delight, as he quickly moved off again, after muttering "very good", at her.

The mare whinnied and Elizabeth gripped the reins tightly. She was truly petrified for a moment; it was all so foreign to her, the smell of the horses, the saddle and the strange side to side movement of her mount under her, as the animal shuffled restlessly, obviously keen to be off. Robert stroked the mare's mane again and whispered into her ear to steady her.

"What's the horse's name?" Elizabeth asked him.

"She doesn't have one yet, ma'am. 'Tis your horse, brought down from Scotland on the instructions of the master, you're to name her."

"Oh," was all she could say. She'd supposed he had come up with the notion of having her learn to ride only yesterday. That a horse had been procured for her many weeks ago was strange news to hear, and that it had come down from the Scottish estate, gave her much pause for thought. Had he thought of her then, while in Scotland? Had he seen this young mare while he'd been away and chosen it for her? It seemed a ridiculous thing to have done when he'd had no true notion of whether she'd ever actually ride. Oh, he had managed to get her on horseback today, but if she had truly put her foot down and refused, she doubted he would have had the nerve to manhandle her onto it. Was the horse a present? Then why not give it to her directly? Oh teasing, obtuse man. It was not a present at all; it was an instrument of torture and nothing else. If he had wanted to gift her something, he might have bought her a book, sheet music, anything in the world other than a horse. He knew her not at all.

And then they were off, and it was not so very bad. After five minutes or so at a very sedate pace, she relaxed enough to enjoy the air and began to feel a little pleased with her own bravery. Robert, true to his word, rode very close behind her. It would have been even more pleasant if Mr Darcy had not circled back to ride alongside her at intervals and bark instructions. *'Hold the reins tighter'*, *'hold them looser'*, *'straighten your back'*, *'relax a little'*. She had no riding crop, but if she had, she would have been sorely tempted to use it - though not on the horse.

Georgiana, having been allowed to leave off mourning clothes for the outing, was very resplendent in full riding habit with a neat little hat on top. She did look remarkably fine, and although she was not one to care much about clothes, Elizabeth did feel some envy and wished her own gown was not so dowdy. The colonel was in high spirits and continually made comments to Mr Darcy, before throwing his head back to laugh at his own jokes. Mr Darcy would glare back at him. Elizabeth was not close enough to know it all, but she did overhear the colonel say it was *'the duty of all husbands to give their wives a good riding lesson.'* She was sure he inferred something by this that didn't involve horses, but what it was *exactly,* she couldn't say. Yet it made her think of how Mr Darcy had surprised her in her nightgown that morning, and of how he'd grabbed her ankle through the covers. She knew the colonel had only meant to embarrass his cousin and the comment had not been intended to reach a lady's ears, but she blushed deeply nonetheless.

They were out for no more than an hour and on their return back to the house, Mr Darcy was more ebullient than she had ever seen him, proclaiming they would go further the next day. He announced he would have her trotting by the end of the week and proficient enough to ride to Lambton and back with a degree of competence by the time he departed for Antigua.

Elizabeth submitted to this new daily routine, rather than fight against it, as she saw how glad the colonel was made by it - on a horse he could move quickly - it was almost as if his injury did not exist. Georgiana, who had ridden since she was a very small child, was very at home in the saddle and the exercise did its intended job of brightening her mood, and Mr Darcy's countenance was not so foreboding either. The three of them were family, of the same strata. They had the benefit of shared experiences and the same blood running through their veins. Elizabeth would watch as they cleaved to each other, while she would fall behind, through her lack of skill, of course, but also through choice. She was the outsider, the odd interloper, the girl who was only there because of a ridiculous set of circumstances, a bad mistake. She would ride with Robert, who seemed to have quickly become *her* groom. He rode always within a few yards of her, looking out for obstacles and supplying encouragement when asked for. He was a handsome young man, no more than eighteen, broad and strong, with a mop of blonde hair that fell across bright blue eyes and he looked to her protection with an unfailing dedication she well appreciated.

They spoke little except of the horses and the park, but she liked him. He helped her on and off her horse after every excursion, jumping off his own mount rapidly to perform the service even as they were coming to a stop. One day he had cause to steady her when she wobbled after dismounting. Her legs had failed her, and her whole being had felt odd after the strangeness of being in the saddle for longer than she ever had before. His arms had been strong and his smile so understanding that she'd found herself leaning against him a little longer than was strictly necessary, while wondering about the strange fluttering of her senses it excited.

It had been a brief encounter, however, as Mr Darcy had come over to take her by the elbow and steer her inside for refreshments, and she dismissed it quickly from her mind.

Twenty seven

"I shall show you Brigham Edge tomorrow, Elizabeth," Mr Darcy said after supper as he paced restlessly around the room. "It's a very fine view."

"It's a long ride, Darcy, maybe too much for Elizabeth," Colonel Fitzwilliam replied on her behalf when she was silent.

"Nonsense, she has been to the edge of the park now, a little further will be no trouble at all."

Elizabeth stifled a yawn. She was tired from days of activity she was not used to, and tired in general, she wanted to go to bed. Her throat was sore and she shivered, even though she was as close to the fire as could be. Mr Darcy had accused her some days ago of never being sick, but she was getting a cold, she was sure of it. It was as if his words had dared illness to come forward and defy her normal strength, her generally excellent health.

"It is quite a jaunt. We'd be out for a few hours at least," the colonel added.

"I have told Mrs Reynolds we will require a picnic." It was clear Mr Darcy had made up his mind about the excursion, whatever the feelings were of the rest of the party, they were obviously all expected to acquiesce to his wishes. "Elizabeth will do well, she walks miles every day," he said decisively, without looking at her, and as if she were not even in the same room. "Brigham Edge was my mother's favourite place. We used to go regularly in the summer, do you remember, Richard?" His face held a wistful quality for a few moments and Elizabeth was lost in contemplation of his countenance, never having seen him so reflective before. "I should very much like to see it again before I go away," he finished, then got up and quit the room rapidly, declaring in an off-hand way that he had some business to attend to.

"And there he goes," the colonel said, chuckling. "He has arranged it all just as he pleases, 'tis very kind of him, is it not, Elizabeth, to save us the bother of thinking for ourselves?"

Elizabeth had never heard him criticise his cousin before and she was tempted to add her own low opinion of Mr Darcy's officious behaviour to his gentle chiding, but refrained, saying only, "he has the great power of choice. I do not know anybody who seems more to enjoy the power of doing what he likes than Mr Darcy."

"He likes to have his own way very well," replied Colonel Fitzwilliam, "but, so do we all, I suppose. It is only that he has better means of having it than many others, because he is rich, and many others are poor." The colonel took a long glug of the amber liquid in his glass. Elizabeth wondered if maybe he'd had one too many and his tongue was loosened by it.

"You are so unlike him," she said, "and yet you grew up in very similar circumstances."

"You don't take into account his being, for many years, an only child, the longed for and much cherished heir to all this." The colonel swept an expressive arm to indicate their surroundings.

"You mean that he is spoilt."

"Oh, I don't mean to disparage him so, I do love him, truly, I do. And I promise you, Elizabeth, underneath all that hauteur, a truly good and kind man exists, but he does test my patience occasionally."

"Only occasionally, Colonel? Then you show great forbearance. He tries my patience constantly."

"And are you a particularly patient person?"

She laughed. "No, perhaps not."

"Well, I think I shall be as dictatorial now as your husband sometimes is, and I will insist you go to bed, for you are fading fast where you are."

Knowing he meant this dismissal kindly, she thanked him and went upstairs much earlier than was her habit. She moved slowly, feeling odd and out of sorts and entered her room quietly, hearing the chatter of maids who were turning down her bed and stoking the fire. They obviously did not hear her behind them at the door, and carried on talking, one more loudly than the other.

"...heard the master was in her room this morning, but I checked and there was no need to change the sheets. Clean as a whistle. He don't fancy her, don't blame him, skinny little thing. He never comes to her at night, ever, makes my job easier s'pose." This came from a stout, short maid with a hard face and a gruff voice, called Daisy, who Elizabeth had never warmed to, finding her a smirking, lazy annoyance, rather than of any true assistance.

The other maid's voice was lighter and gentler. "Don't talk so, it isn't right, she's never give a cross word to no one."

Elizabeth shut the door firmly and both of them turned quickly, their faces ashen in fear. "Oh, Mrs Darcy," Daisy stammered. "I did not see you there, I beg your pardon."

"Yes, I rather think you should," Elizabeth said and fixed the girl with a look that left her in no doubt that she had overheard her. She opened the door and nodded towards it. Daisy went scurrying out and Elizabeth closed the door before turning to the other maid. "You are not normally upstairs. Don't you sometimes attend to the downstairs fires?"

"Yes, Mrs Darcy. I'm upstairs because everyone is feeling rough as...they are all right sick with the cold." Her voice was little more than a squeak, and she dared not look Elizabeth in the eye. "I'm a scullery maid, really, but the house is short."

"And what's your name?"

"Rose, Rose Kiddy, madam." She dropped a curtsey.

"That's a fine Derbyshire name. Well, Rose Kiddy, now the fire is lit and the water is here, I don't require anything further tonight, other than the unlacing of my corset, do you think you might manage that?"

The girl's eyes widened and her hands shook, but she managed to undo Elizabeth's gown and corset. She stepped away and gave another awkward little curtsey. "I hope you don't think I am like Daisy, I do not talk about you in the servants hall or the kitchens. I don't agree with her neither, I think you are very pretty, and kind."

Their eyes met in the mirror. There was something about the girl which was comforting and Elizabeth was gratified by her compliment, but did wonder if she spoke only because she feared she was in trouble. "Thank you, Rose. You may go, and do not worry, I may speak to Mrs Reynolds, but you'll not suffer."

"Shall I get your nightgown for you before I go?" Rose asked, a broad smile crossing her face, obviously keen to please.

"Yes, alright, go on then," Elizabeth answered with a smile of her own.

Full of purpose, Elizabeth swept downstairs the next morning, past Mr Darcy who was on his way to breakfast. He stopped and looked as if he would offer to escort her in, his arm was half-raised, but she acknowledged him only with a brief nod and headed for the door that would take her downstairs to the kitchens and servants hall. He caught her up and blocked her way.

"It was some time ago now, I realise, but did we not have a conversation about your going below stairs? About respecting the servants' privacy?"

"Yes, Mr Darcy, and I certainly shall respect their privacy, as long as they grant me the same courtesy in return. Now if you'll excuse me, I have a matter to attend to that cannot wait."

Expecting him to say something further, she was surprised when he stepped aside and allowed her to open the door and take the stairs down. Whenever she had ventured into the servants' hall before, she had been overwhelmed and bewildered at the sheer number of people, the size of the kitchens and the labyrinth of hallways and doorways that greeted her. It was, of course, almost as large as the ground floor of the house above, but darker and much more functional and basic. On this occasion, the chairs scraped back as before, there was a scurrying to find coats as before, but she paid it less mind now, and schooled her features into impassivity. The staff she was met with were not impressed by her presence, seemed more annoyed at it, but then there was a little gasp and a straightening of backs and she

227

realised, without turning around, that Mr Darcy had followed her.

She asked the nearest person to show her to the housekeeper's room and she followed him down several twists and turns to a small cubby hole of an office. It benefitted from a thick door, behind which a private conversation might take place. Mrs Reynolds stood and greeted her with reserve. Elizabeth's intrusion was almost certainly unwelcome, although to Mr Darcy, who came into the room behind her, the housekeeper was all deference and politeness.

"I'll stand, Mrs Reynolds, thank you, what I have to say will not take long, and I would not wish to detain you from your duties. Please feel free to sit yourself."

Thankfully, the housekeeper did. Elizabeth felt the need to have a height advantage over her, so she might deliver her orders. "There is a maid, Daisy, who attends me upstairs. I would ask that you dismiss her from such duties and find another role for her."

"Well, Daisy is a good maid, Mrs Darcy. I have strict regulation over her. In fact she is my cousin's girl."

"I see, well, she does not suit me. I would not have her in my room any more, or Miss Darcy's."

Mrs Reynolds blustered. "If she has done something to offend, I am sure I might speak to her and all will be resolved. May I ask what she has done to upset you?"

"No, you may not, though as she is a relation of yours, maybe she will tell you of it herself. I should like Rose to take Daisy's place."

"We have three Rose's in our employ, Mrs Darcy."

"Do we? My goodness, well I refer to Rose Kiddy, and from today she'll attend me. The other maid, who is normally upstairs with Daisy, might do for Miss Darcy's sole use, though I understand she is unwell at the moment."

Mrs Reynolds face hardened. "Rose Kiddy is a scullery maid. I do not understand."

Mr Darcy stepped forward. "Mrs Reynolds. Mrs Darcy's request is simple. That Daisy be removed and Rose Kiddy, whoever she is, be her replacement. See to it, will

228

you? Mrs Darcy need not explain herself further. We'll go up to breakfast now."

Though the housekeeper fumed, she said no more. They went back through the kitchens and Elizabeth stopped when she saw Rose. "Rose, you will have a new set of duties from today, Mrs Reynolds will speak to you about it." Rose blushed and smiled, and nodded. The cook, standing close by with head bent, started in surprise. "I am sorry to drag her away from you, Mrs Small. I imagine she's industrious and helpful?"

"Oh, yes, Mrs Darcy."

"Well, Mr Darcy and I will leave you all in peace, but may I say before I go that last night's pudding was excellent, Mrs Small."

Mrs Small was pleased with this critique and lifted her head. "Thank you, madam, 'tis a great compliment to me when your dish comes back empty every night."

"Mrs Darcy has a great sweet tooth, Mrs Small. If you were to serve four puddings every night in place of any other courses, she would be a very happy lady, I daresay." With this rare show of humour and geniality, Mr Darcy ushered her upstairs.

Twenty eight

Their excursion went ahead as planned. The picnic, the servants required to serve it and Miss Temple all travelled by carriage, while the rest of the party went on horseback. Elizabeth rode behind, as had become her habit. Mr Darcy, as their illustrious leader, was usually at the helm, though when they had been travelling for an hour or so, he came to ride alongside her, circling back and counselling his horse to match the rhythm of hers. He scratched the side of his head with a finger, as if he were in deep contemplation of something.

"What did she do? The maid you had dismissed."

"I did not have her dismissed, I asked for her to be put elsewhere."

"Semantics, what did she do, style your hair wrong?"

"It does not matter."

"And why was it important for you to be seen going down to Mrs Reynolds to deliver your edict? You were sending out a message, I suppose, regarding what you will and will not tolerate."

"Mr Darcy, you deal with dozens of matters of business every day and never choose to share the details of them with me."

He looked as if he were about to leave and ride on ahead, and not wishing him to think she was being churlish, Elizabeth thanked him for his assistance with Mrs Reynolds. "I did not need or ask for your help, I would have eventually carried my point. Your support made it easier though. She would not question you."

"You struggle to preside over her."

Elizabeth was not sure if this was a question or a statement. "I am still shy of seventeen, and she, well, she is nearer to my mother's age and she runs the house with such great efficiency, that I almost dare not interfere. Would you wish for me to be more assertive, to take a more active role in the household affairs? Your aunt thinks I ought to."

"I have never expected it. Mrs Reynolds, as you say, needs no direction, having been doing the job for so long. My father's death has come sooner than any of us anticipated, which I suppose has brought the question a little more to the fore, but it is up to you. I have to say, though," he said, with a small smile, "your style of management is a little random and unusual. You do realise you have promoted that girl from scullery maid to a position in the household second only to Mrs Reynolds in terms of importance amongst the female staff? 'Tis akin to being a lowly private one day, and a lieutenant general the next, if you think of it in army terms."

"Oh, well that is perfect, Mr Darcy. She shall be my lieutenant. I like the sound of that very much."

"You might hire a proper lady's maid you know."

"What would I do with such a creature? Rose will suit me admirably, I think."

He shrugged his shoulders, pressed his heels into his horse's side and cantered away.

When she had woken that morning, Elizabeth had felt almost normal, as if she had slept her cold off, but by the time they reached their destination, she began to shake and shiver again and had never been so glad to quit her mount. She only wanted to sit and recover, but supposed she would not get any peace until she appeased Mr Darcy by standing in awe of the view they had come so far to see, if only for a few moments. So she climbed the tor, looked out and although now felt very bad indeed, was able to admire it. The rough, rugged landscape of Derbyshire was laid out before her for miles ahead and it was a beautiful scene. She was the first to turn away though and her heavy legs stumbled down towards the picnic spot where she almost fell upon the rug.

The refreshments did something to revive her, though she was quieter than usual, and let the conversation flow over her head, but her attention was required when Georgiana began to speak directly to her. "We are right in the middle of the country now, Elizabeth. You could not be further from either coast. You must take Elizabeth to the coast one day, brother, when you return, for she has still never seen the sea."

Mr Darcy got to his feet and wandered away and Elizabeth wrinkled her nose in disgust at his rudeness. She

231

had no illusions or hopes as to his ever taking her anywhere, let alone on a trip that would give her so much pleasure, but he might have at least given Georgiana a polite reply.

The colonel smiled too brightly, "and Darcy will soon see far more of the sea than he could ever have hoped for. I confess after my last voyage home, I have no longing to go aboard a ship, or near any vast expanse of water, for a good long time."

"I am guessing you were always bound for the army, Colonel?" asked Miss Temple. "The navy would not have suited you then?"

"You assume correctly. All that salty air and strong wind, it cuts a man's youth and vigour most horribly; a sailor grows old sooner than any other man," the colonel said jovially and patted his cheeks. "I am plain enough looking as it is - a sea-faring life would have been the death of all my romantic hopes - imagine me all knocked about and exposed to every climate. I would not be fit to be seen. Dreadful profession, I can't think why any man would choose it, lest he was a complete fool."

Silence reigned and the smile fell from the colonel's face as he looked about in confusion at the pained expressions of the three ladies.

Elizabeth spoke, hardly knowing what she said, something about both the navy and army having everything in its favour. "Heroism, travel, bustle, fashion, soldiers and sailors would always be acceptable to me; nobody can wonder that men chose to be soldiers and sailors."

Miss Temple rushed away as Elizabeth was still speaking, but in a different direction to the one Mr Darcy had taken.

"Miss Temple was once betrothed to a young man of the navy who died at sea," Elizabeth explained to the colonel.

His face crumpled and she saw he might have cursed himself had she and Georgiana not been present. "Shall I go after her, do you think? Is it my business to? Should I apologise?"

"She is the sweetest soul in the world, Colonel, and will not be cross with you," Elizabeth told him, "but I do always think there is everything to be gained, and never anything to be lost, by the issuing of a genuine apology."

He got very slowly to his feet and limped away.

Neither he or Miss Temple came back for quite a while. For so long, in fact, that Elizabeth began to wonder whether all was well and was concerned something had happened to them. Mr Darcy returned in the meantime and kicked at the dirt for a time and then began to speak of returning home. Elizabeth observed that he was a man who lacked the ability to be idle. He could not sit in the same position for long. His mind was constantly active, always wondering what to do next. She felt weary just watching him.

The servants packed up and made them ready for the off. When Miss Temple and the colonel did appear, the colonel gallantly handed the governess into the carriage and then looked around at Elizabeth. "Why do you not ride back in the carriage too? You look dreadfully pale; I believe you are sickening for something."

"Stop fussing, Richard. She's a country girl, very hardy. You'll come and ride alongside me, Elizabeth, there are some views I would point out to you," Mr Darcy said.

The colonel looked at her as if he were waiting for her to protest. Why she didn't, she could not actually say, but she supposed she just wanted to get back to Pemberley as quickly as possible, where she might ring for a mug of chocolate, find a shawl and doze in the library. Robert helped her into the saddle and they set off. It was just the three of them and two grooms trailing behind. Georgiana, having been allowed the luxury of choice, had opted for the carriage for the journey back.

She and Mr Darcy rode mostly in silence, side-by-side, for long stretches at a time, the colonel going on ahead. Mr Darcy would point something out occasionally and she would take notice of it and nod her head, but she had not the energy to answer him. He looked crosser with each passing minute and with each mile she grew more fatigued and light headed.

The colonel came back to them after a while and she heard him speak to Mr Darcy, it was something about stopping, letting the carriage catch them up. Her name was mentioned and then there was the sound of Mr Darcy's baritone, shouting to her. "Have control over the reins, Elizabeth, that horse may take you anywhere it pleases," and then there was nothing, it was all darkness.

Twenty nine

Darcy heard a succession of noises - his own voice berating
her, a rustle and thumping sound from the surrounding woods
as a deer ran quickly through - then her horse; the mare he
had chosen specifically for its calm nature, startled a little,
snorted and shuffled in alarm. It was a common enough
occurrence. If she had been alert and had had a tighter grip of
the reins, she would have easily managed to calm the animal.
But her eyes were closed, her head down, and the movement
caught her unawares. She fell, sliding slowly from the saddle,
her left leg catching around the pommel, which tipped her
almost completely upside down, before gravity did its worst
and pulled her quickly to the earth, head first.

He looked away in horror, unable to watch the
moment of impact on the hard ground and unable to do
anything to save her. There was no one near enough to
prevent it. The loud cracking sound, which he was sure was
her skull breaking in two, sent him cold and sick to his
stomach. He heard his cousin shout something, but knew not
what it was, he was too busy jumping from his horse and
running to her. The groom, Robert, had been riding the
closest to Elizabeth and was bending down over her when
Darcy arrived.

"Get your hands away from her, you forget yourself
boy," Darcy bellowed at him. The groom rocked back on his
heels and withdrew the hand he had been about to put behind
Elizabeth's head. If the boy hadn't retreated quickly back,
Darcy might have shoved him away such was the high state
of his temper, brought on by the sheer panic that coursed
through him. She was so still and lay at such an awkward
angle. His immediate thought was that she was already dead.
He knelt beside her. There was no blood, no visible bruise,
but her eyes were closed and she breathed not, her face was
like death. He gasped and choked and then she made a
similar noise. He feared it was a death rattle, but then he saw
her take another breath, shallower, and then another, and
another.

He called up to his cousin, who must have felt quite useless stuck atop his horse, unable to dismount without assistance. "She is not conscious but breathing, thank God."

"How shall I help?"

"Go back and direct the carriage here." Colonel Fitzwilliam nodded and was gone as soon as the order was received. "And you, boy." He turned briefly to Robert. "You will ride to Lambton and fetch a surgeon to Pemberley. Tell him of the accident, stress the urgency."

Robert went quickly too. Darcy sat on the dirt and gently lifted her head so he might slide his leg underneath to act as a cushion. When she was settled so, he made her as comfortable as he knew how, by removing her bonnet and brushing her hair, now tangled and loose, back from her face. He sat and waited and was lost as to what to do other than to offer up his silent prayers and a litany of apologies. "I am sorry, I am sorry," he mumbled over and over, until the wheels of the carriage could be heard in the distance.

Darcy noted, upon the door of the carriage being thrown open, that Georgiana's face was as pale as Elizabeth's. She said not a word, seemingly struck dumb. Darcy carried Elizabeth himself, but required some help from a footman and the wincing Colonel Fitzwilliam before they were settled on the bench, in much the same position as they had been on the ground. Her head across the top of his thigh, his arms cradling her shoulders to keep her steady as the carriage lurched forward.

"What happened?" Miss Temple asked.

Darcy shook his head, unable to say, unable to relive it. "It is my fault," was all he could manage.

"Rub her temples, rub her hands. I wish I had some salts," Miss Temple said.

Though it seemed like an eon to Darcy, they reached Pemberley within twenty minutes and Mrs Reynolds came running out to meet them, asking what was required. Darcy only barked at her that the doctor was on his way as he got out of the carriage and lifted Elizabeth into his arms again, steadying himself for the journey up the stairs.

"Will I help, sir?" asked a footman.

"No, no. She weighs barely nothing. I'll carry her myself." He took the stairs two at a time, with a trail of people behind him. A quietly sobbing, Georgiana, a comforting Miss Temple and Mrs Reynolds directing maids to bring things. Darcy concentrated only on the small form in his arms. Still, she had not opened her eyes. Coming to a stop at a chamber door, he directed Mrs Reynolds to open it and wondered briefly if his tone had been too harsh, for the look she gave him was one of incredulity. She turned the handle nonetheless and once inside the room, the housekeeper pulled back the covers on the bed, allowing Darcy to put Elizabeth down as gently as he could. He was loathed to let go of her. He had been cradling her for so long that he feared putting her down might signal a change in her condition, that she might suddenly stop breathing.

"Where is the damn surgeon?" he yelled, forgetting the other ladies present. "Forgive me, Georgiana, Miss Temple."

"That is quite alright, Mr Darcy, very understandable, given the circumstances. Georgiana and I will go downstairs and wait for news." Miss Temple ushered his sister out of the room.

Darcy paced for a while until towels, water, cold compresses and salts arrived. A maid, the one Elizabeth had singled out to attend her earlier in the day, now attired correctly and looking less like she belonged in the kitchen, arrived with a nightgown and seeing they meant to change her and make her more comfortable, he excused himself from the room and went down to the hall to await the doctor. He was announced at the door by Hodges just as Darcy reached the bottom step and after showing him the way, Darcy went to the library, where Colonel Fitzwilliam stood over a tray of drink decanters.

"I know you hardly touch it these days, but does a little brandy take your fancy?"

Darcy nodded grimly, accepted a glass and sank into a chair.

"God, that was awful," the colonel said needlessly. "And I, stuck so uselessly atop my horse, unable to be of help."

"Nonsense, you were of great assistance in hastening the carriage there."

"How is she now?"

"The same, she has not opened her eyes." Darcy ran his hands over his face, unable to dampen down his worst fears. "If she lives, she will not be the same."

"Don't say such a thing? Let us hear the surgeon's opinion first." Richard swallowed the liquid that was in his own glass whole, before coming over to sit opposite Darcy.

"I ought to have listened to you, Richard. You said to let her ride in the carriage."

"Come now, Darcy. What's done is done. But, I do wonder…did you not see how tired she was?"

Darcy drank too, throwing the entire contents of the glass to the back of his throat as his cousin had just done. "I wanted her to ride with me, to speak to me, as she does you. She is all ease and friendliness, when she is with you, or that groom."

"Look here, Darcy. I hope you do not think I flirt with her. I do not think of her as anything but a cousin, and your wife."

"I know, I have never doubted you, but she likes you, as a friend. She speaks to you in a way she does not to me. I thought if we rode together, if it was a pastime we could share, it might be easier for us to get along, when I return from the Indies, do you see?"

"And to encourage some felicity you decided she should pursue an activity she detests? You did this in order to make her like you?"

Smarting from his cousin's well deserved reproof, Darcy jumped to his feet and began to pace. "I've a good mind to get rid of that groom?"

"Good God, Darcy, how is it his fault? What will you do then, shoot the mare?"

"I do not like him; he is over familiar. Go and see what the surgeon says, will you, Richard? I cannot bear to go in there again."

His cousin let out a heavy sigh and got to his feet, ambling off. When he had been gone for a while, with no word brought back, Darcy went into the hall, where the butler was shooing out Robert, the groom. "What is it?" he enquired.

Hodges bowed. "The groom was just enquiring as to the welfare of Mrs Darcy."

Robert pulled his cap from his head and threaded it through his hands. "I hope she will recover, sir. I was never so scared in my life."

"You will come to my study, Robert. I have something I wish to say to you."

It was above an hour, and Darcy had well finished his interview with the groom and returned to the library before Colonel Fitzwilliam appeared again.

"And so," Darcy asked him, a little breathless, "what is the news?"

"The surgeon says she has a cold."

"What?" Darcy asked, unable to comprehend.

"A very bad cold and a fever. He believes she fainted when the horse startled, then fell and dislocated her collarbone."

"But, she hit her head, I heard it; t'was the most sickening noise."

"Yes, I thought so too, but it seems her shoulder took the brunt of it. She has a small graze on her temple that'll heal itself, a collarbone that needs putting back in place and a couple of days in bed to get over the fever and the shock, then she'll be as right as rain."

The relief was great, but Darcy couldn't quite believe she had gotten off so lightly. He could not believe *he* had been given such an absolution. He had not taken care of her. His father's last letter to him, written in the last year and left with his attorney, as if he knew he had not long left, had been full of instructions and guidance, and near the end, one line he had paid little heed to, *'take care of Elizabeth, take care of your wife'*. How miserably he had failed in that.

"Is it certain she will be well?"

"He expects a complete recovery. She begins to come round a little, go up and see her, take Georgiana."

Darcy climbed the stairs with Georgiana's hand tightly in his own and they went into the room where he had put her down, which was quiet, but had not the same feeling of desperation occupying it as when he had left. Releasing Georgiana, he took a chair next to the bed. Elizabeth's head rested on a pile of pillows. She looked fragile, and as white as the sheets around her. If it were not for her chestnut curls, she might have disappeared altogether.

Her eyes flickered open and she looked at him for a second, and then at Georgiana, and then her gaze met his again.

"I thought you were dead," Darcy said, a bit bluntly, but he had little control over his emotions as yet. It was all still so raw.

"No, I think I am very much alive," she replied, licking her lips. "Are you terribly disappointed?"

He laughed despite himself. "On the contrary, I am very pleased."

"Where am I?"

Georgiana let out a little gasp. "She has lost her memory!"

Elizabeth smiled weakly. "I have been letting her read too many novels, Mr Darcy. I know who you are, Georgiana, and that I am at Pemberley, but this is not my room."

Darcy looked around him, no it was not her room. He had put her in his mother's room, though now unused for over ten years, he had done so without thinking. He had put her in the mistress's chambers. No wonder Mrs Reynolds had looked at him so oddly when he had asked her to open the door.

"It is huge," Elizabeth said, looking about her in wonder, "and so many windows! I imagine it has a lovely view."

"The best of views, but the décor is perhaps a little dated. 'Tis' the mistress's chambers, yours now, I suppose, whenever you should like them."

She raised a small eyebrow at him and looked as if she might say more on the subject but was interrupted by Georgiana throwing her arms about her and kissing her. Elizabeth winced and cried out.

Darcy looked to the surgeon, who told Elizabeth of the injury to her shoulder and the need to 'pop it back'. She nodded grimly and once Georgiana had left again, Darcy held out his hand. "Should you wish to hold onto something." She did, gripping him tightly and looked down at their joined hands, while the surgeon crept into place on the other side of her. "Richard has passed on some good army expletives to me, these past few years. I might tell you one to use if you would like. I would be willing to overlook a lapse in ladylike behaviour, given the circumstances."

"That's very good of you, Mr Darcy, but I shall manage without. Unfortunately, this is not the first time this particular shoulder has required putting back, so I am aware of what to expect. I fell out of an apple tree two years ago."

"Why does that not surprise me?"

The surgeon moved quickly and while she was still smiling wryly at his reply, there was a crunch and it was done. She let go of his hand, one loud cry escaped her and she fell deeper into the pillows with her good arm over her eyes, breathing hard, beads of perspiration gathering on her brow.

"I'll give her a little something to help her sleep, Mr Darcy."

Nodding at the surgeon, Darcy got to his feet. "I shall come back later, Elizabeth."

Her arm was still over her face, all he could see of her was her mouth, which was set into a thin line. No, he had not taken care of her at all, at this, he must do better.

Thirty

Mr Darcy may have come back to her room some time later that day, but Elizabeth really could not remember; her mind had been so addled with fever and some foul tasting concoction the surgeon had given her, that for the next two days, she woke for only brief intervals, feeling dreadful, her body aching all over and her head pounding. Sleep was too much like a comforting embrace for her to leave it for long.

She did recover though, her periods of wakefulness lasting longer each day, and then she welcomed visitors, though soon realised they had been given instructions to not tire her and to keep their attendance brief. Georgiana came regularly, to read to her and tell her of her studies and the goings on in the house - of how worried everybody had been - but after fifteen minutes or so, she would declare she had to be going and jump off her chair to depart. Mr Darcy, she learned as soon as she was well enough to enquire, had gone to Matlock on some business. She couldn't help but feel dejected at this news. He had seemed so worried for her, immediately after her accident. He had held her hand and teased her with a gentleness and humour she had hitherto not thought him capable of. She wanted to see him, and it was an odd craving. Even if he were only to come to her room for five minutes to frown his disdain for something or other she had done, she would have welcomed his presence. Perhaps she was just bored and lonely and sought different company, but for whatever reason, she wished he had not gone away, and then she learned that even when he did return, he would soon be setting off for the Indies - in a little over a week!

A whole year he would be gone, another year complete, when she would inhabit the same sort of odd existence she had done when he had been in Scotland. Married, but with no husband; the lady of the house but certainly not fit to be its mistress, a half of a life, awaiting the return of a man who did not want her. She was still in the vast mistress's chambers, though she had ventured forth on the topic of returning to her own room, no one seemed to want to move her yet. Her shoulder ached and she still felt a little fatigued, though remaining in bed, where all manner of melancholic thoughts grew louder and stronger in her mind, was eventually unbearable, so she rang the bell beside her and summoned Rose.

Mr Darcy's first words to her, when he arrived back unexpectedly after dinner to find her in the drawing room, were not exultations of joy on seeing her so well recovered, but, *'what are you doing out of bed?'* He came to sit by her on the sofa, where she was occupied with a book. "I left very specific instructions regarding your care before I went, who allowed you up?" he asked.

"Nobody allowed me, I just got up. I am quite well again, you see." She waved her injured arm briefly to show him. She smiled, but then said quietly, under the hearing of the others, "I did not know you had gone away, or when you were to be back." She was unable to help the hint of admonishment that crept into her tone.

After being quiet for a moment, he shrugged his shoulders. "I am still not used to having to consult the feelings of anyone other than myself before I set about my business."

"It is not my feelings you hurt," she told him, "but you tell me nothing. Why have you been at Matlock?"

She thought for a long while he would not answer, or would just tell her it was his business and no one else's, but he did speak, eventually. "I leave for the Indies on Friday and I wished to bid farewell to Lord and Lady Matlock and advise the countess of what steps should be taken if something were to happen to me."

"Don't say such a thing! Nothing will happen to you," she cried, aghast.

"Elizabeth, you asked to know why I went and now I tell you, you act like a child, covering your ears and refusing to accept the possibility. When you fell from your horse it brought home to me how fragile everything is, how we all hang on to life by the slimmest of edges. No matter how careful we are, sometimes, everything is chance. Would you

243

have me leave you or Georgiana unprotected and your future uncertain? It is a long time until you are one and twenty, until you might live on your own. Should anything befall me, all is now arranged."

Looking at her book, rather than at him, she wondered exactly what arrangements he had made for her protection, but as her mind stubbornly refused to accept that anything terrible would happen to him and that he would return to them in a year's time, as proud and as disagreeable as ever, she did not ask. "Do not go, to the Indies," she said instead.

He looked up at her in wonder. "I must. The Fitzwilliams may find themselves in a great deal of financial difficulty if I do not."

She said no more, *let him go,* she told herself. What difference did it make? He was not a husband. They fought more than they agreed. He always did exactly as he pleased and never sought to include her in his plans. "Well, if you are determined, you shall have your farewell present." She got up and went to a side table, coming back with a small parcel, some squares of muslin tied together with a ribbon of deep blue.

Mr Darcy pulled the ribbon open and inspected the handkerchiefs with a broad smile; one that reached his eyes and showed a deep dimple to the left of his mouth.

"I am sure they are quite terrible. You probably possess some very fine handkerchiefs. You needn't use them."

He examined them carefully, taking his time, before folding them back up and tying the ribbon around them, putting them into his coat pocket. "I shall indeed use them. I shall treasure them always." He gave her an intent look which made her colour and look away, only to see that Miss Temple had been watching them with a soft smile. This made her blush more and she would have walked away if Mr Darcy had not spoken again.

"I should not have insisted on you riding, Elizabeth, I feel entirely responsible for your fall."

"But I am well, it is all forgot."

"It is good of you to say so, but you might give it up now, I am sure you will want to, and I will not force you again."

"Give it up! Oh no, I have no intention of doing so."

"You don't? You were not confident to begin with and after this incident, I would have thought you would never want to ride again."

"I am very determined to get back on my horse again, Mr Darcy. I do not blame the animal at all. She did not throw me, I fell. In fact, I shall ride out every day, depending on the weather. I have to admit, that after the first few times, and once I gained a little confidence, I did begin to enjoy it. If I might always have the same groom and the same horse, I should do very well, I think."

She had been standing over him whilst speaking, but now he got to his feet, shuffled them somewhat, straightened his clothing and cleared his throat before speaking. "I will appoint you a new groom. Robert has been dismissed, he is no longer in employment at Pemberley."

Elizabeth wanted to shout, to rage at him, but aware they were not alone and remembering other occasions when her temper had caused her to make an indecorous display of herself, she tempered her response. "May I ask why? You do not blame him for what happened to me?"

"Not at all, he was just not suitable."

"Not suitable! In what way?"

"Elizabeth, the decision was mine to make. It is done and I shall not be questioned about it."

Miss Temple diplomatically interrupted them by taking Georgiana upstairs, and the colonel excused himself too, saying he would take a stroll in the evening air, while there was still a little light outside.

When Richard was gone, Mr Darcy began to make excuses too, stating he would go to his study. She whirled around. "Do not dare. Do not dare go and hide from me."

His temper flared. "I do not take orders from you, madam."

"Why would you dismiss him, when he was of such great assistance to me? It is unjust and ungenerous of you.

I'm sure I would not have gotten on so well riding if it had not been for his encouragement. And he has a family, a mother and sisters that rely on his salary here."

"I gave him more than enough money for his trouble, and an excellent reference, he will soon find another position."

"But why could he not remain here? I liked him."

"Oh I am very aware that you liked him," he said.

"I am not allowed to be attended by someone agreeable to me?"

"I indulged you regarding the scullery maid, did I not?"

"Indulged me! You are so pompous and overbearing. He was *my* groom," cried Elizabeth, with energy.

"He was not *your* groom," Mr Darcy replied angrily, before seeming to get better control over himself. "The matter is closed and I shall speak no further on it."

"Well, I say it is not closed. I demand a proper explanation."

"I am the master of this house," he shouted. His deep booming voice reverberated off the walls and made the glasses on a nearby tray shake. His complexion became pale and the disturbance of his mind was visible in every feature. His fists were clenching and unclenching repeatedly as they hung at his sides.

They stared at each other for some time, Elizabeth wondering whether she dared to speak again, before he offered a slight bow. "Forgive me, forgive my shouting at you. This discussion is concluded. Good evening." And with these words he hastily left the room, leaving her open mouthed and reeling. Suddenly the bruises she had sustained in her fall began to hurt again.

Thirty one

Friday came, as it always did, fast on the heels of Thursday. This one though, found Darcy in a state of waiting and uncertainty. He had arranged to leave at ten, but had been up since six, walking the house, assuring himself that everything he might do to ensure things would run smoothly in his absence had been done. He had spoken at length to Georgiana, to Miss Temple, the colonel, Mrs Reynolds and his stewards. He had attempted to speak further to Elizabeth but her countenance whenever he approached always deterred him from his purpose. She looked very much as though she hated him, and he was so ashamed at having lost his temper with her so very badly that it seemed easier not to try and push past her displeasure. He was leaving most of his affairs in a state of some satisfaction, but not his dealings with Elizabeth. He went over to the bureau in his room and picked up the bundle of handkerchiefs she had given him. Untying the ribbon, he selected one from the pile. It bore a haphazard design of colourful stitches that he was sure must be some sort of representation of wildflowers and then in the corner, in a turn of actual quite clear and fine needlework, his initials. He slipped it into his pocket and threw the rest of them on the bed.

His valet was putting a strap around the last of his baggage, a smaller travelling trunk that would stay with him. "You have not packed these," Darcy said, pointing to the handkerchiefs. He took a last look around the room he had grown up in. When he returned from the Indies he would take up the master's chambers and the thought made his heart heavy. His father would not be present for his leave taking, nor would he be there to welcome him back again after a twelve-month. Such was his preoccupation that he did not pay any attention to the valet, who picked up the handkerchiefs, looked at the trunk he had spent the last fifteen minutes or so struggling to fasten, and then discarded them, reasoning that opening the trunk again would make them late, and knowing Mr Darcy despised tardiness, and that he already had much finer linen on him than these scrappy pieces, he tossed them carelessly onto the bedside table.

Darcy left his room and shook Colonel Fitzwilliam's hand at the bottom of the stairs.

"I shall say my farewell here," Richard said. "Georgiana is outside to wave you off. God speed."

"Thank you." Darcy let go of the colonel's hand and made his way outside, nodding to some of the staff who had gathered. Once in front of the carriage, he kissed Georgiana and was attempting some words of reassurance, when Elizabeth approached. The servants parted the way for her at the door and she stepped out, moving swiftly towards him, with her head held high and a shawl around her. Her look was inscrutable and he was, for a moment, concerned she was about to say something terrible, to send him off in no doubt of her hatred for him. He denied her the opportunity, however. When she was close enough, his arm shot out seemingly of its own accord and his hand went around her neck, crushing her curls to her skin, holding her tight. Then he pulled her towards him and put his lips to her forehead, lingering for longer than he meant to, breathing in the scent of her hair and skin. They neither of them spoke. Georgiana gasped. When he released Elizabeth, she turned immediately to go back to the house and so he was spared the sight of her face, no doubt full of disgust at being manhandled so.

To a person oblivious to their situation, feelings or recent history, it might have looked like a desperate, reluctant, even a passionate farewell. The only sort of kiss a husband could give a wife in front of his house, servants and family. He did not know why he had bestowed it, perhaps because words had become too painful; words often led them to anger and he wanted none of that today. Taking one last glance up at the house, and giving his sister one last adieu, he clambered into the chaise.

Elizabeth stood in the vast hall at the bottom of the stairs, the sounds of the servants boots echoing around her as they came in from outside, their low murmurs reaching her ears but not really attended to. She listened instead to the noise of the carriage wheels on the road as they grew fainter and fainter, until they could not be heard at all. *He was gone then.* Colonel Fitzwilliam was stood at the door to the large study that had been George Darcy's, then very briefly had become Mr Darcy's, and was now to be temporarily occupied by him. He was looking at her carefully, a book in his hand.

"You see, I went outside, like you said I ought to," she told him.

"Take heart," he replied. "He will be back. A year will go quickly."

"I do not care. Let him never come back. What can it matter to me?" She ran up the stairs and away from them all, but it seemed everywhere she went there was someone. Georgiana had come in and was headed for the music room, Miss Temple was bustling between the schoolroom and the library with arms full of books. When she went to her own room, Rose Kiddy was busy sorting through her clothes to decide which ones needed mending. Maids were everywhere, cleaning and chattering, so she kept walking, thinking of the old deserted schoolroom she had once commandeered as her own and wondering if it would be too chilly to sit there now. She had not felt the need to hide herself away for so long, but now she sought calm and peace and who would have thought it would be so difficult to find, in a house the size of Pemberley. She turned towards the old schoolroom, then changed her mind and decided to go downstairs. She would go down and write a letter - to anyone, but her spirits were in such a tumult, she knew not what to do and doubted she had the patience required to sit and write. She walked listlessly for a good while around the first floor, before stopping beside an open chamber door, Mr Darcy's room, but now empty. She stepped inside, curiosity getting the better of her, as she had never seen inside it. It was distinctly masculine and still smelt slightly of him, but it was a pleasant aroma and she stood looking around, thinking that surely it could not be an invasion of his privacy when he had quit it and was going to be gone for such a long while.

She looked at the wall hangings and wandered over to the windows. On his bureau were a pair of worn out riding gloves, with holes appearing at the tips of the fingers, discarded, obviously not considered necessary for his trip and probably too threadbare now to be useful for any purpose. She picked them up, opened a drawer and threw them in, before her eyes fell on the bundle of handkerchiefs, knowing what they were immediately by the blue bow she had tied around them. "You shall treasure them always, will you, Mr Darcy?" she said, her voice loud in the otherwise vacant room. Snatching them up, she took them downstairs and went to the library, where there was always a fire. Without hesitation, she threw the handkerchiefs on it. Miss Temple was in the room and heard the hiss and spit as they caught light and came over to stand beside her. She did not ask what Elizabeth had burned, perhaps it was not her place to, or perhaps she knew. For the blue silk ribbon was the last thing to catch light. Suddenly, Elizabeth knew not how to support herself, and from actual weakness sat down and cried for half-an-hour, while Miss Temple said nothing and held her close.

"I was wrong," Elizabeth said between sobs. "I think I do need a governess after all."

Volume Three: Eighteen

Thirty two

"My felicitations, congratulations, very best wishes and many happy returns of the day."

Elizabeth laughed at the colonel's enthusiastic greeting when she entered the breakfast room at Pemberley. Georgiana and Lady Matlock also wished her a happy birthday, and she smiled in response, but try as she might, could not summon up any feelings of genuine pleasure; though her mood did lighten when Hodges brought her letters in. Both Jane and her Aunt Gardiner had written to her, obviously having taken the trouble to try and arrange for her to receive their notes on this very day.

Georgiana presented her with a very fine shawl and Lady Fitzwilliam surprised her with a book of verse she had once expressed an interest in reading. Though deeply touched by their thoughtfulness, she could not rouse herself out of the flat, serious mood she had woken in. The colonel pushed a small, rectangular velvet box along the table in her direction, "and this is from Darcy."

She could not hide her incredulity, "truly?"

"Of course," the colonel replied, but Elizabeth saw how he would not meet her eye. "He wrote and asked for it to be bought on his behalf. He told me exactly what he wanted to get you."

"Open it, Elizabeth. I want to see what it is," Georgiana said, leaning over the table and almost out of her chair in excitement, before being told to sit up properly by Miss Temple.

Elizabeth prised open the box to find a very sweet bracelet, made of gold, with pretty links in the shapes of birds and flowers. A lovely gift and so obviously chosen by the colonel that the sight of it overcame her and she blinked back tears.

She said nothing, however, until Georgiana had gone, and it was just she and the colonel left in the room, lingering over their respective cups of coffee and tea. Then she pushed the box containing the bracelet back towards him.

"I know it is not from *him*, and you should not be so extravagant with me. Please take it back."

He raised his eyes to the ceiling and although looked a little ashamed of his deception, even still did he try to convince her of it being Mr Darcy's gift.

Elizabeth would have none of it. "Colonel, you are too kind. I never met a kinder man. Why you are not married. Why there are not six thousand women violently in love with you and pressing against the gates of Pemberley demanding access to your fine person, I cannot fathom. But Mr Darcy has never yet acknowledged the anniversary of my birth. I can hardly credit that he would do so now. Please take it back. I know you acted with generosity and from the goodness of your heart, but I would hope that we are good friends now, and friends do not lie to one another."

The colonel looked reluctant, but took the box from the table and put it into his pocket, just as Lady Fitzwilliam wandered back into the room.

"We are to have a very good dinner tonight, Elizabeth, in your honour. I have just left instructions with Mrs Reynolds, and I have sent a note to your friends at the parsonage to ask them to join us."

"Thank you, Lady Fitzwilliam, but if you'll excuse me now, I'd like to read my letters. I shall take them out into the park."

Lady Fitzwilliam watched Elizabeth go before turning back to her son. "She is dreadfully low, she smiles, but it does not reach those lovely eyes."

The colonel nodded but said nothing.

"Shall we attempt a little walk too, my boy? We should do well enough, with two good legs and two sticks between us."

They went slowly out and walked the length of the terrace. Elizabeth was in the distance, sitting under the branches of a tree in the park, her letters in her hand. "Does Darcy ever write to her?" Lady Fitzwilliam asked.

The colonel shook his head. "I have never seen a single piece of correspondence pass between them. I am not sure a letter from him would be well received in any case. She might treasure it, or she might rip it into a thousand pieces, who knows?"

"She seems very angry with him? For something that happened while he was here, or because he stays away?"

"Both, I should imagine, and she is simply bored, mother, and dreadfully lonely. I have once or twice tried to arrange for her elder sister, Jane, to visit, but it has never been possible. The Gardiners have been away, or not able to bring her, and I've not been able to go to Town when it might have been convenient. She has no close friends here; to the ladies of Lambton or Kimpton, she is Mrs Darcy and a great unapproachable lady, though it is far from the truth."

"What of the party from the parsonage, those who you had me invite to dinner tonight?"

"The parson is called Mr Smythe and he is very pleasant, newly married and his wife, again, is pleasant, but she is six and twenty to Elizabeth's eighteen. She is full of home-making and dreams of children. She has not Elizabeth's intelligence or liveliness. They get along well enough, but I hold out no hopes for a close companionship. The Smythe's have a niece visiting soon, who may be better suited, we shall see."

"What is Darcy about, staying on so long in the Indies when Walter has been home above three months now? Surely his business is concluded?" the countess asked.

"I know not. His letters to me are full of instructions and vague references to opportunities. I can only believe he simply does not *want* to come home."

"I am exceedingly angry with him. He shirks his responsibilities. I ought to write to him myself."

"Well, if a direction from you does not bring him back, nothing will."

The countess let go of her son's sleeve and turned to face him. "I have another concern. In fact, it is one that was brought to me yesterday by Miss Temple. She was very embarrassed to have to speak of it, but I suppose she felt so strongly she could no longer remain silent; such a steady, thoughtful, kind lady."

The colonel smiled. "Isn't she? I am glad you like her, mother. She has some very fine qualities in my opinion."

Eyeing him steadily the countess continued. "Yes, very fine, she is an excellent governess, but we would *all* do well to remember that's exactly what she is - *a governess* - she has been here so long there might be a tendency to treat her with more familiarity than is possibly wise, but never mind that for now, what she brought to my attention yesterday was the issue of clothes."

A small frown creased the colonel's face. "I do not follow. There is a problem with Miss Temple's clothes?"

"No, none, only that they are a good deal finer than her employer's. She very delicately suggested that Elizabeth's skirts are too short, and she is right. Please tell me she is not still wearing the same gowns she came here with? When did she last have anything new?"

The colonel laughed. "You are asking me, what do I know of female finery?"

"She has no finery, that is the problem. Mrs Darcy should look like *Mrs Darcy*, and that is something which can only be achieved with a trip to London."

"Not possible I'm afraid. You know very well how Darcy feels on this issue. He does not want Elizabeth to go to London."

"Does he expect his wife to wear rags?" Lady Fitzwilliam protested. "Oh come now, you said yourself how dull she is, such a trip would be just the thing to restore her spirits."

"He has entrusted me with her care, I don't think I should go directly against his wishes. If something were to happen to her in London…"

"Oh, blame me if it does," his mother interrupted, waving away his concerns. "He could not rage against an old crippled woman for long."

The colonel laughed and stopped walking, considering for a while, before banging his stick on the ground. "Oh hang him! You are right, let's take her, and let's go soon."

Elizabeth, who was coming up from the lawn with her letters folded up in her hands, was beckoned over by the countess.

"Elizabeth, we are to go to London."

"Oh, when do you leave? Might you take a parcel for me?"

"You might take it yourself, for you will be going too, on a matter of vital importance. You require new gowns."

Elizabeth's smile was wary, as if not quite believing the truth of the intelligence. "New gowns are of vital importance?"

"Quite so, along with hats, gloves, boots, nightgowns and a great many other things; the requisition of such items are indubitably necessary for a young lady whose income is as fine as her figure."

The colonel gave a polite cough to interrupt his mother. "If there is to be talk of figures and nightgowns, ladies, I shall depart before you have me blushing," he bowed slightly and left them.

Elizabeth offered the countess her arm to lean on as they made their own way back into the house at a slower pace, falling deliberately behind the colonel. "Am I really to go? You would not tease me?" she asked. When the countess assured her it was so, she frowned. "Do you think Mr Darcy would approve?"

"Perhaps we ought to ask him," Lady Fitzwilliam made a great show of looking around her. "Oh, but it seems he is not here, so we cannot. Well I for one am quite happy to assume his compliance, given the desperate circumstances we find ourselves in. I feel certain he would not only give his agreement, but also urge us to spend a great deal of his money."

"Desperate circumstances, Lady Fitzwilliam?"

"Very desperate, Elizabeth, you have grown in height, and in other ways too." Lady Fitzwilliam nodded towards her bust. "Do not bend down too far in front of the poor parson tonight, my dear, your gowns are struggling to contain you."

The colonel had departed for fear of blushing, but no embarrassment he might have suffered could match the deep crimson colour that overtook Elizabeth's cheeks upon receiving Lady Fitzwilliam's remark, and its accompanying sly smile. They walked into the house with Elizabeth very consciously tugging up the neckline of her dress.

Thirty three

Less than three weeks later, and with a sense of disbelief that such a thing was really happening, Elizabeth found herself in one of two carriages pulling away from Matlock, leaving the north behind and heading south for London. The journey would take three days. Such long hours confined to a carriage were bound to be arduous, but what pleasures were awaiting her at their destination! Lady Fitzwilliam was opening her own house in Mayfair but Elizabeth had been allowed to make up her own mind as to where she would stay, and that would be in Gracechurch Street, with Jane. To add to her joy, after she had completed her shopping in London, she and Jane were to travel into Hertfordshire together and visit their mother and sisters for some weeks, before she was eventually obliged to return to Pemberley. She was quietly overflowing with happiness but had been forced to temper her enthusiasm during her farewells to a cross, sulking Georgiana, who had been left at Matlock under the care of Miss Temple, Beatrice and Walter.

The colonel, sitting across from her, was still shaking his head, for he had lately been the unfortunate recipient of most of Georgiana's ill temper. "Whatever ails her?"

"It is nothing more than a mild case of being fourteen. She wanted to come with us, she does not like being left behind," Elizabeth told him.

"Well, I am left in no doubt that we do the right thing in leaving her behind, and I beg you not to feel any guilt about it. This is your trip, for you to spend time with your family, you should not spend it supervising Georgiana, and nor am I in the mood to watch over her at present. I think I require some time away from Pemberley as much as you do."

Time away from Pemberley? Yes, Elizabeth most certainly did require that, and time apart from Georgiana too, for while she loved her little sister by marriage dearly, and felt the deepest sympathy for her, she had most definitely reached a trying age. Georgiana could be ecstatically happy one moment and in floods of tears the next and the unpredictability of her moods made her difficult company.

Elizabeth understood the girl's tumultuous feelings – she was not so distant from fourteen as to forget the torture of it - and what the colonel did not know and what Elizabeth would not dream of sharing with him - was that the girl had just begun her courses. To add to the usual confusion this right-of-passage brought upon a girl, Georgiana suffered from terrible pains and her complexion had deteriorated. She was a tall broad, strong girl, very much in frame like her brother, which made her especially self-conscious. She had gone from being somewhat introverted, to cripplingly shy, within the space of a few months. If a boy, or heavens forbid a fully grown man, be him married or single, looked at her after Sunday services, even if they only did so out of curiosity, Georgiana would crawl so far behind Elizabeth's cloak or skirts as to try and make herself invisible. She would meet no one in the eye and her voice had become little more than a squeak. Elizabeth, not of a shy nature herself, was at a loss as to how to help her, other than to reassure her about her looks - for despite all this, she was not a plain girl - though she ought to be described as being striking, rather than pretty. Her appearance, together with the Darcy name, meant she drew notice wherever they went and the more notice Georgiana drew, the more she retreated behind her companions.

Elizabeth had briefly ruminated on the idea of taking Georgiana to London, and then to Hertfordshire with her, thereby forcing her into company with her own noisy, rambunctious family, in the hopes of bringing her sister out of herself. She had been on the verge of applying to the colonel for his agreement to the plan. In the end though, she hadn't, but for an entirely different reason. For when Georgiana was more rational and talkative, she became even more infuriating to Elizabeth; for she would become extremely effusive on the general wonderfulness of her brother. Mr Darcy was, in his younger sister's eyes, some sort of God-like man to be idolised and lauded to the heavens. Perhaps it was because he was the only intimate family Georgiana had left, but the girl was enamoured of him. She refused to see a single fault. He lavished her with presents (something ridiculously expensive would arrive at Pemberley every six months or so) and he would send her the odd letter, but certainly not as many as she sent him. As a brother, he was away more than he was at home, and when he was there, he was distant with Georgiana, and showed no real interest in her other than to note her accomplishments, and decide how marriageable she was making herself. Elizabeth found herself having to hold her tongue, or bite her lip, or sometimes leave the room altogether, to refrain from commenting when faced with a barrage of nonsense about Mr Darcy's supposedly manifest perfections. Elizabeth hoped that some time away would restore and fortify her patience in this regard.

As the miles passed, the colonel became brighter, freer of the weight of his responsibilities. They made good progress, and Elizabeth, fascinated by the places through which their route thither lay - Bakewell, Derby, Birmingham, Kenilworth, Blenheim and Oxford - found the journey more pleasant than she had previously imagined. Her only other memory of such a long trip was the one she had made three years earlier in the opposite direction, and that had been such an altogether surreal experience that she had paid little attention to the delights of the places they had passed through. If she had noticed them at the time, they were all now forgot, and all she passed seemed new and exhilarating.

They went in a grand and extravagant procession; the Fitzwilliam's coach was particularly large and luxurious. Elizabeth had questioned why one of the many Darcy carriages was also required, seeing as the party consisted only of Lady Fitzwilliam, the colonel and herself. Colonel Fitzwilliam had replied that the second carriage was, of course, for her use in Town and in Hertfordshire, which had made her laugh heartily. How odd that she should have risen to such a lofty position; to be travelling in her own carriage, with her own maid, her own footman and John the coachman at the helm of it all, with a whip in one hand, a pistol down the back of his breeches and a knife in his boot.

They would often alter their travelling arrangements when a stop was made, swapping carriages and company as the mood took them. When they neared London, the colonel decided to ride his horse into the city while Elizabeth sat with the countess.

"The earl does not come on this trip?" Elizabeth enquired, noting that they had started to rattle over London cobbles.

"He grows worse by the week, Elizabeth. It matters not to him if he is at Matlock, or Pemberley, or London. Once I was the only person who could bring him back to himself. He always knew me, even if everything else was a mystery, but now, even I am not fixed in his mind."

"It must be very hurtful for you, and so painfully confusing for him."

"I think I would almost prefer an illness of the body to an illness of the mind; something to treat, something palpable that I could see, would be infinitely preferable to this, the vanishing of his memories and senses. He was once so vital, so dashing and handsome, and now I can scarcely give credit to him being the same man I married."

"And you were married very young, like me."

Lady Fitzwilliam nodded. "Not quite as young as you, but yes, I was only seventeen."

"Why so young? Was it truly your choice?"

"It was not so unusual then, we are talking of a different time, forty years ago now; a time when a girl came out at sixteen and was usually betrothed by the end of her first season. The earl spotted me at a ball and approached my parents. They were concerned, but he was an earl and perhaps they feared if they asked for a delay his attention would wander elsewhere, and he would be lost. I was cajoled by my parents, but a girl was expected and encouraged to make the best match she could, and so while frightened, I was also thrilled to have engaged the affections of such a man. I managed to convince myself that I loved him and raised no objections. I do laugh when I think of it now though - a few dances, some stilted conversation in a parlour, one walk through Rotten Row - and I thought I knew enough about him to commit myself for evermore."

"But you have been happily married, haven't you?"

"My dear, after forty years, if the principals are mostly on speaking terms, and can be in the same room for above fifteen minutes together without harbouring dark thoughts and planning the other's demise, then a marriage should be called happy."

Elizabeth smiled. "Well then, I shall call yours an exceedingly happy marriage, for I can tell you love Lord Matlock dearly."

The countess smiled. "You must be very excited to be seeing your sister, Elizabeth. I have heard you talk of her often. Jane, isn't it?" Lady Matlock asked.

"Yes, she was the most goodly creature in the world to me when we were growing up. I can't tell you how much I have longed to see her again, though now I am on the verge of it, I find myself nervous. I fear she will not like me anymore."

Lady Fitzwilliam tutted. "Foolish girl, who could not like you? I was very determined to disapprove of you when Darcy brought you to Matlock, but you have rather eaten away at my disapprobation."

"Or maybe you have just grown used to me. Perhaps I am like an uncomfortable shoe you have finally worn in."

"You are an odd fit, that's for sure," Lady Matlock said as the carriage pulled around the corner into Gracechurch Street.

Elizabeth was handed down by the footman outside her Uncle Gardiner's address and immediately pulled into Jane's embrace, setting aside any fears she might have had regarding the warmth of her welcome. They both cried and laughed, Jane taking Elizabeth's face between her hands to look upon her carefully.

"Oh Lizzy, I have been looking out for you all morning. You don't know how wonderful it is to have you here."

Behind them, Elizabeth heard the sounds of the Fitzwilliam's carriage preparing to move away and looked around to see the countess nod at them briefly through the window, and then she was gone. Lady Fitzwilliam obviously had no wish to stay and be introduced to Jane, or the

Gardiners, and had no intention of stopping long enough to be seen in Gracechurch Street. The countess had become important to Elizabeth, a friend of sorts, and certainly someone she looked to for advice and guidance. She was now family, and that her ladyship would not acknowledge her other relations, her dearest blood relations, gave rise to painful emotions, but Elizabeth tucked them away, saved them for closer examination on another day. The colonel, now a much beloved cousin, friend and guardian, was dismounting to greet her sister, and he did so with much humility and amiability, making a swift excuse for his mother's not stopping, and moving them all inside where Elizabeth was swept up again into another's arms, those of her Aunt Gardiner. More tears were shed, but her aunt's weeping was of a different kind, and her expression melancholic. She stared at Elizabeth, patted her arms, listened to her every word and did not leave her side for much of the day. It was only when Elizabeth went to bid her goodnight, and her aunt bade her further into her bedroom that she began to understand what had made Mrs Gardiner so uneasy.

Patting the edge of the bed, her aunt asked her to sit. "So often you have talked of coming to visit, and it has been over two years, Elizabeth. I have missed you."

"And I you, but we shall have a very pleasant few weeks together now." Elizabeth smiled broadly.

"And how have you been? Truly, tell me? You look very well, but I have tortured myself with the memory of how I turned away from you. I feel I let you down, as your aunt. You put such trust in me and I let your uncle insist on the match, without brokering any real opposition. I wish I had taken you away myself; that we had all upped and gone somewhere new."

"Oh, but that was impossible, I know that. My uncle's business would have prevented it."

"But still I regretted it, wished there had been another way. You were so small and young, standing in that church, calling out your vows to a man who was a stranger to you. It seemed to be the only solution at the time. I know you write, but you never mention him. Your letters are full of witticisms and what you have been up to, but never a word about Mr Darcy. Please, tell me he isn't cruel."

Elizabeth laid herself down next to her aunt and let her hair be stroked and her brow kissed. "He is not cruel," she said and then remembered she had once called him cruel, perhaps she had even shouted it at him, in a fit of petulance. "He is not here to be cruel, Aunt. He remains abroad and I don't know when he will return. Not anytime soon, I expect."

"But when he has been at home? Oh forgive me, now I am prying..."

"Your prying can be forgiven, for it is born out of concern, but please do not worry. I have nothing to give me any great cause for displeasure, with the exception of being so very distant from you and Uncle Gardiner, my little cousins and of course, Jane. I have nothing to plague me. I am a very carefree creature, mostly at leisure." She kissed her aunt back and got to her feet again, afraid that if she stayed longer, she might say more. "And now I am quite fatigued. I shall go to bed and fortify myself with a good night's sleep, for tomorrow I am to buy up all the lace London has to offer."

"Well, I hope you have much fun doing so," her aunt replied.

She did have fun, out in her own carriage, with only Jane and Rose Kiddy for company. Her status as a married lady meant she was able to chaperone Jane. They were free, independent to a degree and giddy with the novelty of being able to do just as they pleased. They went first to an establishment where she was not only expected (the appointment having been arranged by Lady Fitzwilliam) but fawned over, admired and extolled. The modiste had recoiled in horror when Elizabeth had first removed her spencer to reveal the ill-fitting simple country gown beneath it, but recovered from the shock and smiled broadly, turning her this way and that, raising her chin to look into her eyes. *'Oui. Oui'* she said simply, before taking out her measuring tape, excitement overcoming her. She began to run on and on, in such fast French, that even Elizabeth, whose grasp of the language was very good, could not catch every word. Jane, whose French was much poorer, looked on, bemused and wide-eyed. '*Excellente figure, une belle peau. De magnifiques yeux*'. Yards of silk, satin and muslin were rolled out before her and held up against Elizabeth's face. Patterns and drawings were mulled over and within two hours, she had ordered two evening gowns and four day gowns for herself, and one for a protesting Jane. Then they were back out on the street again, into the carriage, and on their way to a milliner's shop recommended by Lady Fitzwilliam. Here they spent another delightful hour, trying on hats, looking at lace and purchasing stockings, before they left in a little procession, Rose Kiddy's arms overflowing with hat boxes and parcels.

"Well, I think that will do us for today, Jane," said Elizabeth, throwing herself back against the plush velvet of the carriage bench and blowing out her cheeks.

"For today? You mean to go shopping again? Do you not worry about the expense? You have already ordered some lovely gowns," Jane said.

"And I shall order many more before I am done. I have been told to spend at will. I have three years of unspent pin money to get through, according to the colonel. And, do you know, I am enjoying it. I have never before put any importance on clothes, but being here in London, watching all the elegant ladies go by, I can see the appeal of wanting to look one's best and all my current gowns are quite dreadful, they are so old. I think I shall reinvent myself."

"Do not become too elegant, Lizzy, or I shall not know you," Jane smiled.

"I fear there is not much chance of that. I am sure one country walk will undo all my endeavours at becoming *une personne de la mode*."

At Jane's frown, Elizabeth rolled her eyes and laughed. "Your French really is terrible."

They took their purchases back to Gracechurch Street and laid them out on Elizabeth's bed, where Mrs Gardiner came to view and admire them also. "No caps, Lizzy?"

265

"Caps?"

"You really ought to wear one, I notice you do not. A lady wears a cap to let others know she is married."

Elizabeth's nose wrinkled. "I don't wish to, it is not strictly necessary, is it? Besides, I am mostly at Pemberley where everybody knows I am married."

"Does Mr Darcy not object?"

"I doubt he's ever noticed one way or the other."

This earned her a surprised look from Jane and thinking she had probably said too much, she got to her feet and started to gather her things into a pile. Rose would make a much better job of putting them away later.

"And will one of your many new gowns be ready to wear by Friday next, Lizzy? We are invited to a small private ball given by some friends of ours." Mrs Gardiner said.

"Oh, I am sure at least one of them could be made ready in time. A ball, how wonderful!" Exhilaration fizzed through her, setting her senses alight. To go to a ball, in a new gown, and meet new people, where there would be dancing and everything that was thrilling, and with Jane for company, it was too much happiness!

Thirty four

Elizabeth's time in London passed quickly, in a flurry of shops and appointments. She was summoned to take tea with Lady Fitzwilliam twice and went to dinner there once, but as the rest of her family weren't invited, she went begrudgingly and was not good company, which earned her some questioning looks from the countess, but even this did not dampen her buoyant mood too much.

The colonel had accompanied her back after the dinner, obviously on his way to another party, somewhere where later hours were kept and the company was a little less formal, she surmised. On route, he ordered the carriage down a particularly fine street and had her look at a smart black door. "The house yonder is your London home, are you curious about it, would you like to see inside?" he had asked.

Elizabeth had shaken her head. "Home, Colonel? Home is a place where there is love and family, sometimes arguments and troubles. Home, to me, means security and comfort. No, I have no interest in seeing inside."

"I have described it wrong then, your London *house*, Mrs Darcy."

"Call *it* what you wish, call *me* what you wish, but I find it means little."

"You're a strange creature," he had told her, "I don't think I ever met another girl like you."

There were truly lovely excursions though, to the theatre and out to the park with all the Gardiners and Jane, her little cousins running quickly about, ruffling her skirts as they swept past. And there were moments when she felt more sanguine than she could ever remember being, certainly since before her father had passed away. All the while, her shopping continued apace and an impressive wardrobe was gathering about her. She had to admit there was a certain deliciousness attached to her wealth and position; to walk into a shop or warehouse and know she might have anything she desired and with a nod of her head, it was purchased. The winter clothes to be sent to Pemberley, the summer ones to remain with her, or follow her to her mother's house.

She was mulling over her return to Hertfordshire, thinking of the changes she might encounter there, and waiting for something to be wrapped in the milliner's shop, when two ladies entered; obviously wealthy, ladies of quality and high society, gossiping gaily. They pushed past Elizabeth on route to the counter and began giving instructions to the girl behind it, a very sweet young lady who had served Elizabeth on several occasions recently.

"Millicent. I am desperate for a new hat. Bring me out something that will not bore me to tears, or astound me with its ugliness. Bring out a selection," one of them said.

Elizabeth felt their rudeness and saw they thought themselves so above everyone else to not require manners. They were interesting to watch but so disagreeable she wanted to move to a different part of the shop, and would have done so if Millicent had not spoken.

"I shall be happy to show you some hats, Miss Cartwright, as soon as I have finished serving Mrs Darcy."

The ladies' heads spun around quickly to look at Elizabeth, inspecting her closely. "Mrs Darcy? You are not Mrs Darcy," the taller of the ladies, who was wearing a green turban, proclaimed. "Mr Darcy is a *very* dear friend of mine, I had no notion he was married. Are you quite sure of this lady, Millicent?"

Elizabeth felt anger and indignation, and she had a certain amount of sympathy for the poor shop girl at having been asked such a question.

Millicent, however, had obviously worked there for some time and was not the least abashed. She ignored the question. "Shall I have this parcel sent to Pemberley, Mrs Darcy, or your London address?" she queried, looking directly at Elizabeth.

Elizabeth smiled as she had already given the delivery instruction before the other ladies had entered. "To Pemberley please, Millicent."

Rose Kiddy jumped up from her seat at the back of the shop. "Are we done, madam, shall I fetch the carriage?"

Elizabeth felt ashamed of her inability to defend herself. She was silent and useless, while a shop-girl and maid came to her rescue. She was humbled by their sweetness. "If you will, Rose, yes please."

Rose rushed away but still the lady in the green turban was not satisfied, and turned to her friend, whispering, but not quietly enough for Elizabeth not to hear her in the still of the shop. "Mr Darcy is abroad. I am sure she must be some sort of charlatan. Look at her!"

"I think you are right," her friend replied. "He has never mentioned being married, who on earth is she? She has never been introduced in any decent company, I am sure."

"Maybe she doesn't wish to be introduced," Elizabeth said, with more courage than she felt. "Perhaps her notion of what is decent company is different to yours, and she is surprisingly content in a different sort of society, one where politeness and civility mostly prevail, and who could blame her?" Her cheeks burned with fury and frustration, but she managed a soft goodbye to Millicent as she stepped out on the street. Rose, bless her good, kind heart, had ordered the carriage to pull up right outside the shop, so that the lady in the turban and her friend might see Elizabeth board it. The footman jumped down to hand her in and John doffed his hat to her.

She did not look back at the ladies in the shop. She did not care who they were, or that they were *'very good friends'* of Mr Darcy. Let them believe whatever they chose to. But what rankled and hurt, sneaking through her entire being like a snake, was that she was such a secret, someone not even to be *mentioned* to his friends, let alone be allowed to make their acquaintance. And she had married him for nothing! There were clearly people who did not even remember that Mr Darcy had once been at the centre of a scandal. She supposed other persons, more interesting and notable, had disgraced themselves since, behaving far more disreputably than she was alleged to have done, and now her ruination and absolution was very old news. If she *had* been sent away to wait out the storm, without marrying him, might she now have been able to enter society again? Rose, sitting opposite, saw her pain but could not speak unless Elizabeth introduced the subject. The girl kept her eyes to the floor and quietly passed Elizabeth a handkerchief.

By the time she arrived home, preparations were well under way for the ball and the house was full of nervous energy. Maids ran hither and thither with ribbons and shoe roses. Elizabeth sank into a chair in the parlour and decided to delay her own preparations. Rose deserved some tea and rest before tackling her bath and hair in any case.

The colonel was announced and shown in. He sat down opposite her, whistling and smiling in his casual way, before he really looked at her, then he was all tender concern.

"Whatever is the matter?"

Elizabeth blinked rapidly. She had thought she had restored her appearance to normal, after her cross tears in the carriage, and was surprised at him having noticed something amiss, but they had lived together for a long time now. Perhaps he knew her as well as anyone, better even than Jane.

"Does Mr Darcy have a mistress?" The question shocked her as much as it did the colonel. The thought had only just occurred to her as she had sat considering the lady in the green turban and what constituted 'a very good friend'. "I am sorry," she said, as the colonel floundered for a response. "I shouldn't ask you. You wouldn't betray his confidence in any case and I assure you, I do not really worry about such things. I was just curious."

The colonel was silent for a long while, and Elizabeth wondered whether he was so still and quiet because it were true, but at last he rubbed his bad leg and spoke. "I know of none, but he is a private man. I doubt it, but I could not completely assure you one way or another. What has brought on this pensive mood, Elizabeth? You were in very lively spirits when I saw you not two days ago."

"Oh, and I shall be so again. Do not worry yourself. It is a silly matter of no consequence to anyone but I. And how are you? Has the countess found you a lovely heiress yet?"

"Not yet, I continue to foil her attempts." They were both amused by Lady Fitzwilliam's efforts to make a match for her son since their arrival in Town. The colonel had been to a succession of dinners and parties and put before every rich eligible lady of the countess' acquaintance; from young debutantes to middle-aged widows. He had amused Elizabeth during his visits by recounting tales of his usually disastrous dealings with them.

"So none of the ladies currently in Town can please you, Colonel? Not one has caught your fancy. I am incredulous, come now, there must be someone you admire?"

"Certainly there is someone I admire, but she is, unfortunately, not someone my mother would consider suitable."

"Ah ha!" Elizabeth cried, thrilled at the soft smile that crossed his face, certain he was thinking of his unsuitable lady. "I must know more."

"You must not," he answered sternly and then they were interrupted by Jane coming into the room to enquire how Elizabeth was after her shopping trip.

Her sister looked lovely, truly beautiful. Elizabeth watched the colonel get to his feet and bow to her and was struck with the idea he might be in love with Jane. He certainly took the trouble to call at Gracechurch Street often enough. Of course, who could not be taken with Jane? And it was true that she was neither wealthy, nor suitable. The countess would heartily disapprove. It was an impossible, doomed admiration, and she felt for the colonel. Thankfully, Jane appeared oblivious to it, and so she at least, would not be hurt, but oh, how the poor colonel must be suffering!

"Oh, 'tis your ball tonight, isn't it?" the colonel said. "I shall leave you to prepare. Though how such loveliness can be improved upon, I know not! I shall take myself off to my club."

"I suppose we do need to go and dress, Lizzy, although my Uncle Gardiner sent me to you, Colonel. He wonders whether you will do him the honour of joining him in his book room. He wishes to escape from *female frippery,*

271

lace and hysteria' and wonders whether you might join him in a glass of something."

"I have been to many a party, soiree and dinner these past couple of weeks, but I promise you, Miss Bennet, that is the best invitation I have had so far. Excuse me, ladies." He bowed again and was gone, leaving them to their preparations.

The colonel was still there when they descended the stairs some time later, coming out of Mr Gardiner's book room, slightly wobbly on his feet and with a very wide smile. "Miss Bennet, excuse my impertinence, but I must tell you how utterly lovely you look."

Jane blushed and smiled. "Thank you, Colonel."

"Now, would be so kind as to introduce me to this charming and lovely creature by your side? And then, you must tell me what you have done with Elizabeth."

She swatted his arm.

"All jesting aside, Elizabeth, you look truly beautiful."

He had spoken with great sincerity and Elizabeth was touched, but deflected his compliment. "I think everyone will look handsome to you tonight, all swathed as they must be, in a sea of fine brandy."

"I am not so in my cups as to not know handsome from unhandsome. I wish Darcy could see you now."

Now it was Elizabeth's turn to blush.

"You know," the colonel said. "I think we should have your likeness taken while we are in London, nothing that would cause you too much trouble, just a miniature. It might only take one or two sittings. I could have it mounted and sent to him."

"You will not. I will not," she cried, aghast at the idea and pleased when their aunt came to whisk them away from the colonel's admiring, teasing gaze.

The ball was at a house only a few streets away, not a fashionable address, but everybody was merry and pleasant and welcomed them. Elizabeth noted how the young men began to nudge one another and slowly crept closer to

272

where she and her aunt stood, hoping obviously to be introduced to her sister, they fought for the best position. Jane stood serenely chatting to their hostess, oblivious to the attention she drew. Her ignorance of her beauty, and the commotion she could cause simply by entering a room, was endearing.

Mrs Gardiner took pity on one of the potential young lovers and beckoned him over. He was obviously an acquaintance of hers. He bowed low and smiled engagingly at all of them, but his gaze rested on Jane, who lowered her eyes bashfully and looked away. He was not deterred easily though and Elizabeth saw him step a little closer to her sister, gently asking after her health and for her opinion of the ball, before applying for her hand for the next set. Jane agreed with a shy nod of her head and the gentleman beamed with pleasure. Then he had a tug on his sleeve and a cough from his friend who had come over with him. Elizabeth had been so amused watching Jane being courted, that she hadn't noticed the second young man. He was dark haired and dark eyed, an intense looking gentleman, who reminded her a little of Mr Darcy, though he was not nearly so tall, and much younger.

"I beg your pardon, Miss Bennet, Mrs Gardiner, this is my friend, Mr Burton, who I don't believe you have met before. He is currently studying the law."

Mr Burton gave a deep bow, bending almost double at the waist. He then rose crisply up and puffed out his chest a little, before nodding at Elizabeth, who had kept herself a small distance away. "I am very pleased to meet all of you," he said, very properly. "I very much hope *both* of the young ladies you bring with you tonight might dance, Mrs Gardiner?"

"Mr Burton, Mr Carter, I am remiss." Mrs Gardiner brought Elizabeth forward and put a hand on her arm. "May I present to you my niece, Jane's sister, *Mrs* Darcy." Elizabeth noted the soft look her aunt favoured Mr Burton with. He swallowed hard and his countenance was overcome with disappointment. Elizabeth looked back at him for longer than was polite, their eyes meeting; her curiosity making her forget her manners. *He admires me!* The realisation was a shock.

She half expected him to excuse himself and retreat to the other side of the room, but instead he proved to be as gallant as he was earnest. "Will you do me the honour of dancing the next with me, Mrs Darcy, if your husband has not already engaged you?" He looked around the room for such a man.

"My husband is abroad, but you must excuse me, sir. I am not inclined to dance this evening and will sit out."

He bowed his head and when the strains of the new dance started, he took the chance to move away. Jane went away too, with her partner.

"Well, shall those of us *'not inclined to dance'*, retreat to the chairs?" There was something sardonic about Mrs Gardiner's smile as she took Elizabeth's arm and led her across the room. "That poor boy," she muttered, "how very sweet he seemed, why did you not want to dance with him?"

"I did," Elizabeth replied. "I did want to dance with him."

Mrs Gardiner's brow wrinkled in confusion, but she asked no more as she was being approached by another lady of her age and they sat down to watch the dancers and talk. Elizabeth found herself ensconced in a group of chaperones and married ladies, with her back against the wall of the room, oddly detached from the scene around her, suddenly not enjoying herself at all. To think she had been looking forward to the evening with such excitement and now the world seemed dismal, the music dull, the colours muted. She was wearing the most flattering, most expensive gown she had ever owned, her hair had been arranged beautifully by Rose, who was learning her trade well, and yet she felt miserable.

She *had* wanted to dance with Mr Burton, so very much, but she had wanted to dance with him as Elizabeth Bennet, not as Mrs Darcy. He had looked kind, intelligent and steadfast, interesting and handsome. Elizabeth Bennet would have been half in love with him by the end of their set and wanting him to fetch her some punch so she might prolong their time together, steal a few more words from him. Elizabeth Bennet would have been hoping he would ask her for a second dance later in the evening, this Mr Burton, who was probably a second son of a country gentleman, and a perfect match for Elizabeth Bennet. She imagined him asking her aunt for permission to call upon her, to take her for a walk. She saw them strolling side by side, fingers brushing accidently, or maybe on purpose, who knew, who cared? He would get up the courage, after a few weeks, to put forth a particular question, she would assent. Her uncle would ask him to wait until his studies were complete, he would agree and when they had to be apart, they would write long letters of devotion, promises and longing. And after they were married, what then? A smart, little house somewhere in Town, two children, maybe three? Oh, there would be no fine carriages, no vast estate, no great library for her to lose herself in, no Colonel Fitzwilliam, no Georgiana or Miss Temple, no countess for an aunt. She would be Mrs Burton, unexceptional to everyone but her nearest and dearest, but at least she would spend her days knowing what it was like to be looked at with love and affection. She might find out what passion felt like. She would be kissed and touched, pressed down underneath a firm, broad chest, wrapped in cool white sheets, her legs tangled around a strong, masculine frame. She was hot, then cold, confused and then oh so clear about her real future, and it stretched out before her in horrible clarity, years of being married, but alone.

As she watched Jane being courted so assiduously, dancing and laughing, white hot anger and envy ran through her, and then she was ashamed, for nothing was Jane's fault. Hating herself, she closed her eyes and put her hands over her ears to drown out the happy, lively music which seemed to taunt her. She knew not how long she sat so, before she felt her arms being pulled down by Mrs Gardiner. "Lizzy, my love, are you well?"

"No. I am not anything."

"You are in a very strange mood tonight, I am sorry. I thought you would enjoy the ball."

Elizabeth spoke in a low voice, so as not to be overheard by anyone but her aunt. "I lied to you when I said Mr Darcy is not cruel."

Mrs Gardiner squeezed her hand and looked as if she might cry. "Tell me of it, please. What does he do?"

"He ignores me." Elizabeth trembled all over, disturbed by her own words. "Am I silly, to speak of it as a cruelty? He does not strike me, or abuse me, but, you see, there is no Mrs Darcy, she does not exist. I do not exist."

Her aunt understood her immediately. "There is nothing silly about it at all and it must hurt a great deal. Tell me how I may help, would you like to go home?"

"Yes, I would like to go home, back to Hertfordshire. That is where I would like to go," she said, thinking there was no embrace more certain to soothe a troubled child and ease her pain, than that of her mother's.

Thirty five

Upon setting down in Meryton three days later, Elizabeth soon discovered she'd had the right of it - there certainly was no embrace like Mrs Bennet's. She clutched Elizabeth to her, and then threw her backwards in order to look at her, before hauling her suddenly back into her arms again. This was done thrice over, much to Jane's amusement. "Let me look at you, let me look at you," she cried over and over again.

"Do you find her much changed, Mamma?"

Mrs Bennet both nodded and shook her head, so her answer was never known, but she did expound greatly on how *'grand'* Elizabeth was, before her eyes alighted on the carriage. "Oh how very fine," she exclaimed, "and this is yours, Lizzy?"

"Well, it is one of the Darcy coaches, yes."

Her mother then proceeded to climb into the carriage for a closer look, trying out both benches for comfort and exclaiming loudly over the fittings and upholstery. Elizabeth hung her head at her mother's display. The house the family now occupied was only a little short of the main thoroughfare and the whole of Meryton probably had their eyes upon them. When she looked at Jane, though, and saw the indulgent smile she wore whilst looking upon her mother's embarrassing antics, she laughed at her own proudness and then at her mother too, who was demanding Mary, Kitty and Lydia clamber up to join her.

Kitty and Lydia did as they were requested but Mary hung back, her face solemn. When Elizabeth told her how pleased she was to see her again, Mary only offered a serious hello in return, with no kisses or embraces. Elizabeth looked to Jane, whose expression suggested they would talk more of Mary later.

Their mother finally quit the carriage and they all moved to go inside. Mrs Bennet held Jane back and ushered Elizabeth onto her right hand, so she would be first through the door. "Ah Jane, Lizzy takes your place now, and you must go lower, my dear, because she is a married woman."

Though the etiquette of it was correct, Elizabeth felt for her sister, but Jane shrugged to show she did not care and they went indoors, shutting the door behind them. Reunited. All of them, five sisters, one mother, together under the same roof for the first time in nearly three years - there was much talking at once. Lydia and her mother were exceedingly loud. Lydia was tall, pretty and very developed for thirteen. Elizabeth was as much astonished at the change in her appearance, as she was in her self-assured manner. The girl babbled on and on, asking her lots of questions without giving much thought to the answers and sometimes without even waiting for one. Most of these questions involved pin money, gowns and jewels.

"You are very glamorous, Lizzy. You don't look anything like I remember," she asserted.

"You do not look anything like I remember either, Lydia. Do you know I have not seen you since you were ten?"

"Oh, eleven, you are wrong, I was eleven," the girl replied, confidently.

Elizabeth smiled. Lydia was almost exactly five years younger than her, their birthdays were in the same month, but she had no wish to argue the point. Lydia spoke in dramatic declarations, throwing her arms around. She dominated the room in a way which seemed unseemly for a girl of such tender years, particularly when there were five other ladies in the room, all her elders. Mrs Bennet did not seem to care however, and looked upon Lydia fondly, chuckling at her antics, rather than shushing or checking her.

"You must take me to London next year, Lizzy, and buy me lots of gowns, and take me to parties."

"She will take me, Lydia, not you. I am older," Kitty protested.

"You are both too young for London," Elizabeth said.

"La!" cried Lydia. "How can you of all people say such a thing, when you were married by fifteen?"

Elizabeth blustered a little. "I pray you do not use me as a yardstick. I was too young, I would even suggest Jane now, at twenty, should wait a while."

Lydia laughed. "Oh, I shall be married by her age. I would be embarrassed to not even be betrothed by then. Do you mean to be an old maid, Jane?"

Cringing at her sister's rudeness, she sought to send the silly young girl from the room and declared to Lydia and Kitty that she had brought them all presents and that if they saw Rose Kiddy in her room, they might claim theirs. Kitty and Lydia squealed and left quickly. Jane went after them, saying she feared for the safety of Elizabeth's trunks and gowns, and a little for Rose. Elizabeth was left with Mary and her mother.

"I have a present for you too, Mary."

To this Mary very gravely replied, "far be it from me, my dear sister, to depreciate ribbons and lace; those trinkets and baubles which are doubtless congenial with the generality of female minds. But you must know, fripperies hold no charm for me - I should infinitely prefer a book."

"Well, how fortunate then, that books are what I have brought you. I very much hope you will enjoy them."

"If they are of some intrinsic value to my moral or spiritual education, I am sure I shall."

Mrs Bennet rolled her eyes. "She spends too much time with Mr and Mrs Collins."

"Ah, yes, our cousins at Longbourn," Elizabeth said.

"I go there as little as possible, of course," Mrs Bennet told her. "Oh, there was a dinner last week. Very bad table, Lizzy, not as I would have kept it. I go there very little. And we took tea there on Tuesday and Thursday, but I do not enjoy it, I do not like to go to them I assure you. I call there rarely, only once or twice a week."

Elizabeth smiled. "But you enjoy their company, Mary?"

"I find their godliness, humility and religious devotion very inspiring. If you will excuse me, I am due at the church now, to assist with preparations for tomorrow's services." Mary left the room without curtsey or even a nod. Elizabeth noted that Mary's own godliness and humility did not extend into her manners, having neither thanked Elizabeth for her gift, or greeted her with any warmth.

279

"Do you think maybe she spends a little too much time with Mr and Mrs Collins, Mamma?"

"Oh, I cannot dissuade her, heaven knows I have tried."

Elizabeth suspected her mother had not tried very hard at all, just as she had not quieted Lydia or Kitty, but as it was her first day there she thought it best to keep her own counsel for a while. She had no immediate wish to go looking for faults in those she loved. "The house is charming, Mamma. Much more spacious than I had imagined."

"Yes, Mr Darcy has been very kind, very kind indeed."

"Mr Darcy!" Elizabeth repeated.

"Yes, to think we would still be in that horrible little cottage if it were not for his contribution to our income."

"Mr Darcy provides you with an income?"

"Of course," Mrs Bennet was indignant. "And why should he not, when he is so rich, and is married to my daughter. Of course he should provide for us."

Elizabeth had been sending letters to this new address since her first few months at Pemberley. Her mother and sisters could not have been at their original cottage for very long and she realised Mr Darcy must have been supporting them ever since she had been married. But which Mr Darcy had made such arrangements and been so generous?

"It was instigated by George Darcy I suppose," she said, voicing her thoughts out loud, feeling it would have been the sort of grand philanthropic gesture the late Mr Darcy would have made. But then, she remembered all the talk of settlements and financial arrangements that had accompanied those strange days in Gracechurch Street, when marriage had been decided upon as the only possible solution to the scandal that had surrounded her. Had her husband rescued her mother from her state of genteel poverty? But from whichever Mr Darcy this altruism had stemmed, Elizabeth was thankful and relieved to see her mother was living in very good comfort.

"We are invited to the Lucases tonight, Lizzy, and perhaps you will come too, if you are not too fatigued from your journey?"

"Not at all, Mamma, 'tis only half a day's journey from Town. I am recovered already and should be glad to see the Lucases again. You are even closer to them now, I think, than when we were at Longbourn. Lucas Lodge must be a very convenient stroll from here. I suppose you walk there for such parties?"

"Walk? Yes, we do, often, but then we have no choice, having no carriage of our own, though Sir William orders his for us, when the weather is foul." Mrs Bennet frowned and looked out of the window. "I do fear that it may rain tonight, Lizzy."

Elizabeth feigned innocence and looked out of the window too. "Oh no, it looks very fine to me and will be plenty warm enough, and you know how I love to walk, Mamma."

"Yes, my dear child, you are a fine walker, as am I. I would happily, of course, walk there and back ten times, and take great enjoyment in it. But I worry for Kitty's chest, she coughs so, you must have heard her."

"She does appear to have a slight cold," Elizabeth admitted. "Maybe she ought to stay home, while the rest of us go?"

"Oh no, there is no call for that, though if I had a carriage at my disposal, that would make me easy about her comfort. I would surely call for the carriage, if I had one."

"Hmm," Elizabeth paused, hiding her smile. "Do you think perhaps we should take mine, Mamma? You would not object to being deprived the pleasure of the walk?"

Her mother let out a small gasp, as if this thought had only just occurred to her. "Oh, Lizzy, you are very good, that would be just the thing, I think, for Kitty's sake."

"I would not wish to be the cause of any deterioration in Kitty's condition, Mamma."

"No, of course not and perhaps you might tell the coachman to stop right outside the Lucases' door, so she is not out in the night air for long. Though Lady Lucas only has a small barouche, and very old it is too, with shabby bench seats and a cracked window, she is not the sort to be resentful that I have such a rich daughter, able to carry me about in splendour and comfort. So we should not worry about pulling up at the front door, even though from there we will be seen by the whole party assembled in her drawing room. She is not the sort to call us ostentatious."

Elizabeth quit the room a few minutes later, both shaking her head at her mother's shamelessness but smiling at the thought that she was able to provide her with a little pleasure.

The Lucases and the Bennets had always been intimate. Sir William Lucas had acquired a living in trade, then been risen to the knighthood after an address to the King and retired to Meryton, where unshackled by the concerns of his previous business, instead occupied himself with being industriously civil and pleasing to all. They were received with the utmost cordiality in his drawing room.

Lady Lucas was a valuable neighbour to Mrs Bennet, as being not particularly clever, not very rich and not too handsome; she could be much talked above and easily impressed. "You see us arrive in good time, Lady Lucas, for Mrs Darcy was kind enough to transport us here in her coach. I did tell her she should not trouble the coachman and footman for such a short journey, but Mrs Darcy insisted."

"Yes, we saw the carriage, and heard it too, in fact we could not hear one another talk for a few moments, when it first pulled up, such was the rumble," Lady Lucas said.

Elizabeth stared at her shoes, but her hand was caught in Jane's and she was led away from her embarrassment and further into the drawing room, where they stopped at the fireplace, near a tall girl with dark hair. Elizabeth remembered her instantly as the eldest of Lucas girls, but she was much plainer, and not as fair of figure, as Elizabeth remembered. She recalled once thinking of Charlotte Lucas as the very model of all that a young lady should be - wise, kind, pretty and charming and was a little shocked to find her such an ordinary woman, but she did have such an engaging smile and a true, warm, inviting way about her, that Elizabeth immediately liked her once again.

Charlotte Lucas took hold of Elizabeth's arms, turning them over to closely examine her elbows. "But this cannot be little Eliza," she said, exclaiming with some drama. "There are no scrapes upon her elbows and no grass stains on her skirts!"

"Perhaps I have grown up a little since you saw me last, Miss Lucas," she ventured.

Laughing, Charlotte Lucas assured her that she had, and they fell into such easy, lively and interesting conversation, that Elizabeth began to feel very happy, though her mother's conversation with Lady Lucas could be easily overheard and was a source of discomfort.

"I don't suppose you saw Mrs Darcy's gown, Lady Lucas?" Mrs Bennet said. "Is it not very fine, and do you know, when I asked her how much a yard the material had cost, she could not answer me, for she had paid no attention to the price. Can you imagine, being so wealthy as to not even enquire? Fourteen new gowns she ordered in London, Lady Lucas, fourteen!"

Charlotte caught Elizabeth's eye and gave her a soft smile.

"If it were possible to die from the pain of embarrassment, I might expire on the spot," Elizabeth said.

"We are well used to your mother, Eliza, do not worry and I confess, I much prefer her company to that of the new occupants of Longbourn."

"I notice they are not here tonight." Elizabeth was pleased by their absence, remembering her only encounter with them in London, when she had been the subject of their disapprobation and judged morally corrupt on the briefest of acquaintances.

"No, my father does not care for them. Where he sees joy and light, they see corruption and sin. Dancing, music and youth are a delight to my father; to Mr Collins such things are a cause for horror and astonishment. Have you met them since your return to Hertfordshire?"

"No, I only came back today."

Elizabeth was interrupted by her mother, who had overheard the talk of the Collinses. "We will not call on them, until they come to call upon Mrs Darcy, they ought to give precedence where it is due," Mrs Bennet said.

Here, Elizabeth had cause to blush again. She could not imagine putting herself in so elevated a position that such civilities were necessary. She was therefore surprised to hear Charlotte Lucas agree with her mother. "Yes, let them call upon you, Eliza, I think that would be the correct way of things."

There was eventually some music and Jane was approached by the eldest of the Lucas boys; a lad of no more than seventeen, who led her to the floor with such an exultant look, that it gave Charlotte and Elizabeth much amusement. And then, Elizabeth was approached by another local young gentleman, but declined, sending him away.

For this, she overheard herself called proud by two muttering ladies of the parish and seeking to prove she was anything but, she offered to play while others danced. Her skills at the pianoforte, though much improved, would have perhaps been called passable in London, but she positively amazed Meryton's chief inhabitants, who proclaimed her a genius of the highest order. When they went away at the end of the evening she was in a tumultuous state, pleased to have made a very good new friend in Charlotte Lucas, but concerned with how she was seen by her mother's neighbours. The carriage, her dress, her musical abilities, her refusal to dance had all singled her out. Her accent even, had changed, she realised, and this all disturbed her enough to make sleep difficult. She tossed and turned until the small hours of the morning, and when sleep did find her she dreamed of boats, crashing waves and ladies in green turbans.

At breakfast, she was horrified to hear her mother forming a plan of Elizabeth accompanying her on some sort of tour of Meryton society, in order to show her off. It was most definitely not why Elizabeth had come back to Hertfordshire and the idea made her shudder. She had made her own plans for the day and they included taking a long walk with Jane and Charlotte Lucas. Keen to be allowed to do just that, but wanting to please Mrs Bennet, she sent her off with the carriage, and instructed John to take her mother wherever she pleased. Kitty and Lydia went with her and the trio waved gaily from the windows as they pulled away.

Elizabeth retired to the parlour after they had gone and found Mary deep in the study of human nature. She had copied out some extracts from a weighty tome which she called upon Elizabeth to admire, and then she proceeded to expound some extraordinary observations on threadbare morality, collected from their very ordinary evening with the Lucases, which left Elizabeth lost for words and patience. She nodded, however, and tried to understand Mary's thinking, but as it was so different to her own, she feared they would never share anything other than a distant kind of sibling cordiality towards one another.

Jane saved her from Mary's readings by wandering in with her bonnet in her hand, ready to meet with Charlotte. They invited Mary to go along with them, but she shook her head violently and spoke of another three long extracts which needed her perusal and possible replication.

Their walk with Charlotte, through the woods and by the streams of her youth was worth the two hundred miles of travel alone, such was her enjoyment of it.

Elizabeth was able to voice her concerns regarding Kitty and Lydia openly, and found that Charlotte and Jane much agreed with her.

"Does my mother allow them everywhere? They are surely not fully out?"

"They are full young, but she does allow them to do pretty much as they please. Not assemblies, or balls, but otherwise they go with her. Lydia is such a force of nature that she overthrows immediately any of your mother's attempts to discipline or restrict her, and where Lydia leads, Kitty follows, even though she is the older of the two," Charlotte said.

"And Mary? I remember her as a serious child, much indoors, but her piety and didactic attitude to others concern me. What of her relationship with the Collinses?"

"She receives much attention from them. They are an odd pair, mean-minded. On his arrival here in Meryton, Mr Collins scared off our local clergyman into retirement and delivers the sermons in his place. I think to save himself the cost of the living. I suppose it ate into the Longbourn income. Mary sees them daily and they pray together. You will hear Mr Collins give his sermon on Sunday, and it will be very different to what you are used to. We are all heathens, on a certain route to hell if we do not follow his virtuous path. He scares some of the young children half to death."

Elizabeth shook her head. "I can well believe it. I met Hogarth Collins briefly in London, before he took possession of Longbourn. I very much doubt he or his wife will call on me. I apparently have a terrible badness about me and am also *'destined for damnation'*. I think that is what he said. You were there, Jane, do I have it right?"

"Do not forget, Lizzy, that 'the devil is on your shoulder' and you must *'repent, repent, repent,'*" Jane said, with a very serious expression but a laugh in her voice.

"Oh, believe me, Jane, I have done much repenting since that day," Elizabeth said.

Charlotte threw her a curious look, but perhaps felt she did not know Elizabeth well enough to ask after her true meaning, so instead she turned her attentions to Jane. "Now, how is Miss Bennet? Surely at least one of the young men who pine so vociferously at your aunt and uncle's door must come forward soon and declare themselves. Who is the forerunner in the race for your hand?"

Jane would not be drawn. Elizabeth teasingly mentioned Mr Carter. "He danced twice with her at the ball we recently attended, and would have ventured a third if he thought he could have gotten away with it. And he has called at Gracechurch Street!"

"Well this all sounds very promising, but why on earth have you come away now, Jane? You may lose the opportunity of fixing him. There are very few of us who have heart enough to be really in love without encouragement. In nine cases out of ten a woman had better show more affection than she feels. You ought to be in London, helping him on a little."

"But, I do not know him very well, I am not even sure I would welcome his suit, or whether he is the sort of man I could love," Jane said, taking Charlotte's advice seriously, though Elizabeth was sure she must be in jest.

"Oh that matters for naught. When you are secure of him, then there will be more leisure for falling in love as much as you choose."

"Secure him!" Elizabeth cried. "When she is still unsure of his character?"

"If she were married to him tomorrow, I should think she had as good a chance of happiness as if she had studied his character for a twelve-month. Happiness in marriage is entirely a matter of chance."

"You make me laugh," Elizabeth said, "but your theory is not sound, unless all one wants is any sort of husband, rather than the right husband. You would never act in such a way yourself, Charlotte, I am sure."

"Would that I had the chance too," said Charlotte with a pout. "Though, even my opportunities for dancing and falling in love may increase soon. I have it on very good authority that we are to have a militia regiment settling in the neighbourhood any day now. How do you like a man in regimentals, Jane?"

Jane merely smiled, while Elizabeth's thoughts turned to Kitty and Lydia. They, she thought, might like regimentals a little too much.

Thirty six

The Collinses did call upon Elizabeth, with great ceremony and a surprising amount of deference. Hogarth Collins bowed very low indeed and his wife smiled in a way she must have thought pleasing – though her attempts to ingratiate herself simply annoyed Elizabeth. As Mrs Darcy, she was apparently no longer *'the devil's own child'*, as she had been three years ago, now her grace and favour was to be courted.

"Mrs Darcy, we hope to see you in church tomorrow?"

"Of course," she said simply, hoping that by speaking as little as possible she might hurry the visit along and get them out of her mother's house.

"A man of my standing and position cannot be insensible of your husband's great influence in the church, madam, and I cannot tell you how delighted it will make me to see you among my flock."

"Delighted," his wife added.

"You may find my sermons somewhat different to what you are used to, Mrs Darcy, but I do like to speak plainly and warn my parishioners of the dangers of exposure to too much sin."

"Too much sin," said Mrs Collins.

Mary, who was sat in the corner, nodded.

"There is corruption and vice everywhere, we must be on our guard. It is everywhere, lurking in every corner, in every house in the land," Mr Collins extolled, with passion.

"*Everywhere*, Mr Collins, you include Longbourn, I suppose?" Elizabeth asked.

"Oh, not at Longbourn, I assure you. We are a God-fearing household."

"I hope you do not mean to imply, my home, Pemberley, is a house of sin, Mr Collins?"

"Oh no, Mrs Darcy," Hogarth Collins squirmed uneasily in his seat.

"Is my mother's house full of sin? Should I be wary here?"

Elizabeth saw him look around, while perspiration gathered on his brow. He was so conflicted, so conscious not to offend. "When I say *'everywhere'*, you must understand, I was speaking of generalities. Perhaps I made too sweeping a statement?"

"Yes, there can be a danger in those," she said, "but perhaps you are right and sin is all around us, I am sure I am not able to throw the first stone. Who among us have not been occasionally guilty of such things as say, a lack of charity, or of turning our backs on those who are going through troubled times?"

"Mrs Darcy, I cannot imagine you behaving in such an unchristian way. You are all goodness, I am sure."

Elizabeth got to her feet. "I wonder, theologically, what you think of hypocrisy, sir. Do you consider that a sin of sorts? To my mind, there is nothing worse than a hypocrite, but perhaps that is a discussion we will have to save for another day, for now, you must excuse me, I have some correspondence to attend to." She walked towards the door and held it open for them, not caring if he thought her rude. She was apparently rich enough to give offence wherever she chose, for they continued in their compliments, bows and curtseys as they got up to leave the room.

Elizabeth sighed, realising that the very worst thing about their call was that she would have to repay it within a couple of days. Even fifteen minutes in their sanctimonious company would be too much to bear, and to see Hogarth Collins presiding at Longbourn, and to see the insipid, vapid Mrs Collins playing hostess in her mother's old parlour would be agonising. She supposed the younger girls and her mother had gotten used to it, but she did not think it would sit so easily with her.

Before they parted the couple mentioned their son would soon visit. "William is to take orders soon, and as soon as he finds a living, I am sure he will want to furnish his new home with a wife. We cannot be otherwise than concerned at being the means of injuring your sisters. Be assured of my son's readiness to make every possible amends." Mr Collins glanced over at Mary, who sat with her eyes closed and her hands in her lap, as if praying for such a thing to befall her.

Elizabeth was horrified at the idea that they might be grooming Mary for a daughter and sincerely hoped this was one issue on which Mrs Bennet would see sense and flatly refuse consent. Mary, she feared, might do whatever the Collinses instructed her to, and would probably be only too pleased to escape the noise, silliness and mild depravity of the Bennet household. Only her mother might prevent the match.

When at last the horrible couple went, Mrs Bennet looked up at her. "Whatever did they mean, Lizzy? Such odd people!" Mrs Bennet considered for a few moments before her face lit up with excitement. "Do you suppose he meant young Mr Collins means to marry one of my daughters? That one of them should be the future mistress of Longbourn?" Mrs Bennet looked fondly at Jane, who had been sat sewing in the corner. The thought of Mary being so closely related to the Collinses was terrible enough, but to think of Jane being married to their son was truly a cause for anguish. Elizabeth fervently hoped he was not handsome, or charming.

Her hopes, it turned out, were not in vain. When he happened upon her a few days later, Elizabeth thought William Collins was perhaps one of the least attractive men she had ever met.

He started badly, by importuning her on the street in Meryton, approaching with a gait that was half hop and half run, his head bent so low as to make her fear he might topple over; for he had quite a large head and very small feet. She was bracing herself for the impact of it, when he suddenly stopped before her and his face rose up to meet her curious gaze. He was a tall, heavy-looking young man of around three and twenty, his nose large and his eyes bulbous His hair heavy with pomade and perspiration. "You will excuse me, madam, but having been in the butchers just now, and when speaking to the man there, I made the most astonishing discovery that you are one of my fair cousins, and not just any one of them, indeed. Do I have it correct? Do I have the honour, nay the very great privilege, of addressing Mrs Darcy?"

Though a little revolted at his squirming manner, Elizabeth could not help being amused. "Mr William Collins, I presume. I am Mrs Darcy, though I will leave you to decide upon the level of honour and privilege attached to meeting me. Perhaps when we have been properly introduced, and you have known me for a whole hour altogether, you might think my acquaintance a punishment."

He looked confused and knew not how to take her comment, his air was grave and stately and his manners were very formal, she sensed he suffered from an incurable lack of humour.

"I did wonder whether I should be so forward in coming over when you do not know me, but for this, I am sure I will be forgiven. There is a wide difference, you know, between the established forms of ceremony amongst the laity, and those which regulate the clergy. Give me leave to observe that I consider the clerical office as equal in point of dignity with the highest rank in the kingdom – provided a proper humility of behaviour is at the same time maintained."

Elizabeth sorted through this mess of loquaciousness and found his meaning to be that he felt free to approach anybody he liked, from pauper to king, as long as he wore a clerical collar. "I did not think, Mr Collins, that you had already been ordained. Your parents gave me to understand you had not yet taken orders."

He waved this concern away. "It is a matter of weeks."

"I see. It is a point of semantics in your eyes then?"

He suddenly looked concerned, worried that he had affronted her and then began to apologise at length for detaining her, but kept her stood on the street for another ten minutes or so. When she eventually managed to interrupt him, assuring him she had taken no great offence, he began a long soliloquy on the subject of her gracious condescension and affability. The man was ridiculous and while in the right setting and mood Elizabeth might have found keen enjoyment in observing his absurdity, she now only wished to get away from him.

She made her excuses while he bowed and thanked her again and again. Two minutes after leaving him, she came upon Kitty and Lydia, who had come from home and were headed into Meryton.

"Oh, Lizzy, will you turn around and come back with us? The regiment comes today and we are going to see them march in."

Elizabeth raised her brows at them. "No, I will do no such thing, and neither will you. You will not stand out on the street gawping. I forbid it and insist you come home with me."

"Oh Lizzy, having you at home is not as much fun as I thought it would be," Lydia complained.

"It is not proving to be much fun for me either. Come now, indoors with you." She gave them a stern look, and luckily, was senior enough for them to obey her.

Elizabeth was beginning to form a plan of writing to her Aunt Gardiner, to propose that it might be best if Lydia were to stay with the Gardiners for a while, while Jane remained in Meryton to help her mother with Kitty and Mary. She had mentioned the idea the previous evening to Jane, who had been surprisingly agreeable to the switching of their positions; wishing to be of use and assistance, and also being concerned about Lydia's lack of decorum.

Thirty seven

When two days had gone by and they'd still had no sight of a red coat, the two youngest Bennet girls began to whine and protest. An invitation to supper and cards from their Aunt Phillips added to the discord and their noise became cacophonous. Jane and Elizabeth, knowing that some of the officers had been invited, insisted Lydia and Kitty were too young to attend, but their mother wavered, wanting to appease all of her daughters at the same time. For a while Mrs Bennet looked to be siding with Kitty and Lydia, complaining that her nerves could not stand any more of their crying, until Elizabeth won the day by saying that if the girls were to go, she would not, and neither would the carriage. So, only the four of them went, with Mary protesting as fervently about being forced to attend, as Lydia had about being left at home.

"I do not know why you were so worried, Lizzy," Mrs Bennet said as they approached the Phillipses' house. "They have been to my sister's parties many a time before."

"Not when the militia are expected, Mamma. Lydia is only thirteen, but to a man who does not think to ask her age, she might seem much older and her head is already full of beaus and flirting. Please do not let her out so much in society, there is a danger in it. You must think of her reputation, because she will not. She will imagine herself violently in love with one of them and do something silly, I would hate to see her disgraced and ruined."

"Oh, such a thing would not happen."

"Such things do happen, Mamma. It happened to me."

"That was different, Lizzy, and it has done you no harm, look at how well you are married."

Distressed by her mother's logic, Elizabeth turned to the window.

"Lydia just wants to look upon the officers. I remember a time when I liked a red coat myself - and, indeed, I do still at my heart," Mrs Bennet said.

"Maybe you will fall violently in love with one of them then, Mamma."

This remark, from Mary, so contrary to her usual solemnity, made them all laugh and when they went into the Phillipses' party, they were still smiling. Elizabeth was pleased further when she realised it was definitely to be an evening of cards, a few games of lottery tickets and a hot supper. There was no music and no expectation of dancing. Her aunt insisted on parading the three girls around. Elizabeth hung at the back of each introduction and once it was known she was married, she was of as little interest to the officers, as they were to her. Only one of them caught her eye, a young lieutenant of most gentlemanlike appearance, with an air that seemed to court attention - he certainly seemed to have the eye of every lady in the room. He had a good figure and very fine features, almost beautiful. He was unscarred and unmarked, with high eyebrows and a full mouth. Elizabeth saw he was taken with Jane immediately, as were most of the officers, but he glanced her way too. When he heard her name, though, he started most visibly, was clearly astounded and stared. He soon recovered and bowed, but his face was ashen, his countenance wary.

"You are Mrs Darcy?"

"Yes, sir, I am sorry, I did not catch your name, there are so many to remember."

"I am Mr Wickham, Lieutenant George Wickham. You are not, surely, one of the Pemberley Darcys?"

"I live at Pemberley, yes."

"How extraordinary! You are Mrs Fitzwilliam Darcy?"

Elizabeth nodded. "Yes, I am she; you seem to be one of the many people I have met recently, to whom my existence is a complete surprise."

"You'll forgive my stupidity in asking so many questions, but I am astounded at the coincidence of meeting you here. I grew up at Pemberley, you see." He tugged uneasily at his coat and looked away. "Have you never heard my name? Your husband has not mentioned me to you?"

"Oh, should I know you? My ignorance must offend. Are you a friend of the family?"

"No, I was not born so high as to earn the title of friend. My father was the son of the late Mr Darcy's steward. I was lucky enough, *for a while*, to have him as my benefactor."

His tone invited further questioning but at the same time, he inclined his head in a half bow and seemed to be offering to step away. "I should tell you that your husband may not wish you to speak with me. We fell out some time ago."

"Is that so? We have something in common then, Mr Wickham, for I too often fall out with my husband." It was a dreadfully disrespectful thing to say about Mr Darcy to someone she had only just been introduced to, but he laughed at her, favoured her with the most charming of smiles and she sensed he liked her boldness.

"Mr Darcy is not with you in Hertfordshire?"

"No, he is in the Indies on business. He has been gone for over a year now and is not expected back any time soon."

His eyes swept over her form and then his gaze returned to her face, to examine her more closely. "And, is it true what they say, does absence make the heart grow fonder?"

She demurred, refusing to answer. Feeling she had been familiar enough with him already, and sensing the danger of it, she walked away.

It was not the end of their dealings, however, and when cards were arranged, he took the seat next to her with a questioning look, silently asking if he were welcome. She said nothing either way, so he remained, and after a few moments, embarked on some conversation. He stuck to the safe topic of the weather at first, remarking on the wetness of the evening, but Elizabeth found he rendered even the commonest, dullest, most threadbare topic interesting, such was his skill as a speaker. She was taken in and they soon moved on to more interesting topics, while, of course, allowing for the demands of the game. He eventually spoke of his love of Pemberley, of his favourite views and walks thereabouts.

"You will get no disagreement from me as regards the beauty of Pemberley, for there is much to approve of," Elizabeth said.

"Yes, Mr Darcy is truly the luckiest of men. His estate is a noble one, with a clear ten thousand a year; he has a home, I think, where there is something to admire and adore at every turn." His look was shamefully intimate and flirtatious, and made Elizabeth shiver. "You'll forgive my rudeness when we first spoke," he said quietly. "I did know there was a Mrs Darcy in existence. It is just that I had not expected to find her so alluring. I wonder at Darcy's going away for so long, I would loath to be separated from Pemberley and *all* my beautiful things for any great length of time. How my heart would pine!"

Elizabeth felt hot and was reddening under the full force of his considerable charm. "There was some necessity to his going, I believe," she replied, knowing she ought to add a rebuke for his forwardness, but she was flattered and wondered what he would dare to say next.

"I suppose he has more responsibility now, with his father gone. The late Mr Darcy was one of the best men that ever breathed and the truest friend I ever had. I have a thousand tender recollections of his kindness towards me."

"It seems a shame then, that you are no longer welcome at Pemberley. May I enquire as to the source of the disagreement between my husband and yourself?"

"It is not my place to speak ill of the husband to the wife, I have not such bad manners."

She shrugged, sensing he was playing with her. "Do not tell me then. I might get on tolerably well with the rest of my life without knowing."

"But you are curious?" he said, leaning forwards, his eyes sparkling, his velvety tones mesmerising her.

"Who could not be? You look at me as if you consider yourself a wronged party, what has he done to wound you?"

"The late Mr Darcy bequeathed me the next presentation of the best living in his gift. He was my godfather and excessively attached to me and meant to provide for me amply. The living came empty shortly after his death, but it was given elsewhere."

"I wonder then, that you do not seek legal redress."

"It was an informal promise. I have no hope of success through the law. A man of honour could not have doubted his father's intentions and wishes, but his son makes some excuse for not giving it, asserting that I have forfeited it through extravagance or imprudence – but I really have done nothing to deserve to lose it. I have a warm, unguarded temper, and perhaps I have spoken of him, and to him, too freely. We are very different sort of men and he hates me simply because his father loved me."

Elizabeth focussed her attention on the cards in her hand, rather than on him, for his look was appealing and hard to resist. "I do not claim Mr Darcy does not have it within him to be harsh at times and maybe his relationship with his father was not always easy, and yet…"

"And yet?" he asked.

She shrugged a shoulder. "He *is* a man of honour. What would you say if I told you I do not believe you?"

Mr Wickham merely laughed. "You dislike him as much as I do, I can see it in your eyes."

"My feelings for him are very personal to me, and neither here nor there to your situation, but if his father had made you a promise, I don't believe Mr Darcy would fail to fulfil it without good reason."

"I shall not attempt to denigrate him further then, if you are determined I am the liar in the case, but I will say that there is more to our tale than this. There are things I cannot mention in a drawing room - other dealings I have had with him. I have done nothing so terrible, except to injure his damnable pride. I have paid for minor offences in a most spectacular way, and I shall suffer from the effects of our disagreement for the rest of my life."

He caught her attention with this, and in his looks, there was truth. She could well imagine Mr Darcy taking umbrage at some silly mistake Mr Wickham had made. Their discourse returned to safer topics, but throughout the evening he continued to be near her and paid her most assiduous attention.

She went away with her head full of him. She could think of nothing but Mr Wickham, and what he had told her, all the way home. His manners had recommended him to everybody. Whatever he said, was said well; and whatever he did, done gracefully. In bed, when she shut her eyes, she saw his penetrating, mesmerising gaze, so focussed on her. She related his tale of the lost living to Jane in private the next day. Her sister tried to get her to take a more balanced view, concluding that perhaps it was a sad case of two very good childhood friends falling out, and maybe both of them were feeling some injury as a result. By now, however, Elizabeth was much preoccupied in going over all the injuries Mr Darcy had done to her and, influenced by her own prejudices, became convinced her husband had not been fair to Mr Wickham.

Her mother was delighted by the officers and invited them frequently to tea, and once to dine. An Elizabeth who was not so enamoured of her new friend Mr Wickham might have objected at their presence in the house, but he excited and thrilled her; flattered and tempted her to such a degree that whenever he left a room, she found herself longing for the next sight of him. Her fears for Mary, Kitty and Lydia drifted to the back of her mind, so caught was she in her fancy, and though a part of her knew she was being undutiful and not diligent, she could not focus her mind enough to care.

They were immersed in a game - a playful flirtation, which Elizabeth never intended to cause anybody any harm, and which she thought must have its boundaries. Wickham would speak the words lovely, beautiful, pretty or handsome, often, in the context of any dull conversation, but then would cast a glance her way. Even in a drawing room or parlour full of people, he could make her feel wanted. She would push him away with caustic words, tease and taunt him, before pulling him back with a warm look, a welcoming smile. He manoeuvred himself to her side at every opportunity and they would spend far too long speaking alone, talking only to each other, while laughing and flirting.

When Jane took her aside for a walk one day, she half expected the sort of lecture an older sister was well within her rights to deliver, even to a married sister, but it seemed she had been so caught up in her own amours, she had failed to notice Jane had an admirer of her own.

"I think he is on the verge of an offer," Jane said.

Elizabeth was confused and astonished. "Who?"

"Why, Mr Collins of course. You must have noticed his marked attentions towards me."

To her shame, Elizabeth had not. She had thought Mary had been earmarked as the future Mrs Collins and had been vaguely watching their interactions. She had been pleased when William Collins had not made any direct overtures, but this news shocked her. How dare he single out Jane? She was so far above him, in every way - looks, manners and grace, that it seemed impossible he would try for her. "Please tell me you are not considering him?" Elizabeth said.

"Mamma believes I should encourage him, that he would be an excellent match." Jane's forehead was creased in thought. "It would be a great comfort to her to think of me as the future mistress of Longbourn, and it would do honour to Papa as well."

"Jane, be serious. Papa would turn in his grave to see you married to such a man. Longbourn, for all our happy memories of it, is not worth forty years of misery, unless you do actually admire him?"

"Well, I do not think him unkind, I would not be mistreated. But he is perhaps a little…." Jane covered her mouth before anything further could spill from it.

"Go on, Jane. You may say it. I know it goes against your very nature, but there are people in the world so worthy of contempt, that a bad thought or two may be given voice to."

"But he is not worthy of contempt, Lizzy. Though his manners are a little trying, perhaps."

"Well, if that's the worst you can do, I shall have to be satisfied." At Jane's look, she was a little penitent. "But do you truly like him, Jane?"

"He is a man of the cloth, and to be a clergyman's wife would be very acceptable to me. His prospects are excellent."

"What of your prospects, for happiness? Does he make your heart race? Does he make your soul sing?" Elizabeth sank onto a nearby log, using it as a seat, and her head fell into her hands. If only the colonel were independent enough to make Jane an offer. How happy it would make her to see her sister as Mrs Fitzwilliam and married to a man who would truly appreciate her.

"No, but Lizzy, I have never yet met a man who does rouse any strong emotion in me - and are such things the most important consideration in accepting a man, what of comfort and a good home?"

"You are asking me?" Elizabeth cried. "Please do not think I have all the answers. You know my situation and how it was arrived at, but Jane, I do wonder whether at least one woman in the world might be lucky enough to have everything; a man she truly loves, who would love her back with equal passion, and is it too much to expect that he might also be a good match for her in terms of fortune and status? Can such a miracle happen? If it can, then I wish it with all my heart for you. Be patient a little longer, let love be your watchword, and give me some faith that good things can happen to good people."

Jane looked unsure and sat beside her. "What if I never receive another offer? I am twenty and this would be my first."

"You will, how could you not?" Elizabeth said firmly, but no sooner had she finished trying to persuade Jane that William Collins was entirely wrong for her; than the man himself was before them, with an ingratiating smile and many bows.

"Your good mother told me I would find you walking in the shrubbery, and sent me out to join you."

Elizabeth got to her feet and put herself between her cousin and Jane as they walked the paths together. Thinking how well it would do to put an even greater distance between

Mr Collins and her sister, she talked of his going away to take orders and where he might settle afterwards.

He looked glad of this opening and made a great long speech about it, during which Elizabeth's attention wandered, but she was finally roused back to interest by his mentioning Lady Catherine de Bourgh and how he had applied to her for a living, which was soon to become vacant, but where it was to be bestowed, was still undecided.

"I understand she is your aunt, Mrs Darcy. I am sure a recommendation, from such a close relation as yourself, might have some influence over the matter."

"Oh," Elizabeth suddenly understood the Collinses eagerness to please her nowadays. She had attributed it just to a deference for the Darcy name, and all the sway it held within the church, but now she saw they had a direct, more personal reason, to win her approval. "Mr Collins, I would, of course, gladly assist you if it were within my power to do so, but I am no great favourite of Lady Catherine. She is an aunt through marriage, but I have never met the lady. There is current discord between my branch of the family and hers, my recommendation would more likely do you harm than good."

He stopped, clearly disturbed at the information. "I see." Where he had been all obsequiousness and sycophancy to her before, he now tossed his head and looked cross at having applied to her. "The living of Hunsford, near Rosings Park, which Lady Catherine has within her power, would have suited me a great deal and placed me in the happy position of being able to take a wife very soon." He looked sideways at Jane with a tight smile. "I have heard Lady Catherine sets great store by a man of the cloth being settled, and I believe she would approve of my taking a wife who was an active sort of person, such as one of your sisters, Mrs Darcy, a gentlewoman but not brought up too high and quite used to a small income."

To be talking of such things in front of the woman he hoped to marry made him insufferable in Elizabeth's eyes. He spoke of her sisters as if they were livestock he wished to purchase. His only concern seemed to be that they had arms and legs aplenty and would suit his needs - he would certainly never give a care for theirs.

"Well, I wish you luck with all your plans, Mr Collins." And then declaring herself cold and unable to walk any further, she went inside and took Jane with her.

Thirty eight

They went for dinner at Lucas Lodge the next evening, a place where the Collinses were not usually invited and Elizabeth was pleased to see them absent, but there was a large party, thanks to the presence of the officers. She looked for Wickham, unable to help herself, wishing for his company and his notice.

When she did not immediately see him, she drifted towards Charlotte Lucas who raised a brow at her by way of greeting. "He is not here yet, but he has been invited."

"Who do you speak of?"

"Mr Wickham, it is he you look for, isn't it? Take care, Eliza, people are beginning to notice your preference for him, and he makes no secret of his for you."

"Am I not allowed to have a friend?"

"Not one who looks at you as he does," Charlotte warned.

"I need no advice from you, Charlotte, I promise I have no intention of causing a scandal. If there is flirting, it is quite harmless. Please leave me to my own business, as I will you to yours, and Jane needs no guidance either. You have filled her head with the notion that she ought to accept the first man who can offer her a home with a decent front parlour, whether she likes him or not."

Offended, Charlotte gave a curt bow and looked to move away, before Elizabeth caught her arm. "I am sorry, forgive my sharp tongue. I know you mean well."

"I do mean well, Eliza. My family and yours have been friends for many years, and I have become very fond of you, since you returned to Hertfordshire. I have to tell you that I do not trust Mr Wickham. He has told his tale of woe to the whole town; everybody knows he considers himself cheated by your husband. By all rights, you should hate him for the way he slanders Mr Darcy."

"But, perhaps he *has* been mistreated by him. I know my husband, Charlotte, and he can be stubborn and unyielding in temper. He does have a tendency towards thinking he has the right of everything. I can well imagine him taking against Mr Wickham for the slightest misdeed."

"Well then, I have said all I intend to on the matter, and you have been so kind as to listen. I hope that it will be the only subject on which we ever disagree, and we can continue to be friends."

Elizabeth smiled and nodded, but when dinner was called and Wickham appeared suddenly at her side to escort her in, she dared not meet Charlotte's gaze. He seated himself next to her. The Lucases had invited more guests than the table was designed for and so they sat very close, elbows brushing. The room was warm and loud and they could converse freely without being overheard, as long as their tone was lowered. Elizabeth ate little, so attentive was she to his conversation, and she drank much without really noticing it, her glass being readily refilled by him every time it became even half empty. Lightheaded and happy, she did not chastise him when he spoke of her beauty, and said nothing when his hand brushed her knee under the table. His direct look told her it had been no accident.

He followed her around after dinner. There was some impromptu music and dancing. He asked, but she declined.

"You are right," he said, "far better to sit at the back of the room here, where we might talk, rather than up there on display." He nodded at the dancers. "I shall fetch you another glass of wine."

"Oh, I am not sure I should..." She got up to stop him and stumbled a little, bumping into the back of Jane's chair.

"Lizzy, are you well? Perhaps we ought to go home," Jane said, turning to her, full of concern.

She was about to protest and then noticed the room spun about wildly and Jane's features were blurred. She could not even remember her last conversation with Wickham. What had they been talking of, and how late was it? Just how much wine had she taken?

"Yes, I think I should go home. Would you tell Mamma and order the carriage brought round please, Jane?"

"Of course."

She went to give her goodbyes to their hosts and wondered if her voice was slurred. There was an odd look on Sir William's face, half amused and half concerned, but he bowed and wished her goodnight.

She went out into the hall and then into the empty, dark coat room to fetch her wrap. Then she found herself grabbed by the arms and pushed backwards against the wall.

"Kiss me, quickly, before someone comes."

There was only the faintest of slivers of light from a candle in the hallway and it did nothing to illuminate the place, but even in the near pitch black, she knew it was Wickham. She knew his voice, his scent, his height and they were all enough to nearly overpower her senses, to make her lean her face up towards his.

"You are mad," she said instead.

"I am mad for you. You are all I can think of. I cannot sleep. I toss and turn and hear your voice, your laugh. I dream of your eyes, your hair, your lips. A kiss, I beg you."

"I cannot."

"But you want to, you cannot deny what you feel for me, this is dangerous I know, mad, as you say, but meet me tomorrow. Name the place, the time, somewhere we will not be seen and I will be there."

Shaking her head, Elizabeth pushed past him, half expecting him to haul her back, but there were footsteps heard in the hallway which perhaps deterred him. She dashed from the room, and luckily, he did not expose her by immediately following. Jane was there and within five minutes she was in the carriage heading home, still trembling from the risky encounter.

Elizabeth groaned and put her hands over her eyes when the curtains were drawn back the next day by Rose Kiddy.

"I'm sorry, madam. Did you want to go on sleeping? Just it's nearly eleven and so far past your normal hour for rising, I thought I had better wake you."

"No, it is fine, but I have a terrible headache, Rose, and I am so thirsty."

Rose giggled. "It is the wine, Mrs Darcy, you were well in your cups last night. You passed out on the bed the minute I got your nightgown on, and that was no easy task."

Memories of the previous evening assailed her, none of them good. She had fawned over Wickham, embarrassed herself in front of Sir William Lucas and then there had been that incident in the coat room. She ought to have screamed the place down, revealed him as a seducer; instead she had merely run off, her head full of his words and her body in danger of succumbing to his pleas for kisses.

Rose approached her with a piece of paper that had been folded over many times, to make it very small. "I have been into Meryton already this morning. A gentleman asked me to give you this."

"A gentleman!" Elizabeth said, knowing instantly it was a note from Wickham. She took it from the maid, and struggled with her conscience briefly, before handing it back to her unopened. "Rose, I don't expect you to run notes for me. Don't let him importune you again, refuse on my behalf if he approaches you, and I shall not give you anything for him. Throw it on the fire."

Looking relieved, Rose did as she asked. "I am glad. I would do anything you asked of me, of course, but I did not like it. Will I fetch you a tray?"

"Please, I don't think I could eat anything other than toast, though." Her head still pounding, Elizabeth groaned and wiggled further under the covers. "I don't think I am fit to face the world today. Shall we swap places, Rose? You can go and be Mrs Darcy, I am tired of her."

Laughing, her maid went off to fetch her some sustenance. Elizabeth thought of how little wine or spirits Mr Darcy took, and could now understand why - he was a man who liked to be in control. The alcohol had lowered her inhibitions and made her careless, and now she felt dreadful. She resolved never to take more than two glasses in one night ever again.

She flipped onto her back and stared up at the ceiling, speaking quietly into the empty room. "How are you,

Mr Darcy? And do you ever think of me; do I ever cross your mind?"

Oh the lecture she would have endured if he had seen her behaviour of the previous evening. She could almost see his frown, feel his disapproval.

Elizabeth was beginning to think Charlotte had been right to warn her off Mr Wickham, and for the first time since the evening when they had first become acquainted, she gave serious thought to his character. Rising gingerly from the bed, she threw on the dressing gown Rose had left draped over the bottom of the bed and went over to the table by the window, where she had left her elegant little writing set.

She had gotten out of bed resolving to write to Mr Darcy, but after taking a blank piece of paper, she sat in front of it, immobile, for some considerable time. She wanted to ask about his dealings with Mr Wickham - for his version of events - thinking that even if the letter took months to reach him, and even if he deigned to answer, and that letter took months to travel back to her at Pemberley, she would still be interested in the answer. She also wanted to ask how the business of her mother's income had been arranged, and to thank him, if it had been his doing. But when Rose returned with her breakfast tray, she had not committed a single word to ink, and she pushed the paper and pen aside. Why would she write to him? They had been married for three years, separated for most of those, and she had still never received a single letter from him. Instead, she ate and dressed and went downstairs, going out of a side door so as not come across anyone. Determined to have no company but her own, she set out along the paths and lanes of her childhood, stopping briefly outside the walls of Longbourn to wallow in tender recollections for a while, before moving off down towards the farms, hardly knowing where she was bound, but wishing to be away from any kind of society.

Encountering Mr Wickham on the path towards Oakham Mount astonished her.

"You received my note then?" he said. "Thank you for meeting me."

If in a better mood, she might have laughed at the irony of it, to have not read his note and still ended up there, with no one else in sight, was bad luck indeed. If she had opened his missive, she would have known how to avoid him. "Mr Wickham, I am going to turn back now, towards Meryton."

"No, please come up to the Mount with me. Or at least stay here and listen to my apologies. My behaviour last night was unpardonable. I thought my advances, my overtures, might be welcomed. If I had it wrong and offended you, I am indeed sorry."

She shook her head. "Let us forget it, I was at fault too, if I led you to believe, that I would wish for…" the words would not come. "I shall turn back and that will be the end of the matter. Perhaps it might be best if you do not come to the house so often."

She had not gone ten paces from him before his voice stopped her.

"Elizabeth, I am falling in love with you."

"I have never given you permission to address me so," she replied without turning around.

"Do not be cold to me, I beg of you. Such words are like a knife through my soul."

She turned then. "Mr Wickham, I am married, what could you have possibly hoped for, or expected?"

He approached and took one of her hands in his own. She attempted to pull away, but he held on tight. "I expect nothing, but what I hope for is that you will admit to wanting me too, and that you do not want him."

"And then what? That we conduct some sort of torrid affair? I know some women in my position take lovers, but I cannot imagine such an existence for myself. I could not cope with the level of deceit it would involve."

"No, you misunderstand me, Elizabeth. I would not want you to lead two lives. For you to lay in my arms, for us to know heaven, and then to send you home to him. I do not wish to share you, my love, I want you all for myself."

She supposed her face must have shown her anguish, because another voice came from behind her - someone had seen a need to intrude.

308

"Is this man bothering you, Mrs Darcy?"

Wickham dropped her hand and looked over her shoulder. "Run along with you, boy, this does not concern you."

"I think it does. I'll stay here unless the lady wishes me to go."

It was a country accent, not at all refined, and she was not surprised at Wickham trying to dismiss the boy, but there was something familiar about the voice that made Elizabeth turn towards it. She saw rough clothes and large heavy work boots. She blinked into the sunshine, trying to make out the face.

"Is that a way to address a gentleman and an officer?" Wickham complained.

"I'm no soldier. I'll address you how I like. I'd be happy to escort you home, Mrs Darcy."

Elizabeth could not help but smile, for one moment she was wondering how he knew her name, and in the very next, she realised she knew him. "Henry? Henry Jones?"

He grinned back at her in response and nodded. "How are you, Lizzy?"

"I am very well, Henry, and so pleased to see you." He was so tall and so broad, such a strong-looking young man that she did not wonder at his standing up to Mr Wickham and his courage gave her the impetus to do likewise. "We will have to speak on another occasion, Mr Wickham. Henry Jones is a very dear friend of mine, a playmate from my youth and I was walking this way to call on his mother, to give her my respects."

Wickham's jaw twitched and he scowled at Henry before looking back at Elizabeth. But then his face broke into his usual easy smile, and he pretended nothing of any import had happened. "We have some things still to discuss though, Mrs Darcy. We shall speak again soon I hope."

She nodded and he went, with a crisp bow at them both.

Elizabeth watched Wickham go before addressing Henry. "I do not know what to say to you first. What you just saw may have you thinking bad things about me, and I do not say you are incorrect to do so."

"It is none of my business, but what I saw was a man trying to persuade a lady around to his way of thinking, and that the young lady was reluctant. You do not mind me having stepped in?"

"No, not at all, Lord, I hardly knew you, Henry. You are so different. So…"

"So what?" he prompted.

She wanted to say 'manly', but it would have made her blush to do so. "You are a man and not a boy."

"And you are a lady, not a boy!" He laughed in a rich deep way she remembered well. "The last time I saw you, you were running off into the woods in breeches and cap."

"Oh do not remind me of how foolish I was then."

"I know you were trying to get rid of that fellow just now, but you know, my mother would like to see you, if you have some time to spare, and you look as if you could do with a sit down."

She agreed and they walked down to the Joneses' farm together, him telling her news of the tenants, which her sisters and mother had not been able to supply.

Mrs Jones put a hand to her chest and truly did not know her. She looked at Henry, wondering what he was about, bringing a lady home with him.

"It is Lizzy Bennet, Mrs Darcy now," he told his mother.

"Well bless me, of course it is, now I see that smile full of cheek, I would know you anywhere," Mrs Jones covered her mouth. "Oh you will excuse me."

Elizabeth laughed and was pleased to sit down at their plain, well-worn kitchen table. Mrs Jones bustled around her, trying to tidy a few things away and smoothing down her apron. Children ran in and out constantly, and though she was told their names, they were too numerous for Elizabeth to remember them all. A girl of three or four climbed onto her lap without ceremony or invitation and sat mutely, staring up at her.

"Oh get her off you, Mrs Darcy. She will make your lovely gown all muddy."

"I truly do not mind, Mrs Jones," Elizabeth said, stroking the little girl's hair. "Tell me of Mr Collins, is he a good landlord?"

Mrs Jones pursed her lips and shared a look with Henry, who was stood leaning casually against the dresser. "We preferred it when Longbourn was in the hands of Mr Bennet," he said evenly.

"As did I," Elizabeth replied. "Thank you for making me feel so welcome, Mrs Jones, you have a lovely family."

"Oh, we don't do so bad." Mrs Jones truly was a cheerful woman and seemed content, despite her lot as a farmer's wife, with more children than were manageable scampering about the place. Elizabeth could imagine, but not truly comprehend, the extent of her daily toil, and felt her own luck then - realised how privileged she was, and terribly spoilt. If she wanted something, she rang a bell for it. Dozens of people attended her whims and fancies and cared for her. She might have ten baths a day and eat cake in bed, if she chose - very good cake at that. She sat in splendour, yet was often found in scowling complaint, and she resolved to do better. No, she did not have the life she might have wished for, but she had a very good one. Perhaps, fortune had favoured her by giving her not so much what she wanted, but everything she might need.

"The farm does well, and the house is a very good one," Mrs Jones said. "They say you married well. Your new place must be a bit bigger than this, I s'pose?"

Elizabeth tried not to smile. "Just a little bigger, yes." She was sitting in a house where there were, in total, four rooms, two downstairs and two upstairs. Comparing it to Pemberley, where there were two rooms set aside just for the practising of music, and one very grand room for the listening of it (that one room larger than the whole of the Joneses' house entirely), was ridiculous.

She did not stay too long, not wishing her presence to make them uncomfortable, but was sent away warmly. Henry offered to walk her home but she declined.

"Your friend will be long gone by now, I should think," he said.

"Yes, I think he will. It has been lovely to see you again and know you are well."

"Hold on a minute, Lizzy." Henry disappeared but returned quickly, his hand gripped tightly around three or four letters, which he passed to her. "I never knew what to do with them, but I didn't want to put 'em on the fire."

Recognising her own handwriting, Elizabeth knew they were the letters she had sent him when she had first gone to Pemberley. She gave him her thanks and they smiled at each other. "I am sorry to have written such drivel to you, Henry. I gave you much to read on the subject of my youthful sulks and misplaced misery. You were very kind to reply."

"I would not have been able to, if you hadn't taught me my letters, how patient you were with a dim-witted farmer's boy."

"You are not dim, Henry. It was no chore to teach you."

They were both silent for a while, she thinking of more innocent times. Of how they had once stretched out, flat on their stomachs, pouring over books under an old oak tree, she sounding the words out for him, while his young brow furrowed in concentration.

Saying a simple, fond goodbye, she left him to walk back to Meryton.

Her ruminations on the past took her to the churchyard, where she sat in her father's company for a good half hour, trying to fix in her mind all the things she was starting to forget - his laughter and the twinkling of his eyes. She thought of how his unshaven chin would gently scratch her cheek on those occasions when she would crawl onto his lap as a small child, creeping into his study before the rest of the house had woken. She had once thought him perfect, but now, although all her former affection still prevailed, she could see faults. His derisive treatment of their mother and total lack of conjugal obligation had been obvious to her - even at thirteen or fourteen - she had noticed how he had lacked decorum and made Mrs Bennet a foolish figure before her

312

own children. And she, Elizabeth, he had favoured unfairly; ignoring the younger ones almost completely, calling them 'silly' and dismissing them at every opportunity - and what steps had he taken to protect his family in the event of his premature death? Had he saved money for them? No. His last act had been to call in an old favour and secure a favourable position for her; he had done nothing for her siblings. If she hadn't gotten herself into so much trouble and Mr Darcy hadn't been forced to marry her, her sisters and mother would not have such a comfortable home. Her idiocy had done more for her family's fortunes than her father ever had. His laconic, slightly scatty, impracticality had been charming but had done them no favours. And yet, she loved him still, because she supposed, everyone had defects, faults and it was one's level of tolerance, or ability to overlook them, that decided the depth of the affection. She rose from the churchyard bench and began the walk back again, thinking of how Mr Darcy would not play so loosely with her security. He had ridden to Matlock, she remembered, to talk to the countess about what would happen to her and Georgiana if he never returned from the Indies. He had an odd notion of kindness and caring perhaps, her husband, but she didn't worry for one moment that her current levels of comfort would diminish if anything terrible happened to him.

Her fears, instead, were to do with how things would be when he *did* return. How was she supposed to feel about him? How was she supposed to act around him? Did she hate him still? No, that was too strong a word, a silly immature emotion. Breathing deeply, and running a hand along the hedgerows as she passed them, she put him from her mind. He was too complex a subject, and her feelings for him were so interwoven with the painful recollections of some of her previous folly, that she could not think on him for too long without bringing on a headache.

Thirty nine

Wickham was waiting in the parlour when Elizabeth reached the house and she was dismayed to learn that her mother had invited him to stay for dinner. Knowing he was bound to contrive some situation where they could be alone, she thought it better to deal with him directly. She threw the letters, along with her bonnet and gloves, onto a small table and took him on a tour of the pleasant little garden at the rear of the house.

"I meant everything I said, Elizabeth, most sincerely," he began, as soon as they were out of the sight and hearing of anyone else.

He reached for her, perhaps to take her into his arms, but she stepped deftly away. If he held her and she enjoyed it, there was no telling what other things she might succumb to. His eyes were imploring, full of love and desire. He was handsome, intoxicating, exciting, but it was so wrong. "I cannot act as I choose, Mr Wickham. If circumstances were different, then I'm sure I would welcome such attentions, but as things are, I think we ought to say goodbye privately and avoid each other as much as possible until I return to Pemberley."

He stopped, his voice became firmer. "But you have not heard me out. What I propose is that we go away together. There is a place by the sea in Kent where we could go, where nobody knows you. I would introduce you as Mrs Wickham and why would anyone think you are not?"

"And…?" she asked, incredulous.

"And what?"

"Have you thought no further than that? It will be fine for us for a few days, I suppose, to pretend. What happens when I am missing? What will my family think? It would be a monumental scandal."

"Of course I have thought of that. Darcy will seek a separation. Divorce might not be possible, and it pains me to think you will never truly be my wife, but I think he would pay to have you live quietly away from him somewhere. He might pay very handsomely. We might live very well."

Elizabeth could hardly believe he would suggest such a thing and wondered at the excited expression on his face when he spoke of Mr Darcy paying them money. She moved away but he pulled her into his embrace, before she had time to protest.

"I will not let you go back to him; you ought to know what it is to be properly loved by someone other than Darcy. His heart is caked in ice. I would make you feel things he cannot. I would make you cry out with pleasure, Elizabeth," he whispered furiously into her ear. "I would lay money that he never has."

"Do you truly love me, or do you merely seek to injure him?" she said, trying to struggle free, new ideas and doubts occurring to her.

"Oh my love, you misunderstand me. It is all about you, of course."

Elizabeth heard a footstep, a crunch of twigs beneath a boot and looked up in astonishment to see Colonel Fitzwilliam standing a few feet away. Wickham released her immediately.

"I came to surprise you, Elizabeth," Colonel Fitzwilliam said, coming closer, "but it seems I am the one very much surprised. Will you go indoors?"

She nodded and fled, leaving the two men facing each other. As she went into the house, she looked back to see Wickham's head hung low for a moment, before he raised it and smiled, trying to affect bravado. The colonel was still and silent, but his fists were clenched at his sides. Elizabeth went in, where she saw Mrs Gardiner talking to her mother. She looked up at Elizabeth to greet her, but instead her face crinkled in concern.

"Whatever is the matter? Did the colonel find you? I got your letter and think your proposal an excellent one. I spoke of it to the colonel and he was kind enough to bring me. You do not look very pleased to see us though."

"I am glad to see you, very much so, but…excuse me." She went to her room, where she retreated into a corner and sat curled up in a ball on the floor, with her arms around her knees. She did not cry, her fear was too great, held too tightly within her. Rose came to her after fifteen minutes or so, with a soft knock on the door, but she sent her away, and would not admit her mother either. She had no idea how long she remained so, and closed her ears to the noise of the house, of people moving around downstairs, doors opening and closing. Her own body seemed paralysed.

Mrs Gardiner came in the end, not waiting for permission to enter, and sat on the floor beside her. "The colonel wants to see you."

"I can't face him."

"He is a good man, Elizabeth. He will treat you fairly."

"Is Mr Wickham gone?"

"Yes. He was despatched long ago. I wish I had known you had come into his company, but your letter did not mention him and I couldn't have expected that he would end up here." Mrs Gardiner wrung her hands together.

Elizabeth's head finally rose up. "You know him?"

"I know of him. I grew up in Lambton, remember? I am afraid he is not of good character, Elizabeth. He got a girl in trouble there and left her to go to London. He eventually returned to marry her but only after her father went to George Darcy to complain of it. Mr Darcy settled a sum of money on Wickham so he might afford to take a wife, and purchased his commission for him."

"He is married?"

"Yes he is married, and has a child. He spoke nothing of this to you, I suppose?"

"Oh I am so stupid," Elizabeth cried. "I am a silly, foolish, horrible girl and I don't know why anybody is ever kind to me. I am completely undeserving."

"What has happened between the two of you? You may be honest with me, I will not judge," Mrs Gardiner asked.

"Oh nothing, not even a kiss. I thought I was clever, I felt like one of those fashionable society ladies who flirt with impunity. It was fun, a silly game and I was flattered."

"It was a dangerous game."

"Yes, I began to see that and sought to withdraw, but when I tried he began to speak of love - he wanted us to go away together. And he is married? As bound to someone as I

316

am. Would he have just abandoned her do you think, his wife? How could I have not seen him for what he was?"

"It seems to me he is a practised and accomplished seducer, Elizabeth. You have lived so quietly at Pemberley these past years, that you have probably not come across a man of his ilk before, and as unhappy in your situation as you are, you were probably more open, more susceptible to his charms." Mrs Gardiner took her into her arms and kissed her forehead. "The important thing here is that nothing happened and he is gone, you are safe. Though, I think, perhaps you would have extracted yourself from the danger, given a little more time, you would have seen sense."

She heard the colonel's distinctive shuffling walk in the corridor, the rap of his stick on the floorboards. He had obviously grown tired of waiting for her downstairs and appeared in the doorway. "I would never dream of invading your privacy normally, Elizabeth, but I am conscious of the time. If we are to make it back to London tonight we need to leave in an hour. I shall send Rose up to you, to help you pack."

"I cannot leave so suddenly, without a proper leave taking, and farewell visits," she said.

"You will not reside another night anywhere where George Wickham is also present," he insisted, spitting Wickham's name at her. "You'll be in London tonight, and we'll leave for Pemberley tomorrow."

Elizabeth let out a sound of anguish, and throwing off her aunt's embrace, got to her feet and whirled at him. "I am so sick of being told what to do by men. Don't run, sit still, stay at home, be this, be that. I am eighteen. I am not a child anymore."

"No, you are not." The colonel was cold towards her. "But you will be leaving in an hour. I made a promise to my cousin that I fully intend to keep. Be ready."

It was a mixture of the warning in his voice, her longstanding affection for him, and her own shame at having been seen in another man's arms that eventually made her do as she was told. She came down less than an hour later in her travelling clothes and went to the parlour to say her goodbyes. Her mother was bewildered with all that had passed and wailed and moaned at Elizabeth going away again so soon after she had come home. It was mostly theatrics. Elizabeth sensed Mrs Bennet would be as glad to be able to talk of Mrs Darcy to her neighbours, as she would be to have her second daughter near. Still, it was lovely to be embraced by her and wept over. She kissed her sisters, knowing it would be a long time before she saw them again. Jane, she learnt, had been given the option of returning instantly to Town with them, but had elected to remain with their mother a little longer. The farewell from her was the hardest to endure but she managed it, asking her sister to give her excuses and apologies in the neighbourhood.

"I am sorry to have to part from you again so quickly," she whispered into Jane's ear.

"It is perhaps for the best, Lizzy. People were starting to talk."

"As if I have not embarrassed you all enough in the past, I sought out more trouble. Will you say goodbye to Charlotte for me?"

Jane agreed and Elizabeth gave her hand one last squeeze before looking about the parlour. "Where are my letters?" Elizabeth asked, going to the table where she had left them. "I brought some letters back with me, when I came in from my walk. They were just here, has someone moved them?"

Her sisters all looked at her blankly, but Mrs Bennet was able to solve the mystery, though the answer sent a shiver of terror through Elizabeth. "Oh, those. Mr Wickham took them. I supposed they were his and he went off to post them."

"They were not his, they were mine," she said, though no one seemed bothered by her plight. She tried to remember what they contained. Nothing so terrible, she was sure, but Henry had been her closest friend at the time they had been written, and she had been honest with him, as she had not been with any of her other correspondents. That Mr Wickham had taken them was a cause for disturbance. What could he have meant by it? Did he just want something of

318

hers, or did he mean to use them to try and wound her in some way?

There was no time, however, to dwell too long on the subject, for the colonel awaited her at the door. He said not a word as he handed her into the carriage. Mrs Gardiner squeezed her hand.

"You have come all the way from Town, only to have to go straight back again. I am sorry," Elizabeth apologised.

"I can come to see your mother another time and speak to her of Lydia and Jane. It is only half a day's travel for me. Do not concern yourself."

When they had gone ten miles and the colonel had still not spoken, still not acknowledged her, Elizabeth began to despair that she had lost his confidence forever. "I cannot blame you for being angry with me," she told him. "You placed your trust in me, and I let you down."

He finally looked her way. "Wickham, Elizabeth, of all people! Did you choose him deliberately?"

"Elizabeth did not know who he was, or what he was, Colonel. I don't think spite was her motivation," Mrs Gardiner said.

While grateful for her aunt's defence of her, Elizabeth wondered secretly whether there had been some element of her wishing to seek revenge. She had known of Mr Darcy's and Wickham's dispute on the very first night she had met him. Had that been part of the attraction?

"You'd better pray there are no repercussions," the colonel said, bitterly.

At first she thought of the letters Wickham had taken from the table, and then of the whispers and glances that had been directed their way while out in society, and then she realised the true meaning behind the colonel's words. Both shocked and disgusted, she raised her arm and banged on the carriage roof, shouting for it to stop. It did, suddenly, causing them all to slide in their seats. Elizabeth recovered first, pulled the door handle and jumped herself down. She strode down the road a little way and then realised the stupidity of it. She could not walk all the way back to Meryton and so began to come back. The colonel met her halfway.

"How dare you?" she raged at him.

"What do you expect me to think?" he said. "You were in his arms, I heard him talk of taking you away to live in sin with him."

"Then you might have also have heard me refuse. He held me once, today, I swear it. And I was trying to say goodbye to him. I know I have acted badly, but upon my honour, I have done nothing so very terrible, and I would hope we are good enough friends for you to believe me."

The colonel's jaw twitched and he smiled a little. "Look at us, screaming at each other in the middle of the road like a couple of fishwives. This is what George Wickham does to people; he's a cur, Elizabeth, a mongrel. I detest the man. I wanted to hurt him, very badly."

"What *did* you do to him?"

"Nothing, I warned him off, then went to see his commanding officer. He'll deal with him as he sees fit. Come on now, back to the coach and I will tell you a few things about Mr Wickham."

Once they were seated again, the colonel appealed to Mrs Gardiner for her discretion and leaned forward. "They were once the best of friends. Where Darcy was reserved, George was gregarious. Where Darcy is cautious, he was daring and amusing. It suited Darcy well to have such a friend, at first. When they completed their studies, they went to London and raised all sorts of hell, and a few eyebrows. Darcy's father was furious and Wickham was summoned back to Pemberley while Darcy remained in London. I think the idea was to separate them, and George needed closer supervision and guidance. However, when he arrived back in Derbyshire, he seduced a local girl."

"And had to marry her, yes, Mrs Gardiner has since told me."

"There is more to it than that, I'm afraid. He knew he had gotten the girl in trouble and ignored her pleas for help. He was given the opportunity to go back to London on an errand for George Darcy and took it." The colonel shifted in his seat. "Unlike Wickham, Darcy had taken his father's warnings more seriously. He had sobered up and began to court Emma Balcombe. They had met as children but hadn't seen each other for years. She was an incredibly beautiful girl."

Elizabeth nodded. "I have seen her, once."

"Yes, but within the family, there had always been an expectation that he would marry Anne de Bourgh, and because of this, and because of his nature, he was restrained and slow in declaring himself. Wickham arrived in London, Darcy introduced him to the Balcombes and well, I'm sure you can imagine what happened next."

"She preferred Mr Wickham?" Elizabeth ventured.

The colonel nodded. "They began in secret. Her family would never have accepted him as a suitor, and I think the daring of it appealed to her. She became mad about him. Darcy caught them together, in what I'm given to understand was a compromising position, though he does not speak of it. By this time, George Darcy had come to know of the girl in Lambton, and Wickham was persuaded to return to Derbyshire and was married to her."

"Persuaded with money," Elizabeth interjected. "I am a terrible judge of people. I have always believed in first impressions, but I was entirely wrong." Though when Elizabeth thought about it, she remembered that she *had* been wary of Wickham at first. She saw that she had been worked on and cajoled, and silently vowed to never again allow someone to make such a mockery of her and abuse her trust. She blinked and was brought back to the present. "And what of Emma Balcombe and Mr Darcy?"

"Emma Balcombe was heartbroken and made a very great fool of herself in London, she wailed and cried and fainted at a ball, began to act very irrationally. Then she tried to attract Darcy back, made very public overtures towards him, but he quickly distanced himself. There was a lot of talk and embarrassment. The Balcombes, who never knew of Wickham's involvement, blamed Darcy. To them it looked like he had withdrawn his attentions without any gallantry and that he was the cause of Emma's distress. Emma Balcombe hates Darcy now, though he never meant to cause her harm, and of course Darcy and Wickham do not speak. Wickham forfeited all rights to any kind of living from George Darcy, though I believe he likes to tell people he has been cheated out of it."

"Yes he does." Elizabeth blinked back tears. "I was not his object at all, was I? He was not in love with me. He only wanted to embarrass Mr Darcy by seducing his wife. He wanted to be paid to stay silent; to extract more money from him."

"Undoubtedly," the colonel said, knowing her well enough to know she would not appreciate any softening of the blow.

She put her head back against the cushion and closed her eyes. Of course Wickham hadn't been madly in love with her, why would he be? She was the less handsome sister and the *'tolerable'* wife of a man who couldn't abide her.

On reaching Gracechurch Street, Elizabeth refused supper, saying she had a letter to write. Her little writing set was unpacked and she composed a letter to Lady Catherine de Bourgh. She had heard enough of the woman to believe her arrogant and conceited, and so crafted her introduction in a way she hoped would flatter Lady Catherine's sense of self-importance. Putting aside her own feelings, she wrote with humility and spoke of her potential gratitude should she be favoured with her ladyship's great condescension and kindness. Elizabeth read it back and admired her own work; she'd managed such an extraordinary level of sycophancy that she quite fancied her chances of success. On the other hand, if Lady Catherine decided to throw it on the fire, what did it matter to her?

William Collins had, after all, asked her for help and she had dismissed him. He might be a pompous nitwit, a complete oddity, but Jane had been right, there was nothing truly bad about him - no small miracle given the evil of his parents - and he was her cousin. This act of charity made her feel somewhat better. If Lady Catherine gave him the living after her interference, it might make William Collins return and petition Jane for her hand, but who was she to decide whom Jane should marry? She, who was in such a splendid mess herself - if Jane truly thought she could suffer to be Mrs Collins and wanted to be mistress of Longbourn one day, then that was her decision. Elizabeth would do nothing to prevent it. She felt ill-qualified to give advice.

After sealing the letter, she called for Rose and confessed her exhaustion. She was helped into a clean nightgown and tucked into bed like a small child, before the sun had even properly set.

Forty

Colonel Fitzwilliam stepped out onto the street in London, the day after returning from Hertfordshire, and looked at his pocket watch. He'd wanted to be off early and had resolved to leave before breakfast, to make as much of the day as possible. He was in a great hurry to get Elizabeth back to Pemberley, where she might recover and be safe for a while, and where they might return to their easy ways with each other. She was much altered by her time away and until her encounter with Wickham in Meryton, he had thought all the changes were for the good, that she had benefitted from the trip. He had briefly seen her sparkle and laugh during her first two weeks in London. This morning however, she had looked beaten and resigned, her head bent to the floor and uninterested in anything except getting into the carriage and being away. Dressed in travelling clothes, she had been waiting for him at the appointed time in the hallway. They were giving their adieus when Mrs Gardiner had requested they delay by a few more minutes so she could take Elizabeth for a short walk in the nearby park.

Now they were coming back, and the colonel wondered what had passed between them; these two very interesting women, for Elizabeth's chin had risen slightly and her expression was more thoughtful, rather than full of woe, as it had been before. She looked up to the grey sky when she reached him.

"Rose must sit inside, for it looks very much like rain. I will not have her catching a cold." This was delivered with regal command and the colonel was amused because she sounded a little like Darcy, though he dared not voice the thought out loud. And then, after a last embrace from Mrs Gardiner, their journey to Pemberley began.

Elizabeth spoke rarely on their trip. When she did, it was mostly to Rose, rather than him. She stared out of the window much and slept often. When she was awake, he left her to her private meanderings, which looked plentiful and complex. When they turned into Pemberley Woods, after three weary days on the road, she sat up straighter, squared her shoulders and breathed deeply. Like she was preparing herself for something - as if she were a soldier going into battle - and he was at first worried that she found the prospect of many more months cooped up at Pemberley a trial; something to be endured and faced up to. He was therefore surprised when Rose asked her if she were glad to be home and Elizabeth smiled in response.

"Will you stop the carriage, just before we cross the bridge, on first sight of the house?" she asked him.

He agreed and they did.

"I'll get out for a moment, you needn't come with me and I won't keep you waiting long," she said, allowing him to hand her down.

"I will come with you, if you have no objections. Perhaps we might walk the rest of the way?" When she agreed, he told the carriage to go directly to the back of the house, and Rose Kiddy rode off in the luxurious equipage by herself, looking a little bemused and a little scared.

"It is a beautiful house," Elizabeth said, gazing up at the impressive stone mansion. The lake in front of it was shimmering under a setting sun and the building was bathed in golden light.

"I have never seen a finer one, though don't tell my mother. Having been born there, I am required to love Haddon Hall above all others."

"I loved Longbourn as a child, but once my father had gone, it was not the same. I had to go back there, whilst in Hertfordshire, to call upon the Collinses and I thought doing so would give me much pain, but I realised it was just another house, with creaky floorboards and overstuffed sofas, poky parlours filled with trinkets, but Pemberley - I do love Pemberley, very dearly. I did not realise it until we turned into the woods, but it is home now. It is where I belong and I ought to stop pretending I am a visitor and quit constantly looking for escape." They were walking over the bridge and Elizabeth pointed to a natural recess underneath it, where a log lay, ideal for a makeshift bench, a canopy of grass and earth overhung it. "'Tis a marvellous place to hide, Colonel, sheltered as it is from the wind, with a good view of the house and the road. One is able to see all the comings and goings, without being noticed. I spent many hours there during my first summer here."

"Doing what, may I ask?"

"Nothing. I have spent three years doing nothing."

"Oh that is not true, you have practised music and taken care of Georgiana, and…"

"And nothing, Colonel, and that simply will not do," she said, with some force, and a shake of her head.

He stopped her so he might look into her eyes. "I am intrigued to know exactly what Mrs Gardiner said to you. Whatever it was, it appears to have made quite an impression."

"She told me I should stop feeling sorry for myself. It is not, after all, a very attractive quality, and she also enquired after the location of my backbone - she was concerned I might have misplaced it somewhere."

"A little harsh!"

"No less than I deserved."

"This business with Wickham, please do not let anything he said or did affect your sense of your own worth."

"Oh it will not; my vanity and confidence might be a little wounded, but luckily I have a plentiful supply. I shall draw from my reserves, Colonel," Elizabeth said, laughing at herself. "I will be well, I promise you. In fact, I shall be more than well, I am quite determined."

They walked on towards the house and Elizabeth did so with Mrs Gardiner's rebukes at the forefront of her mind.

Her aunt had asked her a series a questions and become incredulous upon discovering that she had never inspected the household accounts at Pemberley, was not involved in the welfare or management of the staff, other than Rose, and had not visited any of the tenants.

'You have tremendous power and need not be ruled over, or dictated to, by any man,' Mrs Gardiner had insisted. *'You may become your own woman; you may command your own ship, and you may do tremendous good, if you should*

choose. This is your life now, and you ought to make the most of it. Wishing for something else will not change things and you are wasting your life away if you carry on letting others take on the duties that ought to be yours.'

Elizabeth had not been able to refute any of her aunt's claims about her previous indolence and disinterest.

As they walked up to the front door, Georgiana came running towards them and Elizabeth braced herself for the impact. Arms were thrown about her and she was kissed thoroughly, on both cheeks, many times over. "I have missed you so."

"You are home! I am so surprised to see you. I thought you still at Haddon," Elizabeth said.

"I asked to be brought home when I heard you were expected back earlier." She clutched at Elizabeth again. "Oh please don't go away again. It has felt like forever."

"It has been but a few weeks," Elizabeth said laughing, and remembered something else her aunt had said. *'You crave love, Elizabeth, I see that, but there are many types of love to be enjoyed. And one day, you will experience the all-consuming, demanding, enduring love that a mother has for her child.'* Elizabeth had admitted, in a low whisper that Mr Darcy had never come to her bed, and that though she would like to be a mother one day, it was a difficult thing to accomplish if one of the necessary parties insisted on remaining on a different continent. Her aunt had looked surprised, but then smiled sagely. *'But he will not stay abroad forever, he will come home, and he will want an heir.'*

It had been a new idea to occupy and disturb her. Elizabeth had assumed they would always be distant, two strangers with nothing in common but their names; that he would return to Pemberley now and then for a short while, before going off again to do just as he pleased. That they might conceive and raise children together, seemed impossible now, but would he expect it of her one day?

When Georgiana eventually released her, she turned to Mrs Reynolds, who had given her a brief hello.

"Are we to have something delicious for dinner, Mrs Reynolds? I confess I am absurdly hungry."

"Game pie, madam," the housekeeper answered.

"Wonderful, a favourite of the colonel's, if I remember rightly. Now, if you will attend me upstairs, Mrs Reynolds, in the mistress's chambers, so I might approve the menus for the rest of the week, I should be very grateful. Perhaps someone might bring tea." She was already on the stairs by the time she had finished speaking and was stripping off her own gloves, while Rose, who had arrived by one of the back doors, scurried up after her, eager to help with the removal of her outdoor things.

"The mistress's chambers, madam?" Mrs Reynolds called up after her, doubtfully.

Elizabeth turned on the stairs and fixed Mrs Reynolds with an unwavering look. "Yes, I am mistress of Pemberley, and that is where you will find me."

When she had cleared the stairs and was out of sight of the others, she turned to Rose. "How was that, authoritative enough?"

"I think she understood you, Mrs Darcy."

They went into the mistress's chambers and shut the door behind them. "I am sorry, Rose. I will make plenty of work for you this afternoon. My things will need to be fetched from my old room, as well as my trunks unpacked. And this room requires airing, but we will get you some help."

Rose nodded and took Elizabeth's bonnet and cloak from her. When the maid was gone off to see to the fetching up of the trunks, Elizabeth stood against the door and paced all the way to the window. Sixty-two steps, what a ridiculously big room! Looking about at the dated furniture and faded wall hangings, the musty rugs and threadbare patches on the arms of the chairs, she realised there was much to do, not just here, but in the rest of the house also. She could think of many downstairs rooms that were now wallowing in fast fading grandeur and were badly in need of refurbishment.

The housekeeper entered. Elizabeth heard her huff a little as she dipped a hurried curtsey. She waited with her hands clasped together in front of her.

"You must sit down, Mrs Reynolds, we may be a while and we can have some tea. You did order the tea?"

Elizabeth sat on a chaise lounge by the vast windows and invited the housekeeper to sit at the other end of it.

"Yes, I did, but I did not realise you meant for me to join you. It is very civil of you, Mrs Darcy, I daresay, but not how things are done here, at Pemberley…well, Lady Anne would never have countenanced such familiarity," Mrs Reynolds replied, her look showing her astonishment.

"I am not Lady Anne, Mrs Reynolds. I could never hope to be. I'm afraid my ways will be different and I should warn you that I mean to impose some of them here at Pemberley. Please, do sit. While I was away I thought of a few changes I should like to make."

Mrs Reynolds reluctantly perched on the very edge of the chaise. "I am not sure Mr Darcy would like there to be a great deal of change while he is away."

Elizabeth leaned forward. "Oh, is Mr Darcy very fond of the curtains in the music room? Is he a great connoisseur of fabrics? Do you think he might notice if I moved a few small tables around? Or brought the garden room back to life with some new planting?"

Smiling, the housekeeper shook her head, and Elizabeth saw she was beginning to feel at little more at ease. "Is that all, Mrs Darcy? You wish to redecorate some rooms? I had thought you…" Mrs Reynolds put a hand to her chest. "I thought you sought to reorganise the staff, and since we have never had much to do with one another, I feared you might wish to bring in someone more to your liking."

"Oh goodness, Mrs Reynolds, Pemberley would crumble to the ground without your direction and supervision. Heavens no, that is the furthest thing from my mind. It is true we have not worked together as we ought, but that is entirely my fault, we shall do so from now on. I am sure to blunder and crash my way through for a while, but I hope, in time, to become familiar with my role as mistress, and while I am learning, I trust you will do me the great favour of quietly correcting my mistakes and forgiving my ignorance. Your task is to make it seem to everyone else as if I know what I am doing. Do you think you could manage that?"

"I daresay I can."

They were interrupted by the arrival of the tea, which Elizabeth poured while the housekeeper protested about being served by her.

"If it will make you feel better, I shall let you do the honours in future. I believe we shall require a great many such conferences and a great amount of tea." Putting down the teapot, Elizabeth came back to the chaise. "You will find me very fair, I hope, but in the past there have been occasions when you seem to have doubted my right to make decisions." When Mrs Reynolds was about to interrupt, Elizabeth put up a hand. "It seems to me that a person can have several different existences within one lifetime, and today feels like as good a day as any to begin a new life. But, before I can go on, I shall tell you that while I trust your judgement and bow to your expertise, I will not be undermined or questioned. There can only be one mistress, and she will be me."

"And if I may say so, madam, I think you will grow into a very fine one," Mrs Reynolds said, after a pause.

Their eyes met, and in the housekeeper's, Elizabeth saw nothing disingenuous. "Thank you, true compliments are as rare as fine jewels, I shall make sure I keep and treasure yours, and I hope to one day become worthy of it. Now, let us roll up our hypothetical sleeves and get to work, we have much to do."

My Dear Brother,

I hope this finds you well. We are all much the same as when I last wrote and life at Pemberley is mostly peaceful. I am diligent in my studies. Music though, I think becomes my main passion, and I confess to devoting much more time to it than anything else. I miss you (and Papa) terribly, but you deserve my thanks for leaving me in the care of the colonel, Elizabeth and Miss Temple. They are all so good to me.

Your last letter is a much treasured possession. It is so good of you to write such long accounts of your life and travels around the Indies for my benefit. They cause excitement of an unquantifiable kind when they arrive here at Pemberley, and relief too, because they tell us you are safe and well. Elizabeth is always much taken with your detailed descriptions of the towns and plantations, the harbours and ships, and the people you meet - she had me read your last letter out loud to her three times before she was satisfied. I wonder that you do not write her a letter of her own, I am sure she would be very glad to receive it. She has explained to me that you are probably very much engaged with your business and she has never expected you to write - I cannot pretend to know the goings on between a husband and a wife - perhaps you understand each other so well, that words on a page are unimportant, insignificant perhaps.

Tomorrow is Elizabeth's birthday and there is to be a small dinner in celebration of it. Lady Matlock is here, but the earl was too ill to travel. We are also to be joined by the party from the parsonage....

Darcy threw Georgiana's letter aside without finishing it. He had read it properly the evening before and knew the rest of it was full of studies, some new friends they had made in Lambton, and other matters of great import to a young girl, but largely uninteresting to him. He had fallen asleep soon after reading it, but had woken this morning filled with remembrances of the beginning of her letter. There was something in it that cried 'home' to him. He could imagine his sister reading his letter out loud in the drawing room after dinner, or maybe the breakfast room. He saw her sitting at the pianoforte, he could almost hear the notes she played. He saw in his mind's eye, Mrs Reynolds bustling about, the colonel relaxing into a chair by the fire, a glass of port in hand and an easy smile creasing his features. He could not, however, conjure up a picture of Elizabeth.

She'd had another birthday! How old was she? He looked at the top of the letter and took note of the date - it had taken over three months to reach him. He counted back in his head. The date of their wedding he remembered well, she had been only fifteen, he could not forget that. She must be eighteen now and yet he could not imagine her so. He still saw short wavy locks, gowns that swamped her, a freckled nose. Eighteen! He could not fathom it. Three years gone by. It seemed like she had been a part of his life, one of his responsibilities forever, and yet, incongruously, three years also seemed to have disappeared in the blink of an eye.

Putting on the wide-brimmed straw hat he had taken to wearing to protect him from the sun and his lightest coat, Darcy stepped out of his temporary lodgings in the port of St John's. No matter that he had been there for many months, almost a year, the noise and smell, and the heat of the place always shocked him for a few moments. He was an Englishman through and through and there were times when it was all so alien to him, and thoroughly overwhelming. He had gathered many contacts and acquaintances in his time there, largely through his efforts to redirect the Fitzwilliams' fortune into a more reputable line of investment. His life there was not only bearable, but often entertaining. Despite the warm feelings Georgiana's letter had conjured up, he was not yet ready to return home and thought perhaps to look at whether he might use his time there more wisely still; to make a fortune all of his own, not one he had inherited. He did not wish to own a plantation. There was no way to operate one without the use of enslaved men and women, and having seen first-hand the conditions and brutality they were often subjected to, he could not countenance financing such a business. The thought turned his stomach - but he did wish to examine other possibilities, importing, exporting and building.

Travelling had excited him, opened up new worlds, and he saw that there were ways to safely and wisely invest for the future.

Not that he was poor, far from it, he was a very wealthy man, but for generations Darcy men had simply looked after their lands and collected their rents. Nobody had ambition to do anything more than to see that things continued much in the same vein as they always had; duty was always done, but that was all. What might he do to improve his estates, to enrich the lives and homes of those who worked upon them, if he had an even greater fortune at his disposal? He would not operate alone though, he was not an over-ambitious fool; he knew his strengths and weaknesses and saw his education was lacking in certain areas - he needed someone with a greater knowledge of business than he, a partner of sorts, a man of sense, money and business acumen. He did not expect to meet him that day, he did not expect to be saved by him, but serendipity intervened.

Charles Bingley happened to be walking in the opposite direction, observing Darcy for no other reason than he had not met him before and he had thought he knew all of the Englishmen around the port. Seeing the quality of his clothing and the way he held himself, Bingley knew he must be an Englishman of high society and great fortune. As they neared each other, though, the man looked him over, dismissed him, and would have kept walking if he had not been jostled by a porter carrying a large crate full of live poultry on his shoulder. Darcy careered backwards, stumbling towards the water. Bingley made a grab for his coat sleeve and pulled him back, away from a certain fall into the drink.

Darcy stared, so shocked that he forgot to give his thanks. His rescuer was not offended though. Bingley grinned broadly and held out his hand. "Charles Bingley, very glad to be of service, sir."

Volume Four: Nineteen

Forty one

Rising from the pew, Richard Fitzwilliam left the dark, cool church and stepped out into the brilliant June sunshine. He blinked rapidly while his eyes adjusted to the change in light, and then lifted his face up to enjoy the warm breeze.

When he looked about him again, he saw Elizabeth, resplendent in red riding habit, complete with jaunty hat and veil, her crop swinging to and fro from the strap in her hand. Her dark curls were pinned back at the sides, but otherwise hung loosely down, caressing the back of her jacket. Her large, dark eyes were warm, vibrant and intelligent. She was under the shade of a tree, her horse and groom waiting for her on the other side of the church wall. She was a splendid, arresting sight, a handsome young woman in full, spectacular bloom.

"Morning Duchess."

She laughed and approached him. "I saw your horse and waited for you. I did not know you came to church in the week."

"Only occasionally," he indicated a bench where they might sit and she followed him, "when my stores of patience run low."

"Oh dear, do I give you much trouble lately?"

"You? None at all. In fact, all of my three ladies are a blessing to me."

"Your *three* ladies?"

"You, Georgiana and Miss Temple. No, when I mention patience, I speak of having the forbearance to bide my time. I want things that seem to be currently out of my grasp."

"Out of your grasp, or do you simply not desire them enough to try harder?" Elizabeth asked, tilting her head to the side, waiting attentively for his answer.

He nodded. "You are right, in a way, but others do have some power over our happiness. We must consider family and friends, and whether we have twenty pounds or twenty thousand pounds, we must always consider money. Everything changes and twists and we must bend with it, or be broken." He took a letter from his pocket and held it out to her. "Your husband comes home."

"Oh," she said.

He had noticed that, over the years, Elizabeth had learnt to school her expressions. She was a woman of great emotion, who felt much, but she knew now that it was not always wise to display it so readily. She could be enigmatic at times. Her eyes avoided the letter and she would not take it.

Richard sighed. "The great man comes back; the wanderer returns - gone nearly three years - this important person in your life. And yet, you, probably the most eloquent woman I know, has nothing to say on the subject other than 'oh'. Come now, Elizabeth, there must be more than that?"

"When does he arrive?"

"The letter is dated almost three months ago, so quite soon I imagine, a matter of weeks. Will you not read it?"

"I am not in the habit of reading other people's post, thank you, Colonel."

"Richard, or cousin, if you prefer," he corrected her. "I would like it if you didn't call me colonel any more. It is a long time since I wore regimentals, and even longer since I felt like a soldier."

"But it is a title you have earned, and I'm not sure I can get used to anything else," she protested.

"Well, you must, I insist. And will you do me another great favour?"

"Yes, *Richard.*" She answered, her playfulness returning. She stood and started walking back to the horses.

He followed a few steps behind her. "Will you try not to be so adversarial with Darcy when he is here? He is a decent man, a good man, scratch the veneer and you will find oak, I promise you. Do not be so prejudiced against him."

Elizabeth said nothing as she was being helped into the saddle, but when she was seated she looked down at him. "I will not be so adversarial, if he is not so vexing, so proud and tyrannical."

"Elizabeth," he pleaded.

"Very well, I shall make you the only promise I can make, when faced with such a challenge. I will endeavour to do my best." She turned her horse towards Pemberley. "But you are wrong to call him an important person in my life, his return means nothing. I should wager he'll stay a few weeks, decide he must visit Timbuktu, or some other such place, and then he'll be gone again, leaving us all in peace." She paused and then grinned impishly. "I shall race you back."

"Well, hang on then, I am not even up yet," Richard protested. He had perfected a way of working around his stiff leg and could now get into the saddle without the assistance of a groom, but it took him a minute or two.

Laughing, Elizabeth kicked her heels into the side of her mount and was gone in a flurry of hooves and a shower of dust.

Sitting across from him in the carriage, Charles Bingley was ebullient and could not stop smiling, though Darcy was not completely sure of his own feelings about being back in England, it was clear his friend was delighted to be home. Bingley was a good-looking young man of six and twenty; the only son of a wealthy family from the north, who had acquired a great fortune in trade. Darcy now hated to admit it, but his first instinct, when he had learned of Bingley's background, had been to balk and shy away from the acquaintance. Bingley, however, had shown such genuine pleasure in Darcy's company and seemed to value his advice. His easy manners and happy company had drawn Darcy in, and he had eventually concluded that what Bingley lacked in breeding, he easily made up for in his deportment, dress and education - in his upbringing he was every inch the gentleman. He had come to value Bingley greatly as a partner in business too, for all his gaiety and unreserved liveliness, he was a clever man, who knew how to move in all sorts of circles and get things done.

"Dry land, Darcy, at last! What a relief after three months at sea. I shall not be going abroad again any time soon," Bingley said. "I have missed England."

They both looked out of the carriage window and saw they were moving out of the grimy, noisy docks, through the warehouses, markets and shops, bound for a better part of Town.

And tonight, just think, we will have some decent food. Will your family be at your London house?"

"No, they will all be at Pemberley or Haddon, I doubt anyone I know is in Town at this time of year."

"Then you must dine with us and meet my sisters, if you are not sick of the sight of me," Bingley offered. "The Hursts are here permanently, they have no other residence."

"I have not had an invitation from Mrs Hurst."

"None required, Darcy. We are not from your high circles."

"Very well, but if you are sure it will not be an imposition or inconvenience?"

"Of course not, I beg you not to talk such nonsense. I have written to Caroline and Louisa often of you, from the Indies, and they are very keen to meet you in person," Bingley said, firmly. "It is a fixed thing and you will be there, at six-thirty."

"I will," Darcy replied, suddenly glad of the invitation; the thought of dining alone, possibly from a tray, in a house that had been shut up for years, was a depressing one, though he supposed he might have gone to his club.

The journey was completed without incident and when they parted outside Darcy's townhouse, Bingley shook his hand. "Until tonight, my friend. Get some rest. We have had some great adventures, haven't we?"

"That we have," Darcy agreed, looking about him in wonder at the tree-lined pavement and the tall, neat rows of houses; all of them decked with a white façade and black door, thinking how odd their uniformity was to him now, as used as he had become to the rawness, the heat and slow bustle of places like Kingston and Saint Kitts. "I am, I suppose, glad to be home, but it is the strangest of feelings. Nothing looks as I remember it, or perhaps it looks just the same, but I am altered."

"Yes, it will take some time to get the hang of London again, to adjust to it. But once we have, perhaps we shall have more adventures. Two young men, devilishly handsome, exceedingly rich as we are, why, we cannot fail to cause a stir wherever we go."

Amused by Bingley's unquenchable thirst for life, Darcy said a brief but fond goodbye. He waited on the pavement, until the carriage was out of sight and when he turned, the housekeeper and butler were on the doorstep, ready to greet him.

After washing and changing, he took a slow tour of the house, trying to grow accustomed to the place, wondering if he had he ever known any happiness within its square, rigid walls. As a boy he'd been taken to London once a year by his father, and while he remembered those trips with fondness and could recall how excited he'd been by the amusements Town had to offer, his mother's refusals to join them, and his missing her, had often caused him pain.

He had been about twelve when he'd first noticed the divide between his parents. They were awkward together, happier when apart. Both of them were excellent people in their own right and good parents too. His father, though strict and wanting much for him, had always spared his time and given him good advice. His mother's love was of a more demonstrative kind. She had thought nothing of sweeping him into a tight embrace at any time of the day, of kissing his face over and over again, and stroking his hair, no matter who was about, servant or guest. As he'd grown from boy to young man, he would become embarrassed by her great shows of affection and shrug her off, but she would refuse to let him get away and would laughingly pull him back. He remembered her great joy when Georgiana had been born, and how his father had been very happy too. For a while, it had seemed as if the red-faced, screaming bundle of lace had united them in a way his presence had never managed to. But as time had gone on, and Georgiana had grown, they had reverted back to their normal ways. Their children had free access to both of their apartments, running in and out of them, but never between them. Though there was a door that would have allowed such access, it had always remained shut, unused, unnecessary.

Elizabeth! His broad frame sunk against a nearby wall and lost its usual very particular posture. His father and mother had entered into their mismatched union with willingness, and perhaps with some hope that love would grow between them, while *his* marriage had been merged out of desperation and fear, but nevertheless, he was struck with the notion that history was repeating itself. His destiny was the same as his father's, married without warmth, trapped in a cycle of distance, separation and coldness. Could it be fixed? That was the question he had pondered for many an hour during the three long months he'd spent in the close confines of a ship's cabin.

He had thought of a life in London, while she remained at Pemberley, or another trip abroad, somewhere, anywhere would do, but eventually, he had seen he could not run away from duty and responsibility forever. He would have to go home and stay at home, try to make a life with her. He had previously been too much embarrassed by her age, too mournful about what he had lost, and had thought that anything they sought to create would be a pale imitation of what a marriage ought to be. But wouldn't even that be better than nothing? He could start out for Pemberley now. Why unpack the trunks here? He had been travelling for months after all, what was another two or three days? Something stopped him though and he gripped the bannisters, not yet quite ready. What would be the harm of a couple of weeks in London first, to enjoy himself and continue to pretend there was no Elizabeth Darcy, and then he would begin anew. As he went back downstairs to sit in the study, he was assailed by another memory - that of his mother's ring flying out of the carriage window on their wedding day, and Elizabeth's horrified face, eyes wide, hand clutched to her mouth, short curls almost standing on end in fright. He had been livid at the time, but now the memory of it made him chuckle to himself. The ring was still at Pemberley, secured away with the rest of his mother's jewellery. He had never had it altered and she had never asked for it back. An odd, strange beginning, but hopefully they would overcome it, and he vowed faithfully to himself that he would try to be a better husband, and an altogether better man.

Darcy's first dinner with the Hursts was a success and led to further invitations. He and Charles, and Charles's sisters, Caroline and Louisa, saw each other out and about a fair bit. Whatever was left of London society in the middle of summer gradually came to know of his presence in Town and began to solicit his company, and Darcy was glad to be of assistance to Caroline Bingley, who had made some inroads into the first circles, but had not yet gained full acceptance. Louisa was the elder sister and married to Mr Hurst, a man who drank, played cards, ate and did little else. Still, it seemed to be a decent match for her and as she required no company or conversation from her husband, just his respectable name and connections, she was happy. Caroline, however, was more favoured in figure, had an excellent dowry and a handsome face. Darcy felt she would do better in the marriage mart than her sister had and attending functions and the theatre with him brought beneficial introductions her way. He hoped their brother would do better still because Bingley had everything in his favour.

Darcy enjoyed Caroline's company and wondered whether she would have done for him had he been looking for a wife, despite her trade connections. He was not falling in love, or even in lust, with her, but he did think her clever and accomplished, and there was nothing about her appearance that would have dissuaded him. Her only fault, he found on closer examination, was that she sometimes thought meanly of others, and though she was mostly in good humour, she was often more inclined to laugh at people, rather than with them, and she liked to hang off his arm in a way that he sometimes found irritating, pulling at him, rather than just resting her hand, as a lady ought to. But other than this, he liked her well enough and she was very presentable.

Feeling in debt to the Hursts after having dined there two or three times, Darcy invited them back for dinner at his townhouse one evening and they were on the last of many courses when the butler announced the surprise arrival of his cousin at the front door.

Darcy gave instructions for Richard to be shown into the room and asked for another chair to be brought in.

Richard came, dressed informally. He bowed and smiled at them all, but looked at Darcy with a raised eyebrow and a tight smile. "Excuse me for interrupting. I did not think you would have guests."

"Not at all, I am glad to see you," Darcy said, rising and shaking his hand vigorously. He then turned back to the company. "This is my cousin, Richard Fitzwilliam, second son of the Earl of Matlock." He introduced them all and Richard sat tentatively on the chair that had arrived. He refused any wine and hardly spoke. Darcy saw he was tense and when Miss Bingley laughingly offered to lead the ladies out, he saw Richard's jaw clench and the tight smile he had worn, disappeared altogether.

When only the men remained, Richard stood again and asked if Bingley and Hurst might step out and give them some privacy. Bingley looked surprised but quickly agreed and bundled Hurst out of the room with him.

"That was a little rude; we might have gone elsewhere, if you wanted to speak to me in private," Darcy said.

Richard gave a wry laugh and took the port decanter and a spare glass from the sideboard before the footman could do it for him, then he sent the footman away too.

"Has something happened, Richard, what are you doing here? Why are you not at Pemberley?"

A bitter chuckle escaped his cousin as he walked heavily back to the table and sat himself down awkwardly. He looked tired, in pain and as ill-humoured as Darcy had ever seen him.

"But those are the questions I came to ask you, Darcy. When did the Mauritania dock? More than eight days ago now, and yet, I have had no word from you, your sister has had no word from you, and Elizabeth has had no word from you - although she neither expects to, or probably

343

wishes to - being well used to your lack of attention and I imagine long past the point where it actually bothers her."

"You are angry with me, perhaps rightly so."

"Angry? Yes, I am angry. I am fighting the urge to knock you flat on your posterior, Darcy. You are fortunate, both that you have a house full of guests, and that I have lately sworn off violence." Richard took a long swig of the port. "Are you thinking of returning to Pemberley any time soon and relieving me of the duties you gave me? Something you promised to do after a year, nearly three years ago!"

"If you were unhappy with the arrangement, Richard, you ought to have written and told me so."

Richard wiped his mouth on a nearby napkin and then threw it angrily down on the table. "I have not been unhappy. It is your assumptions that rile me, and the way you have treated others, who have become dear to me."

Darcy got up and walked around the table, putting a hand on Richard's shoulder. "I know my own failings; I have travelled long and far, and have had time to reflect on many things. I aim to always do the right thing in future, and I have missed you these last years. Please do not let us fight, we are more than cousins, I hope, more like brothers, and most definitely friends."

"'Tis a pretty speech, Darcy, and I do not say you have been wrong as such, I even understand, to a certain extent, why you have stayed away, but enough now, why are you still in London? And why is that dreadful, smirking peacock presiding over your table, acting as if she is mistress? Or is she a mistress?"

"She is nothing of the kind, she is my friend Bingley's sister and she means nothing by it, 'tis just a joke."

"Then she knows you are married? Or is she one of those women who doesn't care?"

"She is a very respectable woman, Richard, there is nothing untoward. I have become close to the Bingleys, and in answer to your question, I have remained in London while I attended to some business, but I will be leaving for Pemberley soon. Tomorrow, I will send Elizabeth a letter informing her of my plans. So, given you are here, I suppose your mother is at Pemberley, or Beatrice and Walter?"

"No, they are at Haddon."

"And who manages Pemberley in your absence?"

Richard laughed at him. "Elizabeth is there."

"You cannot leave two young girls and a governess to their own devices," Darcy protested.

"I can and I have, and not for the first time either." Richard continued to laugh. "You are so funny, Darcy. Do you think time has stood still while you have been away? You are in for a shock, when you do deign to go back. I wish you very good luck."

"The truth is, well, I dread it a little. I am married to a girl who is simply all wrong for me, and when I was last home, it was so difficult. I did try with her. She was as unhappy at being tied to me as I was to her."

"Your father had just died, Walter had invested the family fortune unwisely and I was injured on the front. It was a horrible time and you must forget it. Go home, it will be different. She is not the girl you left behind, she is a young lady now."

Darcy pushed his chair out. "As I said, I will, I have already made plans to. Now, why are you in London? Is it just to tell me off?"

"No, I have a few errands to run."

"Come on," Darcy said. "Let's go into the drawing room. Now you have sent the other gentlemen in, I should not leave my guests alone for too long."

Persuaded to his feet, Richard went with him. Darcy stopped him though, just before they re-joined the Bingley party. "You must never think me ungrateful, for all that you have done. I truly never meant to stay away so long. Events overtook me and the opportunities were too good to ignore."

They were in the drawing room before Richard could reply, though he had looked as if he would have said something.

"Ah, there you are, we had thought you meant to monopolise Mr Darcy all night," Miss Bingley said. "I was just about to give you a little music; you would have been loath to miss it, surely, Mr Darcy?"

"Undoubtedly," Darcy replied, with a small bow.

"My apologies, Miss Bingley, I have newly arrived from Pemberley and there were things I needed to relate to Darcy. He is now, it would seem, all yours," Richard said.

"I cannot wait to see Pemberley, I hear it is delightful," Miss Bingley said. "I hope it will be the first of many visits." She purred through this speech like a cat, and fluttered her eyes at Darcy, before focussing again on Richard. "And you are just arrived from there, sir? Then I suppose you will not be going back again so soon. You will not travel with us?"

Darcy saw Richard's look of surprise and sought to explain. "The Hursts and the Bingleys are going north to visit relatives in Scarborough. I suggested we all travel together and they spend a few weeks at Pemberley, before going on. I wished to repay all the fine hospitality they have shown me since I returned to London."

His cousin said nothing and even smiled lightly, but Darcy, who knew him well, saw disapproval in his eyes, and he supposed that arriving back with guests, after so long an absence, was not perhaps the right way to proceed, but he had been put in a position where it had felt wrong *not* to extend the invitation. Conversation returned to safer topics and soon after Miss Bingley took her seat at the pianoforte. She played very well, with great precision, and Darcy was lost in the music for a while, until he became unnerved by how often she looked at him, how intimate her smile was, and that the piece she played was a love song. Thankfully, she did not sing, for he feared it might have been a serenade. Then he recalled how she had picked lint off his lapel at the theatre one evening, and how she always readily agreed with all he said, and laughed at his jokes, even the poor ones. What was she about? What was he about, more to the point, and why had he not noticed and put a stop to it? Had he enjoyed the attention? His cousin's question from earlier came back to him, *'she knows you are married?'* She did, surely. He had never talked about Elizabeth, he rarely did, not to anyone, but surely Caroline Bingley knew?

Perspiration formed between his shoulder blades and he felt it trickle down and pool in the dip at the base of his back. Great Christ, what must Bingley think of him!

He moved away and sunk into a gloomy reverie at the back of the room, where he sat for the rest of the evening, dreading a moment when his cousin would drop a mention of Elizabeth into the conversation. Luckily, Richard seemed exhausted and was struggling to stay awake. Darcy's suddenly sombre mood affected the rest of the room and the evening ended earlier than any of them had probably anticipated. Conversation ran dry and yawns had to be disguised. Miss Bingley tried to enliven them in the hope of staying longer, but it was all in vain.

Darcy caught Bingley's sleeve on the way out, after the goodbyes, and begged a few private words, saying he would supply another carriage to return him home. Bingley, as eager to please as always, agreed. They went through the drawing room, where Richard was fast asleep in a comfortable chair, and carried on to the study.

"You look very serious, Darcy. Well you are mostly always serious, but now you look even more so."

Darcy paced the small room for a while, before leaning on the edge of the desk. "I had not paid too much attention to it until tonight, and it is awkward, and perhaps not very chivalrous of me to speak of it, but it seems your sister somewhat favours me," he said.

Bingley laughed. "I'd say that's putting it mildly," then he suddenly looked concerned. "Oh, dear, is she too much? I rather thought you liked her too, you did not seem to mind."

Darcy ran a hand across his mouth. "It is not that. I'm sure I would be flattered, if my circumstances were different. I have perhaps ignored her attentions because I thought she was aware of my situation. I assumed she realised we would never be anything more than friends."

"What the devil are you on about, your situation?"

"That I am married, Bingley. Have you never told your sister?"

Bingley shot out of his chair. "Well I might have told her. If you had ever told me!"

"Of course I have told you," Darcy replied, beginning to pace again, waiting for Bingley to calm himself down.

"I would swear to it, you have not, Darcy." And he did swear, a proper curse, before muttering an apology. "I truly did not know. You don't talk of her. I have never heard you even mention any woman's name, other than your sister's?"

"Then I am sorry and truly grieved if I have embarrassed you, or Caroline. Would you like some port?" Darcy asked.

"I think I better had. I am truly shocked."

"And on this occasion, I think I shall join you." He poured them both a drink as he began to speak, glad of something to do with his hands, and glad not to have to look directly at Bingley and see his expression. "Her name is Elizabeth. She was very young when we married, I was very young too, I suppose. I have regrets and I am sure, so does she; we do not always get along, our temperaments are very different." He was silent for a few moments before continuing. "It was a dreadful mistake, you see, and not one easily fixed. My father wouldn't have allowed me to even countenance it, but after his death, I considered an annulment, and on a trip to London I made some enquiries. In the end, however, I thought perhaps it might be too messy, too public and I would not want to cause her any distress, or leave her without my protection. I am fond of Elizabeth, in an odd way." He caught himself smiling.

"I see," said Bingley. He still looked incredulous and incapable of any kind of other comment. He took the glass of port and swallowed it in one go.

"If you don't wish to stay at Pemberley, given this, I will understand, though the invitation remains."

"I will discuss it with the others. I take it you are happy for me to relay to them what you have told me?" Bingley asked.

"Of course, it was my hope that you would, and extend my apologies to your sister. I fear I have misled her. You don't hate me, I hope?"

Bingley was thoughtful for some time. "Darcy, you have made a mistake by omission, but I do see there was no direct intention to cause a wound, and I could never hate you."

Relieved beyond measure, Darcy thanked him and sank back into the chair.

Darcy was even more thankful when the morning brought with it a note from Bingley, saying all was well and the whole party were preparing to leave with him the next day, as previously arranged. Darcy immediately set about making his own preparations and only went out once to collect something he had previously ordered from a jeweller's off Bond Street. Richard went out himself and was gone for a great many hours. They met in the late afternoon and had dinner together at his club, followed by a game of billiards. Darcy was dismayed, however, to find that although they still got along, his cousin was more reserved with him, and there was still a hint of rebuke and resentment in his manner.

Any fears he might have had regarding the reception Caroline Bingley would give him were quickly allayed on the day of departure, when they met to begin their trip. She was as gay, familiar and as friendly with him as she had always used to be. Perhaps he had imagined any intimate regard for him, or perhaps she simply did not wish to cause a rift between him and her brother, but for whatever reason, she displayed no obvious signs of ill will, and all he had to worry him was the state of the welcome he might receive at Pemberley. Richard had, again, wished him the very best of luck and laughed heartily while shaking his hand.

Forty two

Georgiana ran in with his letter herself, excited by the arrival of an express, overjoyed at the sight of her brother's handwriting and seal, and seemingly even more pleased that it was addressed to Elizabeth.

"Fitzwilliam writes to you, it just arrived, by express!"

"That seems rather wasteful, I'm sure the normal post would have sufficed," Elizabeth said, irked at his show of drama and extravagance. "Put it down there, I shall get to it in a while. I have a few more notes to write."

"No, impossible, how can you wait? I would have to know its contents immediately. How you must long to see him again. I am sure it will contain the date of his return. Maybe it is sent by express because he returns today!"

Elizabeth wanted to laugh at Georgiana's dramatic tone, the breathlessness in her voice. "Go on now, get on with your practice," she said, affectionately. "I shall read it soon, and if there is any news, you shall know it immediately."

Georgiana pouted. "Oh, how can you be so patient and calm?"

"Practice, Georgiana, which is what you should now be engaged in, *practice*!" Her order was given gently, with a smile, but Elizabeth hoped it would be attended to, for she did not want the girl present any longer, in case Georgiana should see the true state of her emotions. She had not been able take the letter from Georgiana's hands, for fear that her own were shaking.

"I am so stupid, I am sorry," Georgiana said.

"Whatever for?"

"You want to read it alone, of course you do. Of course, I shall go," and then she ran out again.

Elizabeth looked through the window, down to Pemberley's lawns. The Spanish chestnuts, mere saplings when she had arrived, were now well established. They had weathered the storms, survived the winters, and were now deeply rooted and spreading out, growing beautifully into their surroundings. Taking a deep breath, she took up Mr Darcy's letter and sliced it open. Seeing it was no more than a note, with her name at the top and a list of instructions, followed by his signature, she called for Mrs Reynolds. When the housekeeper came she held the paper out to her. "Mr Darcy will return on the sixteenth. He brings with him a small party of guests and has requested rooms be made ready for them."

"I could not take your note, madam."

"Oh please do, it will assist you in your preparations. You should not dread that it contains anything of a personal nature. He might as well have written it to you as to me." Her voice broke a little on her last, and she despised herself for it. How many more times would the man have to upset her before her emotions were forevermore hardened to him? She almost hoped she would find him even more disapproving and cold upon his return, than she had when he had left, so she might close off that small chink in her armour, those miniscule ripples of affection that flowed through her when she heard his name and remembered his rare moments of kindness towards her, or the fleeting looks of insecurity that occasionally crossed his countenance, giving his face an altogether more appealing look.

After Mrs Reynolds was gone and she had sat in quiet reflection for a while, she went to find Georgiana and delivered the important communication. This produced much crying and clapping and it took some time to calm her little sister down and get her to return to the instrument.

Elizabeth wandered aimlessly, even though there were a number of tasks that required her attention, she knew she would be unable to focus on any of them, and she ended her strolling in the gallery, standing before Mr Darcy's portrait. It caught her attention for a good while, particularly the small smile around his lips. She had seen too little of that smile. She was still sat in a chair opposite his painting when Miss Temple found her. "I am reminding myself of what he looks like," she said.

"Mrs Darcy, I do so hate it when you try to provoke me into making comments where I should not," Miss Temple said.

"Oh, you are too good. In your place, I would say all the wrong things and be dismissed from every post I ever held. Mr Darcy comes back in a few days."

"I have heard, and may I speak to you of other comings and goings?"

Elizabeth assented, got to her feet, and they walked the length of the gallery while they spoke.

Miss Temple took a deep breath. "I must be direct, and though only a fool would talk themselves out of such a wonderful position as the one I now hold, I have to remind you that Georgiana is sixteen and not really in need of further academic instruction. Dancing, music lessons and some experience of balls and formal dinners are all she actually requires. She ought to be preparing for her first season and her presentation at court." Reaching the end of the gallery, they turned and began to walk to the other end, while Miss Temple went on. "I think you have retained me much longer than strictly necessary, and I would not wish to think it was because you were afraid you would cause offence by giving me a hint to go. Perhaps I should think about seeking another position?"

Her eyebrows raised, Elizabeth shook her head. "Well, I think that, if you are willing to remain with us, Miss Temple, I should be very grateful for your help. For all that you talk of is quite beyond me. I don't think a Bennet has ever been presented. And in my part of Hertfordshire, being 'out' meant that one day you were allowed to go to the village assemblies, when previously you were not."

"Mrs Darcy, may I ask something of a personal nature? It is really none of my business, but I have always wondered about it, and it is a problem that might be easily solved, if you were to share some of Georgiana's lessons, but I have noticed you do not dance."

"And you are supposing it is because I don't know how?" Elizabeth was amused by the idea. "No, I know them all, I assure you. I grew up taking part in all the childrens dances at our neighbour's houses, and my mother was fond of society. Everything is well ingrained within me."

"Then you do not like to? It is just that I have noticed you always offer to play, whenever we have been somewhere and dancing is suggested."

Not having a sensible answer to give, Elizabeth blithely agreed with her. "I prefer not to, that is all, there is no great mystery. Going back to your earlier question, Miss Temple, I cannot imagine life here without you, and Georgiana would be upset to see you go. However, I do understand that a girl cannot keep her governess forever, and that you may wish for the challenge of a new charge, and seek new adventures. Do you wish to leave?"

Miss Temple was unsettled; Elizabeth saw it plainly. Over the past few weeks, something had happened to disturb and distress her. She was not her usual composed, contented self, but until the governess confided in her, and told her of her troubles, there seemed little Elizabeth could do to help.

"There are people in this house that I am so extremely fond of, that the thought of going does distress me, but I feel it would be for the best, and if it is to be done, it should be done soon," Miss Temple said.

"Very well, but may we delay any further discussion until Mr Darcy returns? I am sure he will have some opinion on it," Elizabeth asked and was relieved when Miss Temple agreed. She then spent much of the rest of the day thinking how unfair an exchange it would be - believing the gaining of Mr Darcy was poor compensation for the loss of Miss Temple.

Forty three

Having woken early on the third morning of his travels, and knowing he could be at Pemberley in a few hours if he went ahead on horseback, Darcy had kicked back the covers and sent for his valet, writing a short note of explanation for Bingley while he'd waited for his man's attendance. The sun had been streaming in through the inn's windows, and for him there had been no hope of further sleep, but the Hursts and Bingleys were all late risers - breakfast was never done till ten and the coaches not boarded before eleven. And progress would be slow - the thought of stopping every mile or so to admire this view and that view, as had happened for the previous two days, made Darcy's mind up to go ahead. Now he was so close to Pemberley, he was suddenly very keen to see it, and every mile he thundered over, driving his horse onwards, made him ever more impatient to be home.

The day was glorious, hot, with only a slight breeze. In high spirits, he rode through the woods, passing through the trees and groves of his youth, but seeing a cart on the road, coming from the house, he steered his horse towards it and hailed the driver, recognising him vaguely as one of his own staff. The man almost fell from his seat in shock when he saw him, but doffed his hat and slowed the cart to a stop.

"Bless you, sir. 'tis the master, isn't it? We wasn't expecting you till later. I'm on my way into Lambton now for some supplies for dinner."

"Very good. You have just come from the house, I suppose. Do you know if Miss Darcy and Mrs Darcy are at home?"

"I think the mistress and the young miss are at the parsonage in Lambton, visiting. They walked down there this morning and John's to go down in the carriage later to fetch them back in time for your homecoming. Stolen a march on them, you have. It's good to have you home, sir."

Darcy thanked the man and sent him on his way, and then turned and rode slowly down to a narrow, secluded offshoot of the lake, where it became little more than a stream and was much sheltered by overhanging trees. Through the dense foliage he could see parts of the house and he took the time to dismount, sit and admire it for a while. The heat made him shed his coat and cravat and he sat back, resting on his hands, resisting the lure of the cool water. How refreshing it would be to take a dip and further up, it was deep enough to swim in. Here, one might only paddle, and he was overcome by a memory of his mother doing just that - of her holding her skirts up and taking him by the hand, leading him as a child of seven or eight, into the stream. The two of them laughing, bending down, looking at their pale feet, as they hopped over the pebbles that lined the water's bed, watching for fish, entertaining themselves on a hot summer's day. Had that really happened? Yes, of course it had. When he looked up and saw a flash of white muslin further down the stream, he wondered at himself, and shook his head, wondering if he was still lost in memory, or if his imagination were playing tricks on him, but the vision, if it was one, was very tangible. It moved and hummed prettily as it came closer.

He recognised her voice and froze as she passed, without noticing him at all. Elizabeth, looking very lost in her own thoughts, her skirts held up with one hand and her boots and stockings in the other, appeared to be walking home from her outing via the water. Choking back a laugh, lest he might be heard, he got quietly to his feet as he watched her progress down the river. Her bonnet might be on her head on this occasion, but she was dishevelled. Charmingly dishevelled, he thought and then wondered at himself. Richard had implied in London that she had changed much, but in spirit and essentials, she was obviously much as she ever was and he was overcome with the sudden notion that he did not *want* her to change.

Getting to his feet, he walked back to his horse and with one last glance at her before she gradually went out of sight, he mounted the animal and urged him forwards, steering him over the bridge, down the road, and behind the house to the courtyard, where he gave him over to the care of an astonished stable boy and raced up the steps, surprising the butler as he walked through the house.

"Sir," Hodges bowed. "I am sorry; you find us ill-prepared." There were servants scurrying everywhere, going back and forth with linen, glasses, jugs of water. "We did not expect you for some hours yet."

"No need to apologise, Hodges. The house looks very good and I can see your preparations continue apace." The house did look in excellent order, despite all the current activity. It seemed cleaner, fresher, more welcoming than he remembered. He glanced about quickly, wondering which door Elizabeth would come through, as there were so many to choose from, probably not the great front door - one of the side entrances certainly. Then, she was there. Stockings and boots back on her feet but her hems wet and a little dirty, coming down a corridor quickly, but slowing when she saw Hodges to throw a greeting at the butler.

Hodges blustered, obviously frustrated at everyone having come back unexpectedly, without notice. "Madam, you are here."

"As you see, Hodges."

"But you were out."

"Yes, and now I have come back," she replied. "Miss Georgiana is still out at the parsonage and will be collected by the carriage later."

"But you have come home early," the butler said.

"As you see," she repeated slowly. She was turned a little away from him, but Darcy could hear the mix of fondness and exasperation with which she spoke, and then perhaps because she had sensed his presence, or maybe the butler had glanced his way and alerted her, she turned and saw him, then looked down at herself, up again, and offered a wry, half smile. "And, I am not the only one who is home early, it seems," she muttered.

He gave a little bow but said nothing. The butler withdrew and Darcy stepped closer.

Recovering from her initial embarrassment, Elizabeth cocked her head to the side and looked puzzled. "Have we met? You look vaguely familiar."

"It has been a long time, but yes, I believe we are acquainted, and you know, I think I just saw, not fifteen

356

minutes ago, someone who looks very like you taking a stroll in the stream through the woods. Mrs Darcy, isn't it, if I recall correctly?"

She bit her lip and hesitated, but for only a moment. "Mrs Darcy. No, Mrs Darcy would never do such a thing."

"Ah, I thought you were she, but maybe Mrs Darcy is still out."

"Perhaps." She looked surprised at him sharing a joke with her, and then looked down at her gown. "I am sure if you were to wait a half hour or so, she might be here, ready to receive you properly, with a good deal less dirt attached to her." She dashed quickly up the stairs, but stopped halfway up to look back down at him. "Welcome home, sir."

"Thank you, it is good to be here," he replied and realised he meant it.

Why was it so often the case, Elizabeth fumed, that a heightened desire to craft a favourable impression, made the chances of actually creating one practically impossible? She had rehearsed his homecoming in her mind many times; imagined herself outside the great front doors, in her finest day dress, with her hair neatly pinned and Georgiana looking pretty beside her. She had planned a low curtsey, her face would be set with no small degree of haughty composure, while she affected an air of cool indifference, one she had been practising for weeks. She had wanted him to be instantly overcome with a sense that she had improved herself, not because she wanted to win his esteem, but almost in spite of him. And instead, he had happened upon her as muddy and messy and insensible as she had been at fifteen. A low groan escaped her as she burst into her rooms and threw her hands up in frustration.

Rose Kiddy appeared without being sent for, with a lovely layered gown of light blue muslin in her hands. "The master is back already, downstairs has gone into flutters."

"Yes, I know," Elizabeth replied, and sank onto the chaise lounge.

"Well, shall we start making you presentable then?"

357

"Oh it is too late for that. He has already seen me. I am now forever to be the milkmaid in his eyes." She sat up. "I was filthy, Rose."

"You often come back from that walk covered in muck, madam, and I can't imagine you ever wishing to stop going there, so I suppose he has seen you as he might often find you in future, and if you don't mind a little dirt, why should he?"

"I should consider those very wise words, Rose, if only they made me feel better, but I am afraid they don't."

Rose bid her to get up and turned her around, undressed her until she was standing only in her chemise, before going into the adjacent dressing room to fetch some water.

Sounds from the room beyond the opposite wall, the master's chambers, made her jump. It was normally so quiet, but of course, Mr Darcy was now in there, no doubt changing out of his riding clothes. Then there were more noises; a chair scraping across the floor, drawers opening and closing, some low muttering. Elizabeth walked over and stood quietly before the door that separated their rooms, listening. How odd to be in her underclothes on one side of the door, while he was on the other side, probably in an equal state of undress. The direction of her thoughts made her hot and confused. When she heard the sound of his footsteps getting heavier, louder, coming towards the connecting door she was stood not a foot away from, she reeled backwards in panic, bumping into Rose, who had been coming in from the other direction with a basin of water in her hands. Some of the water sloshed over onto the floorboards and they both cried out, but her maid was alert enough to save the basin from toppling completely over.

Both she and Rose looked towards the door. The handle rattled, as if it was being tested, but it did not open. After a few moments, she heard him move away again and released a breath she did not realise she had been holding.

Darcy had changed quickly and hurried downstairs again, going through the rooms and noting the significant changes that had occurred in his absence. He stopped at the garden room. It left him immovable, such was its beauty. He was transfixed by a riot of colour. Rows of plants, flowers and small trees were beautifully arranged and all healthy and vibrant. There were chairs and tables arranged carefully about, so the room could be sat in once again and enjoyed. There was one chair that looked particularly comfortable, and on the floor beside it, a small stack of botany books. He walked among the plants and flowers, an outstretched hand brushing over the leaves and petals as he passed them.

"Don't move or damage anything, brother. It is Elizabeth's project and she will get most cross if you do."

He turned and smiled broadly, "Georgiana." Without hesitation he walked to the door of the room where she stood and pulled her into his arms. "How tall you are!" he said when he had let her go to look at her. She was a little shy and overwhelmed by his enthusiastic greeting, but told him how pleased she was to see him. He took her hand and squeezed it. "And where have you been?"

"Down at the parsonage. I have a friend there, Cassandra, she is the Smythe's niece."

"Well, I am glad you like this girl, she shall have to come to tea one day, so I might meet her," he said.

Georgiana laughed. "I am afraid you will find her here more often than not, as we are well past the stage of 'coming for tea'. I am often at the parsonage too. I very much like it there. Mrs Smythe has a little boy. He's such a sweet child."

He was about to congratulate her on how grown up she was, so much like a young lady, when another young lady caught his eye. A flash of a summery blue gown had alerted him to Elizabeth's presence. She was hovering just outside the doors, curiously watching him with Georgiana. He turned and bowed. "Mrs Darcy, I had heard you were out."

She curtsied in response. "Yes, Mr Darcy, but now, as you see, I am home."

He stared, truly taking note of her as he had not done on their earlier meeting. He felt a little drunk, comprehending nothing but how very lovely she was. He had never seen her out of mourning before - and what a crime it would be if she ever had to don drab greys or black again. She ought to always wear gowns the colour of cornflowers, or milkwort, or pansies. He looked for a fault, unable to quite believe the evidence of his own eyes. She was still petite and slim, but now there were curves enough to please any man. Her hair, prettily arranged, with a few curls hanging down to brush against her neck, shone in the sunlight which streamed in through the large windows of the garden room. But it was the sweetness of her face, the small smile playing around the corners of her mouth and her dark intelligent eyes, that truly captivated him, made him unable to look away. "Lovely," he said, without thinking.

"Excuse me," she said.

"The room," he said, gaining some control over himself. "It has not been properly used in years and now it is brought back to life. It looks quite lovely. I understand it is your doing?"

"Yes. It is one of my favourite parts of the house. Particularly when it is raining, it allows me to feel as if I am still out of doors."

"I noticed changes in the master's suite too."

"I did not think you would want it to be exactly the same as when your father had it. If there is anything you dislike…"

"Oh no, I do not mean to complain. I like it very much, I like everything very much. Everything is very lovely."

A quizzical frown crossed her features. He could think of nothing more to say but a hallboy then appeared in any case, to tell them his guest's carriages had been sighted on the road, and they were all required to go outside to meet them.

Caroline Bingley was a difficult woman to impress. Her sister, Louisa Hurst, supposed this was why she hadn't yet married; no man had come close to meeting her high standards. But Caroline's first sight of Mr Darcy had moved her to a quiet state of excitement, her second and third sight of him had sent her into raptures, and by the time he had invited them for dinner in London, despite Louisa's caution, Caroline had already determined upon an autumn ceremony and was mentally choosing wedding clothes. She had been visibly devastated at the news Charles had brought back with him that night; that Darcy was already taken. Louisa had sought to console her but Caroline had brightened quickly, buoyed up by the other things their brother had divulged. "I can be patient," she had said to Louisa in private.

Her first sight of Pemberley, indeed, seemed to renew her determination to be the most patient woman on earth. They were alone in the carriage, Mr Bingley and Mr Hurst were travelling in the other coach behind them.

"Well, it might not come with a title, but I should say it is as good as Chatsworth, or Blenheim," Louisa remarked as they crossed the bridge and started on the gradual descent towards the house.

"In my hands, Louisa, it would be the finest house in the country. The parties I might have!"

Seeing the look of longing in her sister's eye, Louisa spoke sympathetically. "It is a shame he is married, but I admire your forbearance, you have not been at all angry at him for being so dishonest."

"Oh, I do not think him so dishonest; I think he sort of forgot her. The marriage is obviously some sort of terrible mistake. Mistakes may be put right. You heard Charles, Darcy spoke of annulment."

"He said he had *previously* thought of annulment, not that he was considering one now. I believe he has been married some years, such a thing might not be possible."

"Well, he'll be rid of her somehow. Look at Pemberley! He is a great man, with great power. Henry the eighth got rid of his first wife, when Anne Boleyn won his heart, and everyone told him it was impossible."

"Anne Boleyn ended up without a head," Mrs Hurst remarked. "Take care, Caroline. I am a little older than you. I have been around men long enough to know that while many

361

dally in the extra marital pond, few desert their wives. It costs them too much money and causes too much scandal."

"If I had this, if I had him, I would not mind some scandal. A man like Mr Darcy should not have to put up with some horrible, ill-favoured wretch that he does not love."

"Ill-favoured?"

"She must be a fright, why would he hide her away and never speak of her otherwise?"

Louisa smiled smugly, pleased to have more knowledge of Mrs Darcy than her sister, to have the upper hand for once. "I called on my friend, Eleanor Parnell, just before we left Town, and I was speaking of Mr Darcy and how we had only just found out he was married, and do you know what she told me?"

"I am sure you will repeat it, whether I wish to hear it or not."

"She told me she had once met a lady calling herself Mrs Darcy at a hat shop in Town, and though her clothes were a fright, she was very pretty. In fact, I think she described her as being 'unusually pretty' and Eleanor does not dispense a compliment if she can possibly avoid it."

A look of disappointment crossed Caroline's features, but she soon recovered. "Well, she obviously does not please him, and I shall."

Mrs Hurst shook her head and resolved to speak to their brother about Caroline's outrageous notions when she next had a chance, but could say no more to her sister herself, as the carriage was pulling to a stop in front of the grand front doors. She was handed out first and saw that although Mr Darcy and a young girl, who she immediately thought must be his sister as they were both stately and tall, had been standing and waiting their arrival for some time, another lady stepped out only at the last possible moment, and stood a little apart, behind the others. Mr Darcy looked over his shoulder at her, seemingly to urge her further forward, but she paid him no mind. She was the last to be introduced and greeted them all cordially, but there were no false effusions of joy at making their acquaintance, and her expression was fixed, until she was introduced to their brother, whose engaging and happy manners appeared to win her over, as they did most people, and something he said caused a genuine smile to overtake her.

As they went into the house, Mrs Hurst thought her friend Eleanor Parnell had the right of it. Mrs Darcy was unusually pretty, particularly when she smiled properly, from genuine amusement, and not only that, she seemed sensible. She listened more than she spoke, watched them carefully and conducted herself beautifully, offering tea and showing them into a grand saloon. There did seem to be some distance between Mr and Mrs Darcy, more on her side than his - his wife seated herself as far from him as possible as they settled themselves down - but if her sister was hoping to consign Mrs Darcy to a corner to be forgotten, while she flirted with her husband and whittled her way into his affections, Mrs Hurst thought her chances of success improbable. Still, nothing defined Caroline better than her willingness to not see when she was beaten. Mrs Hurst could merely hope that she did not become irrational in pursuit of such a phenomenally unlikely outcome.

Darcy knew he was staring at Elizabeth but could not help himself and was struggling to attend to anything that was said. It was as if someone had torn out a large section of a book. He knew the beginning and saw the ending before him, but what had happened in middle? When and how had this transformation happened? To add to the many charms he had taken note of in the garden room, he was now struck by how graceful and elegant Elizabeth had become. Her voice and her whole way of deporting herself was so altered, and while within his heart he heard some little song of requiem for the spiky, scratchy fifteen-year-old with fiery eyes and a defiant chin, he was so very struck by her now, charmed by what she had become.

Caroline Bingley, fortunately, required nothing more from a partner in conversation than occasional agreement. She spoke at length, expounding on Pemberley's excellence. Darcy liked to hear Pemberley praised, but she went on so much that he quickly grew tired of her. And she was so loud that he could not hear what was being said between Bingley and Elizabeth, who were chatting happily on the other side of the room. He saw immediately they would be friends. Everyone liked Bingley. Darcy eventually managed to excuse himself and wandered over, but at the same moment, Elizabeth commented that it was nearly time to change for dinner and perhaps everyone would like to see their rooms and rest for a while.

They all went out into the hall, where Mrs Reynolds waited to see that everyone was well attended to, and then their guests began to drift upstairs. Darcy remained below and waited until Elizabeth had finished giving some instruction to the housekeeper, a sight which made him smile. When Mrs Reynolds was gone, she looked around, seemingly surprised to see him still standing there. "Well, I shall see you at dinner then?"

"Not so fast, if you please. I have a question for you. I was wondering what happened to the gong?"

They both looked towards the spot in the hall where it had once stood. "Oh yes. I'm afraid the gong is gone."

"Gone? But it indicates what time we are to begin dressing."

"Yes, but you see, in your absence, there are usually only four of us at dinner, a meal which is taken at the same time almost every evening. And we are all of an age where we can be relied upon to calculate, with a reasonable degree of accuracy, how long it takes us to dress and upon consultation we found we were all of us in happy possession of a pocket watch, so you see, I thought to have the gong removed to a store room."

"But all the great houses have a dressing gong."

"That's as maybe, but I confess I hated the thing. If you are so very attached to it, though, I will suffer to have it brought back," her lively dark eyes met his. "So then, Mr Darcy, you may bang your own gong as much as you please."

She took the stairs in a nimble fashion, leaving him standing at the bottom a little lost for words. He consoled himself with the thought that there should be enough time between now and dinner for him to untie his tongue.

Forty four

Elizabeth kept him waiting for more than ten minutes, while Darcy tugged at his cuffs and paced, smoothed his waistcoat down and wondered if he had half imagined her handsomeness before. Had the joy of coming home, of being at Pemberley, made him see everything through a haze? Had she looked wonderful and so different merely because he wanted to find her so?

When the door to the mistress's chambers eventually opened, however, and she came out, he forgot to breathe. Good God, she was a fantasy indeed, but a very real one, who spoke and looked at him with a raised brow.

"My apologies, Mr Darcy, I have been dallying, I had forgot you might be waiting. I hope I have not detained you too long."

"About ten minutes," he replied, and then realised this was probably the crassest answer he could have given. Something along the lines of 'not at all' would have been far better. His cousin might have made some very smooth remark about how such beauty would have been worth waiting far longer for, but compliments did not come easy to him. He feared any attempt to flatter and please would only lead to him making a further ass of himself. "But do not make yourself uneasy," he said.

"Oh, I will try not to," she replied, an amused expression crossing her face.

"Shall we, then?" His hand shaking a little in anticipation of her touch, he held his arm out to her and was stupidly pleased when she put her hand upon it.

"Mr Darcy…"

He cut her off before she could go any further. "I am still Mr Darcy, am I? As long as we have known each other, as long as we have been bound, and even in private, I am Mr Darcy?" They were halfway down the stairs but he had stopped and turned to her.

"You would prefer something else? I hope you are not expecting an appellation of the affectionate kind, I don't think I could manage a 'dearest' or anything similar, not

366

without a great deal of practice. No, I don't think it would do for us."

"I have heard wild tales of married women daring to use their husband's given name, and I have always addressed you by yours. Do you think you could manage that?" he said.

"Fitzwilliam," she mused, drawing it out, her voice low. He was entranced by the sound of it from her lips.

"Yes."

"'Tis rather long, do you never shorten it, to William perhaps?"

"No."

"Fitz?"

"Good Lord, no."

"Mr Bingley just calls you Darcy, without the Mr'. Shall I give that a go?"

"But you are not Mr Bingley, you are my wife."

"Fitzwilliam it is then," she said and put her hand back onto his arm as they began to walk again. "I am only just getting used to calling your cousin 'Richard'. Did you see him in Town?"

"Briefly."

"He went suddenly and seemed out of sorts. Something bothers him, you must have noticed?"

To his shame, Darcy realised he had been far too concerned with his own troubles to pay any attention to anyone else. "I did not," he said truthfully and saw the disappointment that flickered across her face; that he should not have a care for his cousin obviously did nothing to raise him any in her estimation. He wanted to speak more to her, only to her, but they were at the drawing room doors already and he saw that Georgiana had been cornered by Miss Bingley on a distant sofa. The rest of the party were gathered elsewhere.

"Where is the governess?" he quietly enquired of Elizabeth.

"Miss Temple has a headache and asked to be excused," she told him, and then seemingly read his mind, "Georgiana will cope."

She left him and went to speak to their other guests, playing the hostess with consummate ease. He edged over to Miss Bingley and Georgiana, but soon saw his sister suffered a fate no worse than being talked at a great deal without being shown the courtesy of any right of reply. Dinner was announced and he offered Georgiana his arm. Unfortunately, Miss Bingley, being so near, took the other before he could seek out Elizabeth. He looked over his shoulder, unsure how to proceed. She met his gaze, but looked more fascinated than offended. Bingley came to the rescue, stepped forward and asked for the honour of escorting her, and in such a charming way, that Elizabeth smiled and accepted.

Miss Bingley then laughed. "Oh, I am so sorry, Mrs Darcy. Your husband was so kind as to always escort me when we were lately in London, that I have taken hold of him by habit. I am sure you will not mind me borrowing him, not when we are all so familiar and such friends."

Elizabeth smiled evenly. "I'll happily lend you Mr Darcy, Miss Bingley, but I'll keep my rightful place at the table, if it's all the same to you. Shall we lead the way then, Mr Bingley?"

Darcy felt Miss Bingley tense and realised she had been intending to walk in first. What the devil was she playing at! He firmly stood his ground and would not move until Bingley and Elizabeth had passed them and gone into dinner.

The meal was excellent. Elizabeth accepted everyone's compliments with modesty and grace. "Thank you, why you all talk as if I had gone down into the kitchen and peeled the potatoes myself. I shall be sure to pass on your compliments to Mrs Small and her staff."

"You do not have a French cook, Mrs Darcy?" Miss Bingley enquired.

"We did, but he missed Toulouse terribly and so we wished him well and sent him back," she replied.

"What Mrs Darcy does not admit to, is that she favours an English pudding over any fine French pastry," Darcy said.

"I confess to being a woman of simple tastes," she replied. Through the candles, down the length of the table, their eyes met for the briefest of moments, though hers did not linger.

"Pray tell me, where do you hail from, Mrs Darcy?" Miss Bingley asked. "I have never seen you in Town."

"Hertfordshire."

"Quite a distance, it makes me wonder how you and Mr Darcy met."

Darcy searched around for an answer. Elizabeth supplied one readily.

"Mr Darcy nearly mowed me down with his carriage. It was sheer luck I was not killed."

All the ladies gasped. "Oh, you joke, surely. I never heard that before," Georgiana said.

"It is true. You might ask Miss Temple if you do not believe me, she was there and can attest to it. Mr Darcy married me by way of apology."

"My wife loves to embellish a tale with a touch of the dramatic, Miss Bingley. Our fathers were acquainted. They were friends as young men."

"*And*, he nearly ran me over with his carriage," Elizabeth added, making Bingley laugh.

"Yes, yes. There was an incident with the carriage, but if you will go running about the countryside in such a wild fashion, what do you expect?" He looked up to see her smiling at him. He was thrilled for a few moments, until she seemed to remember something and her expression became serious again.

The card tables were brought out after dinner to appease Mr Hurst's appetite for whist. Miss Bingley protested, with an overly-gay laugh, that husbands and wives ought not to sit next to each other and Elizabeth, to his annoyance, readily agreed. He wanted to tell her how well she had done with his guests but couldn't get near enough to her during cards. Later, whenever he moved close enough for a private

369

word, she went elsewhere, leaving him frustrated and confused. But he was nothing if not persistent and bided his time, knowing neither of them could retire until all the guests were seen safely off to their beds.

But just as he thought his opportunity to be alone with her had come, she went towards the stairs with Georgiana, throwing him a breezy goodnight over her shoulder, leaving him feeling thoroughly dispensed with.

He walked around the drawing room for a while, wondering at her avoidance of him. He supposed he had only just arrived back after a very long absence and she might be shy, it would be only natural. He thought this a very good answer until he remembered that Elizabeth had always had great stores of self-possession; she had never been afraid of him. Still, whatever the reason for her reticence, they had the rest of their lives to become reacquainted. He could wait for her to come to him, though he was actually in no mind to be patient. When he recalled how the candlelight had flicked across her face during supper and how her eyes had sparkled and danced as she had laughed and teased Bingley, he felt no tolerance for time at all and he realised it was desire that made him impatient. He wanted her, it was as simple as that, and delightfully there were no impediments. No courtship, engagement, or exchange of vows need occur, she had become an extremely desirable woman, and fortune had favoured him - she was already his!

Lost in these thoughts, he did not immediately notice her when she drifted back into the room. She moved towards him and stopped. His heart beat very quickly.

"I forgot my book."

"Oh."

"You are standing in front of it."

"Of course, sorry." He moved aside and she took the tome from the table behind him.

"Well, goodnight, again," she said, moving away, waving the book at him.

"Do you not have a goodnight kiss for your husband?" he said, feeling bold.

Elizabeth stopped, but did not turn for a few moments. His first sight of her face when she did, told him he had made a terrible mistake, a very grave error. Her eyebrow was raised in challenge.

"You are not known to me, Mr Darcy, as a man of happy humour and jests, but given that you have been away for nearly three years without a single word to me, and that when you were last at home we used more cross words than kind ones, I am inclined to believe you have just attempted some sort of joke, for you could not possibly imagine I might take your request seriously?"

"I beg your pardon, Madam, and *that* I say with all the earnestness you perhaps are more inclined to expect of me," he said. "Perhaps my jokes require some improvement and refinement."

"Your humour, Mr Darcy, amongst other things, is something I have very much learnt to live without," she said, before turning and leaving him.

Forty five

When Elizabeth did not appear at breakfast the next day, despite him taking a very long time over his meal, stretching it out to almost an hour, Darcy was peeved. He found himself very keen for a sight of her, to know what she would say or do around him next. "Where is Mrs Darcy?" he eventually asked the butler, who was directing the footman in and out with salvers of food.

"The mistress does not come down to breakfast, sir, 'tis not her custom. She'll be downstairs about half past ten, or sometimes eleven," Hodges replied.

"Oh, your wife is a late sleeper, Darcy. I could not abide to waste half the day in bed. I would consider myself quite slovenly. I note you and I are early risers." Miss Bingley smiled at him.

On examining his watch, Darcy saw it was a quarter to ten and Miss Bingley had not been with them long. She could hardly claim early habits, even if the hours Elizabeth now kept seemed very late.

"Shall we all ride out, Darcy? You promised to show me some of the estate," Bingley asked, setting his cup down and pushing his plate away.

Reasoning that he could not wait forever for Elizabeth to materialise, Darcy agreed and when Miss Bingley expressed a wish to go with them, he could hardly refuse. He got to his feet decisively and went off to prepare. They convened down at the stables, in order that the Bingleys might choose a horse a piece. Mr Bingley was quickly accommodated from the fine range of hunters available. Miss Bingley walked around for a while before selecting her mount, a grey gelding. She directed a groom to saddle the horse but he looked at her doubtfully.

"That's Mrs Darcy's horse," the groom told her.

"And?" Miss Bingley said. "Saddle him young man."

Darcy overheard the exchange and reprimanded the groom. "The lady wishes to ride the gelding, 'tis not your place to question her."

"I'm sorry, sir, but…'tis Mrs Darcy's horse."

Wondering what had happened to the small chestnut mare he had once acquired for Elizabeth and how on earth she managed on such a bigger, faster-looking animal, Darcy shrugged. There was no reason why Miss Bingley should not be permitted the loan of her horse. "I don't suppose Mrs Darcy goes out often, saddle him boy, and don't question the lady again."

The groom gave a little shake of his head, but went off to do as he was told.

"Really, Mr Darcy, the insolence of servants these days, it's intolerable. Standards are most definitely slipping," Caroline Bingley said. "Charles, when you purchase *your* estate you must run a very tight ship."

Bingley was not listening and was walking out of the stables, a good-natured smile upon his face, already taken with Derbyshire, envious of Pemberley, and eagerly anticipating his ride.

Elizabeth arrived down in the courtyard, only to be met by an embarrassed-looking groom and no horse.

"The other lady went out on him, over an hour ago now, I did try to tell the master she was yours and would have said about it being one of your days for riding, but, well…he's the master."

"Of course, I would not expect you to speak out against him. It is not your fault, Joe, be easy," she assured him.

"Shall I get you another horse?"

"No, I'm not naturally inclined to riding, and in no disposition to attempt to break in another horse today."

"If you'll excuse me, madam, I think you do very well, considering you've not been at it long."

She smiled. "Thank you, Joe. Go and get on with your work, they'll back soon, I expect, and in need of your assistance." As if her predicting such an event had summoned them up, they came back, trotting into the courtyard, their faces full of exhilaration, Miss Bingley riding close to Mr Darcy.

Elizabeth lifted her eyes up to his and seeing her in riding habit, his countenance was all consternation. She had been about to go back inside but waited for them to stop, thinking it would be rude to walk off from guests when they had seen her, and also because she wanted to know what Mr Darcy would say to her.

Miss Bingley, however, spoke first. "Mrs Darcy, my apologies. This is your beast is it not?"

"Do you refer to the horse, or Mr Darcy?"

Bingley guffawed. "Ha! He can be a bit of a beast at times, you are right."

Mr Darcy's jaw clenched. "If you would like to go out, Elizabeth, I'd be happy to turn around and accompany you."

She wandered over to pat her horse's nose. "No, he looks tired. I had planned to ride down to call upon one of our tenants, Mrs Bainbridge, who has been recently widowed, but I can go another day. Think nothing of it, Miss Bingley. If you will all excuse me, Mrs Hurst requested a tour of the house, I think I'll change and take her."

"Oh, I should like a tour, too, very much," Miss Bingley said. "Shall we ladies all go together and leave the men to billiards, or other such dull pursuits?"

"Of course," Elizabeth smiled, but supressed a shudder at the idea. Mrs Hurst was acceptable company. Miss Bingley, however, she was starting to take a profound dislike to and she thought she had better not show them the lake, just in case she should be taken with a sudden urge to push the lady into it.

Forty six

The next few days saw them much engaged in entertaining their guests. Darcy soon found, much to his disappointment, that Elizabeth did not like to be near him for long. If he entered a room and she could reasonably quit it, she did. She accepted his attendance to walk her down to dinner, but never addressed him before he did her, never looked his way willingly, never sought him out. No wonder his cousin had wished him good luck. Her now-perfect manners did not allow her to show her disdain for him in front of others, but in the rare moments they were alone, he felt her aversion, and how much did it pain him, because with every single one of their interactions, his admiration for her grew.

What a marvel she had become. She managed Pemberley with quiet ease and by gentle, charming encouragement. A look at a footman and the servant would know how to proceed. A few words to Mrs Reynolds saw all issues melt away and everything would be as it should be again. She had become more than just their mistress; they had closed ranks around her. They had watched the odd child he had brought them grow up into a capable woman and had taken her to their hearts. She was adhered to more than he. Even the dogs in the house lapped at her heels, desperate for her attention. They followed her down corridors, waiting for her to notice them, hoping to be favoured with an affectionate pat on the head. Darcy had some empathy for the poor animals, as he had similar hopes, but ironically thought their chances greater than his.

He was not a man easily deterred though, and steadily persisted in his attempts to engage her in conversation, if nothing else. When they were all gathered in the saloon for afternoon refreshments, which Elizabeth was overseeing, he walked over to ask for coffee.

"I am sorry you did not get out riding the other day," he said, taking the cup she passed him. "May I ask what happened to the horse I procured for you?"

"Oh, you speak of the little mare, Happenstance. I'm afraid I outgrew her long ago. I have been through two or three mares since then."

"Happenstance?" he queried.

"Life is a series of them, don't you find?"

"Yes," he said, struggling for something else to say. "And, happenstance you might find some time for us to talk soon," he ventured, when a few moments had passed, "a little spot for me in your busy schedule?"

"What did you wish to speak of, is something the matter?"

"No, do you suppose that every time I wish to speak to you, I aim to censure, or find fault? I do not."

She did not reply as they were diverted by the sounds of a carriage on the road, pulling up to the front doors.

"Do you expect anyone?" he asked.

"No. It may be visitors, we get one or two in the summer months, asking to see the house and grounds," Elizabeth said.

"How tiresome," Miss Bingley opined from across the room, "to have strangers trotting in and out. I wonder you do not send them away."

"Oh, it is not too much trouble, Miss Bingley," Elizabeth replied. "They are usually very respectful. I find myself gratified to live in a house that people admire and wish to view. I find it a wonderful compliment."

Mr Darcy had wandered over to the window. "'Tis not strangers, I do believe that is Richard riding alongside a carriage, though the carriage I do not know."

Elizabeth and Georgiana immediately left the tea things and ran from the room, through the hall and out of the front doors, which were flung open for them at the last moment by a footman taken off guard. Mr Darcy trailed in their wake, while the others kept to their seats.

With a majestic wave of his arm from atop his horse, Richard greeted them and then leaned on Darcy to dismount.

"What are you doing back so soon?" Elizabeth asked. "We did not expect you."

"And what sort of a welcome home is that, when I bring you a gift? I do believe you have a birthday soon, Elizabeth."

The footman who had come with the carriage was already opening its doors. The sight of the lady who was handed out caused Elizabeth to burst into tears, though perhaps it was not *just* the sight of Jane that made her cry, as upon seeing her, she suddenly felt all the strain of the last few days come bubbling up and demand release. She moved towards her sister with arms outstretched, and then clung to her. She was not the only surprise, though - Elizabeth's cup truly overflowed with joy because Mrs Gardiner had come too and was the recipient of another fierce embrace. Then they all talked at once, and laughed much. Elizabeth assured Richard it was the best present she could have ever hoped for. Georgiana was introduced and greeted the ladies, not with her usual reserve, but with some considerable warmth, telling them she had heard so much of them from Elizabeth that she felt she knew them already.

Mr Darcy stood at the back, looking quite uncomfortable, and when Elizabeth caught sight of him, she pulled Jane over by the hand to say hello.

"You remember my sister, Mr Darcy," she said, with a challenge in her voice, daring him to disapprove of the person she loved like no other.

He bowed, very formally. "Yes, I regret...I apologise, Miss Bennet, for my...Elizabeth, might you enlighten me? Which one of your twenty-seven sisters do I have the pleasure of addressing?"

Elizabeth could not help but laugh, his confusion was endearing and there was nothing in his countenance to suggest he meant to be anything but welcoming. "Mr Darcy, I have only four sisters, as you well know. This is Jane, who I am sure will not mind you addressing her as such, seeing as she is your sister now too."

"Of course, of course, I thought it was, but could not be sure. It has been a long time since we have seen each other," he said and welcomed her inside.

In the hallway, Jane looked about her in wide-eyed wonder and whispered into Elizabeth's ear. "Lizzy, this is your home!"

"I have written to you of Pemberley."

"Yes but, to actually see it...oh my, it is beyond belief. The size of it, the beauty of it, how do you manage such a big house?"

"Oh, I rule by consent. The staff and I participate in a ruse in which I pretend I am in charge, while they sort themselves out splendidly." Seeing her aunt being escorted into the saloon by Richard, she pulled Jane's hand. "Nobody will miss us for a few minutes. Come and see my chambers. You will laugh to see how grand they are and know that they are all at your ridiculous sister's disposal."

Jane stopped her briefly. "When we planned the trip, we did not think Mr Darcy would be at home, and I see he has guests, will he mind us being here, do you think?"

"I really do not care if he does, Jane. I am so glad to see you."

They ran to Elizabeth's rooms where Jane exclaimed and admired everything and then they lay side by side on the enormous bed, laughing at the pleasure of seeing each other.

"And what news do you have? How are things in Meryton?"

"As I have said in my letters, Kitty is better away from Lydia's influence. She is much improved and begs to be invited to Pemberley. I think she would not disgrace herself if she were, Lizzy."

"I had no idea she would wish for such a thing, then she will come soon. And Mary?"

"Mary is Mary, and I think will always be...Mary."

They both sighed.

"And you, Jane, do you mind being with mamma? Do you miss Town?"

"The Gardiners? Yes. London? Not at all. I think I am a country girl at heart, Lizzy."

"Well then, we must find you a nice, northern, country gentleman so you can keep your sister company more often, unless you are too busy breaking hearts in the south?"

"I confess I have recently had a proposal."

Elizabeth sat up in surprise, not having expected such an answer. "Pray tell me everything, I must know it all."

"Mr Collins returned from Kent. He was very full of praise for his patroness, Lady Catherine, and most particularly asked after you and asked me to thank you again for your assistance in securing him his position there."

Elizabeth rolled her eyes. "I have had about seventeen letters of thanks from him already. I am sorry but I do think he is the oddest of creatures."

"And grows odder," agreed Jane. "Anyhow, he offered, as we always expected he might. It was no great surprise."

Holding her breath, Elizabeth nodded. "Do go on."

"You would have enjoyed the absurdity of his speech, Lizzy. He spoke of all practical considerations, before there was any talk of..."

"Oh Jane, did you accept him or not?" Elizabeth broke in, impatiently.

"No, I did not."

"Oh thank goodness." Elizabeth put a hand to her chest. "You may tell me of his ridiculous speech another time, when I am over my shock and relief and in a fit state to richly enjoy his absurdities."

"Oh I will, but I must tell you the worst part of it. For there he was, professing the violence of his affection towards me, saying of how he had long ago singled me out as the companion of his future life, and could love no other, of how amiable and uniformly charming I was, but what do you think he did after I turned him down?" Jane asked.

Elizabeth shook her head.

"He proposed to Charlotte Lucas, less than two days later! I was the earth, the skies and all the blessings in the world one day, and then the next, Charlotte Lucas was. He was so full of words, Lizzy, but he knows the meaning of none of them."

After laughing heartily for a moment, Elizabeth's face creased into a frown. "And next you are going to tell me Charlotte has accepted him, aren't you?"

"I am afraid so. She has. She is to be Mrs Collins."

"Impossible! She has so much sense, how could she marry a fool?"

"She is almost seven and twenty, she wants a home of her own, and no one else has offered."

"'Tis a high price to pay," Elizabeth said sadly, before they went downstairs again.

In the saloon, when all the introductions were made and she had seen her relations well settled, Elizabeth walked over to Richard who was sat in his favourite chair, a little away from the others, recovering from his ride. "May I thank you again, you must be exhausted, going to Town and then to Hertfordshire to collect Jane, and then bringing them back here. I don't think anyone has ever done a nicer thing for me."

"No less than you deserve. I know how much you love Jane, and you ought to be together more."

"And maybe I am not the only one who will enjoy her company," Elizabeth said with a raise of her brow, remembering how she had once thought him partial to her sister.

Richard looked confused, as if he hadn't the faintest idea of her meaning. "Tell me," he said, lowering his voice and changing the subject, "what do you make of Miss Bingley?"

Elizabeth paused briefly, formulating her answer. "Miss Bingley, it seems, likes me to loan her things. At dinner, she borrowed my husband, the other day she borrowed my horse. I think she would also like to borrow Pemberley from me."

"And?"

"The husband I am indifferent about. The horse I am very angry about. Pemberley, I will only be removed from by earthquake, flood, or on the back of an undertaker's cart. She shall not have my house from me under any circumstances, I have worked hard to earn my place here and aim to keep it."

He leaned forward. "Do you suppose you would be so vexed about her, if you really were indifferent to Darcy?"

It was such an insightful question and she heartily wished she had something clever to say in reply. "I assure you, he has been home some days and we have hardly spoken."

"Is that so? Perhaps you ought to speak more. Since you entered the room, he has looked in no other direction but yours." Richard's eyes flickered over to where Darcy stood against the mantelpiece.

Elizabeth refused to look around. "He is probably disapproving of me talking to you, when I should be entertaining his guests. I am no doubt in line for a lecture."

Richard laughed. "He might have been able to lecture you at one time, but I should like to see him do so now! Actually, I think lecturing you is the last thing on his mind."

"And now you are being vexing. I am off to fetch you a glass of port to keep you quiet."

Darcy had been coming towards them and Richard noted the look of disappointment on his cousin's face when Elizabeth moved away before he reached them. Darcy sat in the opposite chair, but followed her with his eyes.

"Is it good to be home, Darcy?"

"Yes, though, I can't pretend I would not have liked a warmer welcome from some quarters. That was quite a grand gesture, bringing Miss Bennet and Mrs Gardiner here."

"I am sorry if it interferes with any of your plans. It was organised in great secrecy, before we knew of your return, and I had no idea you would have your own guests. You do not mind, I hope?"

Darcy bowed his head. "No, I do not mind. I ought to thank you for making her so happy."

"I thought we might go to Haddon for a picnic on her birthday. I have sent a note to my mother but I am sure she will like the plan. She has grown fond of Elizabeth. Her birthday is the nineteenth, she will be twenty," Richard said, by way of reminder.

"Yes, I know," Darcy said shortly, but then paused, his head bent in submission. "I have been unforgivably remiss in the past. I shall not be so again. I have purchased a gift. Though now it looks like a mere trifle compared to what you have done. I am thinking I might send it back and arrange for something grander."

"No, Darcy, do not, I beg you. She is not one to care about the cost of things. If you have chosen it, I am sure she will like it very much."

"I am beginning to think she likes nothing about me and will not like anything I give her. She hates me, quite rightly. I see today that I have kept her too much from her family," Darcy said.

"You sought to protect her and things have happened, since you have been away, which I think will have increased her understanding of why you might have made certain decisions. But you must know there have been times when she has been desperately unhappy and she has often attributed the cause of her sadness to you. Why do you think I wished you good luck in London?" Richard leaned forward. "How do you find her?"

"She astonishes me. Tell me, when did she grow so handsome?"

Richard laughed. "Oh Darcy, she always was. You just would not allow yourself to see it. Maybe it was her age, or the circumstances, but I assure you, she was always pretty. Though perhaps, she is a little more womanly now. And a fine gown, or an elegant riding habit, does much for a lady."

"That it does," Darcy replied, watching her cross the room to come back to them, a glass of port in her hand, which she pressed upon his cousin with a fond look. The familiarity of the gesture, the easiness they had with each other, which allowed them to communicate without words, made Darcy so envious he got up and stalked away.

Forty seven

There were so many of them now that dinner had to be moved to the old formal dining hall, the one that had been in regular use when his father had been alive. Darcy now remembered those stiff, stilted dinners with distaste - how everybody had sat so far apart that it had inhibited any real conversation. He preferred the smaller room they had been in on previous nights, a room he supposed Elizabeth had fitted out specifically for the purpose. It had perhaps previously been a disused parlour or ante-room. Now though, they just about managed to make the much larger dining hall lively. Richard sat somewhere in the middle, talking with Miss Temple, who was on his right. It looked like an intense conversation, one that Darcy wondered at. Miss Bingley looked happier to be in a grander setting though and had him tell her some of the history of Pemberley, and about some of the paintings that adorned the walls. Elizabeth, seated at the other end of the table, was in lively chatter with her aunt and Georgiana, who she had kept with her once they had entered. He had hoped to have Bingley for some conversation, but his friend was happily monopolised, nay transfixed, by Jane Bennet, who he had connived to be near. The lady blushed and nodded and smiled far more than was necessary. Bingley was soaking her in, revelling in her attentions and giving her much of his own, to the exclusion of all others. He saw Elizabeth glance up the table at them once or twice, curiosity flickering over her lovely features, and he wondered what she made of it. He saw neither approval, nor disapproval, maybe a hint of protectiveness, some concern.

Darcy worried too. Bingley was overly enthusiastic and probably meant nothing by it. Jane might misconstrue him. Bingley seemed to have forgotten what he had vowed to his family, which was to purchase an estate, marry very well and rise up from his humble beginnings to such a position that his sons might truly call themselves gentlemen.

There was music after dinner. Miss Bingley put herself forward quickly and then exhibited for a longer time than was strictly polite, almost leaving no opportunity for

Georgiana to take her place at the instrument. Darcy was keen that she should, having heard how accomplished she had become, but he sensed her nerves. He felt she would always be of a reserved nature, much like her mother, but Elizabeth offered to accompany Georgiana by singing. She was as bold as Georgiana was shy and together, they were charming. They were several entreaties for them to perform again, which Elizabeth refused. "No, no we have acquitted ourselves well enough and that will do. One should always leave an audience wanting more, not begging for relief. We will not have you sick of the sight and sound of us by playing one song too many." She cut a quick glance at Caroline Bingley as she passed her, which went unnoticed by many, including the lady herself.

Sitting next to him, Richard gave a shake of his head. "She has the cheek of the devil."

"But the voice of an angel," Darcy replied.

He had the great pleasure of hearing Elizabeth sing again the next day, stood next to him at church. They had been too frequently surrounded by other people to exchange any words of importance over the last few days, but at least now she was close - very close. Thoughts which had no business occupying his mind in a house of God intruded, as he found his eyes drawn to the sweet curve of her neck and the rise of her chest as it swelled in song. He had a desperate need to touch her, to entwine her slender fingers in his own, or put his hand to the small of her back. Instead he had to be content with how the muslin of her gown would occasionally brush against his fingertips. He let his arm hang limply down by his side so it would. Once services were over, the family lingered in the churchyard while the Bingleys and Hursts, who had no acquaintance there in any case (and how Miss Bingley did complain about being made to stand around in the heat) went on ahead to wait in the coaches. Elizabeth spoke with almost everybody, remembering faces and names and dispensed words of sympathy, or smiles of congratulation wherever appropriate. She introduced Jane and her aunt to everyone.

Many in Lambton remembered Mrs Gardiner and were genuinely delighted to see her, telling her she must visit them soon. Darcy followed Elizabeth around like a perfect dolt, accepting the well wishes of those who were glad to see him home, but not having much to say in return. He had been away long enough for him to feel like a foreigner; and a perfect stranger in his own life.

Elizabeth dictated the time of their departure and when she turned towards the carriages, Georgiana and Miss Temple followed, breaking off from their own conversations and saying goodbyes. He watched his young beautiful wife look for Richard, move towards him and slip her hand though the crook of his cousin's arm, out of habit. Darcy supposed. He had been forgotten from where he had stood, largely silent, behind her. He waited until they were almost out of the churchyard before catching the pair up, stopping them with a little bow, excusing himself to Richard, and taking her hand from his cousin's arm, to settle it on his own instead.

Richard stepped aside, so they might go on ahead.

"You are *my* wife, are you not?" Darcy said to her, leaning down, speaking low into her ear. She smelt as lovely as the rose bushes they passed as they walked the length of the parson's garden wall.

"Did you enjoy the sermon?" she asked, ignoring his possessive display. Whether because she did not mind, or whether because there were too many other people about to make a scene, he could not determine.

He was nonplussed for a moment. It had not been the reply he had been expecting. "I did, yes. Mr Smythe speaks very well. Richard made a good appointment in my absence. It is his niece that Georgiana is very good friends with?"

"Yes, the girl she was speaking to just now in the churchyard."

Darcy hadn't noticed her but did not say so. "And what are her circumstances, what kind of girl is she?"

He felt Elizabeth bristle. "She is from a very respectable family, and like Georgiana, is in the unfortunate position of having lost both her parents at a young age, so she has come to live with Mr and Mrs Smythe. She is a very good sort of girl, I promise you. I would not allow Georgiana to see her so often if she was not."

He handed her up into the carriage and sat opposite her. Their knees bumped and in response, she pushed herself to the very back of her seat, to avoid the contact. He cursed his ability to always say the wrong thing around her. "Elizabeth, I do not necessarily disapprove. It is just that I haven't met the girl yet."

"And Richard's judgement, or my judgement, counts for nothing with you?"

There was no opportunity for an answer, as Georgiana herself was entering the carriage and they were no longer alone. Elizabeth spent the rest of the journey with a small frown creasing the bridge of her nose. Darcy spent it knowing he had the right, but would have to earn the privilege, of kissing her frowns away.

"Will you ride out with me tomorrow, just you and I?" Darcy asked when they were back at Pemberley and busy removing their outdoor things in the hall. "There are things I would say to you, without interruption."

"And there are some things I would say to you, but we have guests that require entertaining."

"Well, we might go early, if you can manage to drag yourself from your bed before eleven," he said jokingly.

Her expression remained even, but she bent her head and licked her lips and looked as if she were trying to bite back a retort. "What time do you propose we go out, Mr Darcy, and I shall do my best to *'drag myself from my bed'* as you put it?"

"At nine perhaps?"

"I shall be there," she promised and walked away.

Her little maid was still hovering in the hall with her mistress's things in her hand and looked up at Darcy as if she wanted to say something to him. He nodded at her, giving her permission.

She spoke very quietly, with her head bent to the floor. "Please, sir. If it would behove you to know some of Mrs Darcy's routine."

"Routine?"

"Mrs Darcy rises between half past six and seven o'clock every day. She dresses herself and walks in the park for about an hour, before returning. She calls me to help her bathe and dress for the day and then has breakfast from a tray in her sitting room upstairs. Mrs Reynolds then attends her and they go through their business - matters to do with the running of the house. Depending on how much they have to do, she is downstairs about eleven, 'cept today, on Sundays, when there's services to go to."

"I see, thank you, Ruth."

"Rose, sir."

"Rose, my apologies." He moved away and such had been her quiet and gentle manner, that he was in another room entirely before he realised he had been taken to task by a maid.

Darcy strode into the courtyard at six minutes past nine the next day and saw Elizabeth leaning against a column, examining her pocket watch in an exaggerated fashion. "You are late, Mr Darcy."

"Fitzwilliam."

"Excuse me?" She put her watch away and pushed herself off from the column, moving through the yard ahead of him.

"We are alone. Didn't we agree to give Fitzwilliam a try?"

The horses were brought round and he wanted to assist her into the saddle but she was quick and her groom efficient. They completed the manoeuvre, obviously much practiced, before he could get close enough to even offer. As he seated himself on his own mount, he dismissed both grooms. "That'll do, you needn't follow, we shall be back in an hour or so."

He was in an ebullient mood as they moved off through the gates of the courtyard and into the park. To be alone with her like this, on such a sweet, fine day thrilled him and he hardly dared speak for fear of ruining the moment. To him there seemed to be noise aplenty, the soft thud of the earth as the horses moved over it, the call of birds, the rustle of the wind as it played across the surface of the lake.

Eventually, he noticed her glance his way, the edges of her mouth quirking upwards in amusement. "I think it will stay fine all day," she said.

"Yes," he replied, before falling silent again. There were so many things he wanted to speak to her about but he could not comprehend where to begin, nor could he gauge her mood.

She let out a little laugh. "It is your turn to say something now, sir. I have talked about the weather and now you ought to make some sort of remark on the beauty of the park, or how pleasant the ride is."

"It *is* very pleasant," he managed.

"Very well," she sighed. "I suppose that reply will do for now."

"I do not see the need to always be saying something," he replied.

"It is called conversation, Fitzwilliam. Perhaps it is a little overrated, depending on one's partner in the exercise, but sometimes it must be attempted and often a very little will suffice. You need not worry about astounding or amazing me, any sort of comment will do, and did you not bring me out here to speak to me? Isn't that why I was *'dragged from my bed before eleven'*?"

He bowed his head in apology, but at the same time was delighted to hear his name fall so naturally from her lips. "Forgive me if I maligned you. I now have a better idea of how you spend your mornings. It seems I have disturbed your routine today. I will do my best to respect it in future."

"I tease you, sir. It is not so ingrained in me that I do not countenance any alteration in it. I like a little change, now and then. Sometimes I wish for more of it."

He felt fresh sources of guilt at the wistful look that crossed her face. She was a bright, lively girl, full of life and blessed with a love of adventure and people, and he had kept her at Pemberley, refused her any kind of excursion or change of scene. He remembered how she had once impressed him with her French and told him how she wanted to travel. He was vowing to himself that he would rectify the wrong, but he had obviously been silent for too long again.

"Well, though you *claim* to have things to say to me, they seem to be buried quite deeply within you, so may I begin instead?" she asked, and then did not wait for an answer. "Miss Temple has suggested we might release her, so she can seek another position."

"And what are your feelings on the matter?"

She looked surprised that he should ask her, but answered readily.

"She has no role here anymore and that must be frustrating for her. Georgiana is too old for a governess. It feels wrong to retain her, and yet..."

"And yet?"

"She has been here so long, and has become such a part of us, that I can't imagine Pemberley without her. You have been away, so perhaps it is hard for you to understand, but Miss Temple has often been our voice of reason, the saner part of us; our steadiness."

"Well it is clear you are very fond of her, but if she has been good to us, then we must be equally good to her and wish her well if she wants to move on. Does she?"

"I think so. Saying goodbye will not be easy, but she is not happy."

"Then we must help her in her quest to find a new position. Do you wish for me to speak to her?" he offered.

"No, no. I shall do it."

She thanked him and he wondered idly what he had done to earn her gratitude. They were at the edge of the park now, moving into the woods.

"I wondered whether I might make the call I was intending to the other day, Mrs Bainbridge, just to see how she does," Elizabeth asked. "It will not take too long."

He agreed and they rode that way. He mostly listened while she spoke and pointed a few matters out to him as they went - issues with drainage, some walls in need of repair, areas for improvement. She spoke with an enthusiasm that grew as she recognised his willingness to listen to her, and he saw that he might make a friend of her by showing her he valued her opinion, and he found he truly did. She was knowledgeable and sensible beyond her years, and obviously cared a great deal about the estate.

He helped her dismount at the Bainbridge's farm and then got back upon his horse.

"Are you not coming in?"

"Please pass on my respects. I shall wait for you."

"You will not sit stupidly out here on your own. Mrs Bainbridge's husband lived and worked upon your land for over fifty years, you'll say hello to the lady, surely?"

"You'll do much better on your own. As you have already pointed out, quite rightly, in fact, I am not good at small talk."

"Then might I suggest you take the opportunity to practice? Get off your very high horse, sir, and accompany me inside."

She was extremely angry and quite fearsome. They stared stubbornly at each other for some time. He was not used to being told what to do and did not much like it, and she was so very lovely in all her fiery indignation that it was almost worth making her heated and cross just to watch her, but then he decided if his ultimate goal was domestic felicity, he had better give in to her now and then, and jumped down.

It was not so very bad. They sat in the elderly lady's kitchen for five minutes and received her great thanks for paying them such an honour. Elizabeth was kind and gentle, unrecognisable from the woman who had told him off just before, and managed the business of them coming and going very well.

When they had ridden away, he sought to explain himself better. "I am a good landlord, Elizabeth, just because I don't visit them all and break bread at their tables does not make me an ogre."

"I know, and neither do I visit them all with any great regularity, only when I feel it is necessary. You are fair and generous and I do not propose any bread breaking, but I do think the courtesy you have shown by sitting with her for five minutes, and paying your condolences in her time of grief, will be long remembered by Mrs Bainbridge and her family."

They were separated for a while by the way becoming a single path. Darcy urged her on ahead so he might keep sight of her from behind and when they were able to ride side by side again, he caught her up.

"The living of Kimpton will become available soon, I think. Mr Rogers is sadly in very ill health. He will not live out the year," she said.

"Yes," he replied. "I have heard."

"How will you choose a successor? Do you have someone in mind?"

"No, but I have the feeling you do. Will you stop dissembling and tell me?"

"I am hoping the man I think of might tell you of his wishes himself; he has not properly spoken to me of it, so it is not my place to say anything. I just wondered if the living was already promised elsewhere?"

"It is not," he said.

They had reached an open clearing and she nudged the horse forward into a brisk trot that quickly became a gallop. He had to dig his heels into the side of his own mount quite sharply to catch her up.

She slowed when the wide expanse became narrower and on catching sight of his face, she tilted her head to the side. "Something is the matter, what concerns you?"

"I confess the sight of you on horseback makes me nervous, and galloping, no less! The last time we went out together you took that terrible fall," he said.

"Oh that. I have had quite a few spills since then."

She waved it away, as if it were nothing, though the memory had haunted and tortured Darcy ever since. The sound of her hitting the ground had never left his consciousness.

They were nearing the house and he realised with some regret that they had been out for the promised hour. It had gone quickly and now she was filling the last moments of it with talk of the estate.

Darcy rode very close, leaning over and stopping her horse with a pull on the reins, and pulling his own horse up at the same time. "Elizabeth, I have seen what you have done with the house. I see how you have grown into your role, how you have had to grow up quickly and how well you manage things. Pemberley is brought to life again and I thank you for all you have done. Might I ask, though, if you would do me the very great favour, now that I am home, of allowing me to manage my own estate? A gentleman likes to. I would feel rather redundant if you took charge of everything."

"I am sorry, the col…Richard and I always discussed things."

"And I promise to always try and hear your opinion," he said, and smiled, "though I cannot see us always being in agreement."

"No, heaven forbid," she pulled a very grave face. "Wouldn't that be very dull of us?"

"But the estate is not what I asked you out here to talk about. I wanted to discuss our…" he paused and waved a hand in the air, letting go of her horse's reins. "Our situation."

The horses moved forward again, finding their own way home, their owners too engrossed in faltering, embarrassing, discussion to assist them.

"I was wondering…"

"Yes?" she asked when he couldn't finish.

"How do you see things?"

"I think that is too general an enquiry for me to be able to form any kind of meaningful reply. What sort of *'things'* are you wishing me to comment on?"

"Well, how we might go on together?" he asked.

"Oh, well I see no great difficulties. As you have just said, we are rarely of one mind about things…"

"I did not mean it quite like that."

392

"But you are so very occasionally at home that it cannot matter too much. I am happy to entertain your guests and when you are all gone away to Scarborough, I shall carry on much as before."

"I shall not be leaving with them for Scarborough. Is that what you thought? Elizabeth, I do not plan on going away again for a very long time, and if I do, I shall take you with me." She looked around at him quickly, but he could not determine her thoughts. "I am afraid that might have sounded like I would pack you up, as if you were some baggage and throw you on the back of the carriage." She laughed softly and it was a delightful sound to his ears and brought him hope. "We may go somewhere in the future, you and I, travel a little together, if it would please you to do so?"

Her head was tilted prettily to the side, he thought her in contemplation of his words, her head full of places she would like to visit.

"Is she your lover, Miss Bingley?"

He was shocked to the core by the question and her bluntness in asking it.

"You must not think me so innocent or ignorant," she said. "Or without understanding for the position you find yourself in, but, you see, I should hate to look like a fool. I will not have you treat me as your wife during the day, only for the two of you to be laughing about me at night. I would rather have the truth of it."

He could not answer for a few moments.

She stared ahead, chin aloft, her countenance set in an air of quiet dignity. "Well, Fitzwilliam, you said you wished to speak of our situation, my question is pertinent to such a discussion. Will I not have the satisfaction of a reply? Or are you one of those men who believes it none of his wife's business and that she has no right to question him?"

They had reached the courtyard and he dismounted and went to her, holding his arms out. She slid into them, but after he had set her down, he felt her start to pull away. Determined to keep her close, he took hold of her elbow. "There are no lovers, no mistresses, I promise you. If there were, do you really believe I would bring them here and flaunt them before you? Elizabeth, you do not know me. I would never dishonour you so."

"No, I do not know you. You have never been here long enough for me to truly sketch your character. Can you blame me for asking, when she is so familiar with you? How could I form any other opinion?" She pulled out of his grasp, taking a step or two away.

"I hardly know Miss Bingley, she seemed harmless in London, and I liked her for being Bingley's sister. I see how badly she behaves here and I am sorry for inviting her," he said.

"As I said, it is nothing to me either way; I just wished to know the truth." She began to walk into the house, leaving him holding the reins of both horses.

"Elizabeth," he called after her. She stopped and turned. "May we go out again?"

"If you wish it, of course."

Forty eight

The breakfast room was not somewhere she often made an appearance these days, but Elizabeth went there in the last hour, knowing all be cleared away soon, to see if anyone still lingered. She found only Mrs Gardiner, sat in front of an empty cup, eyes cast towards the French windows, looking down to the lake.

"Good morning, Lizzy, though I hear you have been up for a while. Did you have a pleasant ride?"

She poured her aunt another cup of coffee, before sitting down next to her. "I'm not so certain I would call it *'pleasant'*, Mr Darcy is not the sort of man you associate with that word. It was enlightening, however, and not wholly unenjoyable," she said. "You are the third person to ask me that question. Georgiana broke off practice to come to my room, to specifically ask it of me."

"Those who love you wish you well, and hope all will be well."

"I think it shall take more than an hour together on horseback to shift some of my prejudices against him."

"Though, if one examines that statement closely, there is a hint in it that you are not wholly opposed to the idea of having those prejudices overcome," Mrs Gardiner replied, with a tease in her voice.

"I am more likely to be overcome by the heat today, 'tis growing warmer. Where is Jane?"

"Walking in the Dutch garden with Mr Bingley, who I think is feeling a little overcome himself." Mrs Gardiner laughed but on seeing Elizabeth's expression, which was very serious indeed, she sobered. "Do you not like him? I would have thought you would have been delighted for her. He would be an excellent match. I hear he has a very healthy income and is looking to buy an estate nearby. Wouldn't it be wonderful for you, too, to have her so near?"

"Oh, I give her leave to like Mr Bingley, she has liked many a stupider person, that's for sure, and I have vowed not to interfere in her business in any case. I should be very happy for Jane, if she likes him and he offers. You are right, it would be a very good match, I just worry about the heartache it will give to others." Seeing her aunt's confusion, she sought to explain. "I consider the feelings of the colonel - I mean Mr Fitzwilliam."

"You think he is in love with Jane?" her aunt whispered, after looking about to make sure no one else was near.

"I do, yes, and feel he would have offered by now, if only he had an income."

"Lizzy, I have recently spent three days on the road with them and I detected nothing of the kind. I believe you are wrong and I hope you do not steer Jane from Mr Bingley because of your fondness for Mr Fitzwilliam."

"No, no, as I said, I shall not interfere. But I hate to think of the suffering it will cause him to see her courted by another. All is *not* fair in love and war," Elizabeth said. "Why does Mr Darcy have so much money and his cousin none at all?"

"Why to keep you in beautiful gowns, of course," Mrs Gardiner said, touching the lace that edged Elizabeth's sleeves, "this is very lovely."

"Yes, Rose has dressed me up rather well for a day at home. I don't know what she was about. She took an inordinately long time over my hair," Elizabeth said, before looking around at the platters of food laid out on the long sideboard. "I suppose they will come to clear away soon. Mr Darcy will be at his crossest if he misses breakfast."

"Oh he has been and gone. He ate quickly and took Mr Hurst off to see about some tackle and rods. The gentlemen are to spend the afternoon fishing," Mrs Gardiner said. "Are you not eating?"

"No, I had something earlier, in my rooms." Elizabeth realised the silliness of her being there. "I only came in to see you."

"Ah," said Mrs Gardiner, with a smirk and a direct look, "to see me, yes."

Elizabeth could not help but blush and wonder at herself. While she had been at her own toilette, she had heard the faint sounds of Mr Darcy changing and the reverberation of his deep baritone through the wall that separated their apartments. She had sat inwardly cursing Rose's long attendance on her, keen to be downstairs. Had she come into the breakfast room for a sight of him? Having vowed to herself, before his return home, to avoid him as much as possible, why was she now seeking him out? Her search for an answer told her it was because she could not make him out - he was an interesting study and she wanted to get to the truth of him.

After some discussion about what they might do for entertainment, Mrs Gardiner recalled how Elizabeth had once joked in a letter about taking her for a drive around the park in a low phaeton with a nice little pair of ponies, whenever she made it to Pemberley. "I confess, I found the idea delightful, and now I am here, I should like it even more. Could such a thing be arranged? If you have not had enough of horses for today, that is?"

Elizabeth stood up, feeling sudden enthusiasm for such an adventure, and went to see about it. Mrs Gardiner had some acquaintance in Lambton she had not yet called on and it was resolved they would extend the tour to include a visit to them. Georgiana and a very flushed-looking Jane were found and gathered up, and off they set.

They did not come back till late in the afternoon, their excursion having been enjoyable and the company so good. As the phaeton rolled into the courtyard, an alert footman stepped out to assist them. They were laughing and talking, and Elizabeth was very happy until she caught sight of Mr Darcy, walking briskly from the house with a thunderous look upon his face. He handed the other ladies down from the carriage with a few words and a tight smile. She, he grabbed about the waist, with little finesse, and set her very firmly down on the ground.

"Where in the hell have you been?" he demanded.

Fortunately, Jane and Georgiana were too near the house, almost inside, to have heard him, but she saw Mrs

Gardiner react to his bluntness and anger, looking away in embarrassment on Elizabeth's behalf.

Determined not to lose her own temper, she walked around him, going indoors and up the stairs to her chambers. Her astonishment when he followed her and shut the door behind him was great. "You were not invited in here, sir."

"I have not yet received the courtesy of an answer to my question?"

"And you will never get one, not if you speak to me in that way again. I will not be sworn at."

He had the good grace to blanch and she saw his temper begin to drain away. "You went off unaccompanied. No gentleman or footman with you."

"Something I have done many times before. I know how to drive the phaeton. How old am I, Mr Darcy? Do you even know?"

"You are nearly twenty."

"Yes, not a child anymore."

"It is not merely your lack of regard for your own safety which angered me. You left the other ladies, Miss Bingley and Mrs Hurst, without a thought to their entertainment or comfort."

He was unfortunately, infuriatingly, right, she had neglected guests. "That was rude of me. I shall apologise to them, but you still had no cause to speak to me that way."

Darcy nodded. "I have just spent three months aboard a ship. The uncouthness of sailors has obviously rubbed off on me."

Elizabeth was still angry, mortified about being told off in such a way in front of her aunt. She could not yet accept his apology and said nothing.

"And, you know, I was forced to amuse Miss Bingley and Mrs Hurst myself, all afternoon. You can imagine how this had quite a negative effect on my mood."

He had said it, of course, to try and amuse her, and she could not help the small smile that tugged at the corners of her mouth.

"Do my jokes improve?"

"Not the timing of them."

They were stood on either side of the bed. She saw him look down at it for a while and then back up at her, before tugging at his cuffs. The heated discussion had meant she'd not noticed the awkwardness of them being there alone. Mr Darcy stepped quickly away and walked towards the window, looking around the room and noting the changes she had made.

"So, I require an invitation to enter your domain, do I?" he asked with a raised brow. "White card, handwritten with all the particulars on it, I suppose?" When she remained silent, his shoulders sagged. "And a good guest should always know when to take the hint to go, of course. You need not worry, I will not bother the lioness in her lair again. Nothing says you are unwelcome quite as emphatically as a locked door."

"A locked door?" she asked, truly bemused.

He nodded towards the internal door that separated their rooms.

Without thinking, Elizabeth went to it, turned the handle and jiggled it in a practised way, until the door swung open. "It has never been locked. I have no key. The catch is a little sticky."

Startled and shocked, he seemed incapable of movement or speech. Elizabeth was triumphant for a while, glad to have the upper hand, before she realised he might take it as permission to go back and forth between their rooms whenever he felt the inclination. She wished for no such thing; and despite being over four years married, felt entirely unprepared for it, should he ever try to force the issue.

Mr Darcy bowed. "I was very rude to you outside but I hope you will show some clemency. I am a man prone to protectiveness and I worry over those I have a care for."

"You must know I would never put Georgiana in harm's way. I love her as you do."

"I was not only worried for Georgiana, Elizabeth. I was worried for you."

He had come close now, both of them standing by the infamous door. "I shall still think of it as quite locked, I assure you, unless you should ever decide to issue an invitation." Then he went past her, through into his own chambers and closed the door behind him.

Elizabeth made it as far as the bed before her legs failed her and she collapsed onto it, pulling a pillow over her head, which was how she remained until Rose appeared to tell her it was time to dress for dinner.

Forty nine

Mrs Gardiner was passing though the hallway when Elizabeth emerged from her rooms, and although Mr Darcy waited for her as usual at the top of the stairs, when he saw her with her aunt, he gave them a polite acknowledgment and went down ahead of them.

"Is all well?" Mrs Gardiner asked when he was out of sight.

"Yes, I am sorry you overheard what you did in the courtyard. His bark is worse than his bite, I assure you, and I am coming to realise that even his bark is not so very bad."

"I think you are right. He came to find me to offer his apologies. He asked me if I was enjoying my stay at Pemberley and we talked for some time, about growing up in this part of Derbyshire. He said, at the close of our conversation, that he hoped I would visit again, for a longer stay, and that on the next occasion, I might bring my husband and children with me. I must say, Elizabeth, I think travelling abroad has changed him from the man who turned up at our front door four years ago, telling us he was *willing to marry you*. Or maybe you have changed him, who can say, but he is a little less proud, don't you think?"

"If he is, then it can be nothing to do with me, but I am very pleased to hear he has some value for my family. I still cannot imagine him being pleased if I should ask Mamma to stay, however."

Her aunt laughed. "Give it time, men will do much to keep their wives happy. I would not bet against hearing your mother's wailings and lamentations reverberating off these beautiful vaulted ceilings before 'ere long," Mrs Gardiner said as they went through to the drawing room. "I was also telling Mr Darcy of Lydia, and the problems we have there."

"She is no calmer?"

"Oh, a little, I suppose. I hope I have had some influence over her, but Elizabeth, she is such a demanding girl and requires so much attention, more than the baby. I am glad of this short holiday and the chance to be away from her for a while. Mr Darcy suggested a good seminary, to finish off her education and would be willing to bear the cost of it. What is your opinion?"

"Yes, that might be the answer and it is generous of him."

"We will have to ensure it is run by a very strict lady and has high walls and lockable doors. Whenever she does not get her own way, Lydia responds by threatening to run away."

"Oh dear," said Elizabeth. "She is more like me than I thought."

They laughed, drawing the notice of Miss Bingley, whose grating tones cut over any other conversation in the room. "Mrs Darcy, there you are, wherever have you been all day? We have missed you so, but your husband readily gave up his fishing to remain firmly by our sides, did he not, Louisa? He kept us very much amused."

"Did he now? Then perhaps you should make him entertain you again tomorrow, Miss Bingley," Elizabeth said and glanced over at him. Though his face wore a polite smile, Mr Darcy was clearly panicked at the idea and she could see his distaste for Miss Bingley. How silly of her to have thought them intimate. He'd obviously had a terrible day. She hoped he was not too fond of fishing and felt guilty that he'd had to forgo his gentlemanly pursuits to cover for her blunder. When their eyes met she tried to silently offer another apology. Then she offered up her penance and his reprieve. "And I am sure he would happily do so, but I have a competitive nature and so must insist you allow me to prove that I can keep you just as well amused as my husband can, if not better. So you are faced with the prospect of my company tomorrow, Miss Bingley, Mrs Hurst. I must warn you that I aim to keep you with me all day. Mr Darcy shall not be allowed the pleasure of entertaining you even for a moment, I shall not allow it - but the choice of activity will be yours, what will we do?"

"Perhaps we might go into Kimpton or Lambton for some shopping? I am very keen to see the milliner's there. They must be the most finely stocked in all the country to keep you so well attired, Mrs Darcy. For Mr Darcy says you never go to London."

She had seated herself opposite Miss Bingley and felt Mr Darcy crossing the room, knowing the weight of his tread above all others. He was hovering at her shoulder now and would hear whatever was said. She glanced at Richard, who looked alarmed, but went on in any case, determined not to lie. "As much as I like to support our local shops, Miss Bingley, I do go to London for clothes. I was there just before Easter."

Miss Bingley sat more upright, and as if sensing the sudden tension in the room, looked around at its occupants, trying to discover the source of it, before settling her gaze back on Elizabeth. "Really, but I have never seen you there. Did you attend Lady Birbeck's ball in March?"

"No, I go only for shopping and to see my family," she replied and then nearly jumped out of her skin when Mr Darcy's hand landed on her shoulder.

"When I said Mrs Darcy never goes to London," he said, "I meant that she does not attend any society gatherings there. Elizabeth was in mourning for her father for a time, and then sadly for my father too - and then I was abroad, of course. We will go to Town for the season next year and the one after, when Georgiana will be presented," he said, smoothly, before removing his hand. He then steered the conversation elsewhere.

If Mr Darcy was angry to discover Elizabeth had been to London in his absence, he hid it well. He gave Richard only a questioning look, and in his every dealing with her, he continued to be more than respectful, he was both solicitous and attentive. She thought perhaps he was trying to compensate for his earlier behaviour after he had pulled her off the phaeton, but whatever the reason for the change, she was grateful. When dinner was announced, he offered only she his arm, and led her into the dining room with great care and no small amount of stateliness, pulling out the mistress's chair and bowing slightly as he left her to take his own seat.

They were seated so far from each other at dinner as to make any intimate conversation impossible, and she was occupied and monopolised with the ladies after they had retired to the drawing room, reminding herself to be concerned with ensuring all their guests were happy, but when it was over and everyone began their goodnights, she lingered in the hope of a word or two with him. It was plainly obvious Richard had never told him of the two visits they had made to London (the first disastrous one had been followed the year after by another quieter, less eventful, trip). Biting her lip, she approached him, but he wished her goodnight before she could begin to speak.

"There is a word or two I would say to Richard. I shall see you in the morning," he said.

Richard nodded towards the door and gave her a little wink. She left them reluctantly, afraid of what would pass between them, not wanting to be the cause of any discord.

What she dreamed of, Elizabeth couldn't remember, but when she woke, it was in a great tangle of sheets and covers and her hair was a wild mess to behold. She teased it into some order, dressed herself in the plainer clothes she reserved for her morning walk, and went quietly out of a side door, as was her custom.

The sight of Richard coming up from the direction of the woods was an unusual one. He was not an early riser, and his wound stopped him from being a great walker.

They greeted each other a little breathlessly and Elizabeth had little patience for niceties. "What happened?"

He was distracted. "What happened? What do you suppose has happened? How much do you know?"

Seeing him look back towards the woods with some concern, she wondered whether they were talking at cross purposes. "You spoke to Mr Darcy last night, after I went to bed, about my having been in London."

"Oh that?" he said and broke into his more familiar easy smile, "Do not worry, he asked me the particulars of it, but was not angry, well maybe a little put out at the deception; that I had never mentioned it to him."

"Truly? I am surprised."

"Though, Elizabeth, I mentioned nothing about when you were in Hertfordshire that first time. That part of it, I will leave up to you to tell him, if you wish to. Maybe he need never know," Richard finished, with another glance towards the woods, which made Elizabeth wonder what he had been doing there before her arrival, and why he was so nervous. He looked as if he had just come back from meeting somebody and she wondered if whoever it was were still there.

"I shall tell him, I think, about Mr Wickham, just not now, perhaps when his guests have gone," she said.

"Yes, that seems wise. Now, if you'll excuse me." Richard limped quickly away, leaving her to take her usual exercise, and as she went, she looked for something, or someone, that would explain his odd behaviour, but her walk remained a solitary and uneventful affair. It did its usual trick though, of fortifying and preparing her for the day, and today she needed much courage, for not only did she face the prospect of a difficult conversation with Miss Temple about her future, but also an excursion to the shops with Miss Bingley. She did not know which she relished less.

By mid-afternoon, having bought all they could, and had as much of each other's company as they could possibly stand, Elizabeth, Miss Bingley and Mrs Hurst returned from Lambton. Jane and Mrs Gardiner were on the terrace both happily occupied with their needlework. Elizabeth joined them but had sat down for no more than a minute and barely had time to tell them of the ugliness of the hat Miss Bingley had purchased before a message came that Mr Darcy would like to see her in his study. She glanced at her aunt and sister. 'You'll excuse me. I mustn't keep the master waiting."

Entering with a soft knock, she stood before him on the rug and gave a little curtsey. "You summoned me."

He sat back in his chair behind the vast desk, the great man at the helm of his great estate and frowned at her. "I did not summon you. I asked Mrs Reynolds if she might watch for your return and tell you I wished to talk to you. Will you sit down?"

In a somewhat playful mood, she eyed the chair opposite his with mock wariness. "I am not sure I want to, am I to have a telling off? I cannot be in this room with you without feeling I have done something wrong."

Mr Darcy shook his head. "You have such a talent for hyperbole. I could count on one hand the number of times we have had cross words in here."

She leaned casually against the chair, but did not sit. Unable to read his mood, she could not properly settle and didn't want him to have the advantage of looking down at her. He passed across the desk a beautifully scripted invitation. It was addressed to Mr and Mrs Darcy, which caused her to pause for a while, never having before seen them entwined in handwriting. She briefly scanned the rest of the card before putting it back on the desk.

"From the Balcombes," she said.

"They are to host a private ball on Saturday, in honour of their daughter Constance's engagement."

"And this has only just arrived?" she asked.

"No, it was here last week, but I did not immediately reply. I was going to send a note over today, declining, but now I am not so sure and I wanted your opinion. The Balcombes are an important family in Derbyshire and we do not have many such neighbours. We have had no contact from them in some time; it is an olive branch; one it might seem churlish to refuse. Our guests are included too, so we might all go."

"My Aunt Gardiner is already engaged to dine with some old friends of her family in Lambton on Saturday night."

"Do the rest of us have any prior engagements?"

"No." Stalling for time, Elizabeth reached for the card again and re-read it. "I am very pleased for Constance, though I only met her briefly, she seemed lovely. She was a great friend of yours once, I think."

"Yes. But I have not forgotten how her mother once came here and was rude to you."

Their eyes met over the card and she couldn't but be pleased at the courtesy and respect he afforded her. Her thoughts were mainly of Emma Balcombe, however, and that lady's name sat heavily between them, unspoken. He had once wanted to marry Emma and she had broken his heart - she would surely be at the ball and Elizabeth wondered how he would react to seeing her again, would it bring him tremendous pain, or was the lady long forgotten? "I thank you for your consideration, but I think I shall leave it up to you. Though, if you do wish for my opinion, I will say that I do not think Constance should be snubbed. She cannot help having some less than desirable relations any more than I can."

"Nor I," Mr Darcy was amused. "I hear from Richard that you have met Lady Catherine and I am sorry I was not there. I would have dearly liked to have been a fly on the wall."

"Oh, it was very dull. We met for tea in Town and I was extremely well-behaved. You would not have known me. I made such a good impression that I have been invited to stay at Rosings any time I should like," she finished.

"Quite a turnabout in her sentiments, she once told my father she would never recognise your marriage to me, however did you manage it?"

"Not by design, it was mere coincidence. My cousin, William Collins, had just taken orders and sought a living. Hunsford had become available and he asked for my support in applying to Lady Catherine for it." Mr Darcy looked blankly at her. "I asked for her help, you see, and she likes to be of use, your aunt. It pleases her to think I am in her debt."

"I see, and you are willing to let her think you are eternally grateful for her benevolence and condescension?"

"Quite so, it makes no difference to me," Elizabeth shrugged. "So, the Balcombes, do we go?"

"Yes we go," he said, firmly.

"And are you prepared for the fuss Georgiana will make if she is not allowed to come with us?" she asked.

Mr Darcy considered for a while and then smiled in way that made him look like the very young man in the portrait that hung in the gallery above their heads. "Georgiana may come if she stays by you and the other ladies, no dancing or introductions. She will be quite excited, I think, it being her first society ball."

"As am I, sir, it being mine too," she said before she left him.

Fifty

"A ball! A proper ball?"

Via the glass above the dressing table, Elizabeth could see Rose's face, her eyes dancing, her mind already assessing her mistress's wardrobe, wondering which gown she ought to get ready. "Yes, on Saturday. Everyone is to go, the day after the picnic. What do you think to my wearing the light blue silk?"

"I hope it won't be out of date," Rose said.

"I should hope not. It was only bought at Easter. I am relieved I shall get a chance to wear it. It seemed like such an extravagance at the time and is to fine just for dinner here."

Rose looked concerned. "These London fashions move so fast. If it was just country society, I wouldn't be so worried."

Elizabeth turned. "Rose, whatever has got you in such a dither? The blue gown will do very well."

"It's just, I don't like people comparing you and finding you wanting?"

"Has something happened downstairs?" Elizabeth asked.

"Miss Bingley's maid says your clothes are too plain, that I don't know anything about how ladies of quality wear their hair; she says I don't make enough of you."

Elizabeth burst out laughing and turned around on the stool. "Well, there is only so much a person can do when there are limited materials to work with."

Rose looked upset and turned Elizabeth around again, so she might finish pinning up her hair. "Don't talk about yourself so."

"I joke; you know I do. I might dress simply compared to ladies like Mrs Hurst and Miss Bingley, but I have no wish to emulate them." She turned around again and fixed her maid with a very serious look. "If you ever come near me with a feather or a turban, Rose, I shall dismiss you on the spot."

They both laughed then before Rose again turned her firmly back towards the glass so she might continue with her work.

"And, is anything else said below?" Elizabeth asked, almost afraid of the answer.

"Not directly to me, but I did overhear Miss Bingley's maid say to Mrs Hurst's maid that Miss Bingley thinks she will make a better mistress of Pemberley."

Elizabeth started at the words though really it was not new information. She had often seen the calculation and jealousy in Miss Bingley's eyes when they swept over Pemberley's rooms and grounds and the sense of ownership she assumed over Mr Darcy, sitting by him, taking his arm, giving voice to opinions that were supposedly his, even when he had not said a word.

"But I speak out of turn. I shouldn't repeat such things and it is all nonsense anyway," said Rose.

They were interrupted by a knock on the door, which turned out to be a footman, come to tell them that Cassandra and Mrs Smythe from the parsonage had come to call.

Elizabeth went down immediately, genuinely glad of the visit. Mrs Smythe was not a great conversationalist and stuck to a few much loved topics, those of her son, the parsonage and the comings and goings of her neighbours, but she was kind and sweet and always glad of Elizabeth's company. Hodges had put them in a cosy parlour, rather than the saloon and when she arrived, Elizabeth saw why. The butler had probably been concerned about some of the saloon's precious antiques, for Mrs Smythe had brought her son with her, a very sweet looking little boy of nearly two, who was prone to sudden bursts of energy. His coordination, however, was not as well developed as his ability to dash about.

Georgiana had got there before her and she and Cassandra were already in close confederation, heads bent close, whispering and giggling together. Georgiana soon asked permission to take Cassandra to the practice room above stairs and Elizabeth, seeing that they wanted to be free to talk without the interruption of married ladies, such as herself and Mrs Smythe, gave her permission readily.

"I am sorry we have not been down to visit at the parsonage lately, but we have been busy with guests," Elizabeth told Mrs Smythe.

"Oh, Mrs Darcy, I would not have expected you to and I am sorry for calling today, and for bringing Henry, but Cassandra has been desperate to see Georgiana."

"And we are delighted to see you."

"We knew Mr Darcy had some important guests and did not wish to intrude."

"You are always welcome at Pemberley, as is Master Samuel," she smiled and went over to ruffle the boy's hair. "Now, young man, shall we see about some cake, because you know it is my intention to thoroughly spoil you, fill you with sugar and send you home twice as naughty as before you came."

Darcy had been at the lake with the gentlemen, but wishing to make some arrangements for their picnic the next day, he began walking back to the house, passing some of the ladies who were out for a stroll. He caught himself immediately looking around for Elizabeth amongst them, keen for a sight of her, and was disappointed to find her missing. Jane Bennet told him her sister had callers, without him having to make any enquiries, and he began to leave them to their walk. Miss Bingley, though, complained of a sudden headache and asked him to escort her back. Darcy noted the look of reprimand Mrs Hurst directed her sister's way and how Miss Bingley ignored it.

Once away from the others, Miss Bingley caught his arm and leaned heavily on it. "I am so happy at Pemberley. I feel I could stay here my whole life."

"Is that so?" Darcy replied. "I am glad you are enjoying your stay, but I am surprised, I would have thought things not lively enough for you. It is a quiet house."

She looked at him through her lashes. "It is tranquil, but doesn't the mood of the house depend very much on its inhabitants? I daresay a change of occupancy might give Pemberley an altogether different feel. Your wife, as she said, is a woman of simple tastes, suited to country living. If she were more disposed to entertaining, as I am, I'm sure your estate would be positively thrumming with society and gaiety."

"Are you supposing that is what I want?" Darcy said.

"What do you want, Mr Darcy?"

"Sometimes, I hardly know," he replied.

"Well, when you decide how things are to be, might you consider letting me know? I have some interest in the matter, you see, and you must always consider me a friend."

If shrugging a lady off and physically removing her hand from his arm were in any way acceptable, he would have done it. What was she suggesting and implying? He thought perhaps it was her odd sense of humour that accounted for it. Was she merely at play? The conversation left him feeling somewhat unclean, as if he had been indulging in something he really ought not to. How quickly his esteem of Miss Bingley was dropping. To think only two weeks ago he had been quite impressed by her.

By now they had reached the house where a small, very old, basic carriage, pulled by two sad looking horses, was sat waiting in the courtyard. He pretended a great interest in it to save him from any further conversation with his companion. "It must belong to Elizabeth's callers?"

"Well," said Miss Bingley, under her breath. "They would not be here for anyone else."

He frowned and when they went in, Darcy discovered he had surmised correctly. Elizabeth was entertaining the Parson's wife. He instantly formed the intention of joining her. Miss Bingley, to his dismay, proved to be unshakable.

"I thought you had the headache, maybe you ought to rest."

"Oh no," she said. "Our little stroll has quite driven it away. Your company was the cure."

He blinked a little in disbelief at her forwardness and started down the corridor with her hot on his heels.

Then he opened the parlour door and fell in love.

Though he had never experienced it before, he knew it straight away. It was the surest emotion he had ever felt. He had burned for Elizabeth before, been desperately attracted to her since the day he had returned to Pemberley. He constantly wanted to be near her and she had certainly ignited that basest, most beastly part of him, his needs and his passions. This was an entirely new emotion, however. It made him shake, such was the force with which it took hold of him. He didn't just adore the sight of her, he realised, he adored everything about her, who she was, what she had become, and what she had once been.

Elizabeth was sat with a small child on her lap, a fork full of cake poised in mid-air, laughing at the boy's cries for more. When Darcy entered, she turned her head his way, but her smile, which usually faltered or disappeared upon seeing him, remained, and its breadth and warmth, the joy in it, sent him spiralling. To think he had just been saying that he did not know what he wanted. Her! Of course, what else was there? Only her. If it took him the next ten years, he would work to win her over. Day by day he would endeavour to strip away her aversions and prejudices.

As Darcy was making his silent vows, however, the parson's wife stood to be introduced and at the same time her sugar-soaked son jumped up from his very comfortable seat across Elizabeth's legs and ran without cause or direction, towards the door, thumping into Miss Bingley, who was still coming through it. He took her skirts in his hands, lifted them to his mouth and used them to wipe his cake covered face upon. Miss Bingley shrieked and the boy, rather than being scared, clung on to her, giggling, until Elizabeth came and prised him off.

The parson's wife was apologising to Miss Bingley, as was Elizabeth, but while Mrs Smythe's regrets were genuinely given, Elizabeth's shoulders were shaking with something Darcy suspected was barely restrained mirth. Miss Bingley's gown was quite smothered in the remnants of one of Mrs Small's very delicious, but extremely sticky concoctions. Elizabeth had the boy on her hip now, while Mrs Smythe tried to assist Miss Bingley with her handkerchief, but was waved off by the lady, who made a great deal of fuss and complained that wiping at it would only spread the mess further. Darcy caught Elizabeth's eye and smiled as he saw the laughter bubbling up in her, trying to escape. Seeing him amused, rather than angry, softened her expression, and for a while they simply stared at each other, until the child cried out and kicked in her arms, keen to be off again.

Darcy reached out and took him from her without ceremony. "Allow me, before your gown suffers an equally wretched fate."

Miss Bingley was fleeing the room.

"I ought to go and offer some assistance," Elizabeth said, remembering her responsibilities and sobering up.

"Perhaps you ought to send your maid up to her, I am sure she is quite experienced at removing cake and dirt from gowns."

Elizabeth looked sharp for a moment, but then understood he was joking and offered him her unreserved, most dazzling smile again, before going after Miss Bingley.

Fifty one

Elizabeth came back down to Mrs Smythe not too long after leaving her. Miss Bingley had declined her help and dismissed her abruptly, reminding her that she did have her own maid who saw to such things. The parson's wife was quite alone and for a moment Elizabeth was cross, thinking Mr Darcy had deserted her guest. Then she saw him through the window, out on the lawn with the boy. Mrs Smythe was not at all offended and was stood at the glass, taking great pleasure in watching them.

"Mr Darcy has introduced himself and taken Samuel outside to look for stones."

Elizabeth nodded. "So I see."

"What a very amiable man he is. I felt so terrible about your friend's gown, but he has assured me he will see to everything and told me not to mind."

"Oh yes, please do not worry. The fault was as much mine as yours."

They watched Mr Darcy making friends with the boy, holding out a large hand for Samuel to place every pebble he found into. Elizabeth recognised something sentimental and affectionate growing inside her, which caused her to take a deep breath, before turning away.

Mrs Smythe expressed a need to return to the parsonage and Georgiana and Cassandra were sent for. Mr Darcy brought Samuel in himself and walked right out to the carriage with the party, handing the ladies and the boy into their very modest equipage with great courtesy - in as easy and as friendly a manner as Elizabeth had ever seen from him. Mrs Smythe thanked him profusely as she sat her son beside her.

"You are so good with him, Mr Darcy. I hope you'll have many sons yourself."

"I hope so too," he said and looked directly at Elizabeth.

Oh! The blush this produced from her.

When the carriage had gone and Georgiana had rushed back inside, Mr Darcy asked her if she was well. "Only you look very flushed, perhaps you ought to rest. This abominable heat is getting to all of us."

"I am very well, thank you. No rest required."

"Is Miss Bingley much distraught?" he enquired.

"Quite upset, but then she will wear satin in the middle of the day."

His look grew quite intent. He took a small step towards her but she took a bigger one sideways.

"I think I'll see if I can catch the other ladies up on their walk, if you'll excuse me," she said, wanting to be away from this sweet, jovial version of Mr Darcy and his very concentrated focus. He was an imposing, disconcerting presence.

Though she did not go far before stopping, "a friend to small children, Mr Darcy, I wouldn't have known it."

"What did you suppose, Elizabeth? That I liked to eat them for breakfast?"

She waved a hand at him in goodbye and left through the courtyard, looking over her shoulder just before she turned the corner, to see him walking slowly back into the house. And now, rather than being uncomfortable about his gaze being so intent upon her, she keenly felt the loss of it.

It was another hot night, without much breeze and Elizabeth lay in bed with only a thin sheet over her and the windows ajar. She had never known such a warm summer, certainly not since coming to Pemberley. She remembered sunny days as a child in Hertfordshire when she had paddled in streams, burnt her nose and acquired many a freckle, but the dry, furious heat they were now enduring, day after day of it, kept her sleepless, restless and ever so slightly irritated. Perhaps the man in the room next door and her mixed feelings for him might be partially to blame for her inability to find slumber, but it was far easier to blame the weather.

A knock made her jump and she stared first at the internal door that joined her rooms to Mr Darcy's, her heart beating wildly beneath her nightgown, but then she realised the sound had come from the main door to her apartments and she heard Jane's voice call out her name. She took up the candle and opened the door to see her sister looking wild-eyed and tearful.

"Has something happened?"

"Oh no," Jane assured her. "No, it is just my own thoughts that make me uneasy. I am sorry if I have woken, or disturbed you."

"Come in," she said, pulling Jane into the room to sit on the bed. She found and lit another candle so they might see each other clearly.

"I could not sleep either." Elizabeth sat next to her and they propped themselves up on the big pillows. "The heat made us all dull and dissatisfied tonight. If it hadn't been for Miss Bingley's constant complaints about children being brought into parlours and taken on visits, there might have been no conversation at all."

Jane's smile was a faltering one.

"What is it, Jane?"

"Do you think Mr Bingley likes me?"

"No, I do not think he likes you," and then seeing her sister's crestfallen face, she burst out laughing, "like is not enough of a word for it. He is madly, deeply in love with you. He has not come forward yet?"

"We have only known each other a short while," Jane reasoned with a shake of her head.

"Well, yes, but a few days where you have been constantly in one another's company. Isn't that the same as a year-long acquaintance, whereby you might only have a few minutes to know one another, every few weeks, in the length of a social call?"

"He asked for my hand for the first two dances at the ball on Saturday."

"Of course he did, and then he shall ask for your hand again, in marriage. Mrs Bingley, how fine that sounds. I cannot wait to address a letter to you in such a way." Elizabeth smiled as Jane shook her head, and then gripped her hand tightly.

"Lizzy, do you remember when I was foolishly considering Mr Collins, and you asked me whether he made my soul sing?"

"Oh, I beg you not to abide by anything I have ever said. That sounds so silly now."

"Mr Bingley does though you see; he is just what a young man ought to be. I have been courted before, Lizzy, there have been interested parties, but no one has ever made me feel the way he does."

"Then I am very happy for you," Elizabeth told her.

"But his sisters today, while we were out walking before you joined us, spoke of what they expected for their brother. They believe he will marry into very high circles. They were, I think, kindly trying to discourage me from forming any strong attachment."

"Kindness, I think, had very little to do with it, Jane. You shall ignore them. Why, you are the sister of Mr Darcy, you *are* of the highest circles."

"If you would be serious though, Lizzy, just for a moment and tell me, am I wrong to encourage him, when his sisters would be so against the match? I cannot wonder that they should be, given that he might choose so much more advantageously and I should not wish to be the cause of any family discord."

"Will they not be the cause of any discord, if there is to be any, by not supporting him in his choice?"

Jane thought on this for only a moment and Elizabeth could see her sister's mind racing, from happiness to uncertainty, and back again.

"I am getting ahead of myself. He may go off to Scarborough and forget me easily."

Elizabeth rolled her eyes and taking the pillow from behind her head, got to her knees, and hit her sister square in the face with it.

Looking very prim and cross, Jane tutted. "Really, Lizzy, you turn twenty tomorrow. Please show a little more decorum and maturity."

She was fooled only for a moment by this stricture, but it was long enough for her to be caught with her guard down. Jane's pillow hit her in the chest with some force, knocking her off the bed and onto the floor. The pillow burst open and feathers exploded into the air, before showering down upon them like snow. Jane gave a short scream of horror, both at the damage she had done to the pillow and fearing any damage she might have done to Elizabeth.

Then she let out a gasp of surprise as the internal door opened and Mr Darcy stood there, dressed only in his trousers and shirt, candle in hand, looking about the room for some unknown danger.

Elizabeth was laughing and got to her feet slowly, before noticing Mr Darcy standing in the doorway and Jane scurrying backwards, delving into the recesses of the bed, trying to hide.

"I heard screaming," he said.

Elizabeth tried to look unbothered, despite being acutely conscious of his having seen her sprawled on the floor, mostly likely with her nightgown in complete disarray. She found a little composure from somewhere. "Thank you for your concern, sir, but I am not being murdered in my bed. Though Jane has tried to kill me, I find myself only a little winded."

He nodded and looked at her as if she were quite mad for a long while, before saying 'very good', retreating and closing the door behind him.

Elizabeth shook her head at her sister. "You do not know your own strength, I fear for Mr Bingley in any matrimonial disputes."

Aghast at being seen in a state of undress by Mr Darcy and at the feathers that littered the bed and floor, Jane put her hands to her chest. "Look at the mess I have made."

"It will be cleared up easily enough."

"Perhaps I ought to go."

"Oh no, stay here. Talk to me more. I cannot sleep in this heat," Elizabeth begged her.

"But I feel I should. Mr Darcy is obviously still awake and well, what if he does not want me here. I may be in the way."

"In the way of what?"

419

"He might wish to, you know, come to you."

Elizabeth let out a little laugh at Jane's faltering words, uttered with such embarrassment. "He will not. I am certain," she said, climbing back onto the bed.

They sat together in quiet contemplation. Elizabeth could almost hear Jane's thoughts and knew there was a question to come, an awkward enquiry, there was a small furrow forming at the bridge of her sister's nose. When Jane did venture forth, she spoke very quietly.

"What is it like?"

The words hung in the air, while Elizabeth swallowed hard, and became irritated. "Oh do not ask me *that*," she snapped, her tone harsher than she'd intended.

Jane flinched. "I am sorry. I should not have pried." She bent over and kissed Elizabeth's cheek. "I will go, though. Try to sleep. You have a big day tomorrow."

An apology and an explanation were forming on Elizabeth's lips, but Jane had hurried away before she could properly express herself, leaving Elizabeth staring at the internal door for a good long while, half daring it to open again.

What was it like?

It took Darcy almost an hour to find Elizabeth. He had woken early with the intention of being the first person to offer her a birthday greeting and had already walked many paths through the woods and park. His search ended when he saw a figure in a plain grey cloak ascending the hill behind Pemberley. He walked quickly and by the time he had reached the summit, he was tired and his bow was a brief, loose one, his greeting abrupt. She glanced up at him from her seat on a bench which had been placed there for the purpose of admiring the commanding views of the surrounding Derbyshire countryside.

She was obviously surprised to see him and looked young and fresh in her plain clothes and unadorned hair.

"I got you this, to mark your birthday." Taking the box from his coat pocket he rather shoved it at her. Cursing his own awkwardness, he wished he had thought of something clever and charming to say before he had approached. He had presented himself as a perspiring oaf.

She took his proffered gift warily, running a small, strong hand over the lid.

"Are you going to open it?" he said at last, frustrated and scared she would not understand, be upset to be reminded.

"I am sorry, I was savouring the moment and, if I am truthful, maybe a little fearful of the contents," her smile was enigmatic.

"'Tis not much", he shrugged and sat down on the bench, but did not presume to move too close to her. "It is less than you deserve, after all you have done, with Georgiana and Pemberley, but I wanted to mark the occasion."

"So much fuss this year, a picnic, gifts, anyone would think I had reached my majority."

"Oh well, if you do not want it," he went to grab for the box, but she held it out of reach, with a laugh that warmed his heart.

"I think I will at least see it, before I decide whether or not to throw it back in your face?"

"You are too magnanimous by far, madam," he looked at the ground as she prised the lid open and swallowed hard. "I said I would replace it, but I never did. I do not like to break a promise, if I can possibly help it."

The thin chain and its delicate cross caught the brilliant, morning sunlight and glinted brightly as she lifted it up to examine it. She turned it this way and that, drew her bottom lip in between her teeth, but said nothing. Her quietness concerned him.

"I am not known for my sensitivity, I ought to take lessons. I see now how such a gift would only remind you of that terrible day - when the one your father gave you was taken from you."

"That day certainly altered the course of my life. I cannot deny I have had occasion to grieve for the paths I might have otherwise taken, and yet, the passage of time

421

renders me able to look back upon things with not a sense of regret, but with acceptance and maybe even some fondness. We are the sum of our histories, and all our mistakes, are we not?" She looked out at the view while he looked at her.

"Am I wrong to surmise, from that speech, that you do not necessarily believe that what starts in mistake and disaster has to end in it?"

"Thank you," she said, not answering his question, closing her fist around the cross, "for this, but now perhaps we ought to go inside and start getting ourselves ready."

She made to get up but he stilled her with a hand on her forearm. "Good God, Elizabeth, let me into your world, just a little. I know I do not deserve it. I have done you a thousand wrongs, but be generous, please."

"I am not sure what you expect of me. I will be the mistress of your house, play hostess for you and even be your brood mare one day if you wish it, Mr Darcy, is that not enough?"

"No, it is not enough," he said plainly, "and my name is Fitzwilliam."

She got quickly to her feet and began to walk away, speaking to him from over her shoulder. "It would be easier, I suppose, to pretend we mean something more to each other than we do, seeing as we are bound with no promise of escape. I am not sure I could live in such a way though, with pretence. Let us always be honest and do the best we can."

"Yes very well, let us be honest, and I shall say that I do not wish for escape."

She stopped and he caught her up, took hold of her by the elbows. Her eyes were soft for a moment then she blinked and they were full of fire. "Tell me, Fitzwilliam, if we were not married, would I still be your choice? Or would I be merely the daughter of a minor country gentleman, quite beneath you and with ghastly relations - tolerable but not handsome enough to tempt you?"

"Your good memory is too good."

"How could I forget such things?"

"My behaviour to you at times has been unpardonable, I aim to be better. Give me the chance to lessen your ill opinion of me. Are the wounds I inflicted so deep they cannot be healed?"

They were standing so close that her breath ruffled his cravat and Darcy cursed, for he felt something shift in her, and much more might have been said and done, if Richard hadn't been coming up the hill towards them, limping, but moving at a furious pace, nonetheless. Darcy realised he was still holding Elizabeth's elbows, so released her and moved slightly away. He prepared to greet his cousin, but Richard's focus was all on Elizabeth - it was her he had come to speak to and that he was displeased about something was obvious by his abrupt manner.

"What do you mean by getting rid of Miss Temple?"

Elizabeth was startled but calm. "I have not *'got rid'* of anybody. We have spoken about her leaving, that's true, but all that has transpired has been at her instigation."

"So, she is to go. After the long and devoted service she has shown this family, she is worth nothing and will be cast off. How could you, Elizabeth?"

"You'll not speak to my wife that way, Richard," Darcy said. "Hold your tongue and mind your manners."

Richard whirled on him, fists clenched. "Your wife and I are well used to sorting out our grievances without your interference."

He was spoiling for a fight, Darcy saw it clearly. Richard was full of rage and it needed to spill before it consumed him. Elizabeth put a calming hand on his coat sleeve though and he was suddenly softer, but still angry.

"Mr Darcy, would you go down to the house? Your cousin and I need to speak," Elizabeth said. He was about to object but she smiled her reassurance, imploring him, telling him all would be well. "Please, Fitzwilliam."

There was something about the way she said his name; how it rolled around her tongue and fell from her lips that laid Darcy bare, and he became her servant. He nodded and left them, though he looked around every few yards as he progressed down the hill. As he reached the house, he turned fully and stared up for a good while, only to see them both sitting down on the bench. His cousin's body had sagged, all

423

the fight seemingly had left him and his head was supported by Elizabeth's shoulder.

"Now, tell me how long you have been in love with Miss Temple," Elizabeth said.

Richard let out a sigh, almost comical in length. "How long have you known that I am in love with Miss Temple?"

"Oh, I have been very stupid. I, who have previously prided myself on my powers of discernment. Would you believe that until recently I thought you were hiding an affection for my sister?" She sat up straighter, pushing his head up and encouraging him to do likewise so she could look at him. "When Miss Temple and I were speaking yesterday, of her future, she expounded on her love of Pemberley and told me she had just returned from a morning walk, and as I had recently seen you do the same, I began to suspect. And here you are again, up very early, and we both know how terribly lazy you are."

He laughed but it was a sad sound.

"Does she not love you?" she asked gently.

"She says she does. In fact, I proposed and she has accepted."

Elizabeth gasped. "But then why are you both so miserable? And why does she speak of leaving?"

"Because after I asked her, I realised I had nothing to offer. She says she does not care - good, wonderful creature that she is, she would live in near poverty with me, but I could not reduce her so, and there is my family; Darcy, my mother, Walter and Beatrice. Lady Catherine! What do you think they'll have to say about my choice?"

Elizabeth could not refute his words. "I do not know about the others but I wish you would talk to Mr Darcy. I cannot say he would approve, exactly, but I see a change in him. I do not think him as proud as he once was, and he owes you much. If he were to give you the living of Kimpton, wouldn't it solve everything? You joke about it plenty, but I think you are called to the church. Take orders, it will take

424

some time, I know, but wouldn't Miss Temple make a very fine parson's wife?"

"That she would," he stood and offered his hand to help her to her feet. "We shall see. Perhaps you ought to talk to Darcy. He seems to hang on your every word these days."

"Oh no, that is your job. If you value your lady, you shall work for her," Elizabeth replied.

"And Darcy his?" he asked, his mood lightening, and then seeing her colour rising, he laughed. "Oh, many happy returns, by the by, I think we shall have a great day."

Fifty two

Carriages stood ready, servants waited. Wine, food and every manner of fine thing was loaded. Their guests chatted excitedly at the foot of the staircase while Darcy paced and awaited Elizabeth, who had still not emerged from her rooms. She was not late, exactly, just the last to arrive, along with her sister, and he suspected they were getting ready together.

Bingley caught his eye and smiled brightly and then looked up to the galleries when flashes of white muslin were seen between the elegant ironmongery. Darcy followed his friend's happy gaze and saw Jane Bennet descend, her head bent shyly, but rising briefly in Bingley's direction. He thought he saw Bingley's hand shake as he offered it up to assist Jane down the last few steps.

"Might we expect Mrs Darcy soon? I fear she might miss her own party," he enquired of Jane, before she could move off with Bingley, his voice brusque, impatient for a sight of her.

"Very imminently, sir."

As Jane spoke, Elizabeth did appear, moving quickly, with light, nimble steps, almost running down the stairs and then stopping at the bottom, turning to Rose, who was trailing in her wake, to take her gloves from her.

It was the difference in her that made Darcy speechless. The young girl in a plain cloak he had spoken to just over an hour ago on the hill, bared little resemblance to the picture of grace and elegance before him now. The odd thing was that he did not know which vision of her he preferred, but in her finery, she was truly something to behold. He could not have said later what colour her gown was, something pale, a slight pattern to it, a sash maybe, but he knew it suited her very well. Her hat was wide and perhaps bore some ribbons, or flowers, but all this was pushed to the periphery, all he really saw was the cross and chain he had given her hanging around her neck. He looked away; too dazzled and too emotional to keep his eye upon her for long and saw that everyone was looking her way. Miss Bingley's face wore a small pout, Richard's a wide grin and Mrs

Reynolds, who was there to see all went smoothly, had a smug, proud look about her as she approached her mistress for a few words.

Elizabeth thanked the housekeeper for something or other and then looked at him with expectation and a raised brow.

"Shall we begin then, this ridiculous business of getting seven ladies and four gentlemen into two carriages, attended by eight servants, and driving nearly twenty miles - all so that I might enjoy a slice of birthday cake on the lawns of Haddon Hall?"

He wordlessly held out his arm and they all filtered out. Still he could not talk because he then became mesmerised by the toes of her boots where they peaked out from under the lace of her petticoats as she walked. His mind was not in the present, but on the sight he'd had of her little bare feet the previous evening, when he had burst into her room after hearing a scream; and of the tantalising amount of leg he'd been treated to a brief sight of as she'd scrambled upright. *Oh, to run a hand up the inside of one of those lean thighs.* It occurred to him that he'd seen her in her nightgown on more than once occasion previously and she'd never been conscious or embarrassed at being caught so. It made him wonder what sort of lover she would make - unabashed, curious, eager? A little ashamed at the direction his thoughts were taking, he remained silent.

She leaned in to him, just before he handed her into the carriage, nudging him slightly with her elbow. "Oh, do be quiet Mr Darcy, I can hardly hear myself think, what with all your chatter."

And still, he could say nothing, but he doffed his hat at her as she settled into her seat and received a wide, full smile in response that rocked him back on his heels.

Elizabeth was pleased to have been seated in a separate carriage to the Bingleys and Hursts. For company she had Mrs Gardiner, Jane, Georgiana and Miss Temple, and wondered whether Mr Darcy had arranged it so.

427

"That is a very fine hat, Lizzy," Mrs Gardiner said. "Miss Bingley is not pleased. You have out-hatted her."

"That is neither word nor expression, Aunt."

"No, but perhaps it should be."

Their arrival at Haddon had Elizabeth worrying over the kind of reception Mrs Gardiner might receive from Lady Matlock. Her heart was somewhat relieved when the introduction was made with brief civilities and no overt disapproval. Elizabeth was left with the impression, when she saw a look pass between them, that the countess had been petitioned by her son for her good graces, long before their arrival, and the countess's present to Elizabeth was to admit the tradesman's wife into her home as a guest. She could not help but feel resentful though, when she saw the Bingleys welcomed with so much more enthusiasm. How were they different? Had not all the Bingleys money been hard earned with blood, sweat and tears, just as her uncle's had?

She held Mrs Gardiner's hand tightly as they walked down to the picnic.

Mrs Gardiner gripped hers tightly back. "Do not fret," Mrs Gardiner told her. "I made my choices long ago, with an open heart and mind. I have never regretted them."

"I would put you above them all," Elizabeth said, ferociously.

"Oh, my dear girl," Mrs Gardiner put a hand to Elizabeth's cheek. "I see that Lady Fitzwilliam adores you, just as I do, and that makes me very happy. Prejudices such as hers are of long duration, built over centuries and passed down through generations. You cannot expect her to change just because you like her and wish her to."

Elizabeth was then pleased by Mr Darcy, who came to give them an arm each and paid special attention to Mrs Gardiner, talking to her and finding her a comfortable seat as they began their picnic on a small hill by the river.

Much amusement was then had by the slow reveal of the dishes, for they were all sweet, mostly cake, Mrs Small's finest concoctions. Those who knew Elizabeth well, laughed heartily, and Mr Darcy looked very pleased with himself for having arranged it so. Only Miss Bingley tutted and complained, saying she did not like overly sugary things, while Elizabeth accepted two slices onto her plate and stole too many glances in her husband's direction. He was still quiet, but not in a way that unnerved or irritated her. She saw he was perfectly happy to sit and listen to others, while he lounged on one arm, relaxed in a way she had never seen him before. He sidled closer and closer, till his head was practically on her lap and she, to her own astonishment, had to stop herself from pushing her hand through his hair and tugging him closer, putting it there. To feel such a physical pull towards him was as confusing as it was thrilling. She had always thought him handsome but in a disconnected way. His attractiveness had never really attracted *her*, yet now she was noticing qualities in him, both physical and in his character, that tugged at her, threatened to undo her. Her eyes settled on his hands, large, strong and unusually tanned for a gentleman and she remembered how they had felt about her waist when he had handed her down from her horse a few days before. Did it signify anything more than her body's treacherous reaction to being touched so intimately when she was so unused to it?

Sensing she had been lost in her own thoughts for too long, she shook her head and looked around the party. The general conversation had ceased and smaller groups were forming. Mr Bingley was quietly and gently teasing and talking only to Jane. His attentions were very marked, and could not have gone unnoticed by anybody. To Elizabeth, the strength of feeling with which Jane received his notice was obvious, but she was guarded in her responses. She did not giggle or simper under them, kept a general composure and her manner remained uniformly cheerful to all. Wine was brought out, which she and Mr Darcy refused, but everyone else partook of. Bingley swallowed two glasses quickly, became garrulous, high on spirits, life and Elizabeth hoped, love. He was a merry, rather than an irksome drunk, and entertained them all with stories of their adventures in the Indies. Elizabeth listened intently, keen to know more of how

Mr Darcy behaved away from Pemberley. The man himself, however, seemed unamused and Elizabeth felt his mood darken. She was dismayed, but not surprised, when he got to his feet and took Bingley off for a walk with him.

"If he interferes in it, I shall never forgive him," Elizabeth said quietly to Mrs Gardiner, who had come closer.

"Oh do not be always thinking the worst of him, Lizzy. Perhaps he just goes off with Mr Bingley to get him away from the wine, and do not be angry with me, when I tell you that I am coming to like him, very much. His behaviour towards me has been very pleasing, his opinions and understanding I find very agreeable. He has a stateliness in his air, that can make him seem proud and unfriendly, on first knowing him; but I see now that he is just possessed of a natural graveness and dignity. He is overly-serious at times, but luckily he has a lively young wife, who may teach him to smile more often."

Elizabeth could not help but smile herself, for her aunt's opinion of Mr Darcy closely matched her own. She *was* beginning to see the goodness that lurked underneath his severity, but her feelings ebbed and flowed constantly.

When the gentlemen came back, Elizabeth saw Mr Bingley was chastened and sat away from her sister. When Mr Darcy approached her, she turned her shoulder to him and ignored his enquiring look.

The entertainment for the afternoon was a treasure hunt, the participants of which had to divide into pairs and follow a trail of ribbons and clues. Lady Fitzwilliam put herself in charge of the pairings, and perhaps sensing Elizabeth's animosity towards Mr Darcy, purposely put them together, ignoring Elizabeth's sigh.

They were the last to leave the picnic site, the least enthusiastic of the hunters, Elizabeth returning Lady Fitzwilliam's departing wave with a very weak one of her own. She saw the countess take out a book, pleased to be left to her own company under the shade of a beautiful willow tree, seated happily on a chair brought out for her comfort.

They quickly found the first clue and ribbon, tied to a tree. Mr Darcy made some comment and read the clue before turning to her with a question about it. Elizabeth leaned against the tree, disinterestedly, idly watching the others disappearing into the distance.

"I would have thought you'd enjoy this," Mr Darcy said. "A run about the countryside, a challenge to your intellect, don't you want to win?"

"'Tis just a silly game."

"Would you rather return? It is your birthday, we shall do whatever you wish."

"Someone other than yourself may make a decision about something? I am all astonishment."

"Will you tell me what offence I have committed? I can think of nothing, but I fear I so easily offend you, that it might be something as simple as the colour of my coat that has you so riled."

Elizabeth stalked away, over to the stone wall, that separated Haddon's park from its surrounding woods. "You know nothing of me, sir, if you think I get upset over inconsequential matters. I have been through too much to worry over nothings. Why do you seek to divide them from each other? You have spoken to Mr Bingley, I know it. You disappoint my sister's hopes, she will endure a misery of the acutest kind. Do you seek to deny it?"

He had followed her over to the wall, his expression angry. "I have no wish to deny it."

"And what are your objections, as if I cannot guess them? I suppose you think he might do better?"

"He could do better."

"Oh, *you*," she cried. "You are as you always were, your arrogant presumption of what you believe should happen, triumphs over all compassion for the feelings of those involved, and you stand there so shamelessly avowing it, as if it were nothing. You are the most abominable tyrant."

Moving so swiftly as to catch her completely unawares, Mr Darcy picked her up under the arms and seated her on top of the wall. She was too high up to jump easily down from it without assistance.

"Let me down," she ordered him as he paced back and forth beneath her.

He looked as if he were trying desperately to control his temper. His jaw twitched and his breath came quickly. "When you are ready to act rationally, madam, and have a mind to listen, rather than jump to conclusions, then I may help you down."

She crossed her arms and looked away. "This is a mean trick. I could very easily get down on my own, you know."

"Yes, yes. I daresay you could. Go on then, ruin your gown and scrape your little boots."

"Your behaviour is unpardonable."

"Sometimes, you must trust me. I am your husband, not your enemy. Why are you always looking for the worst in me?"

"I do not have to look very hard find it." Their eyes met, and she regretted the hurt she saw she had put in his. "What have you said to Mr Bingley?" She asked him in a softer tone.

"I have told him that it would not be fair for him to continue to court your sister, to give her the mistaken impression that he was serious in his designs, if he is not. That I would most seriously disapprove of him; and that it would show him capricious and not honourable. I have the highest opinion of your sister, Elizabeth, and she is now my family too, I will not have her trifled with." He paced some more. "When I said he might do better, I spoke honestly. Bingley is young, handsome and blessed with happy manners and a great fortune. He might marry anywhere."

"I know, I do see that," Elizabeth said, sadly, looking down at her hands where they were linked in her lap.

"He is fond of a pretty face. I am not surprised at his paying attention to your sister, his attraction is natural, but I do not think he considers carefully enough. As you have said, a withdrawal would wound her. I have told him that perhaps he ought to leave Pemberley the day after the ball, if he is not of a mind to commit himself." He stopped, held his arms up and beckoned her forward. Elizabeth fell into them with a rapidity that surprised her. He set her on the ground with great gentleness and she walked away.

She was instantly of a mind to stalk off, but then considered and turned back. "Is this how you will always get me to listen to you, sir, by setting me on a wall?"

"'T'was quite effective," he smiled. "But no, I hope to not require such desperate measures in future."

"You, my silent friend, must talk to me more. How can I not jump to conclusions if I do not know your thoughts and opinions?"

He murmured his agreement and nodded and then they stood in quiet regard of one another, before he changed the subject. "Well now we are at least fifteen minutes behind anyone else, but we might catch up, if you are of a mind to. I remember this hunt from when I was a child. I recognise the first clue and believe it will end at the folly. We might cut across the glade and beat them all, if you will run."

"Run!" A hand went to the cross at her neck, she played with it absentmindedly. "I can't believe you would suggest such a thing, Fitzwilliam. How many times have you ordered me *not* to run, and now I am to take to my heels to appease your competitive spirit and win a silly game? A lady does not run." And then she did just that, peeled away quickly, setting off down the hill in a sprint. She sensed him behind her and looked over her shoulder to see him bearing down quickly, catching her up. He caught her hand in his when he reached her and then pulled her along with him, the two of them laughing as their feet thundered over the long grasses and through the wildflowers until they reached the steps of the folly. He let go of her hand then and leaned over to take a few deep breaths, gasping for air.

"Mr Darcy, are you getting old?" she said, having recovered more quickly.

"You are not as quick as you used to be, Elizabeth. I remember being outrun by you once upon a time."

"And so you shall be now," she said, nimbly ascending the many steps, racing him to the summit.

She turned at the top of the long climb, triumphant, about to tease him and crow loudly at her success, only to be engulfed by his arms. She gasped as he walked her backwards until she was trapped against one of the stone columns of the folly, and once there, he pressed his body flush against hers and kissed her. It was not only unexpected in its timing, but the nature of it was absolutely astonishing. This was no polite brush of the lips, no hesitant touch that asked permission. He took her mouth possessively, demanding much, and though she ought to have protested at being manhandled so, her mind was befuddled by the pleasure his embrace produced. He broke off only to say her name in a half-gasp, 'liz-beth' and where she might have taken the opportunity to push him away, to resist and ask him what he was about, she did nothing except let him kiss her again, because it was delicious. She was vaguely aware of his hands at her waist, gathering the muslin of her gown between his fingers, gripping the material as if he were trying to stop himself from gripping her. And if he had, Lord help her, she feared she would not have protested about that either, she so coveted his touch. He bestowed dozens of kisses, each one more urgent than the last. Her mouth opened, causing an odd guttural sound to come from him that seemed to start in his chest and die in his throat. She was pushed further back against the stonework. Though completely overpowered, she strangely felt no loss of autonomy, instead she felt found, and that a sore emptiness deep inside of her, had at long last been met.

They leapt quickly apart at the sound of footsteps, she going quickly to one side of the folly and he the other. Elizabeth turned to look out at the view, unable to meet anyone else for a few moments; feeling sure whoever it was coming up the stairs to join them would guess what they had been doing. She straightened her gown and then her hand went to her mouth. Kissing! Her only past experience of it had been the quick peck she had bestowed on Henry Jones the day she had run from Longbourn, and that had produced no sensation of any kind. Mr Darcy's kiss, however, had called every sensation to attention, all at once. But then, she had been more than kissed surely, she had been claimed. He had imprinted himself on her, perhaps indelibly.

Fifty three

The intruders upon their scene of unexpected ardour were Mrs Hurst and Miss Bingley. One complaining about the climb and the heat and the other pointing out that she and Mr Darcy had been foolish enough not to claim the treasure. The final ribbon in the hunt was tied around the leg of the stone bench in the centre of the folly. A small box was set on top of it, no doubt containing some trinket. Elizabeth had to turn and face them eventually, politeness dictated it, but she hoped her colour was not too high, her appearance not too mussed. She saw immediately that Miss Bingley was only concerned with the prize. Mr Darcy waved his rights to it away and Miss Bingley fell hungrily upon it. Mrs Hurst, unlike her sister, had some consciousness that she had interrupted something. She played with the rings on her fingers and made some comment to Miss Bingley about going back to the picnic site, with a look of apology at Elizabeth.

Soon, however, they were joined by many others, all reaching the top of the folly one after the other. Mr Darcy received them absentmindedly, offering the briefest of greetings. Elizabeth risked a glance or two his way, but he avoided her eye, frowned deeply and then bowed and left them all, saying to no one in particular that he would ensure everything was prepared for their return journey, and then he was gone down the stairs.

Elizabeth felt her hand caught in Jane's and squeezed. "Are you well, Lizzy? You are quiet."

"Oh yes." Chastising herself into sparing some thought for others, she examined her sister and saw hurt and confusion in her eyes. Mr Bingley was stalking around the other side of the folly, looking uncomfortable, and then he disappeared too, saying he would assist Mr Darcy. "We are in a bit of mess aren't we, Jane?"

Jane squeezed her hand tighter. "There must be a long way back, Lizzy," she eventually suggested. They let everyone else go on ahead of them. Jane would not mention Mr Bingley, even though they were now quite alone. Instead, they spoke of the view, the trees, the beauty of the park. Jane referred to Haddon Hall as a handsome house, which made Elizabeth laugh and tell her she was too polite, for it was actually one of the ugliest buildings that ever was.

The heat had become oppressive in the last hour or so and they were not surprised to have caught up with some of the party, despite taking a lengthy detour. Mrs Hurst and Caroline Bingley had stopped to enjoy the shade of some trees and were talking overly loud, Mrs Hurst chastising her sister. Elizabeth and Jane could not be seen from their position on the other side of the thicket, but a few steps more would alert the other ladies to their presence. Elizabeth caught her sister's arm to stop her from moving, only because she wanted no one's company but Jane's, she did not intentionally eavesdrop, but once they had heard some of what was being said, neither sister could go forward.

"She is only twenty today, Louisa. Good God, she must have been a child when he married her. 'Tis sickening, whatever could have tempted him? There is more to it than meets the eye, I am sure of it."

"It is none of your business," Mrs Hurst replied. "She is his wife and being married myself, I am disgusted by your fawning over him and your attempts to tempt him away. She is your hostess, have you no respect?"

"Respect for her, why would I bow down? She is nothing to me and I am sure she is nothing to him either. He deserves so much better."

"You are blinded by your madness for him." Mrs Hurst paused. "She is not quite the plain, dull, country girl you were expecting is she?"

"I see no beauty in her. Her face is too thin; her nose wants character - there is nothing marked in its lines. Her teeth are about the only tolerable thing about her and I suppose I wished I knew what lotion she used on her skin, for I will allow her complexion to be good. But I declare there is nothing extraordinary about her. Her eyes have a sharp, shrewish look about them, and in her air altogether there is a self-sufficiency without fashion, which is intolerable," Miss Bingley said.

Mrs Hurst laughed. "I believe Mr Darcy finds her tolerable, he looks at her as if he would eat her alive."

The voices faded for a moment and Elizabeth and Jane looked at one another. They had heard too much to reveal themselves now, but oh what a conversation to have stumbled across, how enraged Elizabeth was! She hoped the other ladies had gone ahead, but they must have only moved a little way off, or else their voices had been temporarily carried away by a breeze, for now they could be heard again.

"I am ashamed of you, and one day when you are married, I hope some woman does not torment you in this way," Mrs Hurst said.

"I will be married to him, and I shall let no one even close enough to him to try stealing him away."

"Impossible," cried Mrs Hurst.

"But he has spoken to Charles of annulment. You heard that yourself…"

And then they did go, whatever else Miss Bingley said was lost with the distance. Elizabeth did not think she could have stood to hear anything further in any case. Jane put an arm around her.

"She is mistaken," Jane whispered, "Mr Darcy would never had said such a thing. 'Tis surely a misunderstanding of some sort."

With feelings too tumultuous to be contained, Elizabeth let out a short, angry cry, not caring whether the departing ladies heard it as they moved off. "I begged him not to make a fool of me."

Jane tried to catch her, but Elizabeth reeled quickly away, walking back to the picnic site in great strides, arms swinging and her countenance set in furious indignation. They were the last to arrive back and Jane, perhaps fearing Elizabeth so angry that she would do something unwise, cautioned her with her looks; appealed to her with her eyes. Luckily, Mr Darcy was not present, so there was no immediate opportunity for confrontation. Miss Bingley was also spared a wound from the sharp end of Elizabeth's tongue by being engaged in close conversation with Beatrice Fitzwilliam.

Lady Fitzwilliam begged the use of Elizabeth's arm to walk her back to the house, having had enough of the outdoors. She was a lady who was never to be denied and they walked slowly up to the doors of Haddon, the countess leaning on her. "What has you so vexed?"

Elizabeth shook her head and would not say.

"Come and see your uncle," the countess bid. They climbed the stairs to the earl's rooms, where he lay reclined on a sofa, wrapped in a blanket. Lady Fitzwilliam sent the nurse away and they sat by his bedside. His breathing was light and raspy. He knew neither of them and blinked in confusion, before drifting back off to sleep. "I do not think it will be long, we have come to the stage where it will be a relief for both of us. He is ready to go and I am ready to say goodbye."

"You will send word to Pemberley, if you should need anything, even if it is just my poor company?" Elizabeth asked, softly.

"I shall. Your house seems full of fire and fight at the moment. Ours is one of terrible sadness. We thought until last week that Beatrice was with child, and for a while all was hope, but it has come to nothing and she has suffered. She hides it very well behind that practiced nonchalance, so much favoured by society, but she is a woman living with the great pain of disappointed hopes."

Looking at the countess, and all she was going through, made Elizabeth very ashamed to have been so concerned about her own troubles. They seemed so minor in comparison. They sat in contemplative silence for a while until the door opened behind them and Mr Darcy stepped in. Elizabeth jumped from her seat.

"We will be going shortly, Elizabeth. Everyone is saying their goodbyes downstairs."

She nodded without looking his way and leaned over to embrace Lady Fitzwilliam, holding her tight. "Do not get up, sit for a while. I am sure Mr Darcy wishes to see his uncle." She went from the room but Mr Darcy followed her into the hallway and called out to get her attention. When she

438

stopped, he took her hand, squeezing it tightly between both of his own.

"May I apologise for my behaviour at the folly?"

Elizabeth was all painful confusion. "You are sorry for it?"

"Of course."

"Then, think no more of it. I certainly shall not." She pulled her hand away. "Tell me, is it true you have considered annulment?"

"Yes, I once did."

"As brutally honest and brief as usual, Mr Darcy. Do you *still* think of it?"

"No, not unless you would want it, but I should think it near impossible now, in any case."

"I suppose."

From inside the room, came the sound of the earl coughing. "I should go and pay my respects to my uncle."

Elizabeth, utterly confounded, hurt and miserable, walked away.

Outside the front doors, the carriages were being brought round and the Pemberley party gathered in preparation for the journey back. Stopping short just long enough to regain her composure, Elizabeth then went forward to join them, but saw Beatrice standing alone, a little way off and approached her in what she hoped was a friendly manner.

"How are you, Beatrice?"

"Oh look at your sincere little face. I suppose the countess has told you of my disappointment, and now I am to have your pity. I do not want it."

"You have it all the same, not pity exactly, but I wish there had been a happier ending." Elizabeth did pity her though, particularly as Walter had gone to Town for no specific purpose other than to enjoy himself. That he had left his wife without support, when she was obviously so sad and had been through a terrible time, seemed dreadful.

Beatrice's eyes flickered down towards Elizabeth's midriff. "You shall have no such trouble. Now your husband is home, I am sure you will pop out a dozen little Darcys, your sort of people always breed like rabbits."

Though cross, Elizabeth bit her tongue and reminded herself of Beatrice's pain.

"Still, I shall have my compensation." Beatrice gave a tight smile. "Next time you see me, I will expect a deep curtsey and you will call me Countess."

"Well, I hope that brings you some comfort," Elizabeth replied, saying her goodbyes and moving away.

When she was in the carriage at last and it had rolled away from Haddon Hall, full of those ladies whose company she treasured and felt easy in, Elizabeth drew out the long pin that held her hat on, took it off and threw it aside. Mrs Gardiner raised a brow at her and took up the hat.

"This is crushed. It shall have to be straightened out before you wear it again. Whatever have you been doing in it?"

Elizabeth was suddenly assailed with the memory of Mr Darcy holding her against the stone column, and of how its roughness had felt against her back, while his soft mouth had pressed down on hers firmly. "Too much, today has been far too much. Nothing else can surely happen."

She was wrong. They only made it as far as Lambton before another drama beset them, though it was only the minor matter of Mr Darcy's horse throwing a shoe. The carriages rumbled to a stop and everyone stepped out to stretch their legs for a few moments.

Noise from behind a nearby shop drew their attention and there was a cry out from a few of the ladies and some of the gentleman, when a bedraggled and dirty young man shot past, hotly pursued by a shopkeeper with a stick in his hand. The young man slipped, was caught by the scruff of his neck and was about to be struck, when several of the gentlemen loudly protested. Mr Darcy stepped forward to take the stick from the shopkeeper's hand, reminding him there were ladies present.

"Beg pardon, Mr Darcy. I caught him thieving from the back of the shop, in amongst the crates I put out, he was."

Elizabeth came closer to the scene herself. "Mr Barton," she addressed the shopkeeper. "Are not the wooden crates you put out the back of the shops full of scraps and such, things you wouldn't sell in any case?"

The dirty young man held up his hands in penitence. "That's right, I thought t'was stuff no one wanted anymore."

"'Tis not the point, if you'll excuse me, madam. I've every right to flog him, he's lucky I don't put him before the beak."

"That would be a terrible fate, indeed. I happen to know one of the magistrates who has been absent for a while, but I'm sure he will be invited to sit at the next petty sessions. He's a capricious man, he might be benevolent one day, or send you to Australia the next." She looked slyly at Darcy.

He gave her a questioning look but she detected some amusement, rather than his having taking offence. She looked back to the shopkeeper. "You'll not flog him, Mr Barton, not if you wish to continue providing Pemberley with your wares." Elizabeth then addressed the thief. "What were you taking?"

"Just some bread and rotten fruit. I am trying to get south, to join the navy. I haven't a penny on me, take pity, Duchess."

Trying not to laugh at the appellation, which was what Richard called her when he thought she was being especially grand, she nodded. "Do you have a half-crown, Mr Darcy?"

He reacted instantly and drew it out of his pocket, throwing it into the air. The thief caught it deftly and gave it a kiss. "Thank you, I shall pay you back. Where will I send it, when I get my first pay?"

"You'll send it to Mrs Fitzwilliam Darcy of Pemberley, Derbyshire," Mr Darcy said austerely. "'Tis her kindness that has spared your hide, and to her you are indebted. Get off with you."

He was gone in a flash, throwing up dirt with his heels.

Mr Barton quit the scene, grumbling. Mr Darcy's horse was taken to the smithy, while he began to hand the ladies back up into the carriage.

"He looked like a thief to me, Elizabeth. He'll probably drink that half-crown at the next tavern he comes to," he said to her quietly, as he took her hand to help her up.

"Perhaps, or maybe not. Shall we give him the benefit of the doubt? Maybe your act of clemency might make him mend his ways."

"You are not opposed to the idea, then, that a man can change?"

"Not at all?" she replied. Then realising that they were keeping the other occupants of the carriage waiting, she stepped up and Mr Darcy took the seat opposite her as they set off again.

Distracted and feeling disconnected from the excited chatter that now filled the carriage, Elizabeth stared out of the window and waited for the first sight of her beloved woods. After a few moments, though, she felt Mr Darcy's gaze upon her and looked around to see his face set in a very soft smile. When his eyes drifted downwards, she realized she was swinging her foot back and fro, scraping the floor of the carriage, an old habit, resurfacing in a time of great uncertainty. Mr Darcy tapped a finger against her knee to still her, apparently not caring who might see such a gesture and she blushed and returned his smile. And then she thought back to his apology for kissing her at the folly. She was struck with the sudden notion that maybe he had not been sorry for kissing her, but was contrite about the *way* in which he had kissed her. After all, he had sort of assaulted her. It had not been particularly gentlemanlike. The more she thought on it, the more she felt sure it was the case, and the deeper she blushed. She felt giggly and light-hearted and girlish, and when she risked another glance at him, he looked a little drunk, though she knew he had not touched a drop.

"Are you well, Elizabeth?" he asked.

"Yes, yes. I am very well."

Fifty four

The person Elizabeth found waiting for her in the hall at Pemberley, however, put an end to all feelings of joy - he was a veritable portend of heartache. She had left the carriage first, leaping down with only the briefest assistance from Mr Darcy, keen to get inside with her instructions for Mrs Reynolds, but stopped and went cold as the man stood and faced her, his hat was in his hand, as was hers. His expression was a mixture of amusement and calculation. If he was wondering how he would be received, she was keen to let him know at the first opportunity, that he was not welcome.

"I told him everyone was out, but he insisted on waiting, madam. I've let him no further than the hall," Mrs Reynolds said.

"Mrs Reynolds has been quite cold to me, considering how she used to dote on me so."

"'T'was a long time ago, Mr Wickham, when the old master was still alive. I don't think the new master will be pleased to see you here," the housekeeper replied.

"I agree with Mrs Reynolds. You'll go, sir. Now," Elizabeth told him, with as much firmness as she could muster.

"And here's another lady who was once so warm to me, and has now turned so cold."

She was at once all rage. He was positively sneering at her, laughing and she couldn't abide him. How had she once thought him charming? "I have asked you to go, Mr Wickham."

"I have business with your husband."

"No, you do not, nothing respectable in any case. I am mistress here and I am asking you to go."

Elizabeth felt a footman at her shoulder. Hodges was also moving closer, in a protective manner, but there would be no forcing him out now, she was sure of that, because the others began to file in wearily and no scene could be caused. Mr Darcy was last to come into the hall and she fancied he entered it as if he was looking for her, but his eye fell on Wickham instead and his countenance revealed his surprise and annoyance. He said nothing, but nodded at his one-time friend expectantly, asking him to explain himself.

"I am sorry to intrude, Darcy, I see you have a party of guests, but there are some matters we ought to discuss."

Georgiana rushed forward, recognising Wickham and calling his name, but Elizabeth's hand went to her arm to stop her.

"I thought all our dealings were concluded long ago. I can't imagine what brings you here," Mr Darcy said.

Wickham bowed his head. "I wish to cause no-one embarrassment." He looked directly at Elizabeth. "But I mean to warn you of some possible trouble, a rather delicate matter. Shall we go somewhere we might have a little more privacy?"

Elizabeth saw Mr Darcy consider for a moment before acquiescing and holding out an arm to direct Wickham to his study.

Wickham laughed and told him he still remembered the way, he then gave Elizabeth a brief bow. "Mrs Darcy, 'tis an incomparable pleasure to see you again."

Mr Darcy's eyes were cast in her direction, clearly wondering at how she knew Wickham. She could not return his look.

When they had gone and all the rest of party were standing around with curious faces, Elizabeth sagged against Richard who had stepped forward and put a hand at her elbow. He requested a few words with her in a manner that pretended he sought her counsel on an entirely different matter, and then almost carried her away to the garden room. Once inside, he shut the doors firmly and leaned against them, while she fell heavily into her favourite chair, her head in her hands, and cried briefly.

Richard waited a few moments, knowing she would quickly recover. When she looked up at him, he gave her a soft smile. "So, how are you enjoying your birthday so far?"

Elizabeth let out a sound that was somewhere between a sob and a laugh and took the handkerchief he proffered. "Well it started oddly, became stranger, and the last few hours have been the most perturbing of my entire life. I appreciate your efforts, my very dear friend and cousin, but next year I think I will shut myself in the closet all day and see no-one."

He came to stand beside her. "You are not to worry, Darcy knows what Wickham is. He will send him away and all will be well. He will not believe his lies."

"But do you not see? They are not lies. I did enough wrong without him having to elaborate or embellish." She stopped and got to her feet, too troubled to settle in one place. "I ought to have spoken to Mr Darcy before this, I have erred greatly. How deceitful he will think me." Running a hand across the back of her neck, she dislodged a curl. "I always suspected my actions would not escape punishment."

Richard spoke with some force. "You have punished yourself enough over it, there is no need for others to join in. You are not to send yourself to purgatory over some harmless flirting."

"With a man I knew he hated."

"Wickham took advantage of your naivety. He is the villain here, not you."

Elizabeth looked out through the glass walls of the garden room and across the park. "How beautiful it is. I was saying just lately that I would not give it up for anything, but now I think I would rather walk away than go through all this. How can you bear it, Richard?"

"Bear what?" he asked.

"The uncertainty, the pain of it," she said and excused herself, fleeing through the doors at the rear of the room to the open air, where she might breathe freely. How her emotions raged, crashed and rolled about as she realised she had done the one thing she had promised herself she would not - she had started to feel something for Fitzwilliam Darcy. There was no denying it, he had crossed the burnt bridges, caused the walls to tumble down and seeped into her heart. She must care for him; else she would not be so torn apart by her fears. What was being said to him at that very moment by George Wickham?

Ten days, that was all, she realised. Ten days of his being at home had changed everything. How had he managed to make her feel so much in such a short space of time? Or had a small feeling, a tiny fledging bud of affection grown over time, even in his absence?

And what did he feel for her? He had seemed desperate to reach out to her that morning when he had given her the cross and chain, and his passion that afternoon could not have been fabricated, surely? But was Wickham about to destroy any regard he had for her? And then, would there be a return to animosity and indifference? Or would he pretend at something for the sake of harmony at Pemberley and continue to do just as he wanted elsewhere? It was exactly the future she did not want for herself - to be the silly wife, desperately craving the attention of a husband who picked her up and put her down whenever he chose. It was what she had so diligently and carefully tried to guard against.

Oh, she was irrational, mad thoughts plagued her and it took much walking the gardens and shrubberies before she was calm enough to think of returning. She consulted both her pocket watch and her conscience and decided the responsibilities of being Mrs Darcy could not be shirked any longer, even if the thought of facing Mr Darcy made her want to run for the hills.

When she returned to the house, however, it was to the news that Mr Darcy had left on some urgent business. He sent his apologies, but would not be back until the next day. Richard told her this over tea in the saloon, quietly, away from the guests.

"That is all? Did he mention what had happened with Wickham?"

"He left with Wickham. He said nothing."

"No other message, no note?"

Richard's sad, consoling smile was her answer.

They took an early dinner and the men retreated to the billiards room, while the ladies excused themselves for an early night, in preparation for the next day's ball. Elizabeth ordered a long deep bath, had her hair washed and where she might have previously sat in front of the fire to dry it, she opted instead for a chair by the large balcony windows and left them open.

"I've never known such hot weather. It can't last much longer," Rose remarked idly, as she tidied away after the bath.

"It feels as if a storm is coming," said Elizabeth.

"Good. I like a storm - blows everything about, gives it a good shake and then washes it all clean."

"Yes, that is all very well, Rose, unless you happen to be caught right in the middle of it, then it can be a fearsome, destructive thing." She drew her knees up and hugged them tightly to her. Having quickly become used to sounds from the chambers next door, she now found everything uncomfortably silent and prayed for disturbance and clatter, but knowing it was unlikely. He had, after all, said he would not return until the following day, but she hoped he might all the same. To think he was out there, doing Lord knows what, possibly because of her wretched mistakes and thinking ill of her, caused her misery of the acutest kind.

She had so much to think upon. How much the world, and one's perception of it, could change in a single day. She thought of the Lord Matlock, as he lay dying, lost in a world he no longer understood and surrounded by people he could not remember. What made life so precious that he was so unwilling to let go, what kept him clinging to the edge? She thought of the countess too, a woman who sometimes vexed her with her disdain for those she considered beneath her, but who she greatly revered nonetheless. Who could not stand in awe of the way she managed her house and family and carried her great responsibilities with such grace and easiness? Elizabeth had learnt so much from her and hoped someday to have at least half her fortitude, and her ability to smile through all her adversities. Jane came to mind too, her sweetest sister, who never thought to think of her own suffering. Elizabeth saw, despite the serenity in her countenance, that her sister was confused and pained by Bingley's sudden reserve, but still she did not complain.

It came down to three words. Life, family, love, and they circled around Elizabeth's thoughts and would not leave her be. What did they mean to her?

She saw that she had separated herself. There was Mrs Darcy, the Mistress of Pemberley, a role she played with proficiency, but almost outside of herself. Then there was Elizabeth, a cousin, a friend, an older sister, someone who always tried to do the right thing, who endeavoured to do good by Miss Temple, Richard and Georgiana, and then there was Lizzy, that very private girl, the angry, passionate, defiant, unpredictable creature, who lurked hidden beneath the fine gowns and cultured accent, the big house and luxurious carriages - who truly knew *her?* Jane, Mrs Gardiner, and oddly enough, Rose, who always understood her moods and anticipated her needs - and Mr Darcy, she thought, with no small amount of shock. Yes, he knew Lizzy, and had seen her in all her terrible resplendent glory. She touched the cross and chain still hanging from her neck. Life, family, love, changed into another three words, and she threw her head back and sighed heavily as they settled upon her – *'I love him. Dear God, I love him'*.

Fifty five

Her morning walk was spent looking out for a sign of Mr Darcy's horse, coming back through the woods or over the road. Instead the only person she encountered was a troubled Miss Temple. Elizabeth almost avoided her, thinking she might be stealing a few moments away from the house with Richard, but she appeared quite alone, and when Elizabeth approached her, she was greeted warmly.

"You find me, Mrs Darcy, enjoying the peace of the morning air, before I spend the day with a very excited sixteen-year-old girl, who will be able to concentrate on nothing except her first big party."

"I hope she will enjoy it."

"I am sure she will, she has such a sweet nature, always disposed to be happy, if she can be. I will miss her, when I go," Miss Temple said.

"You will be much missed too, if you do go, and not just by Georgiana." Elizabeth felt all the uncomfortable feelings associated with knowing something and not being able to speak about it openly. Richard's affection for the governess and his offer had been related to her in confidence and she saw it was better that it remained a secret. They were in a precarious position and circumstances meant their happiness might be much delayed, or prevented altogether. "There are others, including me, who will be so very disappointed."

Something happened then that shocked Elizabeth, for she had never seen Miss Temple lose her composure, and she had known the lady for over four years. She broke down suddenly into heavy, mournful tears and covered her face. It took Elizabeth such a disgracefully long time to react and think of comforting her. If it had been Georgiana, or Jane, she would have been there in an instant, with an arm around her shoulders or an embrace.

"Oh, excuse me," Miss Temple said.

"Oh no, you must excuse me," Elizabeth replied and took her by the elbow to somewhere they might sit. Finding a small bench not too far away, she encouraged Miss Temple to rest on it. "I am quite useless in the face of your distress. You are able to speak to me, if you should wish."

But Miss Temple could not speak, not for a long time. She would look cross at herself and shake her head and then dissolve into fresh new levels of misery. "I will be well in a moment; you must wonder what has come over me?"

"No, I do not wonder at it. Yesterday things came over me. Today, they hover somewhere above my head, threatening to descend. I am just about managing to keep from being completely overwhelmed, but it is not easy. I shall give you my handkerchief, but I make no guarantees that it is completely dry."

Miss Temple took the handkerchief, recovered enough to smile a little and eyed Elizabeth carefully. "Your discretion is admirable, Mrs Darcy, but I think I see understanding in your looks. He has spoken to you, Mr Fitzwilliam?"

"Yes, *Mr Fitzwilliam,* or Richard, as we might as well both call him, has."

"I was not expecting to fall in love again, I thought my life was to be one of duty; a calm life of guiding and preparing young girls, watching them grow up and I was perfectly content. He has robbed me of my serenity, Mrs Darcy."

Elizabeth had never felt such empathy for anyone. She completely comprehended the governess's feelings, as they were so like her own. Duty, Georgiana, Pemberley - she had once thought she would be satisfied with such comforts. Yet now she had glimpsed something else. She had been kissed senseless, held, loved for a few moments and she would never again be as satisfied without such joys, as she had been before. "Why do you cry so, Miss Temple? And speak of leaving? He is devoted to you, surely a way will be found."

"I have told him I would live anywhere with him, in any conditions. I should not care if I had to bake my own bread and sweep my own floors, but he will not countenance marrying me unless he can promise me a good situation, and there will be so much family opposition that it seems better if I withdraw. He would not, even though our situation is not known, he would consider himself honour-bound."

"Promise me you will do nothing about a new situation for a while? Be patient."

"Mrs Darcy, I will try, but it is almost as painful to stay, as it would be to go."

Elizabeth squeezed her hand, but felt it wrong to offer assurances. She remembered once being told *all will be well* and it had not been, not for a long time. It was still not.

They were disturbed by Richard coming slowly towards them and Elizabeth saw that she had stumbled unwittingly on a liaison after all.

"Come forth, sir, and see if you can do a better job of stemming this lady's tears than I. If you cannot, you are a poor lover indeed."

Elizabeth left them lost in their own private world of whispers and stolen touches, a little envious. It was only circumstances that kept them apart, at least they were both sure of their own hearts.

Mr Darcy was still not back by the time the other ladies began to speak of repairing upstairs to begin their preparations. To avoid the growing excitement in some quarters about the evening's ball and with the purpose of distracting herself from Mr Darcy's absence, Elizabeth set about her correspondence with some zeal and was writing to Charlotte Lucas when he entered the room and politely stood some way off, until she had put down her pen.

"Good afternoon, I am sorry to disturb you."

"It is quite alright, the interruption is not unwelcome, you find me in the middle of composing a difficult letter," she said. "My friend Charlotte Lucas is to marry the stupidest man in England, and I am writing to congratulate her."

"I rather thought that honour belonged to you." He sat in a chair next to her desk and offered her a small smile.

She laughed and examined his face for any signs of recrimination, astounded to see he was very calm, his manner gentle. "I have never doubted your intellect, sir. I remember once questioning your taste in waistcoats and the length of your hair, but never your mental capabilities."

"And, dare I ask, how do you find my waistcoats and hair now?"

"Far more acceptable."

"I am relieved." He fiddled with his cuffs. "I have just come from Bingley; our guests will depart tomorrow after the ball."

Elizabeth's heart ached for Jane. "I confess there are some in that party I shall be very glad to say goodbye to, and others who it will grieve me to see gone."

"I have also come from your sister. Mrs Gardiner needs to return to London, to her family in a few days and will travel back with some acquaintance of hers who are also bound south, but I have told Jane she is welcome to remain with us, indefinitely, for as long as she pleases. She has said she will speak to you but I think it would be a good plan. Should you like to have your sister with you?"

"Yes, of course. May I write to Mary, Kitty and Lydia and invite them indefinitely also?"

His panicked face amused her and when he realised he was being teased, he lightly batted her arm. "Go on, why don't you? We have bedrooms aplenty."

"If it's all the same to you, sir, I will not. One or two Bennets are acceptable, a whole hoard of them might become more chore than pleasure. I would probably wish Miss Bingley back within a fortnight."

Smiling again, in the most attractive of ways, he got to his feet and moved to leave. "You had better finish your letter." He reached the door before she got up the courage to stop him.

"Fitzwilliam, what happened with Mr Wickham?"

"It does not matter, you are not to worry. He is gone and shall not return."

"Thank you," she said, with great sincerity. "You must think badly of me and now I think you are trying to spare me any pain, which is very magnanimous of you, but I must know it all and I must tell you my account of things, you cannot have only his."

"Not now, another time. Let us enjoy the ball."

She nodded, thinking perhaps he had things to say to her that warranted a longer discussion than the moment allowed. Georgiana appeared then in any case, frantic and excited, wanting Elizabeth upstairs to give her an opinion on how she ought to wear her hair. Elizabeth put away her letters and allowed herself to be dragged away.

When she went to her own rooms to dress, she found Rose in as much of a state of anxiousness as Georgiana had been.

"Oh madam, I have been wondering at you leaving it so late, we do not have long to get ready," she complained.

"I should think an hour and a half plenty, Rose. Particularly for a married lady, who will no doubt spend the evening in a corner admiring lace and drinking tea."

Rose was all horror and dismay. "Oh no, you must dance. You must. You cannot sit down all night," she said, before remembering herself and murmuring an apology.

Elizabeth squeezed her arm. "We shall see."

There was a knock and Elizabeth assumed it was Georgiana again, with yet another question for her. Mr Darcy's valet standing on the other side of the door surprised them both. He was a very upright fellow, with as proud an air as the man he attended. He was very formal in his greeting and offered very proper apologies but asked permission to enter her rooms. Elizabeth assented and he walked to the dressing table, where he laid down a long roll of velvet and then spread it out with a flourish to reveal an astonishing array of jewellery.

Elizabeth heard Rose gasp, but managed to contain her own shock and asked the valet for an explanation.

"For the ball, madam. Mr Darcy asked me to bring them - for you to choose what you would like to wear. The sapphires were Lady Anne's and came here with her, the diamonds and rubies have traditionally belonged to Mrs Darcy."

The idea of Lady Anne arriving at Pemberley with her sapphires and her title, while she had arrived with a nothing but a scowl and some questionable relations, made Elizabeth smile. Rose had gotten over her shock and clapped her hands together, gleeful at the thought of dressing her mistress in them.

Elizabeth's eyes fell on the diamonds, so tastefully set, not too ostentatious, but obviously worth a great deal. Then she saw a ring she well recognised, even though it had adorned her finger for less than an hour before she had managed to temporarily lose it through a carriage window. She picked it up for a closer examination. It was a pretty ring, engraved with a sweet pattern of intertwined vines.

"Lady Anne's also, madam," said the valet.

"Yes, I have seen it before." She put the ring down and addressed the valet. "Will you thank Mr Darcy for his thoughtfulness, but he has recently bought me another piece of jewellery, which I would much prefer to wear."

The valet, well trained, sniffed a little but said nothing and wrapped the jewellery back up in the velvet roll, while Rose tried and failed to hide her pout.

Fifty six

As she descended the stairs, Elizabeth almost regretted her sentimental decision to send the Darcy family jewels away. Miss Bingley and Mrs Hurst were so draped in precious gems that she was blinded by the glare and her hand flew to her neck for a moment, quickly clasping her cross. Her mood was soon brightened, however, by the sight of Mr Darcy, waiting at the bottom step, away from the others, his hand outstretched and seeking hers. Something jolted and lurched sharply within her at the sight of him. He became formal evening dress very well. He was looking down his nose a little and puffing out his chest - those mannerisms she had once ridiculed, seemed strangely dear to her now.

While assisting her down the last few steps, he opened his mouth to speak, but then looked lost for words and an odd sort of cough erupted instead. He was not charming, he failed to flatter and please, but Elizabeth did not care. His faults she liked almost as much as his perfections.

Richard came near and leaned over his shoulder. "What your husband means to say is that you are lovely. Shall we go?"

Mr Darcy frowned at his cousin before turning back to Elizabeth. "I would kick him if he were not correct," he said very seriously, which made her smile and she would have gone to the carriage very happy if she had not witnessed the soft regretful gaze that Richard gave Miss Temple, who was so plainly attired compared to the rest of them. She was not to go, of course, a ball was no place for a governess, but she stood in the grand hallway, loyally giving some last minute steadiness to Georgiana. Elizabeth had seen her and Richard dance together before, at Haddon - very informal family dances - and remembered what a sweet sight they had made. Of course they had fallen in love. How had she never noticed it before, and when would he speak to Mr Darcy?

They reached the Balcombe estate in less than an hour. Elizabeth had no idea of it being so close and though most of the journey had passed easily with some pleasant chatter, they spent the last fifteen minutes of it in a great, very slow moving, queue of carriages, as each one stopped to let out elegant ladies and fine looking gentleman at the great front doors, before moving off again. The stillness of waiting, then the sudden jerking movements, as they inched forward a few feet again, making scant progress, became jarring on Elizabeth's nerves. And the weather was still unreasonably hot; the storm she had predicted the previous day had still not arrived. The air was heavy, the gentleman, in their coats, waistcoats and cravats were hot and restless, and Mr Darcy, she saw by the twitch of his jaw, was tense. Very suddenly he leaned forward and asked her if she were well.

"Yes, I just feel the frustration of being here and not yet being allowed to arrive."

"If I could in any way have us there sooner, to relieve your comfort, I would."

It was such a sweet, gentlemanly thing to say and he looked so sincere, that she could only smile in response.

"Must be two or three hundred guests, Darcy," Richard said.

Nodding grimly, Mr Darcy agreed. "It will be a terrible crush. Too many in a set for the dancing to look at all elegant, it will be an ungainly mess; shoulders bumping and feet being trodden upon, and the smoke in the card room will half choke us. By ten thirty, the place will be full of drunkards. Then, no doubt, there will be as much of a queue to get out of the place as there has been to get in."

"I forgot how much you love a party," Richard teased. "Why don't you give a grand ball yourself soon, show everyone how it ought to be done?"

"I most probably shall," he said with a firm nod. "Though I should not invite three counties and fill Pemberley with strangers. My guests will be drawn from my intimate acquaintance and friends."

"Ours will be a much smaller affair then, sir? Will the ballroom require airing, or might we host it in an ante-room?" The tease fell from Elizabeth's mouth before she had time to check it and for a while, she wondered if he would take offence. Richard chuckled but Georgiana stiffened as they waited his response.

"The ballroom will do nicely," he replied, "we shall invite your twenty-seven sisters, fill it out a bit." There was a ghost of a smile around his mouth and when she met his eyes, she saw their humour was not so very different, as she had once supposed.

At last they arrived and were received by their hosts. Elizabeth went down the line, with some trepidation, but was reassured constantly by Mr Darcy's hand floating near the small of her back. Lady Constance Balcombe smiled broadly when Elizabeth congratulated her on her engagement. Her future husband, beside her, was over a foot shorter than her and a rotund, balding man, but exceedingly jolly and good natured, and so obviously in love with his bride that although they looked like the oddest couple on earth, Elizabeth was left in no doubt that theirs would be a very happy marriage.

"Mrs Darcy, I will be most surprised if you remember me," Constance Balcombe said.

"Of course, most faithfully, I remember particularly your kindness, when I was greatly in need of it, and have long hoped for the opportunity to thank you. Where do you settle, after you are married? I hope not so far away that you would not be able to visit us at Pemberley some time?"

"No, not too far, and I should very much like that," Constance replied, before looking up at Mr Darcy. "You and I, old friend, shall speak later."

He agreed and offered his own congratulations, before they moved on and were before the Viscountess, who looked at Elizabeth for some time, peering closely at her face. "Mrs Darcy, it is a pleasure to meet you."

Elizabeth bit her lip and curtsied. It would not do to correct a Viscountess, so she said nothing of their having met before, and wondered at the woman's memory.

Mr Darcy guided her gently away.

"She did not remember me. Do I look so very different from when I first came to Pemberley?"

"Elizabeth, if *I* had not seen you between then and now, *I* would not know you." He led her into the ballroom, where the musicians were taking their seats. There was much manoeuvring for the first dance, as gentlemen approached their intended partners. She waited, not breathing, while Mr Darcy looked about him, and then, he declared he saw someone he ought to say hello to and left her.

Georgiana was directly behind and Elizabeth reached to take her hand, as much for her own benefit as her little sister's. They went over to a place where they might watch the dancing without being too jostled. Elizabeth noticed Richard was limping heavily as he followed them, another sure sign of an impending storm. His smile, directed at her, was too sympathetic for Elizabeth to bear. "Darcy has never been overly fond of dancing," he said in a low tone, leaning towards her ear while Georgiana was distracted by the grand scene before them.

Feeling tears sting her eyes, Elizabeth willed herself not to cry and blinked them furiously away. "It does not matter."

"Will you stand up with me? I am poor compensation, I know," Richard said.

"You are in pain, you silly man. And I am perfectly happy here. I am Georgiana's chaperone and that is what I shall occupy myself with. Go and find some employment yourself."

He touched her shoulder and was gone, unfortunately to be replaced by Miss Bingley, who had not been asked to dance either and who had no other companion to stand with. Mrs Hurst was dancing with her unenthusiastic-looking husband and Jane and Bingley were dancing too. Jane looked thoroughly miserable and Bingley embarrassed. He had secured her hand for the first two dances at the beginning of the week, when they had both been full of hope and expectation. Now, it was an ordeal for both of them, and tomorrow they would say goodbye. Elizabeth thought his going would be a wound from which her sister might never recover, and though she wished Bingley in love enough to be reckless, she supposed there was something to admire in his prudence. If he were not completely certain, it was right that he should withdraw until he could be, though she feared he

458

would go away and forget; that there would be some beauty in Scarborough or London who would catch his eye and Jane would be nothing to him but a sweet memory.

"Oh please be not fickle, Mr Bingley," she whispered to herself.

Georgiana heard her however and looked over. "I am sorry, what did you say?"

"It was nothing of any importance. Are you enjoying yourself?" Elizabeth looked down at Georgiana's feet which were tapping rhythmically in time with the music.

The girl nodded enthusiastically. "The musicians are very good."

"Yes, it is all very fine; the rooms, the decorations," Miss Bingley said from where she stood on the other side of Georgiana. Miss Bingley looked a little disconcerted and Elizabeth realised the lady was in a room without friends, and was a tradesman's daughter, albeit a very rich one, and was perhaps a little lost amongst the gentry and nobility. If she'd had the acquaintance of someone of consequence amongst the revellers, as she might have had in London, she would have been all superciliousness, but here in Derbyshire, she had no standing, and was nervous.

When Elizabeth looked about the room, she saw one or two faces that looked familiar, older gentlemen, acquaintances of the late Mr Darcy, some of whom nodded respectfully in her direction. She saw Mr Gordon, a widowed landowner who had once visited at Pemberley to discuss some business and afterwards had sat very close to her on a sofa and accidentally brushed against her too many times for him to claim them all accidental. He had eventually been the recipient of a great stare from George Darcy, full of reproach and warning and had never been invited back. She had probably been sixteen at the time and Mr Gordon nearly forty. The thought of it made her shudder and the man's coming towards her filled her with dread.

"Mrs Darcy, delighted."

"Mr Gordon."

"You haven't forgotten me, then?" he asked.

"Oh no, you managed to impress yourself upon my memory, and other places."

"Likewise, I never forget a pretty face." He glanced down at her décolletage and stepped close enough for Elizabeth to smell the wine on his breath and see the sweat on his brow.

Fearing he was about to ask her to dance, Elizabeth put Georgiana a little behind her and hurriedly introduced him to Miss Bingley. "Mr Gordon is the cousin of the Viscount Harewood. He has a sizeable estate nearby," she said, emphasising his connections and wealth.

Miss Bingley was instantly impressed and flattered him with a smile that soon saw his attention drift from Elizabeth onto her and they soon went away to dance. Elizabeth felt satisfaction in watching them go, knowing Mr Gordon would be too forward and that his hands would wander, but dash it all, the woman was a menace who deserved whatever came her way, and was she not forever pawing and clasping at other people's husbands?

Gazing around the room, her eyes alighted on Mr Darcy, but when she saw who he spoke to, her world fell away a little; everything seemed to dim and blur and hush. Mr Darcy and Emma Balcombe were in close confederation. Elizabeth had assumed, as she had not been in the receiving party, that she was not present and had breathed a little easier, but now waves of distress rippled through her at the sight of them together. It had been far easier upon her poor heart when she had despised him.

She could not see Mr Darcy's face, such was their position, but she could see Emma Balcombe's and the small smirk that played around the corners of her mouth. If Elizabeth had been hoping to find her altered, older or less fair of figure for her time away, without bloom, she was disappointed. She was still a very beautiful woman. Fair, tall, long-limbed and voluptuous, everything she was not, and Elizabeth felt so very jealous of her. Though she had stupidly thrown aside his affection for Wickham, Emma Balcombe was a woman who had once commanded Mr Darcy's heart. *Did she still?*

Mr Darcy turned to look at her and smiled in her direction, which took Elizabeth by surprise, and she returned it hesitantly. She watched him bow to Emma Balcombe, who went away without taking a proper leave of him.

"I am sorry to have left you," he said, coming to Elizabeth's side.

"Oh, think nothing of it. Georgiana and I have been entertained watching Miss Bingley dance with Mr Gordon."

Mr Darcy frowned. "Yes, I know Mr Gordon. Promise me that *you* will not dance with him?"

"Most faithfully."

Seeing his cousin approach, Darcy asked him to stay beside Georgiana and held his hand out flat for Elizabeth to put hers on top of. She flushed, thinking he was taking her to dance, but instead he leaned down and said "come". He led her thus into the adjoining drawing room, where the great and good, who were not dancing, had assembled. He took all the care over her one might over royalty, clearing a small path so she was not jostled and securing a cup of punch for her. She then realised his intention, which was to bring her to the notice of his acquaintance. After being introduced to about the twentieth person, she leaned in to speak to him discreetly.

"Is this an attempt, Mr Darcy, to prove to me that you do have enough friends to fill a ballroom?"

"No, I happily admit there are very few people I would call friend. These are merely people you ought to know."

They stopped before Viscountess Balcombe again, who looked less perplexed by Elizabeth than she had in the receiving line, and was now very civil. "Mrs Darcy, I have heard you have a very fine governess over at Pemberley who may leave you now Georgiana is almost grown. My sister in Ireland has a ward, a small girl who requires instruction, do you believe your governess might be tempted by the position?"

"Miss Temple has travelled abroad before and may welcome the chance to do so again, but at the moment, Lady Balcombe, it is not yet decided whether she is to go."

They moved away as another party approached and Mr Darcy frowned. "I thought the governess's fate was quite decided. Did you not speak to her?"

"Yes, I did."

"And?"

"And, to some people she is not merely '*the governess*', let us wait a few days and then we will speak of her again. Will you trust me?" she asked lightly.

His answer was very solemn. "I do trust you, implicitly."

"Thank you," she replied, very gratified.

They had wandered back into the ballroom, where the dancing had briefly broken for the musicians to rest, but it was about to begin again, and a very happy Constance Balcombe was urging everybody who was willing and able to get to their feet. She looked Elizabeth's way and waved her forward. "Now, I should say you are an excellent dancer, Mrs Darcy. Everybody is lazy, everybody is asleep after the break. Come set the example."

"I am ready," she replied, amazing herself, "whenever I am wanted."

"Whom are you going to dance with?" asked Mr Darcy.

She hesitated a moment, and then replied, "with you, if you will ask me."

"Then will you?" he asked, instantly offering her his hand.

"Indeed I will."

Fifty seven

Darcy felt something he had never experienced before - contentedness - an ability to live perfectly in the moment and let all that was joyous about it overset him, without a care for what might follow next. His worries were nothing, his responsibilities were without weight. Opposite him in the set, Elizabeth's eyes sparkled, her smile was ridiculously wide. Whenever her hand left his, as they separated to walk down the dance, he did not feel any great loss, for time and again she came back, and when she did, he gripped her hand tighter and felt the pressure of her fingers squeezing his in return. She teased him after a while, for he had been mostly silent, happy to gaze upon her.

He tried to make a comment about a book he had recently been reading which he thought might interest her.

"Oh books, no! I cannot think of books in a ballroom," she said, before going around him, so light on her feet they barely seemed to touch the floor. "No I shall have to ask you to call forth all your long neglected skills in conversation making and find another subject."

And then just when she seemed to be having such great fun at his expense, her expression darkened, her eyes flitting to the left of them, where Emma Balcombe stood beside a mantelpiece, watching them with some disdain.

"So, Constance is very happy, but Lady Emma Balcombe looks quite displeased with you, sir."

"Is she? She shouldn't be. I only spoke to her to thank her for a good turn she did me long ago."

"Oh?"

"Yes, at the time, I admit, I did not see her actions in a charitable light. Yet I think, or at least hope, she was the odd means of securing my future happiness."

Elizabeth's eyebrow arched but they were separated in the dance, another gentleman had the pleasure of grasping her hand for a few moments.

"And will you not explain yourself any further?" she asked, when they were brought together again.

"No, to say any more would cause me to speak ill of a lady, which I do not like to do, if I can help it. She wronged me, Elizabeth, and she is never to be trusted or thought of as a friend, but maybe she ought to be pitied, for since that time she has had her own troubles to contend with."

"Will you tell me it all, one day? When it no longer matters so much?"

"Perhaps," he nodded, though Darcy could not imagine telling her all the details of his dealings with the lady, and certainly not the sordid tale of how he had once found Wickham flat on his back, with his breeches and boots tangled around his ankles, and a naked Emma Balcombe astride him - taking their pleasure in the master's chambers of the Darcy's London house. He'd thought Wickham was with a whore at first. How astonished he had been when he had recognised her voice, and then her face, as she had turned towards him, horrified, her hands flying up to cover her breasts. He had thrown her clothes at her, told her to dress and when she was decent once again in appearance, if not in character or reputation, he had put her in a carriage home. Despite her embarrassment at having been caught, she had been defiant as he had handed her up. '*It is not wrong, Darcy. We will be married, you will see, and it will be nothing then. If my parents won't consent, we'll run off to Scotland.*' He had silently shut the door on her, his heart had felt mortally wounded at the time, but he had recovered, with surprising speed. Her betrayal had meant little in the end.

It would be difficult to explain to Elizabeth, his conflicting feelings regarding Emma Balcombe. His dislike was now a fixed thing, but when he thought of what promise she had once had, and how poor her prospects were now, he felt melancholic. It was widely believed the child in need of a governess, the ward of her sister's in Ireland that the Viscountess had spoken of before, was Emma's child and that she had been sent there for the purpose of having it discreetly. She had only recently returned and the matter had not been handled with the delicacy and care it should. When he had last been in London, he had heard it tittered about in several quarters. Now the Balcombes sought to marry her off, but no reputable man would want her. Despite her comeliness, she stood alone tonight. No suitors, few friends, another victim of Wickham's want of decency. The thought that Elizabeth had come so close to falling for his charms, made Darcy go cold.

He looked between the two of them, Emma and Elizabeth, and felt there was no comparing them. They were as different as two women could be. Elizabeth was kind, where Emma was mean-spirited; Elizabeth was warm, where Emma was aloof. And while Emma might be overtly handsome, Elizabeth had a quiet, mesmerising beauty that he could not look away from.

Lost in his thoughts, he had not realised the dancing had stopped and went to take another step. She smiled at his error and covered for it by walking forward and pretending he meant to escort her away.

"Will you forgive my clumsy feet, madam, and give me a chance to redeem myself? I should very much like to dance the supper set with you?"

"I shall, but, Fitzwilliam, will you dance with Georgiana now?"

"She is not out," he said, trying to look firm.

"Oh, but you are her brother, it is different. I shall explain to any other gentleman that approaches. Look at her, her first ball. Will you?"

Her eyes were large and imploring, her countenance so engaging, that he found himself agreeing and wondered at her ability to charm him into doing things he otherwise would not. Lord, he would have to be careful in future, heaven forbid she should ever know the power she possessed over him and how persuaded he could be by an intimate glance or two.

As she watched Mr Darcy and a giddy Georgiana take their places for the next set, Elizabeth felt Richard at her shoulder.

"I shall enjoy telling your aunt and Miss Temple of your dancing. We have long attempted to find a decent explanation for your stubborn refusals, and imagined all kinds of reasons. Now, the mystery is solved. You were simply waiting for your husband to ask you."

"Was I?" Elizabeth looked around at him, "perhaps, though I did not really know it."

"I would ask you again now, you know, if I were not so tired of your rejections."

"Do not ask me then," she said casually.

"I shall not. I shall go away again."

"Very well, goodbye," she said and then laughed and took his hand. "Let us dance then, but do not blame me if you are hardly able to walk tomorrow."

"You are worth all the pain you bring, I have said as much to Darcy."

"And *I* am accused of impudence!" she cried, as they went to the set.

Elizabeth had not sat down. Darcy kept careful watch and saw that as soon as she had finished a set with one gentleman, another appeared before her with a bow and a request. She always acquiesced, it would have been rude for her to refuse when she had already shown a willingness to dance, but he did draw a sharp, disgruntled breath when a travelling Italian marquis, an esteemed guest of Viscount Harewood, eyed her from across the room and stepped towards her with great determination, holding out his hand with a flourish, as if he were bestowing a great favour upon her.

After this dance, she came to stand by him and he had never felt more glad to have her back by his side.

"He spoke a great deal," Darcy observed.

"Yes."

"What was he saying?"

"I have not the faintest idea, he spoke no English and, as I have told you before, I do not speak Italian. It did not matter. I found I was only required to nod."

"But he knows you are my wife, that you are married?" At her answering shrug, he tutted. "This, you see, is why young ladies require a thorough education in the modern languages."

"For discouraging foreign lovers, I see. Surely, all a young lady needs to know in that case, Fitzwilliam, is how to say 'no'. That word, I have noticed, is pretty much always understood, in whatever language it is spoken."

"I am not so certain. You might have agreed to meet him at midnight and run away with him for all you are aware."

She lowered her lashes. "Will you think it very bad of me if I confess I find the idea of been thrown over the shoulder of an Italian marquis and run away with quite thrilling?"

"Will you then, meet him at midnight?"

"No," she shook her pretty head. "I do not find him so appealing that I would forsake Pemberley." Again, she looked through her lashes, and her face took on a provocative expression he had never seen before, as her eyes travelled up from Darcy's chest to the top of his head. "And, he was not tall enough."

He couldn't call what he felt at that moment anything other than desire and it raged through him ferociously. He cursed every mistake he had ever made around her but could not find the words to properly convey all his regrets. Would his mouth always be ever so slow?

They danced their supper dance and again, he found himself largely silent, but now she did not tease or laugh at him for it. She was quiet too, as an odd tension grew between them. When he looked at her, she looked away. Her eyes sometimes flashed with a promise of something. Her lips would purse, she would go to speak, and then say nothing. He noticed a tremble in her hand when he took it to lead her into supper and it matched the shaking of his own. The simple cross and chain he had given her caught his eye where it hung around her neck. He had supposed she had worn it to the picnic, out of politeness, as one would on a birthday when it had just been given as a present, but to wear it now, when he had offered such finer jewels instead, what did that signify, was she trying to tell him something?

When he had seen all his party into supper, Darcy thought to look out of the windows and went back to speak quietly to Elizabeth, his mood altered and his responsibilities at the forefront of his mind again. "The wind has picked up. We will leave directly after supper."

"Is that really necessary?"

"Do not fight me on this," he said with a degree of command and perhaps some rudeness, given the brief flash of anger that crossed her features. "I wish you home safe, that everyone gets home safely," he added in a softer tone and with a hand on her shoulder.

She agreed, "I shall tell everybody."

They were the first to go, Darcy apologised to his hosts, ordered the carriage and put them all so quickly into it that they sat without ceremony, wherever was free. Darcy was the last to board and put himself in too small a space between the window and Elizabeth. She might have slid slightly across the bench, closer to Georgiana, to put more room between them, but did not. She stayed close, drew strength from his warmth and comfort from the way their elbows bumped.

Miss Bingley provided some one-sided dialogue about Mr Gordon, of how much he had admired her and how he had talked of going to Scarborough for the express purpose of calling on her there. Only Mrs Hurst, out of sibling loyalty listened, the others paid scant attention. The wind was picking up, whistling around the carriage, making it rock more than normal, but despite the noise and the people, Elizabeth must have dozed for a while, for the very next thing she remembered was a great crack of thunder, a shriek from the horses and the shouts of the coachman. The storm was directly overhead. The coach jerked violently, Miss Bingley screamed, Georgiana clutched at her arm. "John will have no trouble, Georgiana, he'll have the horses under control in a moment," Elizabeth soothed. She looked up at Mr Darcy who was staring grimly out of the window. "How much further?" she asked him quietly.

"A few miles," he replied, and then whispered. "I shall not let anything happen to you, you need not be afraid."

"I know," she whispered back, "I am not afraid."

Yet the wind blew harder and the rain began to lash the carriage windows, then lightning cracked through the sky, bathing them all in its eerie white glow for a few moments and making Miss Bingley scream again. Elizabeth stole a glance at Jane to see if she was scared, but she was oddly expressionless. Mr Bingley was looking at Jane too, his mouth twisted into a grimace, almost as if he were in pain.

Soon after, they made a very sharp turn, which Elizabeth recognised as the entryway into Pemberley's woods. She hoped they'd be home before Miss Bingley had cause to scream again, but the Gods were seemingly angry about something and shook the earth with three deafening roars of thunder that sent the horses into wild panic. They pulled too hard, in different directions and something in the chassis of the carriage snapped. It dropped a few feet, lurched and then stopped, throwing everyone about a little, all except Elizabeth. She had remained firmly in her seat as Mr Darcy had thrown a strong arm across her middle and his hand now gripped her thigh. She ought to have been more disturbed by the peril of the broken carriage, but it was the position of his hand that sent her heart racing and in the few moments of quiet that there always are after such a disaster, she could only gaze at his long thumb where it rested against the inside of her leg. It seemed to burn through her skirts and a flash of white heat crept up into her chest, overspread her neck and settled onto her cheeks. She looked up and saw Miss Bingley, not screaming now, but looking at them both with an air of dejection. She offered Elizabeth an odd smile.

There was a great commotion in front of the carriage, which could not be seen, but easily imagined, as footmen and coachman tried to calm the horses and examine the damage. Mr Darcy left his seat and opened the door, jumping out into the rain, where he was then temporarily blown back by the force of the gale. He managed to adjust himself, set his shoulders to it and forced his way forward, while shutting the door behind him.

Mr Bingley spoke calmly and jovially, trying to assure them all would be well, and in a few moments Mr Darcy came back to tell them that a footman had gone for another carriage, so all they had to do was wait. They filled the time with inconsequential chatter, though everyone was nervous and keen to be back at the house, they did their best to remain cheerful and the new carriage arrived back with greater efficiency than they could have hoped for. It was smaller though, a barouche box, usually only meant for four passengers, not nearly big enough for them all. Mr Darcy proclaimed himself wet through in any case and said he would walk the rest of the way. Richard suggested he would too, though he was limping badly and staggered against the wind in such an alarming fashion that when his cousin told him to get into the new coach, he had little choice but to agree. Mr Bingley, along with Mr Hurst helped the ladies get from the wreck of the broken carriage into the unbroken one, and then they declared they would ride up top with the coachman, which meant the rest of them could fit in at a squeeze. Elizabeth, just as the door was about to be shut, got up from her seat and jumped down onto the road, where she grasped Mr Darcy's arm.

"Do not be so foolish, get inside."

"I shall not, I shall not let you walk on your own, I'll go with you," she said, with determination.

"I would not be able to call myself a gentleman if I allowed you to. You will be soaked through."

"I am already soaked." She was; the rain came down with such unrelenting speed, that to be out in it for only a few moments had made her wet through. "'Tis only a little water," she protested with a smile.

He stared at her in disbelief before raising a long arm and signalling for the coachman to leave. The new carriage went away with a jolt and when it had gone Mr Darcy took up the collars of Elizabeth's cloak and pulled it more tightly around her. Then he pulled her closer to him and kissed her. Not with the same bruising urgency he had done the day before, but with a soft, reverent passion. Putting a hand either side of her face, caressing the wet curls at her neck, finding

470

her lips again and again with his own, his mouth moving over hers with ever-deepening pressure and then breaking away to kiss her cheeks and the tip of her nose, before returning to her mouth again. He sighed heavily, before letting her go.

"Are you planning to apologise for your kisses later?" she asked when she had recovered enough to speak.

"Do I need to?" He looked nervous for a few moments.

"You did yesterday."

"Did I need to then?"

"No, although you did ruin a perfectly good hat."

"I shall buy you another. I shall buy you a hundred."

He took her face in his hands again and kissed her quickly, before gathering her in close to his chest. "The things you do to me, Elizabeth. I have lost my mind. Why are we standing in the rain? Let us go."

Fifty eight

They walked, hand in hand, through the storm, out of the woods, into the more forgiving park, and the gardens, returning home. By the time they reached the courtyard, small streams had formed and water gushed past the bottom of the stone stairs that led up to the house. Elizabeth slipped on the now slick flagstone of the first step but Mr Darcy caught her and lifted her into his arms, carrying her up the rest of the way, while looking down at her wet face, "*'tis only a little water'* she says."

Elizabeth made no complaint at being transported so, and had never felt so safe, despite the storm still raging about them. Mr Darcy, she now knew with great certainty, was a man who would always be there to catch her when she fell.

They burst through the doors to see Mrs Reynolds in the hall with a blanket in her hands and an astonished expression on her face.

Mr Darcy set her down. "There is your mistress, Mrs Reynolds. Wring her out."

Her cloak was removed, the blanket thrown around her, but Elizabeth resisted the entreaties of those who tried to get her to go upstairs to change immediately and followed Mr Darcy, who had walked into the library. He had poured himself a measure of Brandy and was standing in contemplation of the fire that had been lit, one foot on the hearth, absentmindedly drying his shoes. Their guests and family were drifting upstairs already, in search of dry clothes - forgoing lengthy goodnights, or the talking over of the evening's events, in favour of comfort.

Elizabeth and Mr Darcy were alone and lit by only a few candles.

Though he looked deep in thought, he seemed to sense her approach and turned around.

"Tell me it is real, not something we imagine, because it is easier," she said.

He understood her. "It is real, but you are cold and I worry you will catch your death. I should not have allowed you out of the coach. Go and get dry, please," he said.

"I will, in a moment. May I?" she asked, pointing to the brandy, shivering a little. "I have heard it is very warming."

He lifted the glass to her lips himself and she closed her hands around his, tipping some of liquid into her mouth. It made her cough and splutter. Mr Darcy searched around in his pockets and found a wet handkerchief which he handed over to her.

Licking her lips, Elizabeth set the brandy glass on the fireplace. "That is more than enough of that." He looked amused and it made her raise a brow. "What are you thinking of?"

"Of you, long ago, and your first taste of strong cider. Disobedient little hellion."

Looking at the wet handkerchief he had given her, she recognised the stitching and was surprised. "I made this for you."

"Yes, 'tis the only one I can find now. I don't know what happened to the others."

Elizabeth said nothing, only smiled and put a hand around his neck, pulling his face down to hers and putting her lips tentatively against his, without a thought to where they were. He returned her shy kiss and put his arms about her waist, holding her tightly.

Footsteps alerted them to an intruder, but while Mr Darcy's mouth left hers, he continued to hold her, as she hid her embarrassed face in his shoulder.

"Oh, Lord!" Richard said. "I am sorry, cousin, I thought you were alone. Well, actually, I am not sorry to see it, just sorry to have interrupted."

"Your apology is accepted," Mr Darcy replied. "Will you go away again now?"

"Of course, yes. I was going to speak to you, but it may wait."

Elizabeth, thinking perhaps Richard was going to speak of Miss Temple and his hopes, pushed herself away from Mr Darcy. "Oh, please stay, I should go and change. And there is something I need to do. I have a note to write."

She was at the door before Mr Darcy could protest. She bid them goodnight and went.

Rose had dried her off and set her in front of the fire to brush her hair out.

"Will I braid it?"

"No. You can go, Rose," Elizabeth said, and when the maid had gone, she got up from her seat and crossed to her dressing table, where she found some writing things in the top drawer. She sat looking at them for a while, gathering her courage, but hearing Mr Darcy arrive in his chambers next door a few minutes later, made up her mind. It did not take long to write, though she chose her words carefully. Then she blew on it to dry the ink, folded the note and laid it on the floor in front of the internal door. She gave the paper a push, sending it sailing through the gap between the door and the polished wooden floor and waited with her eyes closed, still on her knees.

He was there in what seemed like an instant, the doorknob was rattled, persuaded into operation, and the heavy wooden door whistled past Elizabeth's nose, missing it by mere inches. On opening her eyes, she saw a pair of very large, very masculine, stocking-less feet. Her gaze travelled up to find he was at least still partially clothed, though his waistcoat was gone and his shirt was unbuttoned at the neck. Her note was in his hand, still folded. He had not read it.

"What is this?"

"An invitation, if you were still waiting upon one," she said, wishing she had thought to protest when Rose had put a plain, loose nightgown over her head. She had other, much prettier, apparel she might have worn.

Though when her eyes rose to meet his, any fears about how alluring he found her were put to rest. She remembered overhearing Mrs Hurst saying that Mr Darcy was wont to look at her like he wanted to eat her alive. She had not understood the expression completely at the time, but now, there was no other way to describe his intent stare. He stepped towards her with purpose, just as another great crack of thunder shook the walls and rattled the paintings, and a burst of lightning illuminated the room.

Oh Lord, what have I got myself into, she thought - and then he lifted her off her knees - and she thought no more.

Fifty nine

The storm raged for some time and only quietened at dawn. Elizabeth woke to a bright, but cooler day, which was dawning brilliantly and filling the room with sunshine at far too early an hour. Mr Darcy was at the large windows, closing the curtains. She smiled at the sight and pushed her face into the pillow to cover her blush. How silly to blush now, when he had been naked for hours. It seemed different though, to see him in the harshness of sunlight, rather than by the softness of candle. When the room was darker again, she lifted her face and her eyes fell on his form again. He was striking. Long and lean, strong and square shouldered, as beautiful as any statue she had ever seen, but he was real, made of flesh and bone. Her husband. Turning and seeing her awake, he nodded towards the window. "We have trees down in the park."

Elizabeth, naked herself, got up from the bed, but was more modest and took the top blanket with her, wrapping it around herself as she went to him. He smiled as she drew nearer and pulled the curtain aside for her to look out and examine the damage. "Oh, a shame, but I am relieved it is not the Spanish chestnuts."

"You are fond of them?"

"Very. They arrived here about the same time I did."

"Then may they stand for a few hundred years yet." He brushed her cheek with the back of his hand. "I think we have hardly slept. I would offer to leave and let you rest properly, but I do not want to go."

"Then stay. I will not evict you."

His hand moved down from her face, along her neck, underneath the blanket and travelled down between the valley of her breasts to rest on her stomach. He then used his other hand to open the folds of the blanket, so he might see her better. "You are perfect."

"I am not," she protested.

"To me, you are perfect."

He was so very earnest and she adored him for it. As his hands went to her hips, to bring her towards him, she opened the blanket up, letting it fall to the ground.

Sometime later, when they were both wrapped in the blanket and each other on the chaise - quite ridiculously as the bed was only a very short walk away - she stretched in his arms to look up into his face.

"Tell me about Wickham."

"Oh, Elizabeth, do not let thoughts of him intrude, not when I lie here so contended with you."

"Why were you not angry with me? What did he accuse me of? Did you give him money?"

"Which of those questions would you like me to answer first?" he laughed. She enjoyed the movement of his chest underneath her hand when he did so.

"Start where you think best."

"I suppose you will not let me put it off any longer. Yes, I gave him money. He was owed some. My father did not make it a provision in his will, but in his last letter to me he mentioned that he would like him to be given a small sum of money - if I ever thought him in need of it and if I thought he would spend it wisely. Wickham has decided he would like to take his wife and child to America, and I jumped at the chance to purchase his passage for him, for all sorts of reasons. I dearly hope he makes a life for himself there and does not come back. He did not accuse you of anything, though he mentioned you had been friends when you had visited in Hertfordshire."

Elizabeth sat up. "Then he has been uncharacteristically kind. I was not wise around him. I did not betray you in deed, but in thought…" she shook her head.

Taking her hand, he brought her fingers up to his lips to kiss them, "and did I do anything to encourage your constancy to me at the time? No. Elizabeth, even if something more had happened with Wickham, I would have forgiven you. I did not deserve your faithfulness. But, as I said, he did not try to convince me of an affair between the two of you, what he came to bargain with were some letters you wrote to Henry Jones."

"He stole them from me." Elizabeth closed her eyes. "I left them on a table in Hertfordshire after Henry had returned them to me and Wickham took them. I know I promised you I would never write to Henry again, that I would end the correspondence, and now that seems worse than anything that happened with Wickham. Did you read them?"

"Just one, I had to know what I was being threatened with. I am sorry for the invasion into your privacy."

"I was a silly young girl."

"You were a sad, lonely young girl. I am the one who is to be ashamed. I truly had no idea of how unhappy you were, or of how much you missed your home. You hid it well and I saw only what I wanted to."

Elizabeth shook her head. "I found a new home though."

"I hope you have, but I cannot think back on my past behaviour without abhorrence. How coldly I treated you! I gave thought to your comfort, but never your feelings. And I might excuse myself by saying I thought you hated me and wished nothing to do with me, but I was twenty-three to your fifteen, I ought to have known better, I ought to have *been* better."

"Do not fret. We are fortunate, you and I. We have the power to put all our mistakes away and be done with them. No-one knows the whole of our story except us. The past may be a place only we know. I am only concerned with today. You must learn some of my philosophy, think only of the past as its remembrance gives you pleasure."

He kissed her thoroughly but not in an attempt to ignite her passion, for he was well spent. He kissed her instead with reverence, before breaking off with a sigh. "Sometimes, Elizabeth, the past is difficult to disregard, when it stands in your hallway, with its hat in its hand."

"If your father had known how Wickham behaved around me in Hertfordshire, how he failed to tell anyone there he had a wife and child, he would not have blamed you for

478

not fulfilling his wishes. I wish you hadn't been so generous. Those letters are a tad embarrassing, but hardly scandalous."

"My father was overly fond of him, ridiculously so. Wickham told me yesterday he believes himself to be my brother and I could not refute it. I have always suspected as much myself - born on the wrong side of the blanket - but a brother nonetheless."

"Oh no," Elizabeth cried. "It is not true. You must not think that. If I had any notion that you thought such a thing, I would have corrected you."

"And how, may I ask, do you know it is not true?" He was astonished and sat up, but kept his arms around her.

"There is a letter. I will show you." She left his embrace, taking the blanket and wrapping it around herself.

"You were not so bashful a little while ago, Elizabeth," he said, smiling at her.

"And I note you are not at all, sir," she replied, tartly, her eyes sweeping over him.

"Do I shock you?"

"No, I simply cannot decide whether you are more handsome with, or without, your clothes."

He reached for her, forgetting the seriousness of the previous conversation, tempted again by the arch of her brow, her messy hair and the teasing look in her eye. She stepped deftly away and went to fetch a letter from a drawer. She returned and handed it to him.

"What is this?"

"Wickham's mother had an unmarried sister who visited here and stayed with the Wickhams at the gatehouse. Her name was Alice. She and your father developed feelings for each other, feelings which both of them tried to deny. Though it remained an innocent relationship, she speaks of love. Both were afraid their passion for each other would tempt them too far. She was here for about six months before leaving suddenly, to go to a brother in Sussex. The letter is her goodbye to your father. Of course, it was wrong, but I have to say I found it very touching."

"You are sure of all this?" Darcy asked. "How did you come across the letter?"

"When he fell on the lawn, I had his coat in my arms and his prayer book fell out of the pocket, and then the letter out of the prayer book. I did not know quite what to do with it, knowing the pain it might cause you to think your father loved someone other than your mother. George Wickham is mentioned in the letter, he must have been a boy of two or three at the time, and his aunt was fond of him. Alice asks your father to always have a care for him. It seems he honoured this request and tried to do his best by the younger Wickham. Given this letter and all it relates, and the way it speaks of those involved, I am certain your father was not George's father. I think you will be of a similar mind once you have read it."

"Letters, Elizabeth." He reached for her again and this time she let herself be caught and pulled back down into his embrace. "How they narrate our lives, and with what joy or fear do we open them? What secrets they can reveal, and how they can betray our intimate thoughts, even long after we are gone. Though, I don't think our ancestors are in any danger of knowing much about our dealings with one another from our correspondence, are they? And yet, you write a great many letters."

Her brow wrinkled. "I suppose I do."

"You wrote to Henry Jones, but not me."

"You never wrote to me either, Fitzwilliam. Not once, in all the time you were away."

"No, I suppose I was waiting for you to begin it. It is why I brought you the writing set, I thought you would understand - my going away and the significance of the present - that you might write to me if you wished to. When I heard nothing, I supposed you did not want to."

"That was a gift from you," she said in wonder. "I thought your father gave it to me. He had the desk moved for me the same day. I'm afraid I never even gave thought to the idea it might be from you. And I never thanked you, yet it is one of my most valued possessions. How awful of me. If you go away again, I shall write daily, great long essays. I shall bore you senseless with my inconsequential affairs and news of my afternoons calls. I will list every different type of flower and shrub I encounter on my walks."

"Please do," he said, squeezing her bare shoulder. "But, as I have told you. I have no plans to leave you, not for a good long while."

"Are you going to read it?" she asked, referring to the letter he held in the hand that was not holding her.

He nodded and gently nudged her head towards his chest, encouraging her to rest on him, marvelling at how well they moulded together. He read, while she dozed, and eventually they both slept.

Rose Kiddy entered her mistress's chambers with clean towels in one hand and a basin of water in the other. She pushed the door open with her back and frowned when she turned and saw the empty bed, worried that her mistress had gone out walking on her own on the morning after such terrible weather. When her eyes travelled over to the chaise lounge by the tall windows and she saw Mr and Mrs Darcy wrapped up in a blanket, but also wrapped in each other, limbs entwined and bodies pressed together, and obviously with not a stitch of clothing on between them, she began to creep very slowly and quietly back out the way she had come, breathing a sigh of relief at having not been noticed.

In future, she would have to remember to knock.

She passed Mr Darcy's valet who was carrying a pair of highly-polished boots at the top of the servants' staircase. "I wouldn't bang on his door, if I was you."

"Thank you, little Miss Kiddy, but I think I know my master's habits a bit better than you."

Rose sighed. "I am just trying to offer you a bit of advice."

"When I want some instruction on washing the pots, Rose, I shall come find you. Until then I'll carry on looking after my gentleman the way I always have done, and now is the hour he likes to be woken. I am a fully trained valet, not an elevated scullery maid."

"Well pardon me for speaking. I'll leave you to it."

She was back down in the servants' hall, with bread and jam, when the valet appeared again and sat down beside her.

"Sent you away with a flea in your ear, didn't he?" she asked.

"He wasn't best pleased at being disturbed, no. We might have to work a little closer together, I suppose, Miss Kiddy, from now on," he sniffed.

Rose laughed, wondering how far the valet had advanced into their chambers, and whether the connecting door had been open or shut, before he'd been ejected by his master's command. "Yes, Mr Cramer, though I be a former scullery maid and you an experienced valet, I don't suppose we'll be any a stranger fit than those two upstairs."

Sixty

Elizabeth had first woken to a great shout of *'leave'* from Mr Darcy and had sat up with a gasp, thinking for a truly mad moment that he was ordering her out, until she heard the sound of someone scrabbling away from the master's chambers next door.

He had shushed her like he might a child, pulled her head back down and she supposed she had gone back to sleep, for when she woke again, she was in her own bed, with the sheets tucked up to her chin, and he was gone.

His absence did not concern her. She knew it was late, perhaps as late as nine or ten, and he would be dressed and out somewhere on horseback, inspecting the damage to his park. The location of her nightgown however, did perplex her and when she saw it across the other side of the room, on a dressing table, she threw a hand over her eyes, smiling, recalling how he had lifted it over her head and flung it aside.

Thinking she would send for Rose, she threw back the covers but was stopped cold by the sight of a few very small spots of blood on the sheets. Nothing really, but they were unexpected. He had not hurt her. It had stung, but just a little and only at first, and then it had been exhilarating, lovely, tender, but ever so passionate, nothing like she had expected, nothing like she had been told it would be. All the kissing, his hands everywhere, the overwhelming desperate craving for him - nobody could have explained that to her if they had tried. She got out of the bed and covered the stains up. When Rose arrived she looked down at the floor.

"I know it is not the normal day for changing the sheets and not your responsibility."

"I'll see to it," Rose said a little too quickly.

Elizabeth breathed out and was relieved she did not have to explain herself further. "I am sorry to ask…"

"I shall do it myself, no one else will know."

Defying convention and every rule she had ever heard regarding familiarity with servants, Elizabeth hugged Rose and kissed her cheek. "I would be nothing without you."

"Oh no, stop, that won't do." Rose pushed her off and the two of them shared a look of understanding and great affection, before getting on with the business of bathing and dressing the mistress of Pemberley for a day at home.

The breakfast room was very full of their guests and at the end of it, looking impeccable as usual, was her husband. How different that word sounded to her now, what different emotions it roused. He looked up in surprise at her entrance and got up from his seat, as did the other gentlemen, which started an unexpected blush. Elizabeth turned away to gather a plate and some food, hardly knowing if she had returned anybody's good morning or not.

The only chair available was unfortunately next to his and she took it consciously, feeling as if every set of eyes in the room were turned towards them. It was ridiculous, of course. How would anyone know all of what had passed, or where he had spent the night, but it *felt* like they knew.

"'Tis an unexpected pleasure to have you join us for breakfast," Mr Darcy said.

"I was very hungry," she replied and felt even more embarrassed, so much so she wanted to crawl beneath the table.

"All that exercise you had last night has increased your appetite," Richard said.

She gave him a very pointed stare. "Excuse me?"

"Yesterday, all the dancing, and then walking back after the carriage broke," he explained.

"Oh, yes." She buttered her toast and calmed herself enough to ask Mr Darcy if he had been outside.

"Just the park, I plan to go and see if there is any damage further afield later. Would you like to accompany me?"

Pleased by the invitation and his recognition that she would have a care for seeing how the estate had fared, she nevertheless declined. "I may stay inside today, but thank you." Her eyes drifted towards Jane, and when she looked back at Mr Darcy, she saw he understood. Mr Bingley was to go and her sister would need her.

"The thunder kept me awake long into the night, I have barely had a wink of sleep. Did you sleep well, Lizzy?" Mrs Gardiner asked.

"I…um…yes…no…yes, eventually, I believe," she replied, looking determinedly down at her plate. Oh, it was torture, why had she not just had a tray in her room, as she usually did? When she risked a glance up at Mr Darcy, she saw mirth in his eyes.

"I hardly noticed the storm," he declared, "but then I was well distracted."

Terrified that somebody was going to ask him to explain the nature of the distraction, and cross at him for teasing her when she was struggling not to flee the room in agitation, she jumped to her feet and fetched the coffee from the sideboard. "Were you indeed, Mr Darcy? I suppose it was a good book, or similar? How lucky you were."

"Yes, yes. I feel my luck."

"Then do not push it," she replied quietly, leaning over and pouring for him. She replaced the coffee and whilst on her way back to her own seat, kicked the leg of his chair, causing him to jolt and some of the liquid to spill onto his hand. "Oh, I am terribly sorry."

"Think nothing of it, just a minor scald," he said, dabbing at the coffee with a napkin and still in a very jovial mood. He then turned the conversation onto other matters and their visitors journey further north became the topic.

Elizabeth supposed the ability to sit in a room with him and not think of how his mouth and hands had felt upon her bare skin would come in time. To not be continually embarrassed to be with him in front of other people, knowing how the previous night had passed, might come with familiarity, and in fact, by the end of breakfast, she was almost herself again, until Mrs Gardiner stopped her on their way out of the quickly emptying room and took her chin in her hand, turning her face this way and that way, examining her closely.

"There is something different about you this morning, Lizzy, and I thought perhaps your hair was styled another way, but it is not that. I can't think."

"I confess I feel a little different," she said, relieved when she realised her aunt was guileless, no tease had been intended. "Happier."

Mrs Gardiner nodded, "and if I am not mistaken, very much in love."

"I am in love!" she said, thinking how nice it was to confide in someone. "He is so thoughtful and kind. Oh, he has so many good qualities. I know he is sometimes quiet, but he is perfectly amiable…"

"Lizzy," her aunt stopped her, laughing. "You need not convince me, I can see his worth and he rises in my esteem every hour." Mrs Gardiner pulled her close as they walked into the hall. "And pray tell me, when I visit in future, with Mr Gardiner and the children, might they be promised some little Darcy cousins to play with?"

Now she was teasing and Elizabeth told her off for it.

Sixty one

The Bingleys and Hursts were to go by late morning. Elizabeth took Mrs Gardiner and Jane up to her private sitting room, away from the commotion downstairs, where trunks were being carried about and loaded.

When they came down to say farewell, Mr Darcy picked up her hand and placed a light kiss on her knuckles, as if she were one of the departing party, before tucking it into the crook of his arm to walk her outside.

His gesture did not go unnoticed by Miss Bingley, but Elizabeth saw the lady shrug to herself and when she approached Elizabeth to say goodbye, she did so with a surprising air of civility and great thanks. Elizabeth supposed she had given up all hope of trying to impress the master, and had turned her intentions instead to garnering the mistress's favour, perhaps thinking it was the most advisable method of retaining her rights of visiting at Pemberley. Elizabeth was half tempted to be cold, or offer some thinly disguised slant, but decided to control her temper. If Bingley did return to pay court to Jane, she and Miss Bingley might become related, and so caution ruled the day.

The Hursts were grateful and looked forward to seeing them again. Bingley said all that was proper and grasped Mr Darcy's hand in a firm shake, looked mournfully at Jane, but only very briefly, and then they were gone. Jane turned before the carriage had crossed the bridge and went back inside. Mrs Gardiner said she would go to her and Elizabeth found herself alone with Mr Darcy for the first time that day.

Seeing the carriage disappear from view entirely she sighed. "It was silly of me, but I was hoping, right up until that last moment, that something might move him to stay, or speak."

He will come back, and, if he does not, then he was not worthy of her."

"Well, that is all settled then."

"I am sorry. I do not seek to denigrate Jane's feelings. I know it is not that simple." They began walking back to the house, he guiding her around a large puddle caused by the storm.

"Oh do not be sorry, none of it is your fault. Even a man with your influence cannot persuade another to propose. It is just that you do not know Jane as I do. It will take her a long time to recover."

"I think being here with you will help her."

As sad as her heart was for Jane, she could not ignore the pleasure that thrummed through her at walking so close by him and talking so comfortably with him.

"Are you well this morning?"

She smiled at his careful question. "I am in tolerably good health, thank you, sir."

"I think you understand my meaning."

Laughing, she squeezed his arm. "I am well, Fitzwilliam, everything is well."

They walked on for a few paces before she asked him whether he truly believed Bingley would return.

"I do, sometimes it takes an absence to make us understand ourselves and what we truly desire, I ought to know."

"Hold my hand," she said.

"I am holding your hand." He brushed her fingers where they were tucked into the crook of his arm.

"I think you understand my meaning," she mimicked, speaking gravely, as he had done. "Hold my hand." Elizabeth was so happy she was almost skipping alongside him.

"'Tis up to the master and mistress of the house to set an example, you know, to maintain dignity and decorum."

She only laughed at him as they stepped back into the house through the great front doors together. "Oh, well if you will not indulge me, I will return to duty and responsibility and seek out Mrs Reynolds as I have not seen her today."

"Before you do, will you oblige me by coming to my study? There is something I wish to speak to you about."

Nodding her agreement and fully believing he had something of consequence to say, she went with him, but gasped as he kicked the door shut behind them, gathered her close and kissed her.

"Oh," she said, when she was eventually released, "how much more pleasant than my previous experiences in this room. I far prefer this to a telling off. Do you have anything else you wish to 'say to me?'"

He let out a low moan, followed by a bark of laughter. "I could happily *talk* to you all day, my dearest, loveliest, Elizabeth, but I am sadly engaged to go out very shortly with my steward to inspect some damage down at one of the farms."

"Maybe Richard would meet with him and you and I could continue our *discussion*. You have always been so silent with me before, sir, that this verbose side of you is quite a novelty. *Talk* to me again." Her hands went around his waist and she pressed herself against him, moulded her frame to his.

His kiss this time, however, was merely a gentle touching of his lips to her forehead. "I must go. I cannot ask Richard, he has gone to Haddon."

"Oh?" Suddenly remembering that Richard had approached him the night before when they had got home from the ball, she looked up at Mr Darcy expectantly. "He spoke to you? He told you of his wishes?"

"He did?"

"And? He goes to Haddon to give his mother the news, I suppose."

"He goes to ask her opinion and seek her sanction," Mr Darcy said carefully. "I do not hold out much hope of it being a successful application."

"The countess will not be best pleased, no, but she will come around in time and you will give him the living of Kimpton?"

He set her away from him and his countenance changed as he spoke with warning in his voice. "Why do you suppose he has never approached his mother for one of the livings she has it within her power to bestow? Because he knows she will not grant him anything if he discloses his desire to marry Miss Temple. If I give him Kimpton, I will go expressly against her wishes. It would cause a division within the family. Will you have me go directly against my aunt?"

489

Elizabeth was astonished and suddenly angry. "Yes I would, or you are not the man I thought you had become. After all he has done for you, stood in your stead, been brother, cousin and friend to Georgiana and I, looked after all your interests, you would not do this for him?"

"I have a deep respect for the countess, I could not..."

She gave him no chance to finish, she was already moving, opening the door, striding through the hall, where his steward was now stood waiting. "Elizabeth, stop."

When she kept walking, Mr Darcy dismissed the man with a wave of his hand and followed her through the house. "You are not being reasonable, Elizabeth. You are thinking with your heart."

"At least I have one, sir," she replied, without slowing or stopping to look at him.

"Where exactly are you going?"

Storming through the doors that led to the courtyard and rushing down the steps, she spoke without looking back at him. "I have no idea, anywhere that is far from you."

Mr Darcy slowed down, perhaps considering letting her go, but then she heard his quick step behind her again as she crossed the lawns. "Run away if you wish, but I found you before, and I will do so again, every time."

Her heart beating wildly, both from exertion and fury, she marched onwards towards the woods.

"I do have a heart, Elizabeth," he called out from behind her. "You, my love, currently hold it in the palm of your hand. You are its keeper."

Such a declaration could not be ignored. She turned briefly to see him looking desperate and passionate as he came closer, catching her up. They met under the branches of one of the Spanish chestnuts, but she kept her back to him.

"Do you love me?" she asked, over her shoulder. "Last night I thought you did, I felt you did, but you did not say."

"Don't doubt my affection, Elizabeth. Whatever else fails, that will always remain."

"Affection, sir? I have affection for Hodges."

490

"Whatever you wish me to say, will be said, though you often leave me speechless."

"Oh, so your general disinclination to utter no more than two words together at a time is my fault?"

"Sometimes you do not give me leave or room to speak," he said. "And you run, every time you are hurt or upset, you take to your heels."

He was right, though she only now saw the fault, only now really knew herself. "Run? I am always at Pemberley, I go nowhere."

"That will change, I promise you. And, what I told Richard was that he should speak to his mother first, and do her the honour of letting her know his plans before anything else was decided. It is a delicate matter; her husband is dying. I would willingly give him Kimpton, but I wish to upset neither of them and I wished to speak of it with you too, to hear your views."

"And tell me, what is your true opinion of Miss Temple? What do you think of Richard's choice?"

"I think he has no choice, I used to think we men had some ability to select our partners in life, some autonomy in such matters, but I was stupid and wrong. He could no more turn away from her, than I could allow you to run away from me. He adores her, and I wish him happy. They will marry, and they will be welcomed at Pemberley afterwards."

"I am sorry, then," she said. "I have misjudged you again."

"Despite everything that passed last night, Elizabeth, I sense you are still angry with me for something, and it is more than Richard and Kimpton that bothers you. I feel as if you have not quite made your mind up about me. If I were a suitor, a man coming to ask for your hand, I would not be certain of your acceptance."

"My reply would be yes," she said, immediately. "I love you, I am not afraid to say it, you see." But still she could not look at him.

He moved very close, till he was directly behind her. She could feel his breath on the back of her neck. "I am glad to hear it, but still, I feel I do not have your complete faith. You

491

have been so generous as to forgive me my coldness towards you, and all the bitterness I felt when we were first wed, but there is something you still resent me for. What is it? What is buried so deep within you that you cannot give voice to it?"

Elizabeth rested her forehead against the bark of the tree and bit her lip.

"I fear I have delivered one too many lectures, told you a lady should never lose her temper, never shout, and lately I have been impressed by your restraint, for you have had much provocation. But please, let me have it, Elizabeth," he said.

All was quiet for a few moments. There was no sound around them but the rustling of leaves in the breeze.

"Why did you stay away so long?" It burst forth from her violently, almost at a scream, disturbing the peaceful, beautiful grounds around them. A bird took flight in fear from the tree above their heads. She had shocked herself but he did not react, it was as if he had been expecting such an eruption.

Nevertheless, she sensed he struggled with his answer. "Well, there were times when it was difficult to secure passage, and I had business to attend to."

Elizabeth shook her head vigorously. "That will not do, you are disingenuous. I require the truth."

"I did do much business abroad, but yes, I could have come back sooner," he admitted. "Yet it seemed you all did better without me. I would receive letters from Georgiana and Richard, and you were all so well and happy. I felt myself dispensable here. If you resented my absence, I am sorry, but I will only apologise for it this once, never again. You were a girl when I left and you are a woman now, I think you did better away from me. Did you want me home? I never thought my presence particularly welcome, I thought you found me oppressive."

Elizabeth better understood his reasons, but the sense of abandonment and rejection she had felt at the time could not be so easily forgot.

"Did you want me home?" he asked again, and she felt his fingers lightly touch her elbow. "Did you love me then?"

"No," she said, throwing some of his typical bluntness back at him, but the fire and fight had largely left her. "I do not know what I felt for you. All I can say is that I'm not a girl who gives in easily to tears, yet every time you went away, I cried."

His arms slipped around her, pulling her back against him. He put a kiss below her ear and whispered into it. "If you will allow me, I should like to spend the rest of my days prompting you to happy tears. I have caused too many sad ones. Tell me how I might make you happy, Elizabeth. I am the happiest man on earth just to be allowed to hold you like this. What may I do for you?"

"You may take me to see the sea. I have still never had a proper sight of it."

"Then we will go, as often as you like, as soon as you like."

She turned in his arms and smiled, "though not to Scarborough."

Mr Darcy laughed and looked impossibly handsome. "No, not Scarborough," he held her for a while, and kissed her aplenty. Then, though nothing was said, they knew they ought to go back to the house.

"There is one more thing you might do for me," she said with a tease in her voice.

"Then you must name it."

"Hold my hand."

He gave a great sigh, but it was playful. "Very well, if you are determined to have me act like a love-struck fool in front of the whole house, I will hold your hand." And he did, grasping it tightly as they walked back to that great stone mansion - where a steward waited to be advised by his master, a heartbroken young lady needed consoling by her sister, a governess fretted over her future while she tried to persuade an over-tired sixteen-year-old girl back to her practice, and a housekeeper could not proceed until her mistress had decided whether they would have veal or duck for dinner.

One and twenty

Pulling hard on the reins of his horse, Darcy brought the animal to a sharpish stop as they clattered into the yard of a Hertfordshire coaching inn. A broad smile was creasing his face; the happiness he took from the sheer loveliness of the bright summer's day was amplified by the fresh air, the thrill of the exercise and the love of a good woman.

Elizabeth Darcy was not far behind him, perhaps just two or three minutes, though he had made no exceptions for her and not slowed, or ambled. She had raced, chased and ridden alongside him, over fields, through streams and woods, and he was glad she had insisted (nay fought him!) for the right to travel alongside him on horseback, rather than opting for the comfort of their carriage, which was now probably two or three hours back on the road behind them.

His own entrance into the yard had attracted no attention at all, Elizabeth's drew the eyes of everyone and it was no wonder, for she was an arresting sight atop a borrowed black stallion, dressed in scarlet riding habit and elegant little hat. She had come in faster than him, drawing her horse up quite sharply and the animal skittered about a bit, huffed and puffed and turned a couple of circles before acquiescing to Elizabeth's calls to order.

"You do very well with him, he's not an easy beast to control," he said. Her own horse, her grey gelding, was still at Pemberley, but they had not been there for over two months.

"Luckily for me, I am well used to handling tall, dark, unpredictable males," she replied with a broad smile that matched his own.

Darcy dismounted when he saw a stable boy draw near and gave him a few coins and some instructions. Going over to Elizabeth, he held up his arms to assist her down.

"Do we stop to bate the horses?"

"We stop to bate me, we'll go no further today," he said as he set her on the ground.

She gave him a curious look before peering up at the sky. "There are still a couple of hours of daylight left; we will easily make Meryton before dark if we press on."

"I am sure we would."

"Are you very hungry then?"

"Yes, I am hungry." He saw she started to suspect what he was about, her eyes grew a little darker and there was a slight arch of her brow, a pout around her mouth. "I want you," he said very quietly, leaning towards her ear and wiping a splatter of mud from her cheek, "and I cannot possibly wait an hour and a half."

Elizabeth's brow was still arched a while later, when they lay side by side, their chests heaving, trying to replenish the breath that had been stolen from their lungs. She did not have to speak; her countenance alone demanded an explanation from him. He thought an apology might be more in order.

"I beg your pardon."

She laughed heartily, until tears formed at the corners of her eyes and he could not help but laugh too. "That would be sufficient response, sir, had you stepped on my toes at an assembly."

"I heard no complaints, Elizabeth."

"That was because I had none. I am just surprised. I have perhaps become spoilt and too used to a little more finesse from you. Is it the country air?"

Her left hand moved to his thigh and he enjoyed the weight and sight of it there. His mother's ring was on her third finger, put there over a year ago now - a symbol of her married status which he was glad she was happy to wear - given that she still refused to conform to society's more widely held expectation of married women by covering her hair with a cap. Her decision to flout the convention had caused stern disapproval amongst the older ladies, but envious gazes from the younger ones while they had been in London. Darcy wouldn't be surprised if when they returned in the new year, for the season and Georgiana's coming out, more and more of them would be casting aside their caps. Despite this little rebellion (which she always explained with a simple, 'Mr Darcy likes to see my hair') Elizabeth negotiated London society with ease, and had made a few sensible friends, while remaining distantly civil with the silly and pretentious. Her humour and kindness stood her in good stead; her energy and liveliness carried her easily through days when she was required to make or receive six or seven calls and then attend a ball till two or three o'clock in the morning. It was their second visit and all had gone well, but he felt they never settled properly when in Town and they had not nearly enough time for each other, as they did at Pemberley.

"I am not sorry to leave London, that is for sure," he told her.

"Nor I, it is good we have such a wonderful excuse for quitting it."

She referred to her sister's wedding. Mr Bingley had come back to call on Jane a few months after first leaving Pemberley. He had found her more cautious and wary, more demanding and difficult to woo. She had eventually brought him to his knees, from which position he had begged to be relieved from his suffering, and Jane had taken pity and agreed to become his wife. Jane had asked to be married in Hertfordshire, in Meryton Church, where her father was buried. The much anticipated event was not only bringing Mr and Mrs Darcy from London, but the Earl and Countess of Matlock all the way from Derbyshire.

Richard Fitzwilliam and Evelina Temple had married before he had left for Oxford to study for the church, unable to wait. Richard had taken his new wife with him, and though the countess had not been present at the wedding, she had soon afterwards granted her son a small income, and then had welcomed him back at Christmas, overjoyed to see the new Mrs Fitzwilliam not only blooming in her new role as a wife, but blooming around the waistline too. The countess was not allowed to be happy for long, however. Walter, her eldest son, was lost suddenly - following his father quickly to the grave. The rather simple man had met a simple end, tripping on a London street and hitting his head against a stone column. *'What do you mean he died after tripping up?'* Elizabeth had asked incredulously when Darcy had told her, *'people do not die from such things'*. Yet Walter had, and Richard had inherited the title because his elder brother had forgotten to put out his hands to break his fall.

Walter's death had been a sad time, although a fool, he had been a harmless sort, though quietly Darcy thought Richard a far better addition to the House of Lords and was glad the family had a steadier man at its helm. Elizabeth, for her part, greatly enjoyed dropping deep exaggerated curtseys to the new countess, which the former Miss Temple would roll her eyes at.

"This is a terrible room, Fitzwilliam," Elizabeth laughed, bringing him out of his reverie. "I don't suppose the sheets have been changed in weeks, and the tables and curtains are deep in dust. How dare you ravish me in such a room, do you not know I am Mrs Darcy?"

He was now sleepy and only blinked at her in response.

She sat up suddenly and looked around her. "Are we at Redbourn?"

"Yes, Mrs Darcy."

"This is not the same room, surely?"

Darcy wearily looked around it himself then, having paid scant attention on their entering it, solely dedicated as he had been to the task of removing his wife's clothes. "It might be, I cannot truly remember."

"Is there some significance to your bringing me here?" Elizabeth asked him, poking him in the thigh, trying to keep him awake.

"None."

"I suppose not. It is hardly a romantic memory," she said.

"Do not be so sure. I will confess to you something which I beg you never repeat to anyone, for fear of outraging them."

"And what is that?" Her lovely eyes were wide while she awaited his answer.

"Elizabeth, I think I have loved you since you were a small boy in breeches."

The End

By the same author – available through Amazon

**Ardently – a Pride and Prejudice Variation
by Caitlin Williams**

So much in life depends on chance and sheer luck. How much do we often owe to being in the right place at the right time?

In Jane Austen's Pride and Prejudice, Elizabeth Bennet plans to visit the Lake District with her uncle and aunt, yet ends up at Pemberley instead, just as, by coincidence, Mr Darcy also arrives home. They meet, understand one another better and all eventually ends well.

But what if they did not have such luck? What if Elizabeth actually went to the Lake District and was nowhere near Pemberley, and she and Mr Darcy never met again until another four years had gone by?

Now they are very different people, altered by marriage, time and situation, although, Mr Darcy's failed proposal in the Parsonage at Hunsford still haunts them.

Elizabeth is a companion to her Aunt, Mrs Mountford, a widow of great standing in and 'Miss Bennet' finds herself accepted in the very best of circles. While, Mr Darcy did his duty by his sickly cousin, Anne de Bourgh. He has come to Bath, however, a widower, with his family, the Fitzwilliams, and his sister, Georgiana. Darcy sees Elizabeth, the woman who rejected him, in the opposite box at the theatre and cannot help falling in love with her all over again.

Mr Darcy is still a little proud, still not able to 'perform to strangers'. Can Elizabeth see past his reserve and awkwardness to the decent man underneath?

Made in the USA
Monee, IL
06 June 2020